THE
DEVIL'S
DAUGHTERS

DIANA BRETHERICK

First published in Great Britain in 2015 by Orion Books,
an imprint of The Orion Publishing Group Ltd
Carmelite House, 50 Victoria Embankment
London EC4Y 0DZ

An Hachette Livre UK Company

1 3 5 7 9 10 8 6 4 2

A CIP catalogue record for this book is
available from the British Library.

ISBN (Trade Paperback) 978 1 4091 5030 5
ISBN (Ebook) 978 1 4091 5032 9

Typeset at The Spartan Press Ltd,
Lymington, Hants

Printed in Great Britain by
Clays Ltd, St Ives plc

The Orion Publishing Group's policy is to use papers that
are natural, renewable and recyclable products and made from
wood grown in sustainable forests. The logging and manufacturing
processes are expected to conform to the environmental
regulations of the country of origin.

www.orionbooks.co.uk

To David, who is everything.

Turin, 1 March 1888

The dark changes everything.

She moves quickly through the early winter morning and wishes fervently for the sun to rise. In the daylight this would be an unremarkable journey. But now, in the darkness, the mundane slips seamlessly into the sinister, and threat surrounds her. Every corner is a hiding place for a monster, and every sound, no matter how slight, is from someone or something that wishes to do her harm.

As she makes her way to work through the familiar streets, now shrouded in shadows, she pulls her thin shawl around her in an attempt to fend off the icy cold and damp. It reaches through her clothing right to her skin, caressing her like the clammy hands of an unwanted suitor.

The freezing wind whistles round her ankles as she goes on her way, blowing dust, dead leaves and bits of old newspaper into her path. She blinks, and her eyes water in the cold air. The gas lamps are still lit, but she can take no comfort from them. The flickering yellow flames merely add to the phantoms that surround her. She tries her best to look straight ahead, but every now and again she thinks she hears something, a sharp sound – an unidentified footstep or a door creaking open to reveal . . . who knows what.

She has reached the Via Garibaldi in the oldest part of the

city when her imagined sound becomes real. It is distinct – a cracking sound; an opening perhaps. She is reminded that the gates to Hell are never far away in this city. There is the sound again, sharp and resonating, almost like someone breaking a cane in two. A little way down the street she sees a light, a lantern perhaps, swaying as if someone is looking for something. It seems to be coming towards her. She backs away from it but still it approaches. Instinctively she begins to run. She does not know why. It is only a light after all. Eventually she stops and tells herself to be calm. But then she sees that the light has followed her, so she runs again and tries to lose it, ducking into another street only to find it blocked by a carriage halfway up. The door opens. She hesitates, holding her breath. A gloved hand beckons to her. The gloves are lace. The hand is long and slim.

'Come, child, come!' says the figure in the carriage.

She sees the light again. It seems to be getting closer. She walks to the carriage door and peers inside. There is one occupant – a woman in a large-brimmed hat swathed in a veil.

'Get in, child,' says the woman.

She hesitates. The voice is strange, with a sing-song quality to it. It captivates her. A hand comes over her mouth from behind. It holds a handkerchief and smells odd – like the cleaning fluid the housekeeper gives her to use on the polished wooden floors. She struggles, but it is useless. She is becoming weaker as she is bundled into the carriage.

As they drive away, she slips gently into oblivion. The fears that haunted her have finally come true.

The bearer of the light stops and leans against the wall, trying to relieve himself whilst still holding his lantern. He's getting too old for this. He slumps to the ground and sits with his eyes closed. Everything is spinning. He shouldn't have had that last grappa. But it was a celebration, although of what exactly he cannot quite remember. And it seemed rude to refuse a drink or two, particularly as it was free. 'Come on, Pietro,' they said. 'It isn't a real party without you!' Well who was he to disagree?

Now, though, sitting in a puddle of his own piss in the darkness, he is full of regret. And as if that wasn't enough, he is seeing things – some girl being dragged into a carriage again and spirited away. He takes off his tatty old straw hat and shakes his head at his own folly, but it hurts, so he stops. He drags himself to his feet and starts his journey home to his bed, to sleep it off and forget. The city is quiet again, as if, having been awoken for a few brief moments, it is settling back to sleep. Everything appears to have returned to its former equilibrium. But this is merely an illusion.

1

The morally insane repay hatred with hatred. Even when the cause is slight, they react with anger, envy and vengeance. Incapable of family life, they flee the paternal home, sleeping under bridges and devoting themselves to refined cruelties.   Lombroso, 1884, p. 215

Edinburgh, 18 March 1888

'I know what you are.'

The voice cut through the silence, the edge jagged with hatred.

The mourners stared, first at the man who had made this statement and then at his subject.

The funeral had been difficult enough even before this intervention. James Murray had stood and watched the coffin being lowered into the grave and wondered if his empty heart would ever be full again. He wanted more than anything to regret his father's passing, but instead he felt only relief.

There was Arthur's Seat, rising imposingly behind the church – a green mass giving a hint of colour in an otherwise grey landscape. He and his father had often walked there together, deep in conversation about their shared fascination with the workings of the human brain. He had been the student, his father the teacher. But those were happier times. Now everything was different.

Another memory had lurched into his mind, this time unwanted – his father strapped to a bed in the asylum where he had ended his days, screaming and raving. James had tried to shake the vision away, but he knew that it would haunt him until his own death. He should have done something earlier to prevent this tragedy. Instead, like a coward, he had run away to a foreign city, leaving everything and everyone behind.

Sobbing came from beside him. His sister Lucy was weeping steadily. Wispy tendrils of strawberry-blonde hair surrounded her pretty heart-shaped face. He longed to tuck them gently behind her ears as he had seen his father do. Instinctively he reached out to her, but she shrugged away from him, giving him a reproachful glare. Unlike him, Lucy was truly in mourning, but then she did not know the truth about what kind of man was being buried – a lunatic and a criminal, guilty of the theft of a man's soul.

As the final words were intoned by the suitably gloomy minister, the church clock chimed as if it too was sounding an end to his father's life. James had been about to escort Lucy away when he heard a commotion. A man pushed his way through the mourners and stood for a moment peering down at the coffin. He was smartly dressed in the black frock coat customary for these occasions. His cravat, however, was of a vivid scarlet, and so great was the contrast with everything else that it seemed to glow. James stared at him. Who was he? The man was familiar but he could not place him. Gaunt and pale, he resembled Death himself, but it was his eyes that were his most striking feature. They were steel grey, and when the man lifted his head to focus them on James, it felt as if they were boring holes into his skull.

'I know what you are.'

The words ripped into James, through his skin and through his bones until he felt their icy touch around his heart.

The man walked away. At first there was silence, then what felt like a collective intake of breath among the few that were present. They began to stare at James and mutter to each other. He tried to look straight ahead, knowing that if he acknowledged the man's words it might give them credence, but he sensed the disapproval. He had begun the occasion as the chief mourner, but now he was a source of gossip. That was nothing. He deserved it after all. But Lucy didn't.

Eventually the mourners began to make their way to their carriages. There was to be no wake. At least they had that to be thankful for. It had seemed wrong somehow, given the circumstances.

Lucy turned away, her eyes full of hurt and confusion. James watched her for a few seconds and realised how alone he felt. His parents were both gone, and now even his sister seemed lost to him. But then she stopped, as if she was waiting for him. James walked towards her. Could there be some hope for them after all? The question was still there, an invisible barrier between them as they began their journey home. They sat in silence, together but still far apart, as the carriage with its black-plumed horses, upon which Lucy had insisted, made its way slowly through the narrow, winding streets of the old town to the broad, straight ones of the new.

For a moment James was transported back to Turin, from where he had not so long ago returned. He had gone there to study the nature of the criminal and to find out if his father's evil might have infected him, just as the man at the funeral had suggested. He had learnt not just about crime but also about what it was to love and lose someone. He had put his duty first. He did not regret it, but neither could he quite forget what he had left behind. Still, that was another world and another time. He had returned home to face his fears, but he had been too late.

He glanced out of the window and for a split second he thought he saw her, standing on a corner dressed in a long hooded cloak, a basket in her arms. Everything around him came to a halt, as if he was in a photograph. Even his ability to breathe seemed to desert him. Logic told him that it could not be her, but still the anticipation made every one of his senses sharpen. Then she turned towards him and he saw that she was a stranger. The woman he longed for was in Italy, and he and his duty still belonged in Edinburgh.

'Who was that man, James?' Lucy asked. It was clear from the strain in her voice that she was struggling to keep her emotions under control.

'I'm not sure.'

'What did he mean about knowing what you are?'

James shrugged. He had been badly shaken by the accusatory tone of the man at the graveside but did not want to admit it.

'I just don't know, Lucy.' What else could he say? If he started to tell her of his suspicions, he would not be able to stop. He could not put her through that. It just wouldn't be fair.

The carriage lurched and James and Lucy were thrown together. She leant quickly away from him, as if he was some kind of threat. He put out his hand to hers, but she pulled it away. James understood why she was behaving like this. She had lost her father, and she blamed him. He had abandoned her, and by the time he had returned home, their father was dead. Lucy knew nothing of his sacrifice, and he would not tell her. He deserved her anger, but he would fight for her forgiveness. After all, they had only each other now, and that was all that mattered.

They were not quite alone. They arrived home to find their Aunt Agnes seated primly reading the Bible in the drawing room, grim-faced, like a parasite sucking away at their grief. An ostentatiously devout woman, she had been shocked by their father's decline and the scandal it had threatened to bring upon the family, virtually disowning him since his incarceration. She had even refused to attend his funeral, claiming that it was not decent behaviour for a woman. Lucy, of course, had insisted on being there, notwithstanding – or perhaps because of – her aunt's objections, saying that this was an old-fashioned view and that it was perfectly acceptable these days. James was not certain that she was right, but he did not have the heart to forbid it. Aunt Agnes had merely pursed her lips and stood her ground, her expression making it clear that she blamed James for his father's fate.

Now she sat there in her crêpe mourning gown, having insisted on all the usual customs that accompanied death despite her views on the deceased himself. Agnes Kennedy was small and joyless, embittered by her husband's infidelity. Her mouth was permanently downturned and her thin dark hair was tinged with grey and worn in what seemed to be a mercilessly tight bun secured firmly at the back of her head – an outmoded coiffure that reflected her outlook exactly. He decided not to tell her about the man at the funeral, knowing that it would merely confirm her opinion.

'I'm going up to my room to lie down,' Lucy declared.

Aunt Agnes nodded. 'Very well, child.' She turned to James once his sister had left. 'There is a letter for you,' she said in a faintly disapproving tone, holding out a small cream envelope.

He examined it curiously. It did not have the black borders of a letter of condolence. Who could it be from? Then, as he saw the Turin postmark and recognised the handwriting, his heartbeat quickened with anticipation.

'Who is writing from Italy, James?' asked his aunt, her eyes narrowing suspiciously.

'A friend,' he replied tersely. 'If you'll excuse me, Aunt, I will also rest for a while. It has been a difficult afternoon.'

She gave a curt nod. No doubt, James thought, she was annoyed to be denied further information about the letter. He didn't care. This was for his eyes alone, and was more precious to him than anything in the world.

Up in his room, he stared at the page before him. He lifted it to his face and breathed in its aroma – a faint suggestion of lemons and spice. As he sat there with his eyes shut, he imagined her arms around him, and for a moment he was returned to her. But when he opened them again, he realised that he did not know quite how to feel. Ever since he had left Italy, he had dreamt of hearing from Sofia, and yet he had dreaded it too. He had loved her and left her. They could not be together because their pasts and their futures were so different. All the same, he had hoped that somehow he would see her again. He had continued to write to her, but no reply had come. He had almost reconciled himself to staying in Scotland and making a life for himself there. But now she had finally written to him and thrust him into a state of confusion.

Per favore, aiutami, the letter said in characteristically cryptic terms. Please, help me.

Turin, 19 March 1888

The girl sits alone in what seems to be little more than a deep pit and wonders what she has done to deserve her incarceration. She cannot tell how long she has been there because she cannot see when the night ends and the day begins, but it feels like weeks at least. Too long anyway to be in what she has come to think of as her cell. There is not much in the way of comfort, just a thin mattress, a bucket for relieving herself, and a few cotton strips, presumably for her monthly visitor, which is due quite soon.

Sometimes she hears movement and voices. Maybe she is not alone in her experience, but it is impossible to know for sure.

Occasionally food and water is lowered down to her, but she cannot see by whom. Other than that she is left quite alone with only her own increasingly desperate thoughts for company. Reaching into her pocket, she pulls out a rosary and begins to pray. Perhaps if she does this for long enough, the Virgin Mary will come to her assistance. But the hours pass, as the days have already, and no one arrives to release her. She begins to think they never will.

Yet she is not alone. Through a peephole roughly carved into the wooden cover that is her ceiling, she is being closely watched. Though she does not know it, her release is imminent – but when it finally comes, she will wish that it had not.

2

One need only to look at pictures of women of genius of
our day to realise that they seem to be men in disguise.

Lombroso, 1893, p. 83

Edinburgh, 20 March 1888

James stood outside the door of the lecture hall and listened carefully. A man's voice, soft but authoritative, was holding forth about the importance of observation. 'How does your patient move? Does he drag a foot, suggesting evidence of some former injury? Does he leap around, thereby showing himself to be fit and healthy, if something of a show-off? Does he have any marks upon him – a tattoo, perhaps – gained in some foreign clime, indicating that he has travelled and wishes us all to know it? It is these small things that make up the larger and more significant whole.'

James smiled to himself, remembering when Professor Joseph Bell had given him the same lecture during his own medical training, what seemed like a century ago. He opened the door gently and attempted to sidle in unseen, the better to hear what remained of the lecture. This turned out to be a mistake.

'Ah! I do believe we have a subject, gentlemen!'

James stood and grinned as a ripple of laughter went through the students.

'Come into the centre, sir, and make yourself visible. Now, who can make some observations about our subject? Remember, it is small things we are looking for.'

A couple of hands went up. Professor Bell peered out at them before pointing at a nervous young man sitting at the front. 'Mr Davies, what can you tell us?'

'He looks a bit shifty... up to no good.'

'I see. In what way?'

'It's his eyes. They move about.'

James frowned.

'I see... Anything else?'

'His shoes are scruffy. Looks like he's done a fair bit of walking recently,' someone called out.

'And what might that indicate about his occupation?'

'Is he a policeman?'

'Interesting... Are you a man of the law, sir?' Bell asked James, with a twinkle in his eye.

'I like to think so, but not in the way you mean,' James replied.

'He's a Scot!' a student shouted.

'Aye, he can't be all bad!' said another.

'Let us confine ourselves to the physical for now, gentlemen,' Bell said. 'We've time for one more observation.'

'The subject has a slight stoop,' someone called from the back.

Instinctively James straightened up. 'Not any longer, it seems!' Bell said. 'What does that tell you?'

'He is unsure of himself... or about something.'

'Perhaps he is not confident. He prefers not to stand out in a crowd?' someone said tentatively.

'Well the good doctor has failed in that enterprise today, to be sure!' Bell said to general laughter. 'Yes, Dr Murray is a medical man, and not so long ago sat where you are now, listening to me, poor fellow. Thank you, gentlemen. We shall continue this tomorrow.'

As the students filed obediently out, Professor Bell seized James's hand. 'I hope you didn't mind me using you as a subject.'

'Not at all, Professor. It was, as always, very instructive.'

'Good. That is, after all, what we aim for. Now, how about a drink of something?'

Minutes later they were sitting in the professor's cavernous office sipping at a decidedly acceptable malt whisky. The shelves were crammed with books, untidy piles of papers and one or two jars holding pickled body parts. James felt another twinge of regret for what he had left behind in Turin. His employer in Italy had been similar in many ways to Professor Bell – and yet in others they were almost diametrically opposed to each other. Professor Bell was precise and careful in both his investigations and the expression of his findings. Criminal anthropologist Cesare Lombroso, on the other hand, preferred, as he often said, to let the facts speak for themselves. In practice this often meant that the facts were altered in order to fit the theory, and occasionally vice versa, which made working with him sometimes difficult but never, ever dull.

Professor Bell peered at James curiously over the rim of his glass. 'So tell me, Murray, were any of the students correct in their observations?'

James paused. 'To an extent, perhaps . . . There is a matter that I am unsure of, as one of them mentioned.'

'Is it connected to what happened at your father's funeral?'

'You have heard about that?'

Bell nodded. 'I am afraid it is the subject of speculation in some quarters.'

'I still do not know the man's identity, though I am sure I have seen him before.'

'Perhaps it is best left. It will be yesterday's news soon enough. It is your future that should be occupying your mind now, Murray.'

'You are right. In fact that is why I am here. I wish to ask your advice about something.'

'I see.' Professor Bell paused for a moment. 'I deduce that something is a woman.'

James smiled. 'I suppose I must ask how you reached that conclusion. Was it my demeanour that gave me away, the way I was standing . . . or something I said perhaps?'

The professor laughed and shook his head. 'No, no, my dear boy, none of that . . .'

'So how did you know?'

'When I see a young man wearing a troubled expression, believe me, the cause is almost always a woman.'

'I'm not sure that is quite fair, although you are right on this occasion, Professor.'

'Your tone suggests that she is not the only matter that concerns you.'

'Again you are right. There is more to it.' James hesitated, struggling to find the right words.

'Go on.'

'I want to return to Turin . . . indeed, I feel that I must.'

'May I ask why?'

'The woman I speak of . . . she has asked for my help.'

'And you feel duty bound to answer her call?'

'It is not so much a matter of duty.'

'Ah, I see – a matter of the heart, then. And what else?'

Bell paused. 'You travelled to Italy to study with Professor Lombroso, but you found more, did you not?'

'There was something that had been troubling me and, to an extent, the professor reassured me. I felt that I was just beginning to make sense of his theories when I had to leave. I did not want to go.' As James spoke, the feeling of regret he had experienced became sharper, almost painful.

Professor Bell nodded thoughtfully. 'I have read one or two articles by him. He has some original ideas. I am not sure that I agree with all his methods, but still they are fascinating. I am not surprised that he has inspired you.'

'He is unusual in his approach, but some of his ideas have definite possibilities for the solution of crimes. I would relish the opportunity to work with him again.'

'So what is stopping you?' Bell asked.

'As you know, Professor, I have a sister, Lucy. If I abandon her again, I don't think she would forgive me.'

'Ah, I see,' Bell said. 'So you have come to me because you think I will tell you that your work must take precedence. In other words, you want me to give you permission to leave your sister here in Edinburgh.'

James stared down at his glass and swirled its amber contents round, watching the viscous liquid cling to the sides. 'I suppose you're right, Professor.'

'You must know that I cannot do that,' Bell said gently. 'It is a personal matter that only you can decide upon.'

James nodded miserably. He felt like a fool. How could he ever have thought that asking Professor Bell for advice was the right thing to do?

'Your work is important to you. I understand that. But is a choice really necessary?' Bell asked.

'What do you mean, Professor?'

'Sometimes you're a little slow on the uptake, Murray. There are only two possible solutions. All you have to do is choose one.'

James shook his head in confusion.

Professor Bell smiled at him. 'Give it some thought, young man, and I'm sure the answer will come to you before too long. Remember what I used to say to you at the beginning of each case.'

'Never ignore the obvious. It is often an investigator's only friend.'

'Indeed! I am most gratified that you have not forgotten. Now all you have to do is go away and apply it.'

'Return to Turin! I have never heard such a preposterous idea!' Aunt Agnes declared. 'You cannot possibly be thinking of shirking your responsibilities again! What of your sister?'

'Yes, James, what about me?' Lucy repeated, her eyes flashing with anger. 'Am I to be abandoned yet again?' A look of despair crossed her face.

'No, Lucy, you are not,' he heard himself saying. 'You will travel with me. It would do us both good.'

Lucy looked at him in surprise. 'You want me to come with you to Turin?'

'Yes, I do. '

'You most certainly will do no such thing!' Aunt Agnes got to her feet and strode towards him. For a brief moment he thought she was going to attack him. Instead she stood inches away and wagged her finger in his face. 'Lucy was too young to travel with you before. You admitted it yourself. Nothing has changed.'

'I am older now! I am almost eighteen,' Lucy protested.

'That is still far too young to go gallivanting across Europe, young lady!'

'Things are different now, Aunt,' James said.

She glared at him. 'How, exactly?'

'For one thing I have been there and I know Lucy will be safe.'

'Safe! There were two killers on the loose! That does not sound safe to me.'

'They have been ... dealt with.'

'One has been dealt with. The other is still at large.'

'My employer, Professor Lombroso, is a good man, a family man, with two daughters of an age similar to Lucy.'

'So you have said before, but he is not ...' she paused and took a deep, almost theatrical breath, 'suitable as a guardian for your sister.'

James wondered how else he could persuade his aunt of Lombroso's good character. 'The professor is an eminent scientist, extremely well respected in his field.'

'I do not doubt it, but Lucy is a young lady at an impressionable age. She requires moral guidance, particularly in the light of her parental background.'

There was a pause as James struggled to ignore this slight. 'And she shall have moral guidance, Aunt Agnes. I will make sure of that.'

'I am almost eighteen,' Lucy repeated. 'I require no guidance, moral or otherwise.'

'Your words demonstrate the exact opposite, young lady,' Aunt Agnes said, an expression of deep satisfaction on her face. 'However, I have a solution ...'

Lucy sat in her room with her pencil poised, but inspiration would not come to her tonight. How could it? She was far too excited. Her life was about to change beyond recognition. She was to have a new home, a new city, a new country... and all without the presence of Aunt Agnes. Thank heavens James had put his foot down when she had offered to accompany them! That would have been a disaster. As it was, Lucy would have to put up with some stuffy companion hand-picked by her aunt. Still, that in itself provided a challenge, which was something she always enjoyed. She pictured herself climbing through a window to escape as her companion dozed in an armchair. Yes, she would enjoy pitting her wits against Aunt Agnes's spy, whoever she turned out to be.

Lucy was in the middle of writing one of her stories. Her heroine, the intrepid lady detective Lydia Loveday, was trapped in an underground cavern in the search for some stolen diamonds. The trouble was, having got Lydia into this predicament, she couldn't think of a way of getting her out. She studied the illustration she had sketched last night. Lydia stood with her hands on her hips looking reproachfully out at her. Reluctantly Lucy closed her notebook, carefully tying the ribbons as her father had taught her. 'If you do it like that,' he'd said, 'you'll always know if someone has been poking their nose where they shouldn't.'

The memory of her father made her catch her breath. It still caused her so much pain just to think of him. She cast her mind back to the funeral, and that strange man who had said such a peculiar thing. Who was he, and what on earth had he meant about James? She thought of the expressions on the faces of the few mourners present – an uneasy combination of pity and prurience. Now that they were leaving them all behind, they could think what they liked. It would be a fresh start.

Having no parents made her feel adrift. Perhaps both she

and James needed to put down some new roots. But wasn't that a kind of betrayal – leaving the city where they had lived as a family? Yet the thought of staying here with Aunt Agnes depressed her. It would be like being buried alive, albeit in a silk-lined coffin.

No. She had to go. It seemed strange and somehow wrong that she knew so little of the country where her mother had been born. Lucy's father Robert had been on a walking tour of the Piedmont countryside when they had met. Elena was helping her aunt, her only surviving relative, to run a small hotel in the town of Alba. He was a guest. Her mother would always smile as she told them how he had complained about something and she had argued with him. Apparently he hadn't expected it, and his face was such a picture of shock that she'd laughed. 'Yes,' Robert would say. 'And she has never stopped arguing with me from that day to this!'

Despite the protestations of Elena's aunt, they were married a few months later and returned to Edinburgh. Lucy could only imagine how hard it must have been for her mother to adjust to such a different way of life. Perhaps that was why she had insisted that both Lucy and James spoke Italian. It kept her country alive in her heart. They had often conversed in the language at home and their mother was full of stories about the place, but they had never visited. Perhaps Robert feared that once she was back in Italy, she would not want to return to Scotland. Lucy herself had always dreamt of travelling there with her mother when she was old enough, but it had not been possible, and then it was too late. Her mother had died and her father was never really the same man again.

This then could be a sort of pilgrimage. No – more of a tribute to her mother. She would at last make proper contact with the half of her that was Italian. The prospect seemed inviting. Lucy didn't know whether she was prepared to turn her back on her father and on Scotland completely. Only time and distance would tell.

3

A special type of criminality among females, particularly in the higher animals, is hatred for individuals of their own sex. Envious of her companions, the dove will hide food that she herself does not need under her wing. Among the anthropomorphic monkeys, particularly orang-utans, females treat one another with an instinctive animosity, beating and sometimes even killing one another.

Lombroso and Ferrero, 1893, p. 92

3 April 1888

The train jolted James awake and, for a moment, he wondered where he was. Out of the window he saw the snow-covered peaks of the Alps rising in the distance, and it all came back to him in one glorious rush. It had been only two weeks since he had received Sofia's letter, and now he was on his way back to her. Across from him Lucy was dozing gently, her head lolling onto the shoulder of the woman next to her. Fortunately they were quite well acquainted by now, as she was Lucy's new companion, Miss Euphemia Trott.

'It will not be long before we arrive, I imagine,' she said.

'Perhaps another hour or so, if memory serves,' he replied.

Miss Trott seemed unremarkable in almost every way. She

was in her late forties, short and roundish, with pleasant features and faded-blonde hair that was pinned up rather untidily. She had an air of competence about her, as if little would shake her; this, James presumed, was why Aunt Agnes had decided to engage her. He knew little else about her other than her name, that she attended the same church as his aunt and was fluent in Italian. She seemed nice enough, though a little dull. But then perhaps that was what Lucy needed – someone to keep her grounded in her new life.

Miss Trott sat with her hands folded in her lap, the fore-finger of one tapping on the other as if keeping time with an imaginary orchestra. As James watched, he realised that it was the rhythm of the train that she was marking. Her small round glasses began to slide slowly but surely down her nose, but she did not touch them. How long would she resist the temptation? he wondered.

She turned her head briefly to peer out of the window, and when she looked back, the glasses had mysteriously returned to where they had started, apparently without her intervention.

James stared at her. How on earth did she do that? She raised her eyebrows, as if challenging him to ask. He turned away, embarrassed. It was probably best left. There were other, more pressing, matters on his mind.

He looked out at the Alps again and thought, with an unfamiliar contentment, of what was to come. He was to take up his old position as assistant to Professor Lombroso, and they were to stay with the professor while they found their feet. And that of course meant that he would be in close proximity to the only person other than his sister who really mattered to him – Sofia, the woman he loved. Whatever it was she needed him for, it was surely an excuse, a ruse to get him to return. Why else would she be so oblique? For him their time apart had merely served to emphasise the strength of his feelings, which surely meant that it must have been the same for her.

At last everything seemed to be righting itself to its proper order. He and Lucy had left behind their old life in Edinburgh, with all its difficulties and strains. Finally they could start afresh and everything would be as it should be. He would help Sofia, and somehow, despite her past, they would be together. For once, after the dark days he had suffered, all James saw ahead of him was hope. Because now he had a plan. It had come to him following his conversation with Bell. Its simplicity had surprised him. It was clear that he could not be with Sofia in Scotland. It would be almost as difficult for them in Turin, where everyone knew her background. The answer then was, as Bell had said, quite obvious. They would have to go somewhere else entirely.

'What are your first impressions, Lucy?' James asked as they stood side by side on the platform of Turin's Porto Nuevo station.

'It isn't very... different.'

James laughed. 'What did you expect? People with two heads? Blue rain?'

'Not that kind of difference. Just a feeling that we're not in Scotland.' Lucy had expected some kind of foreignness at least, but all she had seen was... well, sameness. The architecture of the station was almost exactly like that of Waverley. The people rushed about just as they did in Scotland, and she felt as much of a stranger here as she did in her own city. It was even raining, as it had been in Edinburgh when they began their journey.

It was true that there had been plenty of contrast during

their travels, and Lucy had experienced a sense of invigoration with each new experience. The trip by boat had been, in her imagination, a voyage to the new world with a pirate ship on the horizon and the possibility of being shipwrecked on a desert island arriving with even the suggestion of a cloud. The train rattling through the French and Italian country-side towards Turin was the setting for an encounter between her detective and a network of spies. When she tired of that scenario, Lucy had started to peer out of the window at every station and examine the people milling about in almost for-ensic detail. Once she had jotted down a few observations in her notebook, she would set about giving each person a story that she would then relate to James and Miss Trott. The large woman in the dress with the too-tight arms at a small station near the border was wearing an anxious expression because she was fleeing from justice. She had either poisoned her lover or was a retired baby farmer, or possibly both. James had entered into the spirit of it and had suggested that she might be wearing a disguise, because 'no one would wear that dress voluntarily'. Miss Trott had merely kept her nose in her book. Lucy had hoped it would at least be a novel that was holding her attention, but it turned out to be a collection of accounts of the lives of various saints, or what Aunt Agnes would call 'an improving text'. What normal person would read such a dull narrative? she wondered.

Lucy had done her best to give her new companion an interesting backstory, but it was an uphill struggle. In the end she had settled for either a tragic love affair that had come to a premature end when her lover had been killed in a faraway conflict, or some kind of scandal. She liked the idea of an affair much more than the scandal, but had to abandon it due to implausibility. Love and Miss Trott just didn't go together. If propositioned, she would be more likely to raise her eyebrows, give a small shake of her head and walk away rather than do or say anything that might involve passion of any kind. This was based on what Lucy had observed so far, which was Miss Trott variously reading, nodding off or making comments about the weather, with which she seemed to be obsessed. James appeared happy enough with her, although no doubt his criteria were different to Lucy's own.

A sense of disappointment began to overwhelm her. Why wasn't there more evidence of Italian-ness? She could hear the difference in the language, and that was something. But everything smelt of damp and seemed grey when it should have been a new aroma and a different kind of light that had greeted them. Perhaps it was just a matter of the rain.

She watched James, in his element organising their luggage, moving from one trunk to another, checking them off in a notebook. He liked order. Having his equilibrium disturbed in any way depressed him, which was one of the reasons why their father's downfall had hit him so hard. He grinned, and Lucy gave him a small smile. She had not yet forgiven him for his attitude towards their father. He was dead and should be properly mourned, whatever he had done, yet all James had been able to demonstrate, it had seemed to her, was relief.

'I cannot pretend to feel what I do not,' he had said when she had challenged him. 'There are things you do not know.'

'Then tell me!' she had cried. 'He was my father too!'

But it was no good. James would not be drawn on the matter, leaving her trapped in a kind of lonely limbo wherein she could not forgive either her brother or her father, and wondering what the words 'I know what you are' actually meant. She had thought she knew what James was – kind, sometimes funny, protective, impulsive about some things, cautious about others; at any rate nothing bad – at least until her father had been taken away. Then he had changed, becoming secretive and strained, until one day he too had disappeared. She remembered it only too well, for it had marked the beginning of her own incarceration with Aunt Agnes. At least that was over, for the time being anyway.

'Are you ready, dear?' Miss Trott enquired. 'I think we are all set to go. I am told it isn't far.'

She was right. It seemed that they had hardly sat down in the waiting carriage before they arrived at the professor's house. The touch of James's hand was cool and reassuring as he helped Lucy to alight. She looked up at the building with its tall windows and occasional architectural flourishes in the form of scrolls and flowers. Here and there were faces carved into the stone, squinting down at her malevolently as if warning her not to enter. Defiantly she pulled her cloak around her and waited for the door to be opened.

There was only one thing on James's mind from the moment they had arrived in Turin, and that was Sofia. Why had she called him back to her? There had been no communication other than her letter, which had been so brief it had told him almost nothing. Sofia was not one for idle chatter, but still he would have liked at least a suggestion of what help she required. It was as if she knew that her request alone was all it would take. And, of course, she had been absolutely right.

As they stood outside Lombroso's imposing front door, he yearned to see her. He looked at his sister to see if she had noticed anything, but fortunately she seemed oblivious to how he felt. The time would come to tell Lucy about Sofia, but it had not yet arrived. He had no idea how to broach the subject – and that was before he mentioned his plans for all of their futures. For now, though, all that mattered to him was Sofia. He had rehearsed the moment of their reunion many times since receiving her letter, and all he wanted was to see her. But to his dismay and surprise, when the door opened, she was not there.

Instead they were ushered in by a capable housemaid, who showed them into the drawing room. James was instantly transported back to his last meeting with the professor and Ottolenghi, his fellow assistant. They had sat around the fire and reflected on the tragic events that had taken place. Lombroso had seemed humbled by all that had happened, even questioning his own actions. He had been so certain that criminal anthropology could be used to catch a killer, but he had been proved wrong in a very public way. Instead all they had learnt was that science could not always explain criminal behaviour. James wondered what developments in Lombroso's theory of the born criminal this might have led to. It made him realise how much he was looking forward to getting back to work.

The door was thrown open and the professor bounded in, a small, bearded bundle of energy fizzing like a newly opened bottle of champagne.

'Murray, my dear fellow. How good it is to see you! How are you?'

He seized James's hand and pumped it up and down. A grey-haired woman stood in the doorway, watching them and smiling patiently.

'Now, there is much to discuss. I have started a new investigation. We will be revolutionising the study of crime. What do you think of that?' He went on before James could answer, his heavy eyebrows moving up and down, marking time with his words. 'I think – no, I am certain that we will shake the very foundations of criminal anthropology! And there is more... so much more to talk about!'

The woman in the doorway cleared her throat.

'What is it, my dear?' he asked.

She came into the room and indicated Lucy and Miss Trott. 'We do have other guests, Cesare.'

He gave a short bow. 'Ah, Miss Lucy Murray, I gather, and this lady is...?'

'This is Miss Trott, Professor,' James said. 'My sister's companion.'

Miss Trott gave Lombroso a nod of acknowledgement. The professor peered at her and frowned. Steadfastly she returned his gaze. There was an awkward silence, which was eventually broken by the woman with the grey hair.

'Why don't you take Signor Murray to your study, Cesare, whilst I look after the ladies?' She paused. 'I am Nina Lombroso, as my husband neglected to inform you.' She tutted at him, and James was amused to see a sheepish look pass over his face just for an instant before he moved towards the door.

'Yes, my dear... an excellent notion. Come, Murray, we have much to discuss.' With that he swept out of the room without so much as a backward glance.

'I do apologise for my husband,' Signora Lombroso said. 'He is rather prone to getting carried away. He's been so excited about your return, Mr Murray.'

'Should I...?' James said, looking towards the door.

'Yes, do. I think you know the way, do you not?' she said, her eyes twinkling. 'Now, ladies, let me show you to your rooms. Then, later, you must allow me to introduce you to my daughters. They are very much looking forward to meeting you, Miss Murray.'

James took his leave and began to make his way to Lombroso's study. It was almost as if he had never left... except for the one thing that was missing. Where on earth was Sofia?

4

*...the female born criminal surpasses her male counter-
part in the refined, diabolical cruelty with which she
commits her crimes. Merely killing her enemy does not
satisfy her; she needs to watch him suffer and experience
the full taste of death.*

(Lombroso and Ferrero, 1893, p. 182)

Lucy had been left to rest in her room. She was finding it
difficult to settle. Surely the sudden pang she was experiencing
could not be homesickness, could it? She had been so eager to
leave, after all. Still, it was a strange feeling not having your
own home. Professor Lombroso was a funny little man, not
at all the grave and serious scientist she had been expecting.
James had always seemed to be in awe of him. Lucy could
not think why. He was so friendly... almost like a favourite
uncle.

There was a light tap on the door. It opened to reveal two
girls, one of a similar age to herself and the other slightly
younger, perhaps about fifteen – the Lombroso sisters, she
imagined. The elder was taller than the younger and had more
pronounced features. She wore a slight frown, making her
look serious and bookish. Her sister was a little dumpy, with
a rounder face and a flatter nose. Neither could be called

pretty. They both had dull brown hair, and both were dressed in drab school outfits that did nothing to flatter their shape. But there was something engaging about them nonetheless, and Lucy felt instantly comfortable in their company.

'I am Paola Lombroso,' said the older girl, stepping forward and extending her hand. Lucy shook it solemnly.

Her sister grinned. 'And I am Gina. Really, Paola, there is no need to be so formal!'

'I was just being polite. Remember what Mama told us about how to greet a stranger.'

'I hope we shall not be strangers for long,' Lucy said.

Paola frowned slightly. 'We have met, so we can't be strangers now.'

Gina groaned. 'Always analysing!' Paola opened her mouth as if to protest, but her sister interrupted her. 'I know, I know . . . Papa would say that was a good thing, but you can go too far.'

Paola shook her head impatiently. 'How are you finding Italy, Miss Murray?'

'Call me Lucy, please, or should I say Lucia, now that I am here. That is my given name after all.'

'Oh yes,' Gina said, flopping down on to Lucy's bed. 'I like that. Miss Lucia Murray – it is much more serious-sounding. That is what we shall call you – a new name for a new city.'

Lucy nodded. 'Perhaps, though I don't know what my brother will say.'

'Ah yes, Signor James. We watched as you arrived. He's quite handsome, isn't he?' Paola said, perching sedately on a chair.

Lucy considered this view of her brother. 'Really? I've

never thought of him in that way, but I suppose he might be considered so by some.'

Gina laughed. 'Let us analyse, as Papa would. Not tall – more stocky, I'd say – with thick dark hair, pale skin, generous lips, nice smile, grey eyes, I think?'

Lucy nodded, enjoying the game.

'An infectious laugh,' Paola added, 'oh, and a flat head at the back. That might be significant, don't you think?'

'Only if you're Papa,' Gina said. 'I doubt Signor Murray is a criminal!'

Lucy began to laugh, but it turned into a yawn, which she tried desperately to stifle, not wishing to seem rude.

'Perhaps we should leave you to rest a little,' Paola suggested. 'We will have plenty of time to get acquainted.'

'Yes, yes... a good idea,' Gina said. 'We shall see you at dinner. Papa has invited Anna, you know.'

'Anna?' Lucy asked.

'You'll like her,' Gina said. 'She is wonderful.'

'Madame Anna Tarnovsky. She has come all the way from Prague to work with Papa on a new project,' Paola said. 'If we are lucky, they will tell us about it.'

Lucy nodded. 'I think the professor mentioned it earlier. It all sounded rather strange.'

Gina smiled. 'You'll get used to it. Before long, that is all your brother will be able to talk about.'

'Anyway, we will see you at dinner,' Paola said. 'The first of many, no doubt.'

Lucy watched them as they left. Then it struck her. *Plenty of time*, Paola had said, and she was right. They would be here for a few months at least, and who knew what would happen after that. The recent past had not been kind to them, but it was the future that was important now – an unknown and mysterious landscape unpunctuated by the familiar landmarks of her childhood. This was the beginning of a new part of her life.

James was on his way up to Lombroso's study when he saw her – framed in a doorway, the light surrounding her as if she was some kind of vision. He felt a surge of joy travel through him. With her dark hair, almond-shaped eyes and enigmatic half-smile, Sofia was every bit as beautiful as he had remembered. He had fallen for her almost as soon as they had met, but her past had always come between them. She had been working as a prostitute when Lombroso had found her and brought her to Turin. It meant that she and James could never allow their relationship to be anything but a secret either in Turin or in Scotland. When his father's illness had taken him away from her, James had promised that he would find a way for them to be together. Now he thought he had, and he couldn't wait to tell her his plans.

'*Buongiorno*, James.'

He walked towards her, but before either of them could speak, Lombroso called from his study on the floor above. 'Murray, where the devil are you?'

Sofia whispered in his ear. 'I will meet you after dinner. Wait for me on the corner.'

He breathed in her scent – a heady aroma of spices and citrus – and then in an instant she was gone, as ever leaving him wanting more.

'Murray, are you ever going to join me?' Lombroso called out. An indignant face peered over the banisters at him.

'On my way, Professor...' Had Lombroso seen him with Sofia? If so, how would he react?

He ran up the stairs, but when he got to Lombroso's study,

the professor was standing at one of the bookcases that lined it, peering intently at a set of leather-bound volumes, as though he hadn't been calling impatiently for him at all.

'Sit, sit. I'll be with you in a moment,' he said distractedly.

James did as he was told, seating himself on a small, faded velvet sofa to one side and gazing round the room in an effort to reacquaint himself with the world of criminal anthropology. Sitting on Lombroso's desk was a skull belonging to a brigand. According to the professor, it was the artefact that had given him the idea that lay at the heart of all his theories – that some criminals were throwbacks to primitive man and had been born that way. Privately James had thought this a little too simplistic, though it was certainly interesting. He was even less convinced by Lombroso's certainty that one could identify these born criminals by their physical characteristics. Could one really be certain, as the professor maintained, that habitual murderers had a cold, glassy stare and bloodshot eyes, or that thieves had thick eyebrows, thin beards and sloping foreheads? Still he did not know enough to challenge these theories. Hopefully, now he was back, he would be able to learn more so he could reach his own conclusions.

On the shelves were a selection of water pitchers decorated with writing and drawings done by criminals from Le Nuove prison in Turin. There were many more of these in Lombroso's personal crime museum at the university, which was where he kept most of the items he had collected over the years. His aim was to examine such artefacts and by doing so identify signs of criminality. To Lombroso, the items were criminal objects – signs and indicators of the criminal nature of their creators.

James remembered his reaction when he was first shown round the museum. Everything had seemed so strange and alien – as if he was entering a different world. One minute he was in a perfectly ordinary hallway; the next he had stepped into a strange and exotic hinterland filled with death masks, rows of skulls and shrunken heads, a selection of fearsome weapons and even a large facsimile of a carnivorous plant. It seemed like a lifetime ago, though less than a year had passed.

Lombroso finally put down the book he had been studying and sat behind his desk. 'I do apologise, Murray. There was something that occurred to me and I wanted to look it up before I forgot it.'

'May I ask what it was?'

'Oh, just a proverb.'

'Really?' James was intrigued.

'Yes, now how did it go... something to do with deception... "Women always tell the truth, but they don't tell all of it."'

'What made you think of it, Professor?'

'Nothing you need to worry yourself about, Murray. Really, you are so easily distracted. We need to focus on work.'

James decided not to react. 'Is Ottolenghi at the museum?'

'Ah yes, your fellow student... No, he is not.' Lombroso sniffed briskly. 'Signor Ottolenghi has seen fit to take a short sabbatical in order to study with someone else.'

'Really, who?'

'Oskar Reiner in Vienna. They are conducting a study on criminal vampirism, of all things.'

James remembered that his friend Ottolenghi, with whom he had shared his adventures during his last visit to Turin, had been fascinated by Reiner's work. He was not in the least surprised that the young man had decided to take a break from

Lombroso, who, though undoubtedly brilliant in his field, could be difficult to work with. And vampirism did sound interesting.

Lombroso leant back in his chair and peered at James. 'He'll be back with us soon enough, but still it means that we shall have our work cut out. Are you ready for the challenge?'

'Yes, Professor, I believe I am.'

'And what of... other distractions?'

Obviously Lombroso was referring to Sofia; perhaps after all he had seen them together just now. It was difficult to know what to say. He was not yet sure exactly where he stood. A few months ago he had left with promises about their future, but he could tell by her response that Sofia had been doubtful about his sincerity, and indeed his capability of conquering the social difficulties that might impede them. And for all he knew, she was right. For now he would have to bluff his way through and hope it would suffice.

'I will deal with these should they arise, Professor, you can be assured of that.'

'Splendid. I am glad to hear it. I would not want your attention to be diverted from the matters at hand. They are too important for that. Our project must take absolute precedence. I am relying on you.'

'Can you tell me more about what it entails?' James asked.

'All in good time, young man, all in good time. Suffice to say that we shall be conducting some very interesting experiments indeed. Madame Tarnovsky will be assisting us too, bringing some data from Prague.'

'And this is a new kind of criminal anthropology, you say?'

Lombroso looked smug. 'Yes, Murray, in a way. We are certainly going to do something different, something that has never been attempted before.' He stood up and walked over to the window, beckoning to James to follow him. 'What do you see out there on the street?'

'People . . . just people walking . . . and some trams and carriages.'

'Exactly! You have performed what we would call a blind observation of facts, albeit a rudimentary one. You have looked out of this window and given an account of what you have seen from an objective point of view – a scientist's view.'

'So?'

'So, that is how we differ from our contemporaries. They do not approach things objectively, but deduce from universal principles. We, on the other hand, view things empirically.'

'And the new aspect? '

'We will turn our attention to women as criminals and study them in the same way that I have been doing with the male criminal.'

James nodded. 'And no one has attempted this before?'

'Not like this.' Lombroso put his hand on James's shoulder and beamed at him. 'I don't think it is an overstatement to say that we are going to make history in the study of crime.'

James wanted more than anything to embrace the professor's enthusiasm, but something made him pause. Though the subject matter might make them pioneers in the new science of criminal anthropology, he rather suspected that the end result might not have the effect Lombroso yearned for.

The smile disappeared. Had the professor realised what he was thinking? He had often displayed an uncanny ability for such mind-reading. James braced himself, waiting for an admonishment, but none was forthcoming. Instead Lombroso spoke in an uncharacteristically hesitant manner.

'There is another matter that I hope will engage your interest.'

'What is that?'

Lombroso cleared his throat. 'Before we go any further, I need your honest answer to what might seem like an odd question.'

'Go on, Professor.'

'Do you believe in the Devil, Murray?'

5

Everyone agrees that the few violent women far exceed men in their ferocity and cruelty. The brigand women of southern Italy and the female revolutionaries of Paris invented unspeakable tortures. It was women who sold the flesh of policemen; who forced a man to eat his own roasted penis; and who threaded human bodies on a pike.

Lombroso, 1876, p. 67

Lucy had mixed feelings about the dinner that evening. She was excited at the prospect, but she was also nervous. She was loath to admit it, even to herself, but the nerves were there nonetheless, jabbing at her like an impish child armed with a pin. Her life in Edinburgh had been mostly quiet and uneventful. Before her father's downfall, she had socialised with friends from school. Afterwards, just as she was becoming old enough for such things as small gatherings, dinners, concerts and visits to the theatre, invitations had seemed to dwindle until they became non-existent. Then her mother had died and she had gone into mourning. This meant that social occasions were confined to Aunt Agnes's church-related activities, and she was forced to watch as her peers enjoyed all the things that she was missing. Lucy had, therefore, never been invited to a formal dinner that included academics, scientists and thinkers as guests. In Aunt Agnes's social circle, ideas were rarely exchanged, perhaps because everyone held the same opinions about everything. And they were always dull, dull, dull.

Miss Trott had abandoned her, claiming that she had a bad headache and needed to rest. Lucy took some comfort from the fact that both Gina and Paola would be present, which would give her an example to follow.

The door opened after a sharp knock. James strode in. He seemed surprised. 'You look different.'

'How different?'

He shrugged. 'I don't know. Just different, grown up.'

'I'm almost—'

'Eighteen, yes, I know. I suppose I shall have to get used to it.'

'To what?'

'To you being . . . well . . . you know . . .' He cleared his throat and avoided her glance.

'What, James? What am I?'

'I think you know without me telling you. The word is beautiful. Now come on, Lucy. We need to go down. It is not polite to keep our hosts waiting.'

She took a last look at herself in the full-length mirror, turning this way and that to get the full effect. She hardly recognised herself. Instead of the slightly untidy figure she was used to seeing, a young woman stood in front of her – taller, more elegant and more poised than before, red-gold hair piled elegantly on top of her head to reveal a long, swan-like neck. Yes, she liked that expression. Lydia Loveday should definitely have a swan-like neck.

Lucy had always thought it most unfair that it was James who resembled their mother, with his shock of dark hair and fine features, whereas she took after their father's side of the family. Now, however, she was beginning to think that it might not be such a bad thing after all. Still, despite the evidence in front of her, James's words had startled her. Beauty was not something she had thought about very much, but as she stared at her reflection, she wondered if perhaps, just perhaps, he might be right.

Dinner, it appeared, would be less formal than James had expected. It began with a small gathering of guests in the drawing room. He watched Lucy take in her surroundings and smiled to himself at her reaction to the various strange artefacts dotted about the place, mingling with the more normal ornaments and knick-knacks. Even here Lombroso had made his mark.

James had told Lucy all about Lombroso, the museum at the university and its contents, so she was, to an extent, forewarned. Still, he could see that experiencing the professor and his curios in the real world might be something of a shock to the uninitiated, particularly as, on close inspection, even the most innocuous of items sometimes turned out to be anything but.

All were examples of prisoners' art collected by the professor during his career. There were ceramic vases and pots that looked quite ordinary at a distance but were decorated with lurid depictions of various crimes. A small piece of sculpture taking pride of place on the mantelpiece re-created a trial complete with judge and jury. There was even an extremely lifelike object made, according to Lombroso, out of bread and showing an insane thief being strapped to his bed.

Lucy seemed to be taking all of this in her stride, perhaps because of Lombroso's daughters, who were now guiding her through the collection. It was the first time he had set eyes on them, and he could certainly see their father in both of them. The elder girl, Paola, watched studiously as her younger sister talked animatedly to Lucy, waving her arms about exactly as Lombroso did when addressing an audience. Every now and again Paola would interject, her eyes lighting up in her evident passion for her subject. In her expression James could see her father, transported to another world by his ideas and wanting his listener to accompany him there.

James wandered over to take a closer look at one of the professor's latest acquisitions – a small clay sculpture of two men apparently fighting. It was a primitive representation, roughly hewn and resembling a carving on a totem pole or similar, like something from the British Museum. When examined more closely, it was clear that the two men were melded together, almost as if they were Siamese twins. The other thing of note was that one was clearly choking the other, the victim's tongue protruding quite horribly. The perpetrator's expression was determined, ruthless, cold – evil. It reminded James of someone he would far rather forget, a multiple murderer he had encountered in Turin on his last visit. He could see him in his mind's eye – a sharp-featured American carrying a silver-topped cane and wearing a coat with a distinctive astrakhan collar. He was ruthless and calculating, with a quick tongue and a penchant for ripping people to shreds. He had managed to slip away whilst they had been preoccupied with another set of crimes, and now his absence had made him even more of a threat. James and Lombroso had revealed his identity, and he was not a man who was likely to forgive or forget. He was out there somewhere, almost certainly plotting his revenge. The thought made James feel cold, though Lombroso's drawing room was nothing of the kind.

'I wonder who you're thinking of,' Lombroso said, joining him.

'I think you know the answer to that, Professor,' James replied.

'Indeed I do. A finer example of the morally insane criminal I have yet to meet.'

'Where could he have gone?'

'Who knows. No doubt he is perpetrating ever more monstrous deeds in some unfortunate place. He had killed before we encountered him and I see no reason to suppose he will stop of his own volition.'

'I take it there is no chance he has remained in Turin?'

'I doubt it. The city was thoroughly searched. Even Machinetti managed that, though I imagine our friend Inspector Tullio had a hand in it. Still, you can ask him yourself. He will be joining us this evening.'

'You have invited Machinetti?' James said in surprise. Machinetti, Lombroso's nemesis, was a carabinieri marshal whose methods of investigation were almost as primitive as one of the professor's criminal throwbacks.

'Why not? I like to keep an eye on him. Don't worry. I have invited Tullio too.'

James was relieved. Tullio, an officer in the public security police who had also been involved in the case, was a very different prospect from the bombastic Machinetti. He disliked Machinetti almost as much as Lombroso did, and was forever complaining about him.

'Ah, and here they are, together with our remaining guests! Inspector Tullio, Machinetti, I am delighted you could spare the time from your criminal exertions. And Father Vincenzo ... and Professor Gemelli, welcome!'

James grinned at Tullio, who responded in kind. It was

good to see a friendly and familiar face. Something about the inspector seemed to have changed, though. It wasn't so much his appearance – slight in build, neatly clipped beard, well-polished shoes; a picture of understatement and efficiency just as James remembered – as his demeanour. When they'd first met, James had considered him to be a little unsure of himself, which at the time had seemed comforting. Now, however, Tullio had a new air of confidence, and it suited him.

Looking at Tullio's fellow guests, James wondered if Lombroso was operating under the epithet 'Keep your friends close but your enemies closer.' Father Vincenzo, an extremely influential priest who sat on various university boards, disapproved wholeheartedly of the professor's work, seeing his ideas as a direct attack on the Catholic Church. A born criminal could not be held responsible for his actions, which in turn meant that he was not a sinner and therefore did not require forgiveness or salvation. That, as Lombroso had pointed out more than once in Father Vincenzo's company, made the Church somewhat redundant.

Professor Gemelli, dean of the university faculty within which Lombroso worked, was almost as hostile. This was partly due to academic jealousy, James thought, but he too did not support Lombroso's ideas, preferring to criticise his admittedly somewhat erratic methods rather than his findings. Both men had been heavily involved in impeding last year's investigation, although neither would ever admit it.

'I was just saying to Murray here that I think we can be sure, thanks to Inspector Tullio, that our killer is long gone,' Lombroso said.

Machinetti bristled with indignation at being left out. He was wearing his dress uniform, an ostentatious combination of shining brass buttons and gold brocade. His stomach strained at the seams of his jacket and a small bead of sweat glistened as it made its way down one of his temples.

Tullio was about to reply when he was interrupted.

'I hope you are right, Lombroso. It would not reflect well on either you or the faculty if he returned to Turin,' Professor Gemelli said. He was a small, rotund man who had a habit of standing with his chin elevated, as if he were perpetually peering over the edge of something. His hair was plastered to his shining skull in an apparent effort to hide the fact that there was so little of it.

Lombroso smiled patiently at him as if he were a child. 'No need to be concerned, Gemelli. If the killer was still with us, he simply would not be able to resist for long. He would feel a compulsion to commit new crimes and to lay each atrocity out for us in an effort to share them with the widest audience possible. Even Machinetti here could catch him!'

'Now look here, Lombroso . . .' Machinetti's large moustache quivered with indignation.

'I seem to recall that your own efforts in that regard were not particularly fruitful, Lombroso,' Gemelli said. It was the professor's turn to bristle.

'So you are certain that he has left the city?' Father Vincenzo asked, arching his eyebrows. He was an entirely different kind of man to Gemelli. Everything about him exuded understated power, from his bearing – which was upright, almost regal – to his sharp features, including a prominent aquiline nose. He looked a little like a Roman emperor, albeit one dressed as a priest.

Lombroso acknowledged him with a brief respectful nod. 'Indeed I am, Father. It is my considered view that he has gone to a place he knows, a place where it is easy to hide.'

'I hope you're right, Professor,' James said.

Lombroso patted him on the back. 'I am always right, you know that!'

James caught Tullio's eye. The events of the previous year had surely proved that the professor was as fallible as anyone else, given that he had failed to spot the identity of a killer who was right under his nose. Still, he seemed to have recovered from any self-doubt that might have plagued him. In fact he sounded just as he had before it had all happened. And now it seemed there might be a venture into psychical research. Lombroso had been coy about the details. After James had answered his question about believing in the Devil with a puzzled 'not really', Lombroso had declined to comment further. James wondered, just for a moment, whether he had done the right thing in returning to Turin to continue his studies, even if it was only to be a temporary arrangement.

Then the door opened and in an instant all his doubts were gone. There stood Sofia, as captivating as ever, smoothing down her drab grey dress. Anna Tarnovsky passed her in a vivid blue gown with lace around the neck and sleeves and tiny sparkling crystals on the bodice. Her attire was a good deal more elaborate than Sofia's, but she might as well have been standing in a dark shadow for all the impact she made on James. He tried unsuccessfully to prevent himself from grinning stupidly as Sofia walked over to Signora Lombroso and whispered in her ear. Then, without warning, she left the room as abruptly as she had entered it.

James had watched her as she carefully ignored him. She had not exactly been welcoming when they met earlier, but one could never tell with Sofia. She was almost always inscrutable. It was one of the things he had found most enticing about her. Still, at least it would not be long before they met properly. It could not come quickly enough for James.

'Murray!' Lombroso said sharply. 'Madame Tarnovsky is here!'

He flushed at this admonishment, though he deserved it. There was no excuse for ignoring someone so eminent in her field.

Anna Tarnovsky smiled. 'Ah, Mr Murray – how nice to see you back with us in Turin. I see that we have that in common. Neither of us could stay away.'

He stared at her. Was she being pointed? It was unlike her.

'Murray!' Lombroso said again, more impatiently.

James recovered himself and bowed. 'Do forgive me, Madame Tarnovsky. It has been a very long day.'

'Not at all, Mr Murray, though perhaps as we are to work together, we could dispense with the formalities. Do call me Anna.'

'Then please, call me James.'

'I'm "Professor" to you, Murray, before we get carried away,' Lombroso said. 'Now, shall we go in to dinner? I believe I have quite an appetite!'

James escorted Lucy into the dining room. She seemed excited, coltish – skittish even. He supposed it was natural given that prior to this her usual company had been their Aunt Agnes, but still there was something odd about her demeanour. He smiled ruefully to himself. The closer to adulthood Lucy got, the more of a mystery the workings of her mind became to him.

The conversation at dinner was lively, and Lucy was relieved that the atmosphere was a good deal more relaxed than she had anticipated. She was pleased to note that her Italian was sufficient to keep up with most of what was being said, although there were one or two words and phrases that eluded her. Soon, she hoped, she would be as fluent as a native. Other than her brother, the only scientists present were Professor Lombroso and Anna Tarnovsky, and a small man with hardly any hair and what Lucy thought was a mean-spirited expression. They and the rather intimidating priest sitting with them were engaged in their own discussion for much of the meal. This meant that she could watch and listen. She had already learnt something of great interest by doing exactly that, and hoped that further close observation would reveal more. When Anna Tarnovsky had arrived, the change in James had been palpable. His usually pale skin had become flushed as if he was lighting up from the inside, and he had smiled quite stupidly. It was perfectly clear to Lucy what was happening here. She had known that her brother was hiding something from her about his previous trip to Turin, and here it was, plain for all to see if they bothered to look. He was in love with Anna Tarnovsky.

Lucy could understand why. It was true that she was a little older than James, and not exactly beautiful – well, not classically so, anyway. But her face was interesting, some might say striking, with its slightly prominent nose and high cheekbones. She had hazel eyes and a smile that put you immediately at ease. Her hair was a deep chestnut colour – the same hue that Lucy herself had always hoped for instead of her strawberry-blonde locks. But it was Anna Tarnovsky's obvious intelligence and wit that made her stand out. What Lucy admired most was her ability to stand up to the professor, whose opinions were put forward in such a way as to make it absolutely clear that he did not expect them to be challenged.

But had she not been referred to as Madame Anna Tarnovsky? Had James fallen in love with a married woman? Surely not! That would be scandalous. Lucy allowed her imagination to run riot. It must be an unhappy match. She did not even wear a wedding ring. That must be significant. James was no doubt trying to rescue her from her cruel and abusive spouse. He liked to rescue people. It was why he had become a doctor, he had told her once.

Now who might the husband be? Of course! She would obviously be married to a Russian count or similar, who refused to release her from her vows. She had probably met him when she was a student and fallen for his charms. Gradually he had restricted her freedom until she had no option but to escape to Turin. There she had met James and they had fallen in love. No wonder he had been so desperate to return! Poor James and Anna, forced to meet in secret until . . . well, until what? Oh, if only she had thought to bring her notebook down with her. She must observe the interaction between the guests with extra care to ensure that she remembered every last detail.

'It is quite clear that our hypothesis should be that criminal women are inferior to their male counterparts,' Lombroso was stating firmly.

'Now, Cesare, I am not so sure that I agree,' Anna said. Lucy noticed the way she addressed the professor, with an easy kind of informality that made it clear that she viewed them as equals, even if the professor did not. No doubt she was enjoying her freedom from the cruel count.

'Why ever not?' he asked.

'Because it makes no sense to begin there when the figures are so contradictory.'

'In what way?'

'There are so few women criminals . . . that is why. It muddies the ground.'

Lombroso frowned. His face was reddening. Clearly he did not enjoy being contradicted. Whether this was because it was done by a woman, or just in general, Lucy could not tell. The little bald man, who she'd discovered was called Gemelli, was sitting back in his seat, a contented smile on his face. Perhaps he was enjoying the food and wine, which were, Lucy had to admit, rather good. Signora Lombroso had told her that she disapproved of the fashion for serving French dishes and much preferred local cuisine. Having said that, they had dined on chicken Marengo, which according to Paola had been created by Napoleon Bonaparte's chef during his Italian campaign. The aroma of Madeira, garlic and lemon that had wafted across the table was so appetising that Lucy found it agonising to wait for everyone to be served before she could tuck in.

She looked again at Gemelli. No, it was not the food that had made him smile. There was a glint of satisfaction in his eyes that told her it was Professor Lombroso's evident discomfort that he was really relishing.

'A very interesting point, Madame Tarnovsky. What do you say to that, Lombroso?' Gemelli said, smirking.

'It is a question of atavism. These women are throwbacks to their primitive ancestors, as are their male counterparts,' the professor replied.

'I am not sure that atavism is the right way to describe it,' said Anna. 'If they are throwbacks, then why are there not more female criminals? That is what we need to be wary of. What do you think, James?'

James paused. His thick dark hair fell forward over his eyes and he pushed it back impatiently. It must be difficult for him, Lucy thought. He would not want to offend anyone, and yet he would still have an opinion. Would he be sufficiently confident to share, it and whose side would he take? She urged him on in her head. Come on, James, be bold.

'It is a conundrum, that is certain,' he said finally. 'Perhaps before continuing with the experiments, it might be useful to consider our subject pool.'

'Then we are bowing to the critique of the French before we have even got started!' Lombroso said with a note of exasperation.

'Now, Cesare, let us have no more discussion of work,' admonished Signora Lombroso. 'Mr Murray will be tired after his long journey. There will be time enough for that in the days and weeks to come.'

Lombroso acceded to his wife's wishes with a smile, but Lucy could see that he was reluctant to change the subject.

'So, Miss Murray, what will you do whilst James is busy with his work?' Anna Tarnovsky asked.

Lucy frowned. The truth was, she wasn't certain what James had planned for her. Would she have a governess, or would Miss Trott take that position?

'I expect you will do a little sightseeing first of all, won't you, Lucy?' James said. 'Get acclimatised to your surroundings?'

'Could we take Miss Murray to see your museum, Father?' Gina asked.

'I don't see why not,' Lombroso replied. 'I'm all for women in the sciences, am I not, Madame Tarnovsky?'

Lucy noticed Anna Tarnovsky raise her eyebrows ever so slightly.

'Any objection, Murray?' Lombroso asked.

James shrugged. 'If you would like to, Lucy, then I don't mind.'

'I thought she was changing her name to Lucia,' Gina whispered loudly to her sister.

'Ah, a change of identity...' Lombroso said. 'That reminds me of a young female swindler I once encountered. She had the most extraordinarily large—'

'Cesare!' interrupted his wife. 'This is not the time or the place!'

Lucy noticed James hiding a smile. What would Aunt Agnes think if she was here – or Miss Trott, for that matter? The professor really was the most extraordinary person. One simply didn't know what he would say next.

Before long the dinner drew to a conclusion and the ladies withdrew, leaving James and Lombroso in deep conversation about something or other. As she got up to leave, Lucy saw Anna Tarnovsky linger for just a few seconds, but it was enough. She was clearly reluctant to go. How difficult it must be for her. She was excluded from the discussion just because she happened to be a woman, even though she was their equal in every other way. It was so very unfair.

The ladies having left, James sat with Tullio whilst Gemelli and Father Vincenzo talked about this and that, mostly university business from what he could hear. Machinetti sat with them, leaning towards them slightly as if he was hoping to catch them out in some indiscretion.

'How's the family, Tullio?' James asked.

'They are well as far as I know. I hardly get to see them these days.'

'Busy fighting crime, then?'

'It seems never-ending sometimes,' Tullio said. 'We have a devil of a case on at the moment.'

'Go on.' James was not surprised by Tullio's comment. This was a city of devils, after all. The events of the previous year had more than proved that.

'A few days ago a woman's body was discovered in a shallow grave outside the city. We have no leads, and the cause of death is difficult to establish with any certainty.'

'Really? How come?'

'Without going into unsavoury detail, the body is in an unusual state. In fact I would go so far as to say that I have never seen anything like it before. Whoever did this...' Tullio shook his head.

James was quiet for a moment, his mind travelling swiftly to the scene depicted by the inspector. He could only imagine what Tullio had meant, but it was enough to shock him, as evidence of the level of depravity to which a man could sink always did.

'So the state of the body indicates murder?'

'It appears so.' Tullio seemed reticent. James was tempted to probe further, but something about the policeman's demeanour made him pause.

'Have you identified the victim?'

'No, not yet,' Tullio replied. 'But the area is full of seasonal workers, particularly in the rice farms and vineyards, so it could be difficult.'

'Sounds intriguing. Have you asked the professor about it?'

'Not yet. I wondered if you could mention it. I have already asked him for one favour recently, and I don't want to push my luck.'

'What favour was that?'

Tullio furrowed his brows slightly, as if wondering how

much to say. 'I think I'd better let the professor fill you in when he's ready, but if you could mention the other matter...'

James nodded. 'I'll do my best.'

'That would be useful. If you both have time, I'd like you to come down to the mortuary and take a look.'

'I'm sure the professor would be only too happy to lend a hand. You know how he likes a mystery.'

'True enough.'

'What's Machinetti's view?'

Tullio lowered his voice. 'Oh, the usual... pull in all known offenders, whatever their crime, and wait until someone points the finger at someone else. It's time-consuming and won't get us anywhere but, strictly speaking, it is his case, as it happened in the countryside, not the city.'

'How come you're involved?' James asked.

'Intervention from the mayor, who is taking a personal interest in the case for some reason. The marshal doesn't know about my involvement yet, and when he finds out... Let's just say I'd prefer to be out of range, as it were.'

Machinetti's beady little eyes were gleaming as he sipped his brandy and puffed on a cigar. He was a bully, and a stupid one at that. He resented Tullio, who, being educated and intelligent, represented all that the marshal and his ilk despised.

James could see the strain etched on his friend's face. His earlier confidence seemed to be waning. 'Don't worry, Tullio,' he said. 'I'm sure you'll get there in the end... and if we can help, then all the better.'

Tullio gave a wan smile. 'Thanks, I appreciate it, but we will have to be discreet. We don't want the newspapers getting hold of the story until we know more.'

'I'll do my best,' James said, 'but I make no promises. You know that discretion is not exactly the professor's forte.'

'I tell you, Gemelli, we will break new ground here. It can only be good for the university,' Lombroso was booming.

Gemelli looked doubtful. 'I have heard this before, Lombroso. In my experience, you breaking new ground usually means two things.'

'And what are they?' Father Vincenzo asked with an amused smile.

'Large sums of money being wasted on all kinds of...' Gemelli seemed to be searching for the word, 'equipment,' he said with disdain.

Lombroso nodded enthusiastically. 'I'm glad you mentioned that. We will need some new measurement pieces and, of course, components for my lie-detecting machine.'

'And what is the second thing?' Father Vincenzo asked.

'The university being discredited, that's what.' Gemelli was warming to his theme, his face reddening with each word.

Lombroso shook his head. 'On the contrary, we... you will be applauded for your foresight in supporting such pioneering work.'

Gemelli paused, apparently considering this possibility. 'You know as well as I do that all research involving prisoners has been forbidden.'

'I am sure there are ways to circumvent such unreasonable constraints,' Lombroso said.

'No, there are not, and after last year's business you would be well advised to take care with any plans you might have.' Gemelli's voice went up an octave.

'What is this I hear about psychical research, Professor?' Father Vincenzo asked. It seemed like a perfectly innocent question, but James saw from the priest's expression that it had been asked for precise and, perhaps even uncharitable, reasons.

'What's this?' Gemelli said. 'Didn't I tell you to refrain from such activities, Lombroso?'

'Ah, yes . . . well, perhaps unsurprising after what happened last time,' Father Vincenzo said, shaking his head. Machinetti watched in satisfaction as Lombroso blushed.

'That was unavoidable, and anyway, no one was hurt. The shopkeeper was reassured and I paid for the damage . . . most of it, anyway.'

'So you are considering another investigation?' Gemelli asked.

'I am, though it is in the early stages at present,' Lombroso replied. 'I have a venue in mind, although it has yet to be confirmed. As soon as the preliminaries have been completed, I plan to launch a psychical enquiry as soon as possible.'

'What kind of enquiry?' Gemelli asked.

'We are going to be searching for the Devil . . . or possibly demons.'

Father Vincenzo seemed pleased at this, which James thought odd. Surely a priest should be reluctant to endorse any encounter with Satan or those who served him.

'Well think again, Lombroso. I expressly forbid it,' Gemelli said.

'Oh dear,' James murmured to Tullio, 'that's done it.'

Lombroso frowned for a moment, then his brow cleared as if a cloud had moved away from the sun. 'I promise you that I will not embark on any form of psychical research that involves the university.'

Gemelli's expression was one of surprise. He clearly had not expected such a complete climbdown. 'Well, good, just as long as we are clear.'

'Oh, you've been very clear, Gemelli,' Lombroso said, for some reason winking at Tullio, whose mouth twitched slightly. 'Very clear indeed.'

In the drawing room, Lucy sipped at her strong, aromatic coffee and watched as Gina and Paola played at cards, with their mother watching over them fondly. Anna came across and sat with her. 'Your brother tells me that you write literature, Miss Murray.'

'I would hardly call it that,' Lucy said, 'but yes, I do write stories.'

'Then I wonder if you would like to accompany me tomorrow. I am visiting the Marchesa Vittoria Carignano for tea, and I'm sure she would enjoy meeting you.'

'I should like that very much.'

'Good. I think you will find it interesting. The lady is very influential in the city. She seems to know almost everyone, and she is the patron of many intellectual pursuits, including literature and poetry as well more scientific subjects.'

'She sounds fascinating.'

'Oh she is, she is, as is the company she keeps.'

Lucy could hardly wait. She had only just arrived, and already her life in Italy seemed full of possibilities. It would be an ideal opportunity to get to know Anna better and perhaps find out more about her past. She might even be able to ask her about James. Glowing with the anticipation of what tomorrow might bring, she took her leave and went up to bed.

The house was smaller than it looked from the outside. As Lucy climbed the central staircase, she saw that the floors were covered with rugs that had once been vibrantly patterned but were now faded and worn. There were display cabinets holding what she assumed were yet more examples of prisoners' art, as if the professor could not bear to be parted from his work even for a second. She heard a noise coming from downstairs and peered over the banisters.

That was odd, she thought. It was late, almost midnight, time for any sensible person to be going to bed. But not, it would seem, her brother. There was James slipping out of the front door, shutting it quietly behind him as if he did not want to be seen. Where on earth was he going at this time of night? Perhaps he was waiting for Anna Tarnovsky to join him for a romantic assignation. It seemed rather risky behaviour, though typically impulsive. Lucy was tempted to peep out of the front door to see where he was going, but just as she was about to creep down the stairs, Anna emerged from the drawing room and said good night to Signora Lombroso before leaving herself.

Lucy smiled. So she was right. They had to be secretive, given the nature of their liaison. And since they all had to work together, the professor might well disapprove of such a match, so poor Anna and James had to meet in secret. This appealed to Lucy's sense of the romantic. Could she perhaps work it into a story?

A door opened on the landing and Miss Trott came out. She was wearing her outdoor coat and carrying a large canvas bag. 'What are you doing standing about, Lucy? Time for bed!'

Lucy paused for a second and then nodded and did as she was told. There would be plenty of time to find out more tomorrow.

6

Female love is, essentially, nothing more than a secondary aspect of maternity. All those feelings of affection that bind woman to man are born not of the sexual impulse, but from instincts of subjection and devotion acquired through adaptation. Lombroso and Ferrero, 1893, p. 76

James made his way with some trepidation to the corner of the Via Legnano. He had been longing for this moment, but now that it was here, he was apprehensive. A carriage went past and instinctively he stepped into the shadows so that he was not seen. Then there she was, walking towards him with her distinctive gait. His breath quickened with desire at the sight of her. She beckoned to him and he followed.

'Let us walk for a while, *caro*.'

He took heart at the familiar term of endearment. They strolled through the deserted streets side by side, the tension between them forming a barrier that he longed to break through. He remembered their final embrace all those months ago, when they had said their last goodbye. He could bear it no longer. He stopped and gently touched her arm. The feel of her sent a jolt of longing through him.

'Sofia, please . . . we must talk.'

She pointed to a small piazza nearby. A fountain played

at its heart and there were some wooden benches around it. They went over and sat on one of them. The silence was filled only with the gentle playing of the water and a slight breeze rustling through the trees.

'I have come back,' James said quietly. 'You asked for help and I am here.'

Sofia avoided his eye. 'Back, yes, but not alone.'

James was puzzled for a moment at the bitterness in her voice and then realised who she meant. 'Lucy...'

'You are not free.'

'I had no choice. I could not leave her again. It would not have been right.'

'I understand. You have a duty to her. She is your family.'

Sofia's voice was stilted. He could sense her hostility, but he had to try.

'We can still be together. It would have to be our secret for a while, as it was before, until I tell Lucy about us... but we could meet.'

'No.' Her refusal rang out across the piazza.

'But you asked me to come back.'

'That was for another reason.'

'What reason?'

'As I said in my letter, I need your help.'

'Sofia, I will do anything for you, you know that. I love you.'

There was a pause. It told him everything.

She did not look at him. 'We are from different worlds. It is not possible. *We* are not possible. It is as I said when we parted last time.'

'And I told you that I would find a way. Everything has changed since the death of my father. I am independent now.

We could leave Turin and start a new life somewhere else...
America perhaps.'

'America! That is so like you, James. You do not think
things through. I cannot go away. I have a life here. But you
did not think of that, did you?'

'Then why ask me to come back?'

'I had no choice.'

'What do you mean?'

'I need your help. My cousin Chiara. She has been staying
with me. Now she has gone missing. I have to find her.'

'When did she go missing? Do you remember?'

'Of course I remember! How could I forget? It was the first
day of March, her thirteenth birthday. She was on her way
to work as a maid at the Marchesa di Carignano's palazzo. '

There was a pause as James took in this information. Sofia's
cousin was younger than he had thought. 'So why not tell the
carabinieri? You don't need me for that.'

'I tried, but they would not listen. They told me that she
had probably run away, but she is so young – still a child,
though she looks older. She would never have left without a
word like that.'

'There are others you could turn to, surely – the professor,
Tullio, Ottolenghi.'

'None of them would help. The professor is too busy
with his experiments. You know how preoccupied he gets.
Inspector Tullio was sympathetic, but he is dealing with other
crimes and does not have the time, and the *dottore* is away.
I was desperate. That is why I did not tell you in the letter.'

'What do you mean?'

'Everyone else seemed to think that she had run away. Why
should you be any different?'

'I thought you wanted us to—'

Sofia stood up and faced him, her eyes flashing with anger. 'To what? To carry on as before? For me to be your secret mistress, there when you want me and invisible when you don't . . . your whore!' She spat the word out as if she could not bear to have it on her lips.

'All right, I'm sorry. I can see how it looks, but that wasn't . . . isn't what is in my heart. I had planned it all – our escape.'

'*Your* escape, you mean!'

'I thought you wanted to be with me.'

She sat down next to him again. 'It cannot be, James. I will not carry on as before. I cannot live like that – meeting in secret, deceiving the professor. You must understand. No matter what I feel for you, that part of my life is over.'

'But if we went somewhere we could be together . . .'

'And what of your sister? Have you told her of your plans . . . about me?

James looked away just for a moment, but it was long enough.

Sofia threw her hands in the air in exasperation. 'You have not told her anything, have you?'

James shook his head. 'I am waiting for the right time.'

'Oh well, if that is all we are waiting for,' Sofia said, her voice heavy with sarcasm. 'What made you think that she would accept me?'

'She will love you, Sofia. As I do.'

'I doubt that – an ex-prostitute and a servant who steals her brother away and leaves her alone in a strange city?'

'She could come with us.'

'Even better! Two new countries in the space of a year. I am sure she will be delighted.'

'Sofia, we could make it work. We love each other.'

There was silence. Sofia's hands were clenched by her sides as if she was readying herself to fight. Her eyes were dull.

'I do not love you.'

Of all the words he had thought she might utter, these were the ones he had least expected. 'How can you say that, after everything? I said that I would come back, and here I am. Are you really telling me that you do not want me?'

'*Sì.* You ask me to sacrifice everything, but I do not love you . . . enough.'

'Enough?'

Sofia nodded.

'So you just asked me here for my help and nothing else?'

'I am sorry. I have misled you. I can see that. I made you come back to Turin with hope in your heart when really . . .'

'There is none?' Each breath seemed like a labour. How could she be so cruel?

She was still unable to meet his eye. He grabbed her arm and swung her to him, furious now. 'So you have used me. Knowing how I felt about you, you have lured me back here to help you.'

'I had no other option. I was desperate!'

'You are not the woman I thought you were, Sofia,' he said.

'What do you mean? I have not changed.'

'Perhaps it is because of your background . . . your criminal background,' he spat. 'Lies and deceit seem to come easily to you.'

Sofia gasped. 'I see you are becoming like the professor.'

'Why? Because I see you now for what you are?'

Her eyes flashed with anger. 'And what is that?'

The words slipped from his mouth all too freely in his hurt and fury. 'You're a born criminal, Sofia. You cannot help yourself.'

She shook her head. 'It is not I who have changed. You are not the man I thought you were. Goodbye, James.'

He watched her walk away and almost went after her, but he could not bring himself to be near her. He was just too angry – both with her for misleading him and with himself for saying those hateful things to her.

It was only once she had gone that his mind cleared enough for a terrible possibility to enter it. A missing girl, a body in the woods – could they be one and the same?

She hears the stone cover being pushed away. It makes her jump. She can feel someone's eyes upon her.

'Why won't you let me go?' she asks.

There is no answer.

'What are you keeping me here for?'

Again no answer. Unable to contain her misery any longer, she starts to sob.

She hears her captor sigh, as if her weeping is a mere inconvenience. Or could it be that they have realised they have made a mistake?

'Let me go, please.'

'Atone.' The voice comes from above. It is light, almost musical. Is it male or female?

She looks up. 'What did you say?'

'Atone,' the voice repeats, and the covering is slid back into place. Is she being left to consider this advice?

She hears the sound of retreating footsteps.

'No, come back. I don't know what you mean!' she cries out in desperation. 'Atone for what?'

But it is to no avail. She is alone yet again. She does not know when her captor will return, or even if they will return at all. Hours pass, empty of everything – even hope. Despite herself, she dozes off for a little while. She is awoken by a noise. She rubs the sleep from her eyes and sits up eagerly. What is it? She hears it again, a high, keening sound, almost like an animal, but not quite. She recognises the humanness of it because it is a sound she has made herself. Someone is weeping. She is not alone.

'Hello?' she shouts. 'Can you hear me?'

The weeping stops.

'Hello,' she calls again. 'Who are you? Where are you?'

There is no reply. She sits, waits and reasons. Perhaps whoever it is needs time to think . . . to trust. Whoever made that sound must be frightened. When one is removed from everything one knows and placed in the darkness with no explanation, then of course it is difficult to know who or what to believe in.

She tries again. 'Please, we are the same. Tell me who you are.'

There is no more noise at first. Only silence. And then the screaming begins.

7

Women have something close to what might be called an
instinct for lying... Unconsciously all are a little false.
Lombroso and Ferrero, 1893, p. 77

James was walking through the city streets, his mind restlessly
turning over his encounter with Sofia. How could she have
been so cruel? To bring him back to her, knowing how he felt,
just so that he could help her find her wretched cousin, who
had probably just run away... well, that demonstrated how
little she cared about him. He had never been good at affairs
of the heart. Falling for the wrong woman was becoming
something of a habit. Why could he not find some uncom-
plicated, acceptable and suitably adoring young woman to
settle down with? Perhaps love was too much to ask for. It
was not as if he deserved such happiness.

He turned in to yet another dark street. He probably
shouldn't be doing this. Turin was full of criminals, as Lombroso was always commenting, and he was just the sort of
target a thief might be looking for.

A sign was swinging gently in the breeze. As he listened to
it creaking, he realised that he had seen it before. Something
had brought him back to the tavern where he had first been
taken by Sofia. It was only a few months ago, but it seemed

as if years had passed. He paused outside and peered up at the sign: La Capra – the goat, Satan's symbol. The animal stared back at him defiantly as if daring him to enter. He heard laughter. The place was still open despite the lateness of the hour. It seemed like fate. He decided to go in for a drink.

The tavern didn't seem to have changed much since his last visit. The smell was the same – tobacco, stale beer and sweat – the barman, Gambro, was still there, and one of the regulars was sitting in his usual spot, muttering to himself. As James walked in, there was a palpable hush. He was still dressed for a formal dinner in his black tail coat and white waistcoat, so it was hardly surprising.

Gambro sneered as he approached. 'Well if it isn't the Inglese. Back to cause more trouble, are you? I'm not sure I should serve you.'

'Firstly, I'm a Scot, and secondly, I can easily take my custom elsewhere.'

Gambro laughed. 'No, no, I'll take your money. What'll it be?'

'Grappa . . . large.'

'It's like that, is it? Better take a carafe.'

James slammed his money down on the counter and picked up his drink. Despite the hour, the tavern was packed. The clientele hadn't improved. It was still comprised of wastrels and vagabonds, none of whom would have looked out of place in one of the illustrations to Lombroso's *Criminal Man*. There were a few women too, mostly prostitutes, he assumed, judging from their appearance. He remembered from his previous visit that there was a state-registered brothel not far from La Capra, so it wasn't surprising that some of its employees ended up there.

There was nowhere to sit except for a space opposite the

resident drunk, who glared at him as he approached and snatched up his tatty straw hat, hugging it to himself as if it might be worth stealing. James was not in the mood for an argument, so he scowled back and sat down anyway. He planned to stay until oblivion descended in an attempt to blot out his conversation with Sofia.

He drank quickly and steadily, welcoming the warmth of the clear liquid as it burned its way down his throat. Lombroso had once told him that drunkenness caused crime as well as insanity, something James knew about only too well thanks to his father. But tonight he didn't care. He drained his glass and poured himself another. The man opposite shoved out his own glass. James shrugged and filled it for him. He knocked it back in one gulp and held it out again. James poured another glass.

'That's all you get, old man.'

His companion shrugged. 'Woman trouble, is it?' he asked, wiping his nose on his dirty cuff.

'How did you guess?'

'Easy. It's always a woman that makes a man turn to drink. What did she do? Go with someone else?'

James shook his head. 'She lied.'

The old man nodded. 'They all do that.'

'I wouldn't care,' James said as he emptied his glass, 'but she knew I loved her. She used me.'

'I hope you told her.'

'Oh I told her all right. I said some terrible things to her. I wanted to hurt her, you see.'

'Should have given her the back of your hand. It's the only thing they understand.'

James stared at him in distaste. 'I need more grappa.'

'Good idea,' the old man said, burping gently into his

glass and slumping forward until his forehead met the table in front of him.

James went back to the bar and put the empty carafe down. Gambro grinned. 'Are you sure, Inglese? It's stronger than it looks.'

'I'm sure.'

'I'll get this,' came a voice from behind him. 'How are you, Signor Murray?'

James turned and saw a man with a pointed nose and thin lips wearing a bowler hat pushed jauntily to the back of his head. 'Just when I thought the night couldn't get any worse... Baldovino, what are you doing here? Following me again?' They had last met during his previous visit to the city, when Baldovino, a reporter on the local paper, *The People's Voice*, had been shadowing him in the hope of a story.

The journalist smirked. 'That's all in the past, my friend. Let me buy you a drink to make up for that... unpleasantness.'

James waved his hand and made his way to a recently vacated table, well away from the old drunk, who now appeared to be unconscious. Baldovino soon joined him, clutching another carafe of grappa. The sight of his rat-like face reminded James of the terrible events of the previous year. He had arrived in Turin to work with Lombroso just as the first of a series of macabre murders was being committed. Each of the victims was left with a note implicating Lombroso.

'So how are things in the world of crime reporting?' he asked. 'Written any more letters to yourself?' Baldovino had sent letters to his own newspaper purporting to be from the killer. It had led them up a blind alley, delayed the investigation and caused Sofia to be hurt.

'It sold a few papers. What's wrong with that?'

'You know perfectly well what the consequences were.'

'I thought your professor was an expert. It's hardly my fault if he couldn't tell they were fakes, now is it?'

James shook his head. 'I see you haven't changed.'

'Thanks,' Baldovino said. 'I can't say the same for you.'

'I'm having a bad day.'

'I thought you'd gone home to England.'

'Scotland... I did, but now I'm back.'

'Unfinished business?'

'Well I thought so, but now I'm not so sure.'

'How come?'

James ran his hands through his thick dark hair and peered blearily at Baldovino. 'I came back for a woman. She asked me for help. Stupidly, I thought she wanted me too.'

Baldovino nodded sympathetically and poured him some grappa. 'And she didn't?'

'No, she just wanted me to find her cousin, who's probably run away. That's what the carabinieri seem to think, anyway.'

Baldovino raised his eyebrows and sat forward on his chair. 'What is this cousin's name?'

'Chiara.'

'Chiara Esposito?'

James nodded. 'Yes. How did you know?'

Baldovino did not answer him. 'How old is she?'

'Young, still a child really. She was... is thirteen, though apparently she looks older.'

'When did she go missing?'

'A few weeks ago, on her way to work. Why?'

'What was the date?'

'March the first.'

'Drink up, my friend. You're going to need it.'

James peered at him through the fog of his drunkenness. 'What is it? Tell me!'

Baldovino paused, as if wondering whether it was a good idea to say anything more.

'The thing is, I don't think this girl you're talking about is a runaway.'

'How do you know?'

The journalist picked up a copy of *The People's Voice* and pointed at the headline: MISSING GIRLS MYSTERY – HAUNTED ABBEY LINK? BALDOVINO INVESTIG-ATES.

James took it from him and began to read.

Could history be repeating itself? A century ago, girls started to go missing from the city and its outskirts. Shortly afterwards, the nearby Abbey San Callisto was closed and its monks dispersed to other monasteries. There were reports that the monks and the girls had become INSTRUMENTS OF THE DEVIL. The monks were banished and most of the girls were never seen again... except for one. Found wandering in a state of confusion near the abbey, covered in cuts and bruises, the traumatised girl could utter only one word: DIAVOLO.

Now there have been a number of similar disappear-ances in MYSTERIOUS circumstances. Is there a link? If there is, you can be certain that Baldovino will find it.

Baldovino sat back smugly. 'One of my contacts gave me some information and... well, as you can see, your girl is not the only one to disappear.'

'And they are all still missing?'

Baldovino nodded.

'How many?'

'Six that I know of, but there may be more.'

James wondered if the journalist knew about the body in the woods. Presumably not, or he would have mentioned it in his article. 'Is there anything else to connect the girls other than the fact that they're missing?'

'They are all aged between thirteen and eighteen and disappeared in the early morning on their way to work.' Baldovino handed him a scrap of paper. It was a list of names, including Chiara's.

'And the abbey. You mention a link?' James asked.

'My sources told me that there have been reports of strange lights and noises coming from the building, which is odd considering it is practically derelict. I asked around the town nearby, and the people I spoke to all confirmed it. There is definitely something going on up there.'

'Sources?'

Baldovino tapped his nose and smiled. 'You know I can't say.'

'So from what these sources said, you put two and two together...'

'I have to make a living. Besides, the missing girls all have links to the town near the abbey. That can't be a coincidence, surely?'

'Perhaps, though I assume you're not claiming that the monks are back.'

Baldovino grinned and waved at the barman for more grappa. 'Hardly, but they're not the only ones in this city to dabble with the Devil, now are they?'

James had to agree. When he was in Turin before, he had been told of the city's status as a centre for satanic ritual, apparently owing to its location on a pole of both black and white magic. If people believed that nonsense, then it was at least a possibility that someone could be reaching back to the past and drawing inspiration from a century-old scandal. And now that a body had been found, it looked as if it was more than abduction. A killer was at large.

8

The passion that most often leads women into crime is love.   Lombroso and Ferrero, 1893, p. 202

As Lucy awoke for the first time in her Torinese bed, she heard the rain pattering lightly on the window pane. Hopefully it was just a shower. There seemed to be as many here as there were in Edinburgh. She was planning a walk around the city to orientate herself and was looking forward to it so much that even the weather would not deter her. Of course Miss Trott would be there to act as chaperone, but at least it would give Lucy the opportunity to find out a little more about her companion. The older woman had said little of note since they had met in Edinburgh, and up until the previous evening had given the overwhelming impression that she was dull. Now, though, her nocturnal wandering had given her an air of mystery that Lucy was rather enjoying. And there was also the question of James's affair with Anna Tarnovsky to investigate. Things were definitely getting interesting.

Step one in any investigation was to accumulate information about one's suspects. Lucy knew this to be so because it was how Mrs Paschal, the heroine of her favourite novel, *Revelations of a Lady Detective*, would approach such a problem. Lucy was an avid reader of both sensation and detective fiction whenever she could get her hands on it, which wasn't often, given Aunt Agnes's disapproval of such material. This particular volume had been a secret gift from James, and reading it had inspired Lucy to create her own stories.

There was a knock at her door and Miss Trott poked her head round it. 'Are you up yet, Lucy?'

'Almost.'

'Well hurry, dear. We don't want to inconvenience anyone. And you don't want to waste valuable time lingering up here when we could be exploring the city, now do you?'

Lucy observed Miss Trott with a little more care than she had done in the past. Her hair was still the same, fading blonde in colour, pinned up a little untidily, and she was wearing her usual uniform of a plain dress with no evidence of any embellishment. In fact she looked every inch what she was – a lady's companion, hand-picked by Aunt Agnes. But there was something different about her today. She sounded rather tetchy, for one thing, which was unusual, and there was a change in her demeanour. She seemed more guarded in the way she carried herself. It was clear to Lucy that her subject required close study if any secrets were to be uncovered.

'Did you go out last night, Miss Trott?'

'What do you mean, dear?'

'I saw you in your coat when we said good night, and I wondered . . .'

Miss Trott hesitated. Was that a slight flush in her cheeks? 'I just wanted a little fresh air before bed – my headache, you know – so I took a short stroll.'

'I hope it was successful.'

'Sorry?'

'Your headache . . . the walk dispelled it?'

'Yes, yes it did, thank you, dear. Now hurry along. We do not want to waste the day.'

'I'll be down directly,' Lucy said.

Miss Trott paused as if she was about to speak, but evidently thought better of it and merely nodded and departed, leaving Lucy only partly satisfied by the explanation offered. If one was taking a short stroll, why would a large canvas bag be required?

James could not at first work out where he was. He was lying on a shabby settee in lodgings that could only be described as basic. The walls were punctuated with damp patches and the carpet was so threadbare that it did not deserve the name. The place stank of stale sweat with a hint of urine, not unlike La Capra. James groaned as the events of the previous night came back to him and he remembered Sofia walking angrily away.

He tried to move his head but it felt as if someone was burrowing through his brain from the inside. Every time he opened his eyes he found that the room was moving. Slumped in a chair opposite him was Baldovino. His mouth was hanging open and a thin line of dribble was coursing its way slowly down the side of his chin. He shifted slightly in his sleep but did not wake.

It was light outside. James had to speak to Sofia before she went to work. It would be risky. He would have to be discreet. It was important for the sake of propriety that he was not seen anywhere near her lodgings. He would also have to find a way of getting into the professor's house undetected and just hope that he could reach his room before his absence was noticed. He would have to claim a lack of appetite if anyone asked about him missing breakfast. It would not be easy, but he had to try.

Having heard what Baldovino had told him the previous night, James had realised his mistake and knew that he had to put it right, whatever the consequences. He had been dismissive of Sofia's concern for her cousin, and now it was clear that she was not the only girl to have disappeared. Would Sofia have read the newspaper? She hadn't mentioned it. For a moment he considered telling her about the body in the woods but quickly decided that it would be better to wait until he and the professor had examined it. There was no sense in upsetting her unless it became necessary. Besides, first of all he had to persuade her to speak to him, and after last night that might not be an easy thing to accomplish.

Not twenty minutes later, he was standing outside Sofia's rooms. It was raining, and he was ill equipped for the weather. Water dripped down his face onto the end of his nose. He wiped it with his hand and thought what a sight he must represent: haggard from the combined effects of lack of sleep and far too much grappa, and now damp through and through. He looked around him. Fortunately the early hour and the rain had kept most people indoors, and those who were about were too busy getting to their destination to be interested in him.

He had rehearsed what he wanted to say as he walked through the quiet streets of the early morning. But when he saw her in the doorway, his careful words went from his head and he was left struggling to express himself. Sofia did not help him, and who could blame her after the way they had parted the previous evening? Everything about her manner was hostile. Her usual enigmatic smile was gone and her lips formed a thin line of disapproval. He must, he supposed, come across as dishevelled and seedy; not, in fact, unlike Baldovino.

Having made sure that no one was watching, Sofia beckoned him inside. They stood for a moment in the shelter of a small lintel.

'Sofia, I'm sorry.'

'You are sorry... I see. And I am supposed to forgive you just like that? You may have forgotten all you said last night.' She looked at him with disdain. 'Drink will do that.' There was a pause, as if she was trying to retain some control over her emotions. 'As no doubt your father will have told you.' James was shocked by the cruelty of her tone, though he knew he could hardly blame her.

'Sofia, please...'

'I have not forgotten a single word you said to me, and will never do so. You are wasting your time.'

'Wait, please! I know I do not deserve your forgiveness and I respect your decision, but...'

'But what?'

'I have learnt something – some information that you should hear.'

'About?'

'About your cousin.'

Sofia swore under her breath. 'If you are using this, James, so help me...'

'No, no!' he protested. 'I would never do such a thing. You must know me better than that.'

'I thought I did, but after last night...'

'I was angry. It made me say things. I wanted to hurt you because you hurt me.'

She hesitated for a moment. 'You'd better come up.'

James followed her up the rickety stairs to her rooms. He was not stupid enough to think that her invitation changed anything between them, but at least it was a start.

As soon as they reached her small sitting room, he remembered the last time he had been here with her; how they had sat on her threadbare settee and held each other, trying desperately to shut out the impossibility of their situation – two people who loved each other but could never be seen together in public. They had eaten meals at her table, laughing as it wobbled to and fro when James forgot its flimsiness and leant on it. He saw the curtain that separated this room from where she slept and where they had made love. For a moment he was almost overwhelmed by the memories until the smell of coffee wrapped itself around him, reviving him just in time to feel the sting of regret.

Sofia faced him. Her stance was defiant. 'So tell me, what is it about Chiara that I should hear?'

There was no point in prevaricating. 'She is not the only one to have gone missing. Other girls of her age and . . .' He paused.

'Background?' Sofia said.

James nodded and showed her the list that Baldovino had given him the previous night.

'I do not recognise any other names.'

'There is this as well.' He unfolded a copy of the newspaper with Baldovino's article in it. Sofia took it from him and read, a frown spreading across her face. She looked tired. 'It does not say much.'

'I know, but at least it's something.'

Sofia blinked. 'What is all this about the abbey?'

'Baldovino had a tip-off. His source hinted that there might be a connection.'

'I see, and he thought this nonsense would make a good article.'

'That's it. There have been sightings of mysterious figures, and people claim to have heard noises and seen strange lights.'

Sofia shook her head and tossed the newspaper onto the table. 'There have been rumours about that place for years. It means nothing.'

'I know that, but it at least brings the question of the missing girls into the public eye.'

'So six girls have disappeared in the last few months.'

'At least, although Baldovino says that more cannot be ruled out.'

'How much does he know?'

'Only what his source told him, I think. He asked around the town near the abbey, too. Apparently all the girls are linked to the place. '

'*Sì*. Chiara lived there before she came to stay with me. But he has not mentioned the town in his article.'

'I suppose the Devil is more newsworthy.'

Sofia gave a snort of derision. '*Madonna mia!* Young girls go missing and he does nothing except write a story about the Devil and a haunted abbey.'

'The paper wouldn't print it until he got the lead on the abbey, and even then they told him to keep it vague.'

'Of course they wouldn't. Girls like Chiara are not important. They have no money, no status, so they do not matter to anyone. It takes some stupid story about the Devil and a haunted abbey to get it into the paper. Who gave him the tip-off? I suppose he has told the carabinieri?'

'He won't reveal his source. The carabinieri made some initial enquiries, but when they couldn't find anything, they gave up, claiming that the girls were runaways.'

'That is what they said to me... but six of them?'

'Perhaps they will reopen the case now it is in the newspaper.'

Sofia sank onto a nearby chair as if all her energy had been drained away. James went over to her and knelt down by her side. 'Please allow me to help you, Sofia.' He placed his hand on hers, but she shook it away and gave him a scornful glare.

'What help can you offer a born criminal like me? Chiara and I are related. She's probably a criminal too, is she not? No doubt she has fallen into bad company. That's what women like us do, isn't it?'

'Sofia, I am so sorry for saying those things.'

'Maybe, but it changes nothing. Chiara is still gone, and so are those other girls, if Baldovino is right.'

'Sofia, I want to help. Please let me do what I can.'

'What do you think you can do?'

'I can investigate.'

'Like you did with the pilgrim last year? He had to come to you before you found him!'

'I would have found him given a little more time, I'm sure of it.'

There was a long pause. Her face was devoid of all expression. A barrier had come down between them.

Finally she spoke. 'Very well. What have I to lose? No one else will listen. But, James . . .'

'Yes?'

'It changes nothing between us.'

'I understand.' He heard himself say the words but he knew there was hope in his heart. 'I will need your help. You know Chiara; I do not.'

Sofia nodded. 'What do you need to know?'

He took out his leather notebook and a pencil. 'Tell me about her. Tell me everything.'

The showery rain of the early morning had not dispersed, so Lucy and Miss Trott had decided to visit the Galleria Sabauda.

It was a fine old building containing a collection of paintings that had once been owned by the dukes and kings of the Savoy dynasty, whose power had dominated Italy and particularly Turin for many years. There were also examples of the Italian masters and the Piedmont school, as well as a number of Dutch and Flemish paintings. Lucy had readily agreed when Miss Trott suggested it as a destination. It seemed somehow to be a way of reaching out to her mother. A love of art was something they had shared. In fact, so keen had her mother been on encouraging this interest that she had engaged an art master for her, or to be more accurate, two.

The first, Monsieur Rabbe, a tall, skinny young man with a patchy and untidy beard, had escorted Lucy to several London galleries. Unfortunately, he was rather too taken with his charge and was much given to staring adoringly at her rather than teaching her. He was quickly replaced by a much older man, Signor Giovanni: short, stout and in possession of an overly inflated idea of his own importance. Unhappily, he was also enamoured, this time of the bottle. He was asked to leave after an unfortunate incident with a decanter of port and a pair of brocade curtains – he drank the first and pulled down the second, much to the amusement of James and Lucy, but not their mother, who dismissed him on the spot.

It was Miss Trott who had suggested that they visit a gallery, but once they got there, she declared herself to be suffering a moral dilemma. Although, she said, she was herself a champion of self-improvement, and encouraged such opportunities to learn, she also felt that the sight of so much naked flesh might not be suitable for a young lady's eyes.

'Whatever would your aunt say?' she asked anxiously, before doing her best to guide Lucy away from paintings she felt were unsavoury in any way, much to her charge's irritation. Finally they reached a compromise. Miss Trott would go ahead and select those paintings that she felt were appropriate. This, though a somewhat annoying prospect, at least meant that Lucy would have an opportunity to take in some of what she had come to see without her companion's unwelcome and tiresome interventions.

The problem was that the paintings she most wanted to study seemed to be the very same ones that Miss Trott found unsuitable. Lucy wanted to look at works that had some kind of story attached to them, or at least a narrative that she herself could embroider with detail. For example, she had been drawn to a painting of *The Beheading of St John the Baptist* by Volterra, which had a headless body at its heart, with a figure leaning over it picking up the severed head. This work pulled her in not because of its gruesome centrepiece, but because in the background, seen through a window, was a woman looking in at the scene and holding an empty platter. She presumed that this was Salome, who had danced so well for King Herod that he had granted her wish for the head of John the Baptist. Miss Trott, however, steered her away from the painting, calling it 'quite horrid', and instead planted her in front of a tedious picture of *St Peter and a Worshipper* by Ferrari.

'He looks bored, don't you think, Miss Trott?'

'Who does, dear?'

'St Peter. I think he is wishing that his fat little worshipper with the irritating, pious expression would leave him alone.'

Miss Trott frowned at her, though just for an instant Lucy thought she had noticed the beginnings of a smile.

'Come and look at this Rembrandt, Lucy,' she said. 'Isn't the detail startling?'

Dutifully Lucy obeyed. The picture was of an elderly man dozing on a chair. 'I suppose so, but the subject's so tedious.'

'Art doesn't have to be exciting,' Miss Trott replied. 'That is not the point.'

'Is that a severed hand at his feet?' Lucy asked, spotting something in a shadowy part of the painting. 'That would make it interesting.'

Miss Trott peered closely. 'No. It is a pair of tongs, dear.'

Lucy sighed. 'Yes, I think you're right. How dull.'

They continued on their artistic journey, with Lucy being guided away from anything she considered potentially interesting in favour of more wholesome examples, as Miss Trott put it. As they went on, however, this insistence became not just tiresome but suspicious, until it began to occur to Lucy that her companion's piety was not genuine. It was as though that was how she thought she should be, rather than how she was. Lucy was unsure what to do with this idea. Was she creating a mystery where there was none, just to make Miss Trott more interesting?

Lucy was admiring a particularly beautiful depiction of the Madonna and Child by Spanzotti, a prominent member of the Piedmont school, according to Miss Trott, when a light, almost musical, voice interrupted her reverie.

'The form is well constructed enough, but the end result is a little trite, don't you think?'

A tall, slim figure approached her. He raised his hat politely and she saw that he had a mass of dark, wavy hair beneath. She wanted to lean forward and smooth it into some kind of order. Instead she nodded her acknowledgement. 'I don't agree. The word trite suggests that it is ordinary, and in my opinion it is anything but that.'

'Perhaps it is not ordinary, but it lacks a certain spark of life, I feel. It is dull and flat, without originality or realism.'

Lucy had to stop herself from giving a sharp intake of breath as she observed the man more closely. He was younger than she had thought, surely no more than twenty-five, and was like no one she had ever encountered before. His features were delicate, almost feminine, and his eyes were green and piercing. It was the kind of face that, once seen, was never forgotten, and such was its beauty that she did not want to take her gaze from it.

Miss Trott, it seemed, was not quite so smitten, or at least not at first. She had noticed their conversation from a distance and had rushed over to ensure that no further impropriety took place. The man bowed. Miss Trott seemed to start a little but quickly recovered.

'Lucy, I do not think your brother, or indeed your aunt, would approve of you conversing with a stranger.'

The man smiled his extraordinary smile. Lucy felt a pang of regret that it had not been reserved exclusively for her.

'I'm quite all right, Miss Trott.'

'That's all very well, but let it not be said that Euphemia Trott neglects her duties.'

'Euphemia – what an unusual name, and how it suits you, madam, if I may say so,' said the young man. 'I believe it means well-spoken, and so you are.'

Lucy was amused at the compliment. Miss Trott smiled for an instant, a victim of unfamiliar charm. This, however, was only momentary, and she soon recovered her wits.

'It is unseemly for a gentleman, if you could be called such, sir, to address a young lady in such a familiar manner!'

The young man bowed and adopted a sorrowful expression that Lucy suspected was not entirely sincere.

'If I have offended, I am distraught. We were merely conversing as one student of art to another. But perhaps my opinion was unwelcome. Good day, ladies.'

With that he withdrew as quickly and mysteriously as he had arrived, leaving both Lucy and Miss Trott to gaze after his retreating form. The rest of the visit continued without incident, but neither of them was able to banish the thought of the young man entirely from her mind.

She is not completely alone . . . or at least she was not. She does not know whether to be pleased or upset. There was definitely someone nearby, and from the little she heard, they were in the same terrifying situation as her. But when the crying turned to screaming, then . . . she could not forget that sound. A great roar of pain, as if the girl's very soul was being tortured. Dare she call out again? She yearns for human contact until it almost overwhelms her, but does she really want to antagonise whoever it was that caused those screams? Eventually, as she stares into the void that is her existence, she decides to risk it. Even pain is better than this emptiness.

'Are you there?' she cries.

There is nothing for a while, and she thinks she is still alone. Then she hears weeping, and a barely audible 'hello' between the sobs. 'Help me . . . please. It hurts so . . .'

'I cannot. I wish I could,' she calls, tugging at the manacle around her ankle. 'But at least we are not alone.'

There is more silence. She cannot bear it. 'What . . . what has he done to you?' she asks.

She waits, unsure that she wants her question answered. Then she hears the unmistakable sound of a stone being slid slowly back. She has a visitor. It seems that it is her turn.

She sits and stares ahead of her into the darkness. She can

hear her captor breathing. Is it a man or a woman? She cannot tell. All she can see is a shadowy outline. Whoever it is wears a cloak with a hood, like some kind of habit. They have not hurt her, at least not yet, and she supposes she should be grateful for that. But she cannot help but want to know more, even if it might provoke her captor.

'Who was that girl?' she asks. 'What did you do to her?'

Silence.

'How many of us are there?'

Silence.

'What do you want?'

The darkness and the silence press down on her like the stone that her captor slides across when they leave her.

'Clean yourself. Then put this on.' Her visitor finally speaks. It is a whisper – loud, though: a stage whisper. Something is thrown down to her – something soft. A lantern is lit and hung on the wall, and she cranes her neck to see who is there. Then a pail of water is lowered, and a bar of soap follows it wrapped in a towel. The stone is slid back into place and she is alone again. She breathes a sigh of relief. Whatever her captor did to the other girl, he did not want to repeat it... or not yet, anyway. She has survived, and now she has light.

The soft cloth that has been thrown to her is pale, and simple in design. She examines it for a second or two, then catches her breath as she realises what it resembles – a shroud.

9

Criminals and the mad frequently lack affection entirely, showing neither pity nor benevolence nor remorse. They are capable of eating and dancing near the cadaver of their victim, all the while boasting of their crime. In addition they manifest little affection for their companions.

Lombroso, 1876, p. 82

The mortuary was situated in the basement of Turin's main hospital, a building that although not old in years still gave an impression of shabbiness, as if whoever had built it was afraid that to do otherwise might be considered frivolous. When James had returned from seeing Sofia, he had passed on to Lombroso Tullio's request about examining the remains. As he had predicted, the professor had been only too pleased to accept once he was told that some kind of mystery surrounded them.

The two of them sat in the waiting room and waited for Tullio to arrive. Lombroso was bright-eyed and eager to begin. James, though intrigued, had other things on his mind. The thought that the body they were about to examine might be that of Chiara was overwhelming him, making it difficult to think of anything else.

'I cannot think why Tullio did not mention this at dinner,' Lombroso said.

'I seem to remember that he had already asked you for something,' James said. The after-effects of the previous night's grappa were catching up with him. 'Perhaps he didn't want to seem too demanding.'

'Ah yes. That is correct. He did make a request a day or two ago . . . something rather curious, in fact.'

'What was it?' James asked.

'Later, Murray, later. Be patient.'

James knew that it was useless trying to get Lombroso to tell him anything. Besides that, he had a headache and felt queasy. The prospect of examining a dead body in his current condition was not a pleasant one, notwithstanding any secrets that it might be concealing. He was not in the best of physical states to be grappling with body fluids oozing out of every orifice. Already he could smell the familiar underlying odour of decomposition, and they were only in the waiting room. It took all his concentration to stop himself from being sick, knowing that if he was he would never be allowed to hear the last of it.

Luckily Tullio soon arrived and they followed him down some worn stone steps into the largest part of the mortuary, where the body was laid out. Standing to attention next to it was the mortuary assistant, a large man with a face full of dimples, strange unruly blonde hair and an incongruously beaming smile. His name, he informed them, was Boris, and he was happy to help. James noticed that Lombroso viewed him with suspicion, paying particular attention to his ears, which stuck out almost at right angles from his oversized head. No doubt it was the sign of some criminal type or other. If he wasn't careful, Boris would end up having his head measured and appearing in one of the professor's academic papers, or worse, perhaps even being forever preserved after death as an exhibit in the museum.

With a flourish Boris pulled back the sheet covering the body. It was immediately clear that it could not be Chiara. The victim had not died recently. James was relieved. At least he would not have to break such terrible news to Sofia . . . not yet, anyway.

He peered down at the body. It had reached an advanced state of decomposition, being devoid of the telltale swelling produced by the gases of putrefaction. He tried to remember the book that he had been referred to by Professor Bell. What was it called? Ah yes: *Legal Medicine*, by Charles Meymott Tidy – two very handy volumes indeed, particularly for propping open the door to his rooms in the summer months. Professor Bell was especially dismissive of the section on hair and nails growing after death. He was of the view that they didn't, whereas Tidy was certain that they did.

Whatever the truth, they had long since stopped doing so here. James leant over to take a closer look. The body was clearly that of a woman. It resembled a shrunken leather-skinned corpse, bent almost double like a foetus. Next to it were placed what looked to be internal organs, dark brown, almost black, and shrivelled in consistency. On closer inspection the body seemed to be covered in some kind of crystalline substance, not unlike salt. Some hair was still present, but it was sparse – no more than thin brown strands. The jaw gaped open in a macabre smile. A scarlet ribbon was still tied around the head. A picture of the girl when she was alive flashed into James's mind, with glossy hair shining in sunlight and long, slender fingers playing coquettishly with its scarlet adornment.

The flesh, if you could still call it that, was strange – tough and brown. An attempt had been made to open up the body, revealing that it had been stuffed full of vegetation, dried now: herbs, flowers and grasses. The clothes had been removed and lay on an adjacent table. They were mostly intact, though ripped in places – a plain dress of faded blue cotton with an apron tied around the middle. Another picture arrived unbidden in James's head. This time the girl with the long brown hair was standing with an enigmatic smile on her face, her hands on her hips. Her face was Sofia's.

The remains were certainly unusual. 'As you can see, the body is not recent,' Tullio said.

Lombroso peered at it. 'I'd say she has been dead for at least six months... perhaps even longer. Where was she found?'

'In woods outside the city, near a small town called San Callisto.'

'Still no clues on identity?' James asked.

'Nothing solid, as I told you last night. We have made some enquiries in the town and surrounding area, but nobody has noticed anyone missing for that length of time. Mind you, it is a rural community and there are quite a few itinerant workers, so it is hard to be sure. '

'Will you be giving details to the newspapers? Someone might come forward.'

'I wanted to, but the mayor has asked me to keep it quiet for the time being. He doesn't want people to panic.'

'Are they likely to?' In James's experience, the Torinese were not easily shocked.

'I would not think so,' Tullio replied.

'The mayor is hoping for another term of office, is he not?' Lombroso said pointedly.

Tullio nodded and gave a shrug.

'Did you know that the reporter Baldovino has a list of girls who have disappeared?' James asked.

'I am aware that other girls have gone missing, yes,' Tullio replied. 'Marshal Machinetti thinks that they are most likely to be runaways.'

'Even now, with this body?' James said.

Tullio shook his head. 'They have all gone in the last few months, and as the professor has confirmed, these remains are far older.'

'But they are all connected to the town.'

'Do not complicate things, Murray,' Lombroso said. 'Girls like that run off all the time, wherever they are from. It is the way they are made. Indeed, poor women generally are increasingly likely to travel around the country looking for employment as maids, casual labourers or even prostitutes. It is becoming a real social problem. But then what do we expect from women? They are inherently inferior and cannot help the way they are made.'

James could see that he was fighting a losing battle, but he knew he had to persevere. If there was one body now and girls were missing, then there could be more.

'How was the body left?' he asked.

'In a shallow grave,' Tullio said. 'At least it was shallow enough to be dug up by a truffle hog.'

'That's interesting. Any insect activity?' Lombroso asked.

'Some but not much,' Tullio replied. 'Why do you ask?'

'Haven't the French been doing some work on using insect activity to indicate time of death?' James asked.

'Indeed, Murray, though the Chinese started it as far back as the thirteenth century.' Lombroso indicated the pile of internal organs. 'I take it these were removed by the pathologist?'

'No,' Tullio replied. 'They were in a small sealed container next to the body, exactly as you see there.'

'May I look at it?' Lombroso asked.

Tullio nodded, and Boris held up a stone pot with a lid. Lombroso took it and examined it. The handle was fashioned in the likeness of a snake.

'There are no distinguishing marks, though I am sure I have seen something like it before. I can't for the life of me remember where,' he said.

'It is interesting that there is no sign of activity from foxes and the like,' James said.

'Yes, well spotted, Murray. That indicates a recent burial, and yet the state the body is in shows that it is older.'

Tullio nodded. 'That would tally with what the truffle hunter said. He goes there regularly apparently, and claims he would have found the body earlier.'

'Or the pig would,' James said. 'At any rate, it looks like this woman died elsewhere.'

'Cause of death?' Tullio asked.

'It is difficult to say with any certainty, given the state of the body,' Lombroso replied. 'Various things have been done to it, but I cannot tell if that is ante, peri or post-mortem.'

'What kind of things?' Tullio asked.

'It appears that attempts have been made to preserve the body. In order to achieve that, certain procedures must have been conducted.'

James looked again at the leathery bundle beside the body. 'That would explain the organ removal. What other proced-ures?'

'Eviscerate, bleed and dry, Murray. Just as the Egyptians did. The brain is removed through the nasal passage. Take a look and tell me what you see.'

James peered at the girl's face. 'Yes, there is disturbance to the nasal cavity. I think you might be right.'

'Naturally. There might well have been draining of fluids, but that is mere speculation. I would have to ask a specialist to be sure.' Lombroso looked at the body again. 'Yes, see here, Murray, just to the left of the abdomen – an incision. Interesting that the heart has been removed. As I recall, it was usually left *in situ*, along with the kidneys.'

'What is this salty residue?' James asked.

'Natron, I would think. After evisceration, the body was covered with it. It is a kind of preserving salt.'

'Is there any possibility that the woman was subjected to these techniques whilst still alive?' Tullio asked.

Lombroso nodded grimly. 'I cannot rule it out. However, there is damage to the hyoid bone, which indicates strangling or perhaps garrotting.'

'A murder, then,' Tullio said.

'It would certainly seem so,' Lombroso said. 'But it may not have been sufficient to kill her, so it is at least possible that the embalming took place whilst she was living.'

'My God! What kind of animal would do something like that?' James said.

'Someone exhibiting signs of moral insanity... possibly an epileptic,' Lombroso said.

'Really?' Tullio said. 'So that is who I should be looking for here?'

'These are conclusions I have been drawing recently, based on past work,' Lombroso said breezily. 'I have found certain overlaps between epileptics, the insane and born criminals that indicate to me the likelihood of a link. This killer will certainly lack any moral sense and be intrinsically unstable; he will probably be agile, and of course may have a propensity for drinking blood – common in epileptics.'

Tullio and James exchanged glances. It was difficult to work out exactly how Lombroso had reached these conclusions.

Tullio cleared his throat. 'I see. Thank you . . . very useful, I'm sure.'

Undeterred, Lombroso continued, clearly warming to his theme. 'Physically, you are seeking a fairly common criminal type – a voluminous jaw, jutting cheekbones and a propensity towards sexual perversion. I once heard of a very intelligent example who ate excrement as he fitted and also orally masturbated his own penis. Extraordinary!'

Tullio frowned, momentarily lost for words. 'Well that's something to go on, anyhow.'

Lombroso beamed at him. 'Quite so. I do like to think that my work has a practical application.'

'How about the burial site?' James asked, hoping to bring the professor back to something less speculative.

'Yes,' Tullio said with a grateful glance. 'Was the grave shallow because he wanted the body to be found, do you think?'

'I would say that is possible,' Lombroso replied.

'But isn't it equally possible that he thought the location was sufficiently remote to make it unlikely that it would be found?' James said. 'Or perhaps he didn't care either way.'

'Oh he cared all right,' Tullio said.

'How can you be so sure?' James asked.

'Firstly because the body was buried right at the centre of a clearing. The measurement is exact to the last inch.'

'Interesting,' James said.

'And secondly there is the container full of organs.'

'That is unusual,' Lombroso agreed. 'It is almost as if he wanted us to think of them as an exhibit in a museum.'

James frowned. 'No,' he said. 'It's more ritualistic than that.'

'What do you mean?' Tullio asked.

'Think about the care that has been taken here. He made sure that the body was placed right in the middle. The burial indicates to me that he's not putting her on show,' James said. 'He's laying her to rest. And where she was found isn't a museum. It's a graveyard.'

10

Prostitutes have bigger calves than honest women.
Lombroso, 1893, p. 126

'We know, do we not,' Lombroso said as he sat back in his chair, his fingers pressed together in front of him like the steeple of a church, 'that women are arrested and convicted far less frequently than men.'

The professor, James and Anna Tarnovsky were sitting in Lombroso's study at the museum discussing their project about criminal women. James felt his eyes becoming heavy. He had experienced something of a second wind at the mortuary when faced with the mystery of the strange leathery corpse, but that was fast disappearing as he sat and listened to Lombroso. All he could see when he let his eyelids droop even for a moment was a vision of brown wrinkled skin and a red ribbon tied gaily round what was left of a head.

'Murray, try to concentrate! This is important!' Lombroso said.

'Of course, Professor.' Surreptitiously he pinched himself on the wrist – an old trick he had occasionally used during some of his more tedious lectures at medical school.

'And that is the problem, as I outlined last night, Cesare,'

Anna said. 'If you keep to your previous claims about female inferiority, then you may well find that there is a contradiction.'

The professor was nodding sagely and stroking his beard. He did not seem to have noticed the irony of being told that his findings were flawed by a woman who was anything but inferior. It was as if he did not recognise her sex at all.

'I see the problem . . . but what is the solution?'

'James, you mentioned last night about reconsidering our research pool,' Anna said. 'What did you mean exactly?'

'If we look at normal as well as criminal women, then we could do a comparison.'

'That is a capital idea!' Lombroso beamed at him. 'Of course I had been considering doing something of that nature, but I wanted to see if either of you would think of it.'

James caught Anna's eye. Was she angry or amused by Lombroso's claim? It was hard to tell. She was fond of the professor, he knew, but still there was a limit.

'It might be quite difficult to compile that kind of information. After all, how can we be certain what is normal and what is abnormal?' she said.

Lombroso frowned. 'Yes, that might be a problem. Perhaps you could do a little research into existing data, Murray?'

James agreed enthusiastically, eager to start work. It should not be too difficult to fit it around his investigation.

'There is another possibility,' Anna said.

'Which is?' Lombroso asked.

'Prostitutes,' she replied. 'Surely they should be included in the research.'

Lombroso looked thoughtful. 'Perhaps they should. After all, criminal women in primitive times were all prostitutes of one kind or another. Why should today's be any different?'

James exchanged perplexed glances with Anna. He somehow doubted that this view of primitive women was true. He hoped their research would demonstrate some rather more credible conclusions. Still, the role of the prostitute might well be relevant.

'I have some data that might assist,' Anna said. 'I did some work on local prostitutes in Prague this spring and have a number of interesting photographs. I also used a control group for a short while.'

'*Eccellente!*' Lombroso declared. 'I think we are on our way. But I would also like to try to collate my own data. I have some already from a local brothel, so this would be a good opportunity to build on that.'

'Of course, Cesare. Mine was only a small study,' Anna said.

'And we shall use it, I am sure. But as I say, I have been to this particular establishment before, and I think we shall get some interesting material from visiting it again.'

'What establishment is it?' Anna asked.

'Madame Giulia's,' Lombroso replied. 'I've taken some preliminary cranial measurements, but I'd like us to measure other characteristics as well as conducting interviews. They're delightful ladies on the whole, despite their criminality. I hope to arrange it for tomorrow afternoon.'

'It all sounds very interesting,' Anna said. 'I'll look forward to it.'

Lombroso shifted in his seat and avoided her glance. 'I'm afraid it will just be Murray on this occasion. It's not a suitable place for a lady, even when she is as eminent in her field as Madame Anna Tarnovsky.'

'But I did my own research in Prague and no one seemed to mind.'

'That may be so, but I do not want the girls to feel uncomfortable or to upset the owner. I'm sorry, but it cannot be helped. One must always ensure that one's subjects are comfortable with one's methods.'

James thought it most unfair for Anna to be excluded. It seemed that Lombroso remembered that she was a woman only when it suited him. Since they had all begun to work together, he had detected a definite change in the professor's attitude to her. During the symposium last year, Lombroso had been charming, almost deferential. Now he seemed to be undermining her at every opportunity. He also noticed that the professor had not mentioned the body they had just examined. Of course that could be an attempt at discretion, as requested by Tullio, but such things did not usually trouble Lombroso.

'Now,' the professor said in a hearty tone, 'I think we have earned ourselves a decent luncheon. Shall we continue our discussions at Caffé San Carlo over a bite to eat?'

The food was more than decent, James thought as he tucked into a bowl of fragrant wild mushroom risotto and a few glasses of a white wine called Gavi di Gavi that tasted of pears and peaches. The flavours almost seemed to explode on the tongue and revived him after the overindulgence of the night before. But even that could not dull his sense of outrage at his mentor's views on the nature of women.

'They are no more than big children!' Lombroso declared.

'And does this apply to all of my sex,' Anna enquired, her cheeks becoming ever more flushed, either from the effects of the wine or, more likely, the direction of the conversation.

'Or is it just criminals and prostitutes who have never grown up?'

Lombroso nodded enthusiastically. 'They are like men in so many ways, but men who have been somehow arrested in their intellectual and physical development.'

'Cesare...' Anna began.

'Yes, my dear Madame Tarnovsky?' Lombroso said, smiling at her in that way he had – a sort of dreamy confidence, as if he took his own rightness for granted to such an extent that he didn't regard it as needing his complete attention.

'What shall we be asking the girls at Madame Giulia's?' James said, in an effort to divert Anna from a course that he suspected might be unwise.

'I think we should regard Madame Tarnovsky's work in Prague together with mine as an experimental preliminary study.'

'Are you sure my work is sufficiently mature?' Anna asked pointedly.

'Yes, of course, my dear. What a question to ask!' Lombroso shook his head and tutted. 'You really must have more confidence in your abilities.'

'And our questions?' James asked.

'They will be designed to ascertain a propensity or otherwise to dishonesty,' Lombroso said. 'Women lie. It is a well-known fact. Countless proverbs tell us that. The question is, do criminal women lie more?'

'How will we measure that?' James asked.

Lombroso smiled the smile of a man who had a trick up his sleeve. 'We shall use my lie-detecting machine.'

'Really?' Anna said, frowning. 'I would like to see that. I did help you develop it after all, Cesare.'

'Yes, that is true, of course... Ah!' Lombroso beamed at

them both. 'We shall conduct the interviews at the university. Then Madame Tarnovsky will be able to join us!'

Anna smiled in satisfaction. 'Thank you, Cesare. It is much appreciated.'

'Are you sure that is wise, Professor?' James asked. 'Won't inviting prostitutes to the university be somewhat controversial?'

Lombroso grinned. 'I do hope so, Murray. I like people to know what we're up to, and Gemelli will no doubt make sure that everyone hears about it.'

'You must take care, Cesare,' Anna said. 'You know that regulations do not allow for the girls to move around the city outside of their curfew.'

'We shall time our inquiry accordingly,' Lombroso said. He beamed at them. 'I think this will be very interesting indeed.'

At this point Anna took her leave to meet Lucy and Miss Trott. James was delighted that she had taken his sister under her wing. She was just the sort of person that Lucy would admire – independent-minded, intelligent, but with a sense of humour. She would be an excellent role model for Lucy and something of an antidote to the dry Miss Trott. The two women would complement each other and together provide all the guidance that a young girl like Lucy might require, leaving James free to concentrate on finding Chiara and winning back Sofia. That afternoon he intended to visit the place where Chiara worked and speak to her fellow servants. Sofia had already done so but had not learnt much of use. It would be good to do something practical.

'You look pleased with yourself, Murray,' Lombroso said. 'I am glad you are in a good mood. I have something to tell you.'

What now? James wondered. Before Lombroso could say more, a familiar gangling figure came into view and waved at them, almost knocking over some glasses on a tray carried by a short and rather haughty waiter.

'It's Ottolenghi!' James exclaimed.

'Now we are complete,' Lombroso said with satisfaction.

The young man made his way over to them and they shook hands and exchanged greetings. James felt himself relax at the sight of his friend and ally. They had shared so much during James's last visit, and Ottolenghi alone knew how he felt about Sofia. But something about his friend had changed. He was paler, and there were new lines on his forehead. His clothes were rumpled and he had dark circles under his eyes. Whatever it was that he had experienced with Oskar Reiner in Vienna, it did not look as if it was pleasant.

'I was sorry to hear about your father, James,' Ottolenghi said. 'It must have been hard for you.'

'Thank you, Salvatore. It was difficult, but perhaps it is time to look to the future.'

'And it will be a full one, you can be sure of that, Murray,' Lombroso said.

'Have you told our friend about tonight yet, Professor?' Ottolenghi asked, pushing his wire-rimmed glasses up the bridge of his nose.

'Told me what?' James was apprehensive. Expeditions led by Lombroso always seemed to end in trouble, and he suspected that this one would be no different.

Ottolenghi grinned. 'The professor sent me a telegraph in Vienna a few days ago asking me to return. I could not resist!'

'I hope that you have nothing planned for this evening, Murray,' Lombroso said cryptically.

'I haven't, as it happens,' James said. 'So what are we doing?'

Ottolenghi handed him a copy of Baldovino's article. 'We're looking for the Devil, my friend. What else?'

11

Lucy and Miss Trott had arranged to meet Anna Tarnovsky at the marchesa's palazzo, on the hill that rose up from the city and its river. True to her word, she was waiting for them in a carriage outside. The palazzo itself seemed to Lucy to be too small a residence for a woman of such influence and standing. She had been expecting something magnificent and imposing, like some of the buildings that James had told her he had visited when he was last in the city. This, by comparison, seemed quite modest.

Inside, however, the palazzo still bore some of the hallmarks of ostentation that James had described. It was as if whoever had furnished it could not resist the temptation to leave the odd touch of splendour behind – a splash of gilt here and there; a solitary alabaster cherub peeping out from the ceiling as if it had been abandoned when all the others had flown off to somewhere more opulent. They were shown into a large room filled with comfortable chairs. On the walls between the many bookshelves were oriental silk hangings in vivid colours, and every available surface was covered with assorted ornaments and knick-knacks.

The marchesa rose to greet them. She was tall, angular and elegant, with silver hair, and as she talked, she gesticulated gracefully to emphasise her words. The effect was almost balletic. Standing next to her was a girl of about Lucy's age, dark-haired, dark-eyed but with a sulky expression that quite spoiled her otherwise pretty face. Her lips seemed to fold automatically into a pout and her nose wrinkled as if she could smell something sour.

'This is Fabia Carignano, my niece. She is staying with me at the moment.'

Fabia nodded curtly, as if she could only just be bothered to acknowledge them.

The marchesa smiled at Lucy. 'I think I remember your brother from the symposium last year – a handsome young man, dark-haired, rather pale?'

'That sounds like him,' Lucy replied, quite forgetting her host's aristocratic background, so informal did the occasion seem.

'And how does our city compare to Edinburgh?'

Lucy hesitated. 'I have only seen a little so far, but in many ways they don't seem too different, certainly with regard to the weather.'

The marchesa laughed. 'Ah yes, I'm afraid you have arrived during one of our dampest seasons, but soon the sun will shine, I am sure of it.' She sat down gracefully, indicating for Lucy to join her on a large sofa strewn with velvet cushions. 'Now tell me, my dear, what are your plans whilst you are with us?'

'Miss Murray writes stories,' Anna said.

'Ah . . . I thought you might be creative,' the marchesa said. 'Something about your eyes, a glint of . . . well now, what could it be? Yes, devilment, I believe.'

Lucy blushed. She did not know what to say to that. Was it a compliment or a criticism? Before she could respond, a voice came from the doorway. 'I cannot believe that there is anything remotely devilish about this young lady!'

'Francesco! I'm so glad you could join us,' the marchesa said, beaming. 'And Bianca too. How lovely.'

Lucy examined the new arrivals with interest and was surprised to see that the first was the young man that she and Miss Trott had encountered in the Galleria Sabauda that morning. Standing next to him was a dark-haired woman of about thirty, who despite this seniority seemed almost to shrink into his shadow. She was dressed in browns of various hues, which gave her a birdlike quality, enhanced by bright, intelligent eyes and a slightly aquiline nose. She could hardly be described as a beauty. Her features were uneven and her jawline was a little too heavy. This plainness was highlighted by her companion's striking looks. Lucy speculated on their relationship and found herself hoping they were brother and sister. She also noticed that Fabia's expression had brightened considerably at Francesco's arrival.

Francesco strode into the room and kissed the marchesa's hand. 'How could I resist an invitation from the Lady Vittoria? It would be unconscionable.' He caught sight of Miss Trott, who was sitting in a corner apparently trying to be unobtrusive. 'And what a wonderful coincidence! How enchanting to meet you again, Miss Euphemia Trott, and Miss Lucy, the art critic, too. I am spoilt!'

Lucy could not help but smile, though she thought him a little precocious and rude. He had completely ignored both Anna Tarnovsky and Fabia. She could not imagine James behaving so badly. And could their earlier meeting really have been a coincidence as he claimed? As she studied him, she noticed that he had managed to dominate the room to the extent that the woman with him seemed almost invisible.

'I should introduce you formally, even though it seems that some of you are already acquainted,' the marchesa said, with an amused expression. 'Miss Lucy Murray, Miss Trott, Madame Tarnovsky, may I present Francesco Rambaudi and his sister Bianca. You know Fabia, of course.'

Still Francesco ignored the marchesa's niece. Was there a history to his hostility, or was it that his interest in Lucy was feigned in order to make Fabia jealous? Whatever the reason, Lucy was becoming more and more intrigued by him.

Soon after the introductions, refreshments were brought and the conversation began to flow. 'Tell me more of your writing, Miss Murray,' the marchesa said.

'Let me guess,' Francesco said. 'Are you a poetess as well as an art critic, Miss Lucy?'

Lucy blushed again, this time at his familiarity. 'No, I write stories.'

'You are a novelist. How clever of you. Are you published?' Fabia asked, as if she knew the answer already.

'No. They are just short stories. I write them for my own amusement really.'

'That is surely the best of motives for creation,' Francesco declared.

'Have you been in Turin long, Miss Carignano?' Anna asked Fabia.

'I arrived yesterday,' Fabia replied in a tone that suggested it was none of her business.

'I will be throwing a ball next week in Fabia's honour,' the marchesa said. 'To celebrate her eighteenth birthday. Needless to say, you are all invited.'

'How delightful,' Francesco declared. 'And no doubt your niece will be the belle of the ball!'

Fabia blushed and smiled, transforming her face in an instant.

Lucy studied the assembled company as the conversation went on. Ever the writer, she was less interested in the details of the ball than the opportunity it would give her to observe the people around her. She watched Francesco as he entertained the marchesa and Fabia, noting that his easy manner did not seem quite authentic. Beneath the surface was something deeper and more serious. His eyes did not reflect the lightness of his conversation. What lay behind this facade?

At first Bianca Rambaudi, in contrast to her brother, did not utter a word, apparently preferring to allow Francesco to take centre stage. She gazed at him intently, as if everything he said was of the utmost importance. The siblings could not have been more different. Francesco fitted into the marchesa's circle quite naturally, whereas Bianca seemed decidedly ill at ease, fiddling with the tea things in front of her, lining them up in neat little rows as if creating a barrier between her and the rest of the company. It was only when the marchesa asked her about the Rambaudi estate that she appeared to come to life. Lucy gleaned from what was said that the family's wealth stemmed from their rice fields just outside the city, and that since the recent death of their father, Bianca had been running the business almost single-handedly.

'You are to be congratulated, Miss Rambaudi,' Anna said. 'Not many women could do as you have, and with such success too.'

Bianca's face reddened. 'Thank you, Madame Tarnovsky. You are most kind.' Her voice did not match her mannish features. It was light, almost musical, not unlike her brother's.

'Bianca always had an interest in such things,' Francesco said airily. 'Even when she was a child she would follow my father and me around the fields. He was intent on teaching me the business, the old fool, and ignored her. But she was always the one with the brains, just like our mother.'

'You have studied at the university, Francesco,' the marchesa said. 'That hardly makes you a dunce. I remember one of your teachers telling me that you could have been a professor, had you wanted to travel that path.'

'I have dabbled in many areas,' Francesco admitted. 'But without Bianca the Rambaudis would be in a sorry state.'

'What have you studied?' Lucy asked.

'European literature, Philosophy, Art, Egyptology . . .'

'Egyptology! How fascinating!' Miss Trott said.

'Our Museo Egizio holds one of the most prestigious collections of Egyptian artefacts in the world,' the marchesa said.

'How wonderful!' Miss Trott said. 'We must pay it a visit, don't you think, Lucy?'

'And I shall escort you,' Francesco said, much to Fabia's annoyance, judging from the expression on her face.

The conversation rumbled on for a while until it was time

to leave. As they were about to do so, Francesco took Lucy's hand and shook it solemnly. 'I look forward to our Egyptian expedition, Miss Murray.'

'So do I, Signor Rambaudi.'

He bowed and escorted his sister to their carriage, waving at Miss Trott, who managed to nod her acknowledgement and yet simultaneously make her disapproval clear.

'Should you not seek agreement from your brother, Lucy?' she asked.

Lucy watched as Anna left. 'I think you'll find he has other things on his mind, Miss Trott. I doubt he will even care.'

'I'm sure that is not so. In any event, you must ask his permission. And assuming he agrees, I of course must be present.'

As their cab began to trundle towards the Via Legnano, Lucy wondered what it would be like to be free of this endless supervision. It must be wonderful to be male and able to go where you wanted whenever you felt like it. Why should the fact that she was a girl mean that she had to be chaperoned constantly?

Before long they arrived at their destination and Lucy alighted. Miss Trott, though, stayed in her seat.

'Are you not coming in, Miss Trott?'

There was a pause. 'I have somewhere to go,' she said firmly. And with that she leant forward, slammed the door shut and banged on the roof with her umbrella. '*Avanti!*'

Lucy watched as the carriage drove swiftly away. She envied her companion, who, it appeared, thought nothing of exploring the city alone. If only she had thought to stay with her. Perhaps then the evening would hold a better prospect than a quiet dinner and some sitting about until it was time to go to bed. Still, at least she had a visit to the Museo Egizio with Francesco Rambaudi to look forward to, and that promised to be very interesting indeed.

She hears her captor coming with a mixture of relief and trepidation. It is always unnerving, because she does not know what their arrival might bring. Up to now she has been left untouched. Instead that sing-song voice has merely murmured things to her through the bars that form her roof to the world. None of it makes any sense to her. She is urged to atone but is not told what she might be atoning for. She is not a bad person, although some might say she has done bad things. But then what choice did she have? Surely those who employed her have committed greater sins. Why should it be her rather than they who must atone? But she has no influence on anything either here or in the establishment where she worked.

Reluctantly she has changed into her new white gown. Her clothes were beginning to smell and felt scratchy. Her new outfit is soft and scented. It could almost be a wedding dress. She has washed as instructed and waits now for whatever her fate might be. As the hours pass, she has become more and more afraid.

Gradually her apprehension is buried beneath more physical needs. She is hungry. She has not been fed now for at least three days. It might have been more, but she has not been able to keep count accurately in the darkness of her captivity. All she knows is that the rumbling in her stomach has been replaced by an emptiness more acute than she has ever experienced before. Times were occasionally hard during her childhood, but there was always at least something to eat. Her mother made sure of it. A picture comes into her mind – her family sitting round the dinner table; her father cracking jokes and teasing her mother, her brothers and sisters squabbling. A solitary tear runs down her cheek as she remembers how keen she was to leave all that behind in order to work in the city.

And now this.

She realises that her captor is watching her. She can sense the presence in the shadows. The grid is removed and a basket is lowered down to her. The lack of food means that she is not thinking clearly, and she wonders for a moment about grabbing hold of the basket and pulling her tormentor in, but in any event her hunger gets the better of her. As the basket reaches her, she can smell meat and gravy, a rich savoury aroma that makes her feel faint with anticipation. She lifts out a bowl of bollito misto – a stew of fried meats that is a local speciality. Mindful of what her captor said before, she gives a slight smile. 'Thank you.'

She puts her hands piously together and says grace. Once she has finished, she hesitates. Should she eat or wait until she is alone again? Which would be preferred? Throughout her captivity, compliance has become increasingly important. It seems that it might be the only way she is ever going to get out of here.

'Please, eat,' the voice says.

She picks up the spoon that has been thoughtfully provided and does as she is told. She is too hungry to appreciate the flavour or quality of what she is eating, and bolts it down giving no thought at all to her meal. As she eats, though, something does enter her mind. Might she use the spoon to dig her way out? It is only small, so it would take forever – but then perhaps forever is exactly what she has. It isn't as if there is anything else to do. She decides to try to keep hold of it, just in case.

When she has finished, she puts the bowl back into the

basket and watches as it is pulled back up and the grid above is replaced.

'You have atoned,' says her captor. 'Now we can begin.'

A key is thrown down to her and she uses it to undo her shackles.

'What do you mean, I have atoned?' she asks as she rubs her ankle. But she is already alone.

She sits and puzzles over what has just happened. Perhaps the intention is to release her, or to keep her as some kind of slave. At least now that she is no longer shackled, she might be able to escape. If she could win some trust, there might just be a chance. She needs to wait for the guard to slip and then she can get away. And if that doesn't work, there is always her back-up plan. She pulls the spoon from beneath her skirts. Perhaps things are not quite so desperate after all.

She sits back. For a moment or two her eyelids begin to droop and she allows herself to start drifting into sleep. But before she can escape into unconsciousness, she feels herself being lifted from the pit by some kind of hoist. At last she is being liberated. But she is drowsy and her limbs are heavy and useless, so she cannot make a bid for freedom however much she tries in her mind. She is carried over someone's shoulder. She can smell his body – earth and sweat mingling with leather. They reach a garden of some kind. As she is lowered into a chair, she sees candles, food and wine. But there is something else, something so terrifying and strange that at first she cannot make sense of it. When she eventually does, she screams and cannot stop until she is punched so hard that she can no longer open her mouth. She passes out.

Later – she does not know how much time has passed – she wakes, but only just. Her dress is being removed gently by soft, sensual hands. Soon she is naked. She has never felt so defenceless in her life. She wants so much to struggle, but her body refuses to obey her. Now she is being lifted again . . . up and up, higher and higher . . . Someone is touching her softly where no one should without permission as she is held there, suspended in mid-air as if she is floating, helpless. The arms that were holding her let go and she is left to swing. The shock jolts her awake. She is strung up like a carcass – and now the pain, oh such pain, begins.

12

Haunted houses furnish an important factor in the solu-
tion of the problem as to the post-mortem activity of the
spirits of the departed . . . Popular legend, and frequently
history also, attributes the noises heard and the appear-
ance of spectral forms, often blood stained and fierce, to
scenes of violence that happened on the spot many years
or many centuries previous.

Lombroso, 1909, pp. 269–81

According to Lombroso, it was not worth beginning any psychical investigation of a place such as the Abbey San Callisto before nightfall.

'The manifestations will not begin until at least midnight,' he stated with confidence as he, James and Ottolenghi sat in a cab making its way to their dining destination. The abbey was situated in the hills above the city, and Lombroso had declared that this was an ideal opportunity for James to taste more of the local cuisine; there was a little place he knew that served some of the best on offer in the region. The little place turned out to be a trattoria run by a cousin of Paolo, a friend of Lombroso's who had a similar establishment in the city. It was indeed small, with plain wooden tables and chairs and murals of rural scenes on the walls. Outside, though, there was a vast covered terrace with a magnificent view of Turin and the Alps beyond.

It was only early April, but the evening was fine and clear, though there were a few clouds gathering in the distance. The air was filled with the smell of woodsmoke and enticing aromas coming from the kitchens. The hills and the rooftops of the city were glowing gently in the light of the setting sun. James felt that he had finally come home. But for all that, he was more than prepared to leave it all behind if only Sofia would go with him. He had spent the afternoon questioning Chiara's workmates, but discovered that Sofia had been right about them having little to say. Chiara had only been there for a few weeks before she went missing, so they scarcely knew her. Apparently she had seemed diligent and rather quiet — mousy had been one description. Other than that, there was nothing of note. No one was surprised at her sudden absence. He was told that it was quite common for servants to move on without giving notice, particularly in the first few weeks of employment.

'What do you know of the history of the abbey, Murray?' Lombroso asked.

'Not a great deal, except what I read in Baldovino's article. It was secularised a century ago, wasn't it?' He felt uncomfortable lying, but he did not want Lombroso to know that he had been out drinking in La Capra in the company of a reporter, particularly Baldovino, whom the professor despised.

'That much is common knowledge, locally at any rate,' Ottolenghi said. 'The question is why.'

'And that is what no one knows,' Lombroso said. 'It happened a long time ago, after all. There have been rumours ever since.'

'What kind of rumours?' James asked.

'Mostly to do with young girls from the town,' Lombroso replied. 'It is said that they were lured to the abbey with promises of employment and then forced to take part in satanic rituals.'

'Really? What kind of rituals?'

'That is where the mystery lies,' Lombroso said. 'Nobody knows the truth except those involved. The Church was not keen to discuss the matter, as you might imagine.'

'So what happened to the monks?' James asked.

'Once the abbey was closed down, they were dispersed to other places throughout the country,' Lombroso replied.

'Or at least that is what the Church would have us believe,' Ottolenghi added.

James reached for his glass and took a gulp of wine. 'And what of the missing girls that Baldovino speaks of in the article, and the body we examined this morning?'

Lombroso pursed his lips. 'I don't see an obvious connection, given the age of the corpse. Besides, Baldovino is hardly a reliable source of information. Look at how he tried to link the missing girls to events that happened a century ago. His only interest is in selling newspapers.'

'But as you know, several girls have disappeared over the last few months. Do you still not think it suspicious?'

Lombroso shrugged. 'And as I said to you, girls of that type run or move away all the time. It is in their nature. I doubt there is anything to be concerned about.'

'That is not what Sofia thinks!' James knew immediately that he had said too much. Ottolenghi seemed surprised, and Lombroso was frowning.

'What has this to do with Sofia?' he said. 'You led me to believe that the attachment between you was severed. If it is not...'

'It was . . . it is,' James said. 'But she told me about her cousin.'

'Yes, yes, I am aware of it, but that young girl is an example of the type I was speaking of – flighty, incapable of loyalty or any form of commitment. All women have characteristics that bring them closer to the level of savages, as you will see when we continue our investigations.'

'But why should she run away? Sofia said that she had a good position with the marchesa.'

'Oh come now, Murray, it is hardly surprising. They run off at the slightest provocation, wherever they are employed. She has most likely gone in pursuit of some man or other. Girls like that have an inferior moral sense.'

'And is that what you told Sofia when she asked for your help?'

There was a long silence. James realised that he had overstepped the mark, though he could not bring himself to regret it. But still he forced himself to adopt a more conciliatory tone. 'Surely you must at least accept the possibility that the body found in the woods might be linked to the girls who have gone missing recently.'

'Perhaps . . . perhaps not. Really, Murray, I wish you would leave these things to the authorities and concentrate on the matters at hand.'

James glared at him. One minute he was part of something, and the next he had been demoted to the role of assistant. Lombroso's inconsistency was absolutely infuriating, not to mention his stubbornness. Fortunately at that point their host arrived with dinner and the tension was broken.

They began with vitello tonnè – sliced veal served cold in a delicious thick sauce with capers, anchovies and cinnamon. This was accompanied by a white wine made from a grape called Arneis. It had a scented, almost flowery perfume, and the flavour of apricots and melons was so wonderful that James almost did not want to swallow. 'This wine is excellent,' he said.

'Of course. One always gets the best in places like these,' Lombroso said, an expression of satisfaction on his face. He held up his glass. 'Let us drink a toast to our investigation, this evening and beyond. To the Devil and the Abbey San Callisto!'

They raised their glasses. James noticed that there was consternation among their fellow diners, who were muttering to each other and staring.

'What's the fuss about?' Lombroso asked the waiter who had come to collect their plates.

The waiter pulled a copy of *The People's Voice* from his pocket. The professor frowned as he read it, then held it up. James squinted at the headline in the fading light: HAUNTED ABBEY MYSTERY: LOMBROSO INVESTIGATES.

'How did Baldovino find out?' Ottolenghi asked.

Lombroso tutted. 'I told him it was for tomorrow's edition!'

James was incredulous. 'You sold the story to Baldovino? I thought you disliked him.'

Lombroso shrugged. 'He has his uses. Besides, people have a right to know what I am doing.'

'You sound just like him,' James said.

'I don't know why people are so upset about our expedition,' Ottolenghi said. 'The abbey's reputation goes back years.'

'*Sì, Dottore,* but we do not like to speak of it in these parts, particularly now,' the waiter said. 'It is because of *le figlie del Diavolo* . . . the Devil's daughters.'

'Interesting,' Lombroso said, stroking his beard. 'Who are they?'

The waiter looked around, as if worried who might hear him. He bent closer and whispered. 'As you know, it is said that a century ago the Devil walked freely among the monks at the abbey, assisted by his handmaidens, girls from San Callisto he had persuaded to serve him. They disappeared when he did.'

'*Le figlie del Diavolo?*' Ottolenghi asked. The waiter nodded.

Lombroso sipped at his wine. 'I remember the stories, certainly. But surely they belong to the past, as the *dottore* said.'

'If only, Professor, if only. But now it is thought that Satan has returned. Apparently he has been seen walking there at night. And that's not all.' He leant in even more closely. 'When he goes back to Hell, he is taking some of our girls with him!'

Lucy shifted uncomfortably in her seat. It was early evening and dinner had come and gone. The house was quiet, as Professor Lombroso and James were off on some expedition and Signora Lombroso was visiting a friend. Miss Trott and Lucy were sitting in the drawing room reading as Gina and Paola played chess. The two girls had very different approaches to the game. Gina was impulsive, hardly waiting a moment before making her decisions, whereas Paola was more thoughtful. Lucy could almost hear her thinking as she worked out every possible strategy and its consequence before finally making her move.

Miss Trott was nodding off. The book on her lap began to slip down and fell to the floor, waking her. She shook herself, presumably trying to regain her composure.

'I think I'll have an early night,' she said, getting to her feet. 'Don't be too late, Lucy dear.'

'I won't, Miss Trott,' Lucy said, watching her as she left the room. How could her companion bear her life? It seemed so very monotonous, and there was little prospect of change. Admittedly, she had travelled to Italy, which must have provided some variety, but now that she was here, all she did was sit and read, with the occasional visit to a gallery or museum. Not that Lucy's own life was so very different. Still, at least she was young and had the prospect of a future. Observing Miss Trott made her all the more determined to one day break free and forge her own destiny, whatever it took.

Paola looked up from her chess game. 'Miss Trott has left her book behind.'

Lucy went over and picked it up, intending to take it up to her. She was about to flick through it to see what it was when she noticed a small piece of paper marking one of the pages. It was folded carefully in two. Surreptitiously she took it out and examined it. The borders were decorated with a depiction of a serpent, the intricate patterns on its back picked out in red, gold and green. Written in a fine copperplate hand in the centre were the words *Serendipity – 156 Via San Pellico, Torino. Apep.*

'What's that?' Gina asked.

'Just a bookmark,' Lucy said. She was tucking the note back between the pages when Miss Trott returned.

'Ah, thank you, dear,' she said, taking the book from Lucy. 'I like to read a little once I've retired. I find it soothing. Good night.'

'Good night,' Lucy said, watching her leave. She followed her to the door to close it and noticed that Miss Trott had paused by the staircase and was flicking through the book.

When she reached the note, she nodded to herself, apparently pleased to find everything as she had left it, and headed up to bed.

For the remainder of the meal James was acutely aware that they were under intense scrutiny. It did not seem to bother either Lombroso or Ottolenghi, who tucked into their food with gusto. More wine came with their main course – agnello al forno, a fine piece of roast lamb with garlic, rosemary and white wine. It was mouthwateringly good: crisp on the outside, juicy and succulent inside. The wine served with it was a Barbaresco, one of the region's finest, according to Lombroso. It was garnet red and smelt enticingly of violets. The grape, Barbera, also formed the base of the grappa that followed, a pungent but strangely soft drink with a faint hint of juniper at its heart, a far cry from the harsh concoction James had drunk in La Capra.

Following a long lecture from Lombroso on the history of psychical research, they made their way to the abbey. It was not far – a walk of no more than about fifteen minutes up a gentle slope through some olive groves. It was chillier now, and a mist had descended, swirling round them. The clouds parted for a second, allowing him to see the thin crescent of a new moon. As they drew nearer, he could make out a large, imposing building with a tall bell tower at one end. He shivered involuntarily. It could just have been the result of the tales he had heard about the place, but then again...

The bags containing what Lombroso proudly called 'our investigatory equipment' had already arrived and were piled up outside the gates waiting for their arrival. A small, wizened figure was leaning against a wall beside them, hunched over, making him look alarmingly like one of the pictures of early man that the professor was so keen to compare to the born criminal. The man, whose name, they were informed, was Beppe, nodded at Lombroso and looked surreptitiously from side to side before opening the tall iron gates. Lombroso strode through them with great purpose as usual, with Beppe following on behind. Ottolenghi looked down at the bags ruefully, shrugged and then picked up half of them, leaving the others to James. He had no idea what they contained. He was used to the various gadgets back in the laboratory – a craniometer to measure skulls and heads, an algometer to gauge pain thresholds and an Anfosso tachianthropometer for arms, legs, feet and so on. But what equipment would be used to hunt for ghosts or the Devil? And perhaps more to the point, why was Lombroso, a criminal anthropologist, now engaged in psychical research? He still had not made his interest entirely clear. James made a mental note to ask him about it later. He imagined that there would be plenty of time. Something told him it was going to be a long night.

13

*Criminal women exhibit many levels of intelligence. Some
are extremely intelligent, while others are ordinary in this
respect. As a rule, however, their minds are alert; this is
evidently why, relative to men, they commit few impulsive
crimes.*   Lombroso and Ferrero, 1893, p. 189

'So what could it mean?' Gina said.

After some thought, Lucy had decided to share her find
with Gina and Paola. They seemed to have inherited a highly
developed thirst for discovery from their father, and when she
told them about Miss Trott's note, they were well and truly
intrigued. The sisters perched on Lucy's bed while she paced
the room restlessly. '156 Via San Pellico, Torino. Obviously
that's an address, but I've no idea about Serendipity or Apep.'

'Serendipity means a happy accidental discovery. It comes
from the fairy tale "The Three Princes of Serendip". The
heroes were always discovering things they weren't looking
for,' Paola said.

'How do you know that?' Lucy asked in admiration.

'Oh, I expect she read it somewhere, didn't you, Paola?'
Gina said breezily. 'She's always got her nose in a book. The
point is, why has Miss Trott written it down . . . it was her
handwriting, wasn't it?'

'I think so,' Lucy said. 'And what about Apep?'

Gina shrugged. 'It's not a word I've heard before.'

Lucy wandered over to the window and glanced outside at the street below. Impatiently she tapped her fingers on the pane. 'Then of course there is the fact that all of these things are written down together. That must surely signify something.'

'Well there's only one way to find out for certain,' Paola said. 'We'll have to pay the Via San Pellico a visit.'

'How can we do that?' Gina asked. 'You know Mama would never allow it.'

'We'll have to sneak out,' Lucy said. 'After dark would be best.'

Paola frowned. 'I don't like the sound of that. We might get arrested by the carabinieri.'

'Really? What for?' Lucy asked.

'Girls found out on their own after dark can sometimes be stopped and accused of being ladies of ill repute,' Paola replied.

Gina rolled her eyes. 'Where's your sense of adventure?'

Paola was unconvinced. 'Can you imagine Papa's reaction?'

'Then I suppose we should leave it for now,' Lucy said. 'I'm sure we'll come up with something.'

She went back to the window and breathed on it, using her finger to draw in the condensation. She stood back and examined the result – a series of vertical lines. Then, smiling to herself, she rubbed them out.

As they approached the building, James felt a change of atmosphere. The closer he got to it, the more pronounced it became, to the extent that when they reached the large wooden doors beneath an arched stone cupola at the end of the drive, it was almost overwhelming. Before he had been apprehensive, but that was interlaced with anticipation and excitement at what was to come. Now all he could feel was a kind of heaviness and melancholy. He stood next to Ottolenghi and tried to discern whether he shared these emotions, but his friend's expression was giving nothing away.

Lombroso beckoned to him. 'The smaller of your two bags – could you bring it over, Murray?'

James obeyed, glad to see the back of it. It might have been the smaller of the two, but it was also the heavier by far. Lombroso took it from him and put it on the floor before opening it. It clanked as it landed. James peered over the professor's shoulder, expecting to see a camera or a piece of equipment from the laboratory. Instead the bag contained a jumble of jemmies, crowbars, spanners, screwdrivers and other similar tools, along with some lanterns and a set of strange-looking keys. Beppe picked up a slim jemmy and set about opening the door.

'You're breaking in!' James said.

'*We* are breaking in,' Lombroso corrected him.

'You never mentioned burglary!' James whispered.

'Oh, Murray, really. How else did you think we would gain entry?'

'I assumed that you had got the Church's permission.'

'I did ask for it, naturally. It was denied, exactly as I expected. They are somewhat sensitive about what happened here, which is, I suppose, unsurprising.'

'Did you know about this, Ottolenghi?' James asked.

His friend shrugged. 'No, but like the professor, I am not surprised, given the history of the place.'

'What if we're caught?' James asked, imagining trying to

explain a conviction for breaking and entering to Aunt Agnes. 'Baldovino's article makes our presence only too clear!'

'We won't be caught, as you put it, Murray,' Lombroso said. 'You have nothing to worry about. I will explain everything later. Until then, why don't you just concentrate on watching a man at his work? Beppe here is an expert – extremely skilled, in fact. We met last year in the cells at the carabinieri head-quarters. He is a fine example of a born criminal. Just look at his tiny eyes and thick eyebrows! And how about those ears? '

'Sssh!' Beppe said, glaring at them.

'Yes, do be quiet, Murray,' Lombroso said. 'Beppe here needs to concentrate.'

It appeared that the jemmy was not working, so Beppe reached into the bag again and this time picked up the set of what Lombroso informed them were skeleton keys. These were far more effective, and in a moment the doors swung open with a loud and disquieting creak. They were in.

'Thank you, Beppe. I think we can take it from here,' Lombroso said.

Beppe gave a curt nod and held his hand out. Lombroso pressed some coins into it and bowed. James noted that the thief was receiving more courtesy from the professor than he himself ever had. Beppe picked up his bag of equipment and removed two of the lanterns, handing one each to James and Ottolenghi. 'You'll be needing these,' he said gruffly, and with that he shuffled off towards the gates, his night's work completed.

James and Ottolenghi lit the lanterns and followed Lombroso, who was striding ahead of them into the abbey. As they passed the roughly hewn and unpolished doors, James noticed that the locks seemed shiny and new, which was somewhat incongruous given their surroundings. He breathed in and smelt the stench of decay. The melancholy that he had experienced earlier changed to something deeper – a feeling of dread.

He heard what he hoped were Lombroso's solid footsteps to his left and followed them. Stretching before him as far as he could see was a long corridor.

'You go after the professor,' Ottolenghi said. 'I'll try the other way.'

'Are you sure splitting up is the best plan?' James asked.

'I don't frighten easily,' Ottolenghi said, although by the slight tremor in his voice, James thought he was probably trying to persuade himself of the truth of his claim.

'Right, if you say so, but we'll meet back here in one hour. Agreed?'

'Agreed.'

James made his way along the corridor, holding his lantern up to light his way. He had experienced the darkness and strangeness of such a place before. Only a few months ago, he had walked through supposedly haunted tunnels beneath the city, again with Ottolenghi. That was far from pleasant, but this . . . this was a great deal worse. Up to now, he had always been sceptical of all things supernatural, but there was something about this place. Should he be more open-minded? Shadows were everywhere, and the further he went, the more convinced he became that he was being followed. He forced himself to press on. He had to. There was no choice. The professor had come this way. He might be in danger.

That was when he heard the footsteps. They were shadowing his own. Could they just be an echo? He stopped, and so did they, but just for an instant he heard another step. But ghosts don't walk, he reasoned to himself. They float, if they move at all. He wasn't sure about demons. A breeze sprang up and he felt his hair move as if ruffled by an invisible hand. He began to walk faster. The echo of his footsteps started again and he thought he heard heavy breathing in the distance behind him. He had to find the professor before whatever it was found him.

He went on, almost running now. The corridor must be at least a mile long, he thought. The thing behind him seemed to be getting ever closer . . . then he tripped over a loose stone and was left sprawling on the stone floor, helpless as something approached him, something terrible, something deadly. With a surge of adrenalin, he told himself that he refused to die without knowing who or what his nemesis was. He turned over painfully, ready to see the face of his assailant.

14

*Today the wicked man looks for a temperate woman
and the depraved person seeks virtue. Evil men scout
out wicked women to be not wives but only accomplices
in crime. Because cruelty in women is becoming a dis-
advantage and compassion an attraction, women repress
their wicked impulses and simulate compassion, as one
sees all too frequently today in the hypocrites who behave
charitably in order to seduce a man.*

Lombroso and Ferrero, 1893, p. 72

Lucy sat in her room and tried to concentrate on her writing. She was finding it difficult to focus on the page before
her. Her thoughts kept returning to Miss Trott's note and
the strange picture of the serpent that decorated it. As for
Francesco, she couldn't even begin to describe how she felt
about him. Then there was the question of James and Anna
and the mysterious missing husband.

She got up and went to the window. It was dark outside
and the lamplight was flickering in the street. She picked
up her cloak, which she had flung carelessly over the back
of a chair, and left the room. The house was still quiet. She
wondered what James was doing on his expedition. He had
called it 'making enquiries' when she had asked him. There

was no detail, of course, which was typical of him these days. They used to share so much, but now it was as if he had shut her out completely. Or was it perhaps the other way round?

His reaction to their father's death had made her so angry, almost as angry as she had been when he had abandoned her to Aunt Agnes's care without a thought for what she might want. She had hoped that they were close to some kind of a rapprochement since he had agreed to bring her to Turin. But now he was so preoccupied that she might as well not exist. Well, she would show him what happened when he ignored her, whatever the consequences. She made her way downstairs and out through the front door, closing it quietly behind her. So intent was she on getting away from the house that she did not notice the door open again a few seconds later to reveal someone else shadowing her footsteps.

Lucy wrapped her cloak closely around herself as she walked through the dimly lit back streets. The night was chilly and there was moisture in the air, perhaps because of the cover of low cloud that had descended. Or was it mist? Whatever its identity, it enveloped her in a dampness that clung to her skin beneath her clothes. She knew that she was taking a risk by venturing out alone after dark, but it seemed to her to be a risk worth taking. How else could she find out what was at the address that Miss Trott had written down on that piece of paper?

She turned down one of the narrow but fiercely straight streets that criss-crossed the city. There were not many people around. She wasn't sure if that made her feel safer or not, but at least she was experiencing something for herself, something that she could use in her stories. Wasn't that what writers did?

They drew on their own lives and used them in conjunction with their imagination. Now, for once, she would be able to do the same.

When she reached the Via San Pellico, she counted the house numbers — no easy task as many of them were missing — and soon found what she was looking for. It wasn't what she was expecting. Number 156 was a chemist's shop. Lucy peered through the windows. There was not much to see, given the late hour — just a few coloured jars. She had been hoping to find a house with people in it who might be able to shed some light on Miss Trott's interest, but for now it seemed that the mystery was resisting solution. She would have to consult Gina and Paola. Perhaps they would have some ideas about what it meant. She turned quickly. Footsteps! She had company.

'Well, well, well! What do we have here?'

Two men in uniform were standing in the doorway opposite. The one who had spoken was leaning unsteadily on the window. He was tall and skinny. The other, short and squat, had his back to her and was audibly relieving himself.

'What . . . another whore? When will they learn?' he said, shaking himself and doing up the buttons on his fly.

Both men walked over to her. 'Papers . . . You know the drill by now, I'm sure,' the tall one said.

Lucy shook her head, too afraid to speak.

The shorter man tutted. 'Oh dear, oh dear. You know what that means. We'll have to take you in. They'll check you over . . . all over, if you know what I mean . . .' He leered at her. 'All your little nooks and crannies, Bella . . . every single one.'

'I'll look forward to that. I'm sure they'll need witnesses,' his friend said, grinning.

'Come on now, Bella, if we hurry, we can have you all tucked up in your whorehouse before midnight, ready for business.' The short one grabbed her by the arm and propelled her down the street. He stank of stale sweat and garlic.

Lucy struggled. He gave her a slap. '*Puttana!* Do as you're told!'

'Don't you touch her!'

It was Sofia, Professor Lombroso's housekeeper. Lucy remembered Paola referring to her when they were having dinner.

The two men swung round. 'Oh, what's this ... your madam worried about losing some business!'

'She is no prostitute. She is a respectable young woman!'

'If she was, she wouldn't be wandering the streets on her own looking for business, now would she?' the tall one said.

'Neither would you, come to that,' his friend said. 'Perhaps you'd better come with us as well.'

'I wonder what Inspector Tullio would have to say about this?' Sofia said. 'The two of you bothering respectable young women ... not to mention drinking on duty.'

'You know the inspector?' said the short one.

'I work for Professor Lombroso, his good friend.' There was a pause as they struggled to take this information in. Both men seemed to grow pale. 'Well now, it was just a misunderstanding,' the tall one said. 'You go on your way, ladies. We never met. There's no need to tell a soul.'

Sofia took Lucy by the hand. 'Be careful now,' said the stocky man.

Sofia glared at them. The two officers bowed and walked quickly away.

'Are you all right?'

Lucy nodded in relief. 'Thank you. I am so glad you saw me.'

'It is just as well that I did. '

'Who were those men?'

'They were policemen . . . members of what is known as the Morals Squad. Their job is to ensure that the city's prostitutes stay in their registered brothels and do as they are told.'

'And bullying girls is part of that?'

'They would call it keeping the streets safe from unregistered whores. From their point of view an unaccompanied woman should not be on the streets at night; if she is, then she must be there for immoral purposes.'

'Gina and Paola did mention it.'

'Well you should have listened to them. What on earth were you doing?'

'It's a long story,' Lucy said.

'Then I think you'd better tell it to me,' Sofia said. 'My rooms are round the corner. We can wait there until everyone has gone to bed. If we go back to the house now, someone might see us.'

They walked together through the deserted streets. How much should Lucy tell Sofia? Was she friend or foe? Perhaps she was about to find out.

Before he could see anything, James felt a piece of cloth being thrown over his head and tightened around his throat. He thrashed around this way and that, pulling desperately on the material in an effort to free himself, but it was hopeless. He could not breathe and was losing consciousness when suddenly the grip around his throat loosened and the cloth was removed. He heard running footsteps, both away and towards him, as he tried to get up.

'What on earth are you doing down there, Murray?' Lombroso peered down at him. James took the professor's helping hand and scrambled to his feet.

'Did you see him?'

'Who?'

'The ... the thing that attacked me.'

'Thing? What do you mean?'

'Something tried to strangle me.'

'Don't you mean someone?'

'I don't know. Didn't you see anything?'

'All I saw was you rolling around on the floor as I came up behind you.'

'I was following you! How did you get behind me?'

Lombroso tutted. 'The corridor circles the building. I thought I would do a quick tour round, but then I fancied I saw something in one of the rooms. While I was in there, I heard you lumbering past. You are so slow, Murray; it was easy to catch up with you.'

'I do not lumber! Anyway, I thought you were a ...'

'A what?' Lombroso giggled. 'You thought I was a ghost. Is that it? Or perhaps Beelzebub himself? Really, Murray, that is most amusing. Wait till I tell Ottolenghi.'

What had the professor expected after all that talk of the Devil and girls being dragged into Hell?

'I was definitely attacked.'

'You're imagining it, Murray.'

'No, I'm not. Something ... someone ...' He saw Lombroso looking sceptically at him. 'There's something about the atmosphere in this place. Can't you feel it?'

Lombroso shook his head. 'Can't say I do. Have you by any chance been reading Signor Dickens's ghost stories?'

'No, I haven't,' James replied. Had he imagined it after all?

'Good. Science is what we are here for, not old wives' tales or ghost stories. Odd things do happen, but there is always some kind of rational explanation . . . well, almost always.'

'I sensed something, though, almost as soon as we arrived,' James insisted. 'I'm not saying it was supernatural, but I'm sure I saw something . . . or felt it, anyway.'

'Saw what?' Lombroso asked.

James shrugged. 'Shadows, a breeze . . . nothing tangible until I was assaulted.'

'Nothing tangible? Oh really, Murray,' Lombroso said in an exasperated tone. 'What you felt was some kind of reaction of the mind, brought on no doubt by an overactive imagination and imbibing rather too freely of the grappa! We are here to observe real phenomena.'

James was doubtful. Perhaps the professor was right and his mind had been playing tricks on him. It was easy to imagine things in a place like this. Still, it felt real enough. He rubbed his neck gingerly. If he had bruises there tomorrow, Lombroso might believe him.

'Now shall we see if we can find Ottolenghi?' Lombroso said. 'Then perhaps we can do some sensible scientific investigation. Ghosts! Beelzebub! Priceless! There really is no such—'

He was cut off by a blood-curdling scream full of anguish and fear, as if whoever it came from was being horribly tortured.

'What was that?' Lombroso asked.

'I don't know, but I think it came from the centre courtyard.'

'Well what are you waiting for, Murray? You wanted ghosts . . .'

Together they made their way back to the doors at the front of the building and then started to move forward until they reached a large area with a number of stone pillars and graceful arches. At the centre was a statue of an angel, its hands held together in prayer, its wings outstretched. Standing looking up at it in wonder was Ottolenghi.

'Was that you? Are you all right?' James asked.

'I am, and no, it wasn't me. I was in the graveyard outside when I heard the noise and followed it here. I think it was a fox. But look what I found.'

James and Lombroso followed his glance. The angel that he had been staring at so intently appeared to be weeping.

Before long, Lucy and Sofia arrived in a small piazza. Sofia led the way up a rickety staircase in its corner and opened a door to reveal a small room with a shabby sofa and a table and chair in the corner.

'Would you like some coffee?' she asked.

'Yes please.'

She busied herself at a small sink whilst Lucy sank on to the settee. Suddenly her legs did not seem to be able to hold her.

'I shouldn't have done it,' she said. 'I'm sorry, Sofia.'

'No, you should not . . . but it's done now and I think you have learnt something, no?'

Lucy smiled. 'Yes, you could say that . . .' Her smile waned. 'You won't tell James, will you? I don't know what he'd say. Not that he'd care.'

'I won't tell him. Do not worry,' Sofia said. 'But I think you are wrong. He does care . . . more than you know.'

'Are you sure? He has hardly spoken to me since we arrived.'

'He has other things on his mind.'

'Oh, you mean Anna Tarnovsky.' She had not meant to mention it, but it occurred to her that Sofia might know something.

'Madame Tarnovsky? Why would she be on his mind?'

'Isn't he in love with her?'

Lucy heard Sofia bang the coffee pot down on the table. 'What makes you say that?' Her voice had changed. Her usual husky tones had been replaced by a certain brittleness.

'The way he looks at her, I suppose.'

Lucy watched Sofia carefully. Her movements were stiff and the expression on her face was taut, as if she was restraining her emotions. 'Why did you follow me?' she asked.

Sofia hesitated. 'I did not.'

'Then how did you know where I was?'

'A coincidence, nothing more...'

Lucy felt that she was seeing the young woman for the first time. Before tonight she had merely been a figure in the background, but now...

Sofia handed her a small cup of coffee before sitting down next to her. Lucy closed her eyes and breathed in its aroma, letting it take her back to her childhood, and the coffee her mother would brew for her father; a comforting sensation of familiarity and security combined with an almost overwhelming sense of loss.

'Sofia, what do you think of my brother?'

There was a long pause. Sofia looked down into her own coffee cup as if she were seeking the answer in its fragrant depths. 'He is a good man.'

'Is he? I sometimes wonder . . . There are things he has not told me.'

'I do not think you should worry. To me he is someone who tries to do the right thing but sometimes lets his heart get in the way.'

'What makes you say that?'

Sofia blushed. 'I do not know. It is not my business. He is your brother. I do not know him well enough to say.'

The words seemed to tumble out as if she was powerless to stop them; an odd reaction, Lucy thought.

'Now I have a question for you,' Sofia said. 'What were you doing wandering about the streets at night like that?'

Lucy had prepared herself for this question. 'I was researching for a story that I am writing.'

'Oh, a story,' Sofia said, her eyebrows raised. 'How interesting.'

Now it was Lucy's turn to blush. 'I needed some local atmosphere.'

'Of course you did,' Sofia said. 'And I am sure you found plenty . . . more than enough. So you will not need to search for any further inspiration, will you?'

'Er, no . . . I suppose not.'

She was tempted to tell Sofia about Miss Trott's note but decided it was too soon. Sofia seemed like an ally, but Lucy could not be sure that she would not tell James, and he would be sure to disapprove.

'Shall we go back to the house?' Sofia asked. 'I think it is time.'

Lucy yawned and nodded. The evening's events were catching up with her, and she suddenly felt tired. The thought of what might have happened were it not for Sofia's timely intervention made her shudder. Still, the discovery of the address might be important, and the latter part of the evening had been interesting. There was plenty of food for thought, more than enough to keep the most persistent of detectives occupied.

15

What we have seen as true in space, among the various peoples scattered over the surface of the globe, we might view also as occurrences in time, inasmuch as belief in the spirits of the dead has never suffered an interruption, from the earliest ages down to our day.

Lombroso, 1909, p. 215

'What is this place?' James asked.

'This was known as the judgement room, where, it is said, those detained by the monks were left to await their fate,' Lombroso replied. He held his hand out and touched the liquid streaming from the statue's eyes, then put his hand to his lips. 'Interesting, it's salty . . . like tears.'

'What about the scream?' James asked.

'As Ottolenghi suggested, it was probably the cry of a wild animal – a vixen, I would think. We are in the countryside, after all.'

'And the statue? What could cause it to weep?'

'I don't know,' Lombroso replied. 'Perhaps it's some kind of geological phenomenon. Take a sample, Murray, could you? There are some containers in the bags over there.'

James did as he was told and placed the result back in the bag for safe keeping. 'Shall I get out the rest of the equipment?'

'Yes, good idea,' Lombroso said. 'Time to bring science into the equation.'

James and Ottolenghi unpacked the bags and stacked the equipment up against the wall. There were some thermometers, spare lanterns, two cameras and a couple of things that James did not immediately recognise but thought looked familiar. The rest was just for their comfort, it would seem – cushions, a few blankets and enough food and drink to last them several days.

'Isn't that a sphygmograph?' he asked, unravelling a set of wires attached to some small sheets of metal.

'Indeed. I see you are learning, Murray,' Lombroso said. 'And what is it for?'

'Isn't it usually used for measuring emotions through the pulse?'

'Yes, it is.'

'Who are you planning to strap it to, the Devil?'

'Certainly, should he deign to make an appearance,' replied Lombroso, apparently in all seriousness.

'I think the professor means to use one of us as his guinea pig,' Ottolenghi said.

'Ah, I see.' James nodded. 'You want to observe how we react to spending the night in a haunted house.'

Lombroso nodded. 'Correct again.'

'And this?' James asked, holding up another bundle of tangled wires and metal.

'That is my lie-detecting machine ... or at least that is what I hope it will become once I have completed it. It is a plethysmograph – a fear detector, if you like.'

'What are you going to do with that?' James said. He doubted the Devil would agree to be interviewed, and was

143

feeling somewhat aggrieved that he had carried all this along the drive.

'Oh, nothing much,' Lombroso said airily. 'I just brought it along to tinker with. Now shall we get on?'

James exchanged exasperated glances with Ottolenghi. He was tired and cold – the temperature outside was pleasantly balmy, but inside, the stone walls had created a persistent and all-consuming chill. He had come to Turin to complete his training as a criminal anthropologist, not embark on a new career as a psychical investigator.

'We should definitely investigate the crypt,' Lombroso said, picking up one of the spare lanterns and lighting it. 'Apparently that is where much of the activity has been reported. But first we should take a look upstairs, in the dormitory and the great hall. I understand there were sightings there too.'

To James's surprise, the damp and musty smell that pervaded elsewhere seemed to dissipate as they climbed the broad staircase. It was soon evident that this upstairs area differed considerably from the other rooms. The wooden corridors up here were polished, and there was a distinct aroma of incense coupled with beeswax. The latter reminded James of Lombroso's museum, and by association Sofia. It was where they had first met, and he still recalled his initial impression of her – all damaged beauty and pride.

There were a number of rooms leading off the corridor, and Lombroso tried one or two door handles, but to no avail.

'They are locked, and unfortunately I no longer have the means of entering. Beppe has taken my skeleton keys.'

James grinned at the irony. 'Couldn't we break in by force?' He put his shoulder to the door.

'We cannot afford to do any damage,' Lombroso said. 'Everyone in Turin knows that we are here.'

James shrugged. 'I see your point, Professor. Still, it is odd that the doors are locked, don't you think?' He looked through the small gap between the door and the jamb. He couldn't see a great deal, but there certainly seemed to be furniture, and curtains at the only window in his line of sight, which was odd.

'Perhaps I—'

Again there was a scream, followed by another. It sounded almost human . . . almost, thought James, but not quite.

'That definitely came from the graveyard! Follow me!' Lombroso said, running towards the stairs. 'Let's see if it is a fox.'

By the time they got outside, the noise had subsided, to be replaced by an ominous silence broken only by occasional rustlings in the undergrowth, no doubt made by the fox or perhaps even rats. A dense fog swirled round the gravestones, making the place resemble a scene from one of Lucy's gothic novels.

'Look! Over there!' Ottolenghi held up his lantern.

A light was drifting gently through the mist across the graveyard. It was not particularly bright, and the movement was not steady or in a straight line, but seemed to meander from side to side. Lombroso put his finger to his lips and then beckoned for his assistants to follow him as he moved towards it. It seemed to be heading for the building itself. James tried to think of a rational, scientific explanation for what he was seeing. Was it an insect of some kind – a firefly perhaps? It seemed too big for that. Was someone playing games with them? Plenty of people knew they were here, after all, thanks to Baldovino. The waiter from the trattoria and sundry diners had all heard them discussing the abbey, but there would have been little time for them to organise anything as elaborate as this. So who or what could it be?

They followed the light through the doors and towards a narrow stone staircase. The temperature seemed to drop even further as they did so.

'It's going to the crypt!' Lombroso whispered.

Their lanterns flickered, surrounding them with shadows as they approached the stairs. Then the light they were pursuing went out.

They stood in silence for a while, trying to detect any sound that the source of the light might be making. There was nothing. Then they examined the place where it had disappeared, but could see nothing except solid stone walls.

'We might as well go into the crypt ourselves,' Lombroso said, 'since it was what we had planned.'

'What about the equipment?' James asked.

'Ah yes,' Lombroso said. 'I'm not sure what we will need. Still, better safe than sorry.'

Both James and Ottolenghi refused point blank to haul everything down to the crypt unless it was definitely going to be used. Oddly, Lombroso did not protest, agreeing that they could use their eyes and ears until anything interesting turned up. Between them they collected the necessities – cushions and comestibles. They could at least make themselves comfortable during their vigil.

The crypt seemed to be made up of a series of small rooms. They set up camp in a corner of the first one and decided to set about exploring the rest a little later.

'You said that this was the most haunted part of the abbey,' James said. 'What happened here?'

'This is where the Devil appears,' Lombroso said.

'I thought the gates to Hell were in the Piazza Statuto,' James said.

'Hell is a big place. I daresay it has more than one entrance.'

'Why here, then?'

Lombroso lifted his lantern to his face, giving it a devilish glow. 'This is where Satan was summoned by the monks. It is where the rituals were performed that brought him forth, and where the sacrifices took place. It is said by some to be like a centrifugal force: badness swirls around the sides, culminating in a heart of pure evil.'

James was sceptical. 'And the science in that?'

'Something happened here all those years ago,' Lombroso replied, 'and something is happening now, otherwise there would not be reports of sights and sounds that remind the people who live nearby of the legends and stories.'

'These kinds of stories can leave a scar on places and people. I heard plenty of anecdotal evidence of such effects when I was studying with Oskar Reiner,' Ottolenghi said.

'You haven't told us much about that,' James said. 'What was it like?'

There was a long silence. 'It was . . . instructive. He's a strange man and I learnt some strange things from him.'

'Ah yes, he has an interest in sexual murder, does he not – *Lustmord*,' James said, remembering his discussion with Reiner the previous year.

Ottolenghi was quiet, and James sensed his discomfort. 'Salvatore?'

'I cannot say . . . not yet.' Ottolenghi seemed to sigh as he spoke. 'But what I learnt there . . . has changed me.'

'We can discuss it whenever you are ready,' James said. He was perplexed. It was unlike Ottolenghi to be so reticent.

'There will be time enough for that,' Lombroso said abruptly. 'We should continue our investigation.'

They got to their feet and began to move from room to room. James could not see much, even with his lantern, but that air of malevolence was still in evidence. As he approached the final room, tucked right at the back, the feeling of dread almost overwhelmed him. He felt a draught blow around his head. The lantern flickered and then went out completely, plunging him into darkness. He felt frantically in his pockets for a match. It was difficult – his hands were trembling so much that he could hardly hold anything steadily – but finally he managed to reignite his lantern and held it high. He gasped and stepped back. The lantern swayed precariously, casting strange shadows from the macabre tableau in front of him. Seated only a foot or so away from him, dressed in monks' habits, was a row of bodies, strangely preserved, their heads drooping and their mouths hanging open. They seemed to be screaming.

He heard Lombroso and Ottolenghi come in and stand behind him. They too held up their lanterns, revealing the scene in its gruesome entirety. For it was not just the long-dead monks who were seated in the crypt. Propped up next to them was another body. A young girl, pale and beautiful, her lifeless eyes staring straight at them in a monstrous parody of her other corpse companions. Because unlike them, dressed in their coarse brown monastic robes, she was in virginal white, complete with a bridal veil, a bouquet of fresh spring flowers clasped demurely before her. If the monks were the servants of Satan, then she was his bride.

16

. . . the majority of criminals are anything but atheist, although they have fashioned their own sensual and accommodating religion, which turns the God of peace and justice into a sort of benevolent guardian for criminals.

Lombroso, 1874, p. 70

James and Tullio stood together surveying the scene as Lombroso examined the body. He had insisted that it should be Tullio who was contacted, even though it should by rights have been the carabinieri. The inspector's jurisdiction as an officer of the public security police was supposed to be confined to the city, but presumably, James thought, Lombroso could not bear the prospect of the bombastic and always hostile Marshal Machinetti attending. There was also the small matter of them having broken into the abbey in the first place. At least Tullio could be relied upon to be supportive, whereas Machinetti would only have made capital from Lombroso's wrongdoing. They had roused an irritable San Callisto postmaster from his bed to dispatch a message to the inspector by telegram, thus avoiding any unpleasantness, as Lombroso had described it, or possible arrest and imprisonment for breaking and entering, as Tullio had, on his arrival, preferred to put it instead. James noticed that he had brought a couple of carabinieri officers with him, presumably to placate Machinetti, once he was told about their find.

The professor was examining the young girl's body, lifting her hair and picking up each hand tenderly, almost as if she was one of his own daughters.

'Could it be Sofia's cousin?' Tullio asked James. 'Chiara, isn't it?'

'Didn't she give you a description?'

Tullio was shamefaced. 'We did not get that far, I'm afraid. I assumed that the girl had run away.'

James said nothing. He had thought the same at first, so how could he criticise Tullio?

'We will have to ask her to view the body,' Tullio said.

'I was hoping to spare her that,' James said. 'From what she told me, I don't think it is Chiara. The hair is the wrong colour and her complexion is too pale.'

'But you haven't met the girl?'

'No, I haven't.'

'Then I'm afraid we will need Sofia to see the body to be sure.'

James tried to imagine how Sofia would feel once she discovered that a body had been found. He was impatient to get back to the city. It was important to him to tell her himself rather than for her to hear it from an official, even it was Tullio.

'We have two bodies now. There must be a link with the missing girls, surely?' he asked.

Tullio nodded wearily. 'We have already been through this.'

'But you still don't think it worth investigating? We don't even know where Baldovino got the list.'

'James, if I investigated every case where a girl goes missing, I would do little else.'

'Really? Is the professor right, then? It is that common?'

'Yes, it is. Girls of that class disappear all the time and nearly always under their own steam. Either they find a job or take up with some man, or sometimes they are arrested and end up being sent away or working as prostitutes. We just don't have the resources to look into all these cases. I made some enquiries but I came to a dead end and was told in no uncertain terms to stop.'

'And do you think Chiara has run off?'

'More than likely, yes, but I will look at the list again.'

'Why has the body been left here, and in this pose, with the monks? It must have some significance. Remember last year?'

Tullio rubbed his eyes. 'I see what you are getting at, of course, but the body you saw this morning is at least six months old and the monks have been here for many years. Everyone in the city knows about them, though not many have actually seen them. This girl is very recently deceased and yes, the body is posed, but they are so different that to me they seem like separate murders. This might even be an isolated domestic killing. Leave it to us. I am sure that you and Ottolenghi have more than enough to do.'

Ottolenghi was also watching, his features drawn and his face almost as pale as that of the body. Normally he would be keen to assist the professor instead of staying on the sidelines. Something was on his mind and it clearly had to do with his time in Vienna, but what could it be?

The atmosphere was one of quiet reverence. Even the carabinieri officers, who were usually fairly casual in the face of violent death, were subdued and respectful in the presence of such a young and beautiful vision. The girl's features were refined and delicate. She had long fair hair, almost white, which was simply dressed beneath her veil. Her face was also a ghostly white in colour. James wanted to pick her up and take her away from her grim monastic companions. They, by contrast, sat and sagged, as if weighed down by their own evil, their heads bowed in penitence.

Lombroso strode over. 'Interestingly, this girl and the monks have something in common.'

'What is that?' Tullio asked, drawing closer.

'They have, I think, been exposed to a form of mummification.'

Tullio frowned, perplexed. 'What do you mean?'

'I mean that the monks have been here for at least a century, as we know, and for some reason, probably something to do with their physical environment, some kind of natural mummification has taken place.'

'And the girl? She doesn't look mummified.'

'She has been here for less than a day, I would guess, and . . .' Lombroso hesitated and cleared his throat, as if he was finding it difficult to get the words out. 'This young lady has been almost completely drained of blood. Given the marks on the body, I would say that at least some of her organs have been removed – an action that might well have preceded the mummification process.'

'Like the organs left by the body in the woods?' James asked.

Lombroso nodded. 'A full examination will tell us more, but there are certain similarities. I don't think any embalming fluids have been applied, so unlike the previous girl, there does not seem to be any serious attempt at preservation. It looks to me as if some kind of ritual has been performed . . . possibly satanic.'

'Still think it is an isolated domestic killing now?' James murmured to Tullio.

Tullio did not respond. 'Was she killed here?' he asked Lombroso.

'I doubt it. There are no blood deposits . . . unless the draining was done very carefully indeed, so as not to spill a drop.'

At Lombroso's words, James noticed that Ottolenghi was frowning. He sat down on the remnants of an old pillar, pulled out a notebook and pencil and started to write. Lombroso and Tullio carried on their conversation, apparently oblivious.

James went over and sat next to him. 'Are you all right?' His usually placid friend was now hunched over and scribbling furiously. 'Salvatore, what is it?'

Ottolenghi's face was pale and concerned. 'I'm not sure,' he said quietly. 'It has a similarity to something I encountered in Vienna.'

'Go on.'

'If Reiner was here, he would say that the draining of blood from a corpse could mean only one thing.'

'You think that whoever killed this girl might have been satisfying their lust for blood?'

Ottolenghi looked over to the body. 'If Reiner is right, then I think we might be looking for a vampire.'

17

Like criminals, prostitutes tend to lie incorrigibly and pointlessly. This habit flows partly from their disreputable position in society and partly from an awareness of the low opinion that others have of them. Moreover, they are all in fact fleeing from something.

Lombroso and Ferrero, 1893, p. 219

James had arranged to meet Sofia that morning in order to retrace Chiara's last journey before she went missing, so there had been no time to discuss Ottolenghi's observations. He had agreed not to mention them to Lombroso until his friend had had an opportunity to examine his notes and do a little more research.

'I know how it sounds – utterly preposterous,' Ottolenghi had said. 'But if you had been in Vienna and heard what I did, then you would understand.'

James wasn't entirely sure that he would, but he respected Ottolenghi and decided to give him the benefit of the doubt.

Sofia was standing in the Piazza Solferino, beneath a statue of a man on horseback. As James drew closer, he remembered something that Ottolenghi had told him about the sculpture. It depicted Fernando Duca di Genova, a prince who had fought during the disastrous first war of independence. The statue showed the exact point in battle when the prince's horse had been killed beneath him. The sculptor, a man named Balzico, had arranged for a horse to be killed just so he could witness its death throes. The sight of Sofia standing at the foot of this homage to human cruelty seemed fitting, given the news he was about to deliver.

She gave a small tight smile. 'You are late. What happened? Did the professor actually meet the Devil?'

James shook his head.

'What is it?' Sofia asked, a note of alarm in her voice.

He took both her hands in his and looked into her eyes. 'We have found a body.'

Sofia gasped and seemed to stumble for a moment. 'Is it her? Is it Chiara?' as if her legs could no longer hold her upright.

James could not bear to see her distress. 'I do not know for sure . . . It is a young woman, but from what you have told me, I do not think so.'

'How could you know for certain? You have not met her.'

'I don't know, but the girl we found had very fair hair and a pale complexion. You said that Chiara was dark, like you.'

'Hair colour can be changed. You cannot be sure,' she repeated. 'How can I know that it is not her?'

James was silent for a moment. 'There is something else I must tell you,' he said.

Sofia's face, usually such a picture of inner strength, seemed to crumple and tears filled her eyes as he explained about the older body found in the woods, but even though he assured her that it could not be Chiara, she was inconsolable. 'How could you keep this from me? How could you?'

'I . . . I'm so sorry, Sofia,' James said, stepping towards her.

'No!' she shouted. 'Do not come near me!'

'Please, Sofia, I didn't mean to . . . I just wanted to help. We have so little information. Tullio wants you to look at the body later, then you can be sure.'

Her eyes were so full of contempt that he felt crushed by the weight of it. She held her head up high. 'I want to see it now. I cannot wait.'

'You must, I'm afraid. Tullio is having it . . . her . . . brought back to the city. It will take a few hours.'

Sofia paused. 'Then we should retrace Chiara's steps as we planned. We can do that at least.' Now her voice was devoid of anything resembling emotion. But James knew that beneath the facade was turmoil. All he could do was follow her directions and hope beyond hope that she would find it in her heart to forgive him.

They began to walk in silence along the still-deserted streets. It was almost completely light now as the sun rose over the city, whereas in early March it would have been darker. Although this meant that the atmosphere was different, it also made everything more visible.

'It is so quiet,' Sofia said, shivering beneath her shawl. It was still chilly, despite the promise of summer just around the corner. James longed to put his arm around her to warm her up, but dared not try. It was far too soon for even that level of intimacy. She still seemed slightly unsteady. The possibility, however remote, that the body found in the abbey might be Chiara appeared to be weighing her down. James felt useless. All he wanted was to hold her, support her – do something for her. He felt her rejection as keenly as if she had shouted it to him until his ears bled.

'It is not her, I am sure of it,' he said.

'James! You do not know that, and neither do I. And even

if it isn't her, she is missing and two bodies have been found. We both know what that could mean.'

'Are you still convinced that she did not run away?' James asked.

'Why does everyone always think that? If it were Lucy who had gone missing, you would not even contemplate such a thing.'

'Lucy does not go out unaccompanied.'

Sofia raised her eyebrows. 'Chiara had . . . has no choice. She has to make a living.'

'Of course, I know that. It's just . . .'

'What? Just because she is of a certain class, she is more likely to run off? She must be unreliable because she is a servant?'

'Girls like her go missing all the time,' he said, echoing the words of both Lombroso and Tullio from the night before. 'Perhaps all six have just taken off in search of a better life. One could hardly blame them.'

'Girls like her?' Sofia stopped. Her hands were on her hips and her eyes were flashing dangerously. 'We still have our own characters. Poverty does not strip us of that!'

'I'm sorry. I just want her to be safe. That's all.'

'Chiara, as I have already told you, was frightened of her own shadow. She would be far too timid to run away.' Sofia threw her arms up in an exasperated gesture and began to walk away. 'Clearly your heart is not in this.'

'I said I would help and I will,' James said, going after her. 'I have already planned the next step.'

'And that is?'

He spoke carefully, not wishing to make things between them even worse. 'The first thing is to establish who the dead girl is, which I would think will be Tullio's priority, and see if she is on Baldovino's list.'

'It would be a strange coincidence if she is not,' Sofia said bitterly. 'You said that all the girls are connected in some way to San Callisto.'

'The town, not the abbey.'

'All the same . . .'

'That is why I am planning to find out about the backgrounds of all the girls, visit their families and perhaps talk to their friends. I want to see if they had anything else in common, if there is any kind of pattern. Why have these girls in particular gone missing? Could they all have run away? If they did, then what were they running from or to?'

'What about the body in the woods?'

'No one seems to know anything about it. It is as if it appeared from nowhere.'

'I knew that something was amiss. I felt it before. So many girls . . . and now these bodies.'

There was a long pause, but James did not dare to fill it with words, even though the silence made him afraid.

'I am glad that you are here,' she said, her words almost carried away into the distance by the breeze.

James was relieved. Even if this was all she gave him, it was something.

'So you will start today? There is no time to lose,' she said.

'I can't. I have to go somewhere with the professor.'

'What! You put your work before this?'

'I have no choice. You know that. The professor is insisting that our investigation goes on. At least Tullio is working on the case now too. '

'He is not looking for Chiara,' Sofia said. 'So where is it that you go that is so important?'

James tried to think of a way of telling her that would not sound frivolous and offensive. But he could not. 'We are to go to Madame Giulia's, to do some experiments on the . . . girls. '

'You can say the word. They are prostitutes, as I used to be.' Sofia's expression was one of disappointment in him. 'I am not ashamed. I had no choice. But perhaps you should be, to speak of conducting experiments as if those girls are subjects in a laboratory.'

'I have a job to do,' James said. 'We are doing some work on female offenders.'

'There are worse crimes than prostitution.'

'I know, but the professor has his reasons.'

Sofia nodded. 'Well he thinks he does . . . One thing, though, James.'

'What?

'Take care.'

'I'm sure I can manage a few girls, no matter what their profession.'

'No, you don't understand. It's not the girls.'

'Then who?' James asked.

'Just take care, that's all.' Sofia drew closer to him and whispered in his ear. '*Prattica co'buoni, e'sta ben co cattivi.*' Visit the good and keep well with the bad.

'What do you mean?'

'You will know when it matters.' Sofia smiled her half-smile and he felt his heart lift as she beckoned to him. 'Come now. Let us go on with our journey. And, James . . .'

'What is it?'

'When you talk to the girls' families, I would like to be there.'

He nodded. 'Yes, of course.'

They were just about to turn out of the Via Garibaldi into the Via Po when they heard an odd sound, like a cross between some kind of steam engine and a large cat purring. It seemed to be coming from a heap of rags and papers with an old straw hat balanced on top of it, lying on the steps of a monument.

Sofia frowned. 'That's Pietro.'

'Ah, the old man from La Capra.'

'Yes. He must be sleeping it off from last night.'

'Is it worth speaking to him?'

Sofia gave a dry laugh. 'I doubt he would remember anything from last night, let alone a few months ago. Come on. There is some distance to go yet.'

'It is quite a way. Did Chiara walk there every morning?'

Sofia rolled her eyes at him. 'How did you think she got there . . . by carriage?'

They carried on through the pearly paleness of the early morning. The sun had risen now and the day had begun to warm up. James was struck by the beauty of the river as it shimmered and sparkled in the sun's rays. A few people were around now – mostly costermongers setting up their wares, and maids making their way to their various places of employment.

'It is a pity that Chiara's workmates were not more forthcoming,' James said. 'Did they give you the impression that they liked her?'

'They did not seem to have an opinion one way or another. Why are you asking that? Do you think someone there has harmed her?'

'No . . . at least it doesn't seem likely, though they might know something. We cannot rule it out, though, as a possibility at least.'

'We cannot rule anything out. That is why it is so . . .' A

look of utter despair crossed Sofia's face. She shook herself as if trying to dislodge her doubts.

He put his hand on her arm and for a brief moment she did not push it away. 'We will find her. I promise.'

Sofia moved away from him. 'How can you say that? You do not know if we will find her or not, or even if she is dead or alive. I did not come to you for platitudes.'

'I'm sorry. I was just trying to—'

'There is no point. There won't be until I find her.'

James hesitated. 'Would you like me to come to the mortuary with you to see the body?'

Sofia nodded. '*Sì.*'

'I'm sure that Inspector Tullio will help now that...' His voice trailed off as he saw her expression.

'You mean now that others are dead.'

He was struggling for the right words. 'I am sure he will help.'

'He did not seem so keen when I asked him before.'

'What exactly did he say?'

'Just that he was busy. He seemed a little strange. As if...'

'As if?'

'As if he did not want to get involved... No, it was more than that.'

'How do you mean?'

'I know this sounds odd, but it was almost as if he was frightened.'

That same morning, Lucy was sitting in the drawing room after breakfast with Gina, Paola and their mother, Miss Trott having gone out to run an errand. Ostensibly she was reading a book of moral tales supplied by Aunt Agnes, but she was finding them rather hard going. She would far rather read one of her host's articles. Gina had shown her one of them and they looked fascinating. Her mind wandered to the events of the previous afternoon. She had been flattered by Francesco Rambaudi's attention, but still did not know quite what to make of him. And having found Miss Trott's odd little note, she didn't know quite what to make of her either. Everything was uncertain. It was unsettling in some ways, but in others strangely thrilling.

There was a knock at the door and a maid came in with a note. Taking it, Signora Lombroso glanced at it. 'It is for you, Lucy.'

Gina grinned, her eyes full of mischief. 'Who can it be from? Do you have an admirer already?'

Lucy blushed. 'I don't think so.' She opened the note and read it. 'It is from Signor Francesco Rambaudi. He has asked if I would care to accompany him on a visit to the Museo Egizio later this morning.'

'All those mummies . . . how romantic!' Paola said.

'Don't tease our guest, Paola. It is not polite,' admonished Signora Lombroso.

'Do you think it would all right to go?' Lucy asked. 'I should very much like to see the museum.'

'And Signor Rambaudi too?' Gina asked. 'Did you not say he was handsome?'

'Your brother is not here, otherwise I would suggest asking him,' Signora Lombroso said, glancing disapprovingly at her daughter. 'But it would be an excellent educational opportunity, regardless of your escort. I don't think he would mind.'

'Oh yes, Papa took us there last year. It has some fascinating exhibits,' Paola said.

Lucy thought about the invitation carefully. James could hardly disapprove, given his own interest in Anna Tarnovsky.

She was drawn to Francesco Rambaudi and, to some extent, her initial impressions at the Galleria Sabaudi had not changed. His eyes, the intensity of his conversation when they were talking about art and his sense of humour had all enchanted her. But still, her later observations of him at the marchesa's tea party had made her cautious about allowing herself to fall completely for him. There was something about him that she did not quite trust, perhaps because he was so evidently hiding another personality behind his more public face. She needed to get to know him better before she could make a proper assessment of his character. If it came to it, she would ask Anna for guidance, Miss Trott being far too ancient to have a worthwhile opinion on such matters. But for now, meeting him as an acquaintance would surely be acceptable, particularly if Miss Trott accompanied them, as she had already said she would. In her head Lucy began to draft her reply.

As James approached the city's mortuary for the second time in as many days, it was as if he was noticing it for the first time. Appropriately enough, it was a dark, forbidding place, made even more so by the prospect of what waited inside, this time acutely personal in its nature. Tullio was in the hallway and bowed courteously towards them as they walked in. James studied him carefully. There were some signs of change. They were barely perceptible but were there nonetheless – a few extra lines, a greyness in his pallor, nothing more than that. It was probably just overwork, but the new inner confidence detected by James at Lombroso's dinner seemed to have gone.

'Signorina Esposito, thank you for coming. I know how difficult this must be for you,' Tullio said.

Sofia nodded briefly. 'Inspector, can we get it over with?'

'I understand, but first I must tell you about the procedure...'

'I care nothing for procedure. Just take me in, please!'

James touched her lightly on the arm. 'Sofia, listen to the inspector.'

Tullio shook his head. 'It does not matter. Follow me.'

They walked along a panelled corridor. James noticed that it was lined with portraits of portly and self-important men, some dressed in elaborate uniforms. No doubt all were playing their part in the new Italy.

At the end there was a door. Tullio stopped there. 'When we go in, there will be a body under a sheet. The attendant will pull it back for you to see. Then please tell us if it is your cousin, Chiara Esposito.'

Sofia grasped James by the wrist. Her white knuckles were straining through her olive skin. They went in. The body was on a table in the centre, a sheet draped over it. Tullio nodded curtly at the attendant and the sheet was pulled back to reveal the pale face that James had seen at the abbey. She looked even younger than when he had first set eyes on her sitting with her macabre monastic companions. Her fair hair framed her even features, making her appear at peace.

Sofia's grip tightened and then relaxed. 'It is not her...' she whispered.

Tullio leant forward.

'It is not Chiara,' Sofia repeated, louder now, the relief in her voice audible. She seemed to grow taller, as if the release from this terrible tension had allowed her to shake off the burden presented by the possibility of Chiara's death. James was struck by her reaction. She must be close to her cousin. No wonder she was so distraught at the prospect of her being dead. She stepped away, gave a brief nod and walked out, leaving the two men staring down at the body before them and pondering the unspoken questions it provided.

If this was not Chiara Esposito, then who was she? And why was the last resting place of this strange pale girl a crypt in a haunted abbey, full of dead monks?

18

. . . when two women who do not know each other meet even briefly, they look one another over from head to foot; in that glance there is almost an instinctive declaration of war.
Lombroso, 1893, p. 66

The Museo Egizio was in the same building as the Galleria Sabauda. The galleria took the upper floors, leaving the museo to occupy the lower ones with its impressive collection of ancient artefacts. Lucy had been vaguely aware of its presence during her last visit, but such was her desire to see the paintings displayed upstairs that she had tucked it into the back of her busy mind for future attention. Once she was there, however, she wondered how she could possibly have walked through the entrance hall and up a flight of stairs without at least asking Miss Trott to make a detour. She stood and looked towards the doors. They had arranged to meet Francesco there at eleven o'clock. It was now a quarter past the hour.

'This is most fascinating,' Miss Trott said as she peered at a sarcophagus heavily decorated with hieroglyphics. 'Come and see, Lucy. It belonged to Butehamon, the royal scribe of the necropolis, it says here. See the depiction of the wig interwoven with flowers – these are lotus buds to signify rebirth and lilies for purity.'

Lucy glanced over and nodded. Miss Trott was doing her best, but she was no substitute for Francesco. Where was he?

'I fear we may have been abandoned, Lucy,' Miss Trott said gently, apparently noticing her increasing agitation.

'It is of no consequence. We should proceed without him.'

Miss Trott frowned. 'I don't know that it would be entirely polite. We are here at his invitation, after all.'

'It is not entirely polite to be so late,' Lucy replied. 'Let us go on. I am sure Signor Rambaudi will be able to find us.'

Miss Trott agreed, and they were examining a large Sphinx that stood in the centre of the room when a voice rang out from the staircase.

'Ah, Miss Lucy Murray and Miss Trott . . . What are you doing down here still?'

Francesco was walking languorously down the large stone staircase. Behind him was Fabia Carignano, the marchesa's niece, a smug expression on her face. She was dressed smartly in a dark blue velvet gown with a small matching hat perched on her carefully arranged hair. Lucy felt positively shabby in her own somewhat dated attire, selected as it was by the distinctly unfashionable Aunt Agnes, whose default colour was grey and who was only persuaded to purchase new clothes when old ones became so threadbare that they could no longer be decently worn.

'I . . . I . . . there must have been . . .' Lucy stuttered, blushing.

'I'm sure I said to meet upstairs at ten o'clock.'

Lucy was confused. He had said eleven, she was sure of it. Could it be that Francesco Rambaudi was playing with her?

'There has been a misunderstanding, signor . . . All down to me, I'm afraid,' Miss Trott said briskly.

'It doesn't matter, though I fear there is not sufficient time for me to show you all I had hoped,' Francesco said.

'It has been truly fascinating. What a shame you have missed so much, Miss Murray,' Fabia said.

At this Lucy recovered her composure. She was not the sort of person to be toyed with like a cat with a bird. 'Another time, perhaps. Good day, Signor Rambaudi, Miss Carignano. Shall we continue, Miss Trott?'

'Wait, Miss Murray. You cannot go without seeing the Book of the Dead at least!' Francesco said. 'Let me show you.'

Lucy paused. It sounded intriguing.

'I am not sure it is suitable . . .' murmured Miss Trott, but she followed nonetheless as the party accompanied Francesco Rambaudi up the stairs again on to the next floor. Strangely enough, Lucy noticed, the smirk had quite disappeared from Fabia's face, leaving behind her usual sour expression.

Francesco led them through the exhibits until they reached what seemed like a dead end. On closer examination, Lucy saw that there was in fact a small door cut into the wall. He knocked and entered, beckoning to them to do likewise. They walked in obediently, like children following a teacher. The room they found themselves in was unexpected in its dimensions, being large, with windows from floor to ceiling on one side. Behind a small desk in the centre sat a dark-skinned man with a neatly trimmed beard wearing a long embroidered coat and a velvet skullcap. A pair of wire-rimmed glasses was perched precariously at the end of his nose and he was writing furiously on what looked like parchment, humming as he did so. It sounded familiar – an aria of some kind, Lucy thought.

'Professor Donati,' began Francesco. The man held up a hand and continued to write.

They stood in silence as he completed his essay. As was her habit, Lucy took the opportunity to observe her surroundings. The three walls without windows held cupboards with glass doors. On the shelves was a selection of curious artefacts. It reminded her a little of Professor Lombroso's house, although there was one marked difference. His artefacts consisted mostly of primitive items such as crudely painted vases, pots and sculptures, with some bones and skulls thrown in for good measure. In Professor Donati's room the items on display were much more refined. There were pieces of parchment with complex hieroglyphics swarming over them like insects. On a shelf behind the professor's head was a carved facsimile of a boat, complete with oarsmen and other figures standing in the prow looking out to sea. At the back were some people seated beneath a canopy. A cluster of painted stones stood on another shelf, but the workmanship was far superior to the basic daubs of Lombroso's collection. Lucy's eye then went to a collection of four stone jars. Each had a different-shaped carving of a head for a lid. One was a monkey, another a wolf-like creature and another a bird. The professor looked up sharply.

'I see you have noticed the canopic vessels of Wahibra. That is very interesting.' He got up from his chair, unlocked the cabinet and beckoned to Lucy.

'Come, child. Don't be afraid.'

She obeyed and approached him. He lifted one of the pots and handed it to her. 'Be careful now. They are priceless.' Lucy took it and somewhat gingerly began to examine it. The lid was in the shape of a man's head. The eyes seemed to stare at her as if trying to penetrate her mind. She swayed slightly and felt the pot slip from her grasp. Professor Donati caught it deftly and put it back in its cupboard.

'I'm sorry . . . I could not help it,' she said. She felt a little unsteady and put a hand to her forehead. In a trice Francesco was at her side with his arm around her shoulders. 'Take care, Miss Lucy Murray,' he whispered into her ear as he led her towards a small settee.

'I do apologise,' Lucy said. 'I do not know what came over me.'

'There is no need, my dear,' Professor Donati said. 'You are sensitive to such things. It is a gift.'

'What do you mean, sir?' Miss Trott asked. 'Sensitive to what?'

'To death and its rituals, madam, that is all.'

'Go on, Professor,' Francesco said.

'The jars were made to hold the organs of Wahibra after his death and mummification. You were holding that of Amset, one of the sons of the deity Horus. His duty was to take care of Wahibra's liver and indeed his soul.'

'He seemed to be doing a good job,' Lucy said.

The professor laughed. 'Indeed. But not all have the capacity to feel it as you have. I wonder, may I try a small experiment?'

Lucy nodded. She could not wait to tell James. He would be beside himself with envy.

The professor bowed and went over to his desk. He opened a drawer and retrieved a key. 'Excuse me one moment. I will return shortly.' He slipped out of the door, leaving them alone to wait. Lucy heard him humming to himself again as he went. The tune was familiar. What was it? Something from an opera; Verdi, she thought. Yes! That was it. *Rigoletto*, 'La donna è mobile' . . . woman is fickle.

'Feeling better?' Fabia said pointedly.

'Thank you for enquiring. I am,' Lucy replied.

'What a surprise!' Fabia said.

''I do not think that I care for your tone,' Lucy said.

'Come, come, ladies. Let us not fall out over such matters,' Miss Trott said. 'We are guests here.'

Fabia scowled. 'And exactly who are you to tell me how to behave?'

Before anyone could reply, the door opened. The professor had returned. He was carrying a wooden tray with a piece of red velvet draped over it. With some ceremony he placed it on his desk and stared down at it, breathing heavily and swaying a little, as if he was entering a trance. Slowly he began to pull back the cloth.

19

Among criminal women, one thing that can be said with certainty is that, like their male counterparts, they are taller than the insane. Yet they are shorter, and, perhaps with the exceptions of prostitutes, lighter than healthy women.   Lombroso, 1874, p. 57

James stood uncomfortably in the main reception room at Madame Giulia's and stared into the middle distance. He wanted to be out there investigating Chiara's disappearance. Now that a second body had been found, everything had become more urgent, and he found himself wishing that he was anywhere other than a state-registered brothel in Turin. Lombroso, however, had insisted that they continue with his latest project. He sat in an armchair in the corner and scribbled furiously in a large notebook. Occasionally he would mutter something to himself with varying audibility, so that one caught only the odd word or phrase: 'Large hips, I'll be bound!' or 'Anomalous teeth . . . that's the thing!'

James examined his surroundings. They were deceptive. At first glance they seemed plush, palatial, even regal. But when one looked more closely at the deep red velvet hangings and the gilt cherubs, the paintings and murals of gods and goddesses, a different picture altogether began to emerge. The hangings were threadbare in parts and some of the tassels were missing altogether. The cherubs were chipped and the painted deities decidedly faded. It was all for show – a gaudy backdrop to a sordid reality. Would the girls be the same?

He'd expected to be excited by the prospect of doing some real field research for a change, and to some extent he had been. But as the time had drawn ever nearer, he'd become increasingly discomfited by the thought of examining prostitutes who did not have any real choice about their participation. Lombroso, however, seemed to have no such scruples and was almost rubbing his hands in glee.

A woman came in from a hidden side door. She was pale – not in a natural way, but as if she was wearing some kind of white make-up, like a lady from the court of pre-revolutionary France. She even had a beauty spot. This colouring, or lack of it, was highlighted by her hair, pulled severely back behind her head in an unforgiving coiffure, and her plain dress, both of which were coal black. The overall effect was extraordinary – a sort of combination of prison wardress and Chinese concubine, accentuated by a crimson slash where her mouth was meant to be.

'Ah, the *expert* has arrived. *Buonasera, Professore.*' Her voice was harsh and forbidding.

Lombroso bowed, apparently unaffected. '*Buonasera,* Signora Valeria. It is good of you and Madame Giulia to allow us to visit. Are the ladies ready to receive us?'

Signora Valeria nodded and clapped her hands theatrically. James half expected a roll of drums or a trumpet fanfare. Girls appeared from upstairs – slowly at first, and then faster, tumbling down almost like a waterfall, laughing and chattering. It could have been a girls' school at supper time had it not been for the fact that clothes appeared to be almost optional.

They were all dressed to an extent, but quite a few seemed to be in their underwear.

'Dottore!' Lombroso said sharply above the cacophony. 'Prepare the instruments, please.'

James opened the leather case that he had been given and began to remove the various measuring devices and place them on the table ready for use. At the bottom of the bag was a large ledger, which he put next to the instruments.

Signora Valeria began to organise the girls into a queue, using the back of her hand on their behinds when she felt it necessary. The first girl presented herself to Lombroso, winked at him and then pulled apart her blouse to reveal a pair of small breasts. Lombroso peered at them quizzically for a moment, as if he was working out what to do with them. Then he nodded and clicked his fingers.

'The instrument, please, Murray!'

The girls continued to giggle as James handed Lombroso a pair of calipers, which he used to measure his subject's breasts as well as the width of her thighs, calves and arms. The professor called out some numbers, which James duly noted in the ledger. After her weight and height were noted, she was led over to a table where James had set out the craniograph, a metal contraption with various levers. Here she sat down and placed her chin on a small shelf against a ruler. A thin metal bar was brought down on to the top of her head and the measurement on the ruler was recorded. Then another piece of metal was swung round to obtain the circumference.

The whole process was repeated for each girl, although no more breasts were measured, and before long the page was full. The professor had not made it clear what might be significant about the data, but James was sure that he would draw some conclusions from it one way or another.

As the measuring had proceeded, James had done his best to observe their subjects in what he thought was a reasonably systematic and scientific manner. Could any of them be said to have similar characteristics to the few female criminals he had encountered either in the course of his work as a clerk for Professor Bell, or at the criminal asylum where both he and his father had worked? He thought not. Criminal women, like the girls here, were all different. True, some of the female offenders looked older than their years and sometimes had coarse features and raddled complexions, but surely that was down to the way in which they were forced to live their lives rather than their criminality. Indeed, was it not poverty and the resulting despair that led them to crime, rather than in-herited characteristics?

He studied the girls as Lombroso made the final measure-ments. They were sitting and watching intently, occasionally speaking to their neighbours behind their hands. One of them was a statuesque young black woman, apparently named Cleopatra, to whom Lombroso had paid particular attention, no doubt hoping that he could fit her into his 'savage/prim-itive' category despite the fact that her features were refined and delicate and her demeanour somewhat regal. She stared back at James, her eyebrows raised as if admonishing him for looking at her. Beside her sat Ada, a petite redhead with the most extraordinary head of corkscrew curls. She shook her head now and then, giving the air of a lion displaying its mane. As he caught her eye, she grinned and pulled faces at him, which made him smile.

Not all of the girls were young. One, Nora, must have been in her late thirties, James thought. She wore a world-weary expression that seemed to indicate that she had seen and experienced it all – and no doubt she had, assuming that most of her adult life had been spent as a prostitute. There was something melancholy about her. She made James think of Sofia, who had been forced to prostitute herself as a young girl when her father had murdered her mother and run away leaving her destitute. Had it not been for Lombroso coming to her rescue, she might still be doing so, just like the women he was studying. What stories would these girls tell when they were interviewed? How had they ended up here?

Lombroso seemed to have finished his measuring. 'Thank you, ladies,' he said, bowing to them. 'Please be assured that you have made a valuable contribution to science today.'

'*Bene!*' said Ada, tossing her red curls. 'I don't suppose our contribution will transform itself into money.'

'Alas, my dear,' Lombroso said. 'I could not afford to pay you what you are worth to the pursuit of knowledge.'

'That's convenient,' noted Nora, with a wry laugh.

'However, I have given a little something to Signora Valeria, who will, I am sure, distribute it later.'

Nora snorted. 'Minus a small fee, no doubt.'

'I would also like to interview some of you ladies in a day or two. And that, of course, will be remunerated.'

Before any of the girls could reply, Signora Valeria walked between them, clapping her hands at them as if they were children.

'The professor will be in touch with Madame Giulia to arrange it,' she said firmly. She moved towards Lombroso and spoke quietly. 'Madame Giulia would be honoured if you would both join her for coffee, Professor.'

They were shown upstairs into an elegant drawing room – a complete contrast to the somewhat shabby foyer. Everything was understated and uncluttered, quite unlike most of the interiors that James had seen in Turin. The room was dark, lit only by a small gas lamp. The heavy brocade curtains were closed so that not even a chink of natural light was visible.

The door opened and a woman walked in. She was as elegant as her surroundings, and quite breathtakingly striking. Her long auburn hair was worn loose in Renaissance style, and her skin was pale, almost translucent – not made up like Valeria's, but a purely natural beauty. In fact James thought that she looked as if she had stepped from a Titian painting. But there was something else, less tangible than her appearance. One could see from the way she carried herself that she possessed the authority and certainty that came only from knowledge of her own power.

'Professor Lombroso . . . I am delighted to meet you again,' she said, holding out her hand. Lombroso took it and kissed it. 'Signora Concetta Panatti. I was expecting Madame Giulia.'

She put her finger to her lips. 'We are one and the same, but I would prefer it if you kept that to yourselves. I have a number of business interests, of which this establishment is just one, but you know all too well how quick people can be to judge.' Her voice was low and seductive. James noticed that she lengthened each 's', so that her words seemed to linger in the air.

'Of course, Signora Panatti, we will respect your confidence.'

She smiled at James. 'I gather this is Dr Murray, your assistant.'

'Signora Panatti,' James said, bowing and taking her hand. It was cool to the touch. She looked him up and down discreetly, as if performing a medical examination. Her eyes were dark brown but flecked with gold, and their effect on James was mesmerising, making him light-headed and quite unable to tear himself away from her glance.

'I am fascinated by your work,' she said. 'You must tell me more.'

Lombroso cleared his throat. 'It is mostly the professor's work,' James said. 'I am just assisting.'

'I am sure he could not do without you,' she said, smiling slowly at him.

'Perhaps in time he will become indispensable,' Lombroso said brusquely. 'But we are not there quite yet.'

'Do sit down, gentlemen,' Signora Panatti said as a maid entered and placed a tray of coffee and pastries on the table.

James watched as she waved the girl away and began to pour coffee from a silver pot. There was something serpentine about her movements, as if she was about to strike.

'Professor, tell me, what is that you are hoping to discover from my girls?'

'I am examining the female offender generally, Signora Panatti.'

'I do not think they would see themselves as criminals, Professor.' The previously seductive tone of her voice had become almost imperceptibly harsher.

'No, perhaps not... The thing is... you see we're... what I mean is...' Lombroso stuttered uncharacteristically.

'We provide a service. One for which many gentlemen are grateful. Even the state recognises this. I am surprised that you do not.'

'We are examining your young ladies as a separate entity, Signora Panatti,' James said. 'We do not consider them as criminals but as part of our society... a major part, thus deserving of our attention.'

'Oh, I see... Now why couldn't you have told me that, Professor?' she said. 'It puts your work in a whole new light. I was about to forbid any further contact with the girls, but now that Signor Murray has explained it all so eloquently, I am minded to agree to your request. Valeria tells me you wish to interview some of them.'

Lombroso gave a wan smile. 'Indeed we do, Signora. I would like to talk to at least four or five of them, more ideally.'

'And what will you be asking them, Signor Murray?' she said.

'I think we will be enquiring about their pathway to their profession,' James said. 'Is that not right, Professor?'

Lombroso nodded. His lips were pursed and his face was a picture of disgruntlement, but James could see that the only way they would get access was if he smoothed things over. 'We would like to use some new equipment that the professor has developed.'

'What kind of equipment?'

'A lie-detecting machine,' Lombroso replied.

'You think they will lie to you? Well, I am not sure I can agree if that is your view, Professor Lombroso.'

The professor looked crestfallen, like a little boy whose toys had been removed.

'That is not our assumption at all, Signora Panatti,' James said in what he hoped was a conciliatory tone. 'We all embroider the truth, though, do we not, from time to time?'

Concetta Panatti smiled. 'I would have to concede that, I suppose.'

'It is merely a way of testing our equipment. Professor Lombroso wishes to use it in years to come, in the investigation of crime. But we need to ensure that it works before we can do that,' James explained.

'Well, Professor, I will agree under those terms. It would be unpatriotic to do otherwise. After all, we all want to see criminals brought to justice.'

'Thank you, Signora. I am most grateful,' Lombroso said.

'Oh do not thank me,' she said. 'You should be thanking Signor Murray for his intervention. He seems to be quite indispensable after all, I'm sure you'll agree.'

Lombroso nodded. 'Indeed so, Signora.'

'Now if you'll excuse me, gentlemen.' Concetta Panatti rose. 'I have some important work to do.'

Lombroso bowed and made his way towards the door. James was about to follow him when Concetta held out her hand and touched him on the shoulder. It was only a light brush, nothing more, but he felt a strange tingling in his body, as if she had a put a spell on him.

'I hope you will visit me to make the arrangements, Mr Murray,' she said softly. 'I would like you to deal with them personally.'

'Of course,' he replied.

'Good,' she said. 'That will be ...' she moved close to him and he felt her breath on his cheek and smelt her musky perfume, 'enchanting.'

20

Although the female born criminal has intensely erotic tendencies, love is rarely a cause of her crimes. For her love, like hatred, is just another form of insatiable egotism... The impulsivity and casualness of these women's passions are extraordinary. When they fall in love, they need to satisfy their desire immediately, even if that means committing a crime. Lombroso and Ferrero, 1893, p. 187

'This is from the Ptolemaic period,' Professor Donati said. 'Around about 330 BC, we think. Lay your hand on it, Miss Murray, if you would be so kind, and tell us what you feel.'

The papyrus was brown with age. There were some intricate borders in black and a drawing beneath. Lucy closed her eyes and touched it as instructed. She gave a sharp intake of breath at the strange sensation.

'I feel a pain here.' She touched her breast.

'Your heart?' Professor Donati asked.

'I suppose so,' she replied. 'I don't see anything.'

'No, but you are *experiencing* it. That is what is significant.'

Lucy opened her eyes. Fabia was watching, her lips pressed flat in a thin white line. Francesco wore an amused smile.

'Would you tell us more about the papyrus, Professor Donati?' Miss Trott asked.

'It is from the Book of the Dead, a compilation of spells and hymns to the gods. They were said to give you power and influence that would help in your journey to the final destination.' He pointed to the picture. 'What you see here is a version of the Netherworld. Here is the goddess Maat watching as the heart belonging to the deceased is weighed. And here is a depiction of Apep.' He indicated an elaborate drawing of a dragon in gold and green, just like the serpent on Miss Trott's bookmark.

Lucy started at the mention of the name. 'Apep?'

'An evil god, an Egyptian demon, if you will,' Professor Donati said.

Surreptitiously Lucy watched Miss Trott. There was no obvious reaction except for a very slight arch of her left eyebrow, which might not necessarily be significant. Could it be no more than a coincidence that the name appeared both here in the Book of the Dead and on the bookmark? Surely not! Mrs Paschal was not keen on coincidence, Lucy seemed to remember, and perhaps she was right.

Professor Donati turned to her. 'The pain you experienced, Miss Murray, tells me that you are sensitive to these artefacts.'

Fabia snorted. 'Or it could just be indigestion. Might you have eaten too much at breakfast, Miss Murray?'

'I'd rather it *was* indigestion,' Lucy replied.

'Why would the heart be weighed?' Miss Trott asked.

'It represents the soul,' replied the professor. 'The heart is supposed to be the seat of intelligence, so this symbolises the Day of Judgement for the deceased. It is then that the decision is made as to whether the dead person has been pure enough to travel to the realm of the gods, or whether they will be condemned to destruction by the monstrous Devourer.'

Miss Trott peered at the papyrus. 'Purity – most fascinating...'

'Indeed,' Professor Donati said. 'It is often depicted as a lotus flower or a lily. Internal and external purity was considered to be the highest of virtues.'

'Is it usual to have a reaction like that of Miss Murray?' Francesco asked.

'It is unusual but not unknown. The symbolism is powerful – perhaps so much so that it creates a psychic imprint.'

Francesco nodded. 'But you surely have to be a particular kind of person to experience it... is that so?'

'Yes, that is a fair summary.'

Francesco smiled at Lucy. 'A fair summary indeed... I suspected that you were a *particular* kind of person as soon as I met you, Miss Murray.'

Lucy blushed. Was he flirting with her? And if he was, why did he arrive here with Fabia Carignano?

'And now I'm afraid I must take my leave of you,' the professor said, covering up the papyrus and carefully replacing it in its box. 'Goodbye, Francesco, it has been good to see you again, and, Miss Murray, a real pleasure to make your acquaintance.'

With that he gave a perfunctory bow and swept from the room, leaving them to make their own way out of the museum into the heat of what was now the early afternoon.

Miss Trott fanned herself with a pamphlet she had picked up. 'My, my, it is very hot, is it not? Shall we find somewhere in the shade to sit and take a cool drink?'

'Unfortunately Francesco and I are otherwise engaged,' Fabia said as she put up her parasol, almost taking Miss Trott's eye out in the process.

Francesco grinned at Lucy. 'We're expected at the

marchesa's . . . May I call on you later, Miss Murray? Since you are a *particular* kind of person, I think I need to get to know you better.'

'By all means, Signor Rambaudi,' she said, smiling at him.

Fabia adopted her usual sullen expression. 'Come along, Francesco, or we shall be late, and you know how my aunt hates that.'

He was about to follow her when he stopped. A small crowd was gathering by a newspaper vendor. 'Wait a moment, Fabia. Something seems to have happened. Let me see.'

He went over to the crowd and, a moment or two later, emerged clutching what appeared to be the lunchtime edition of the local newspaper, *The People's Voice*.

'Whatever does it say?' asked Miss Trott.

Francesco scanned the front page, then gave a strange little smile. 'They've found a young girl's body, in the Abbey San Callisto.'

James had stayed behind at Madame Giulia's to pack up Lombroso's measuring equipment. He was taking apart the craniograph ready to place it in its silk-lined wooden box when he heard a hissing sound.

'Pssst!'

It was one of the girls, Ada with the red curls. She seemed nervous.

'Can I help you?'

She walked up to him and tugged at his arm. He tried to pull away, but she persisted and he realised that she wanted to whisper in his ear but was too small to do so. He bent down closer to her.

'Are you really an expert in crime?' she asked quickly.

'I'm not sure I would call myself an expert, but—'

184

'Can you find people . . . if they've gone?'

'What do you mean, gone? Who has gone?'

'One of the girls, Agnella. One minute she was here, and the next . . .'

'She works here?'

'Sometimes, but she works in another place as well.'

'What other place?'

'We don't know where it is. We are blindfolded before we're taken there.'

'What happens when you get there?'

'We attend to special clients . . . well, that is to say, they do . . . I have not been chosen yet. Madame Giulia picked Agnella especially on account of her looks. Signora Valeria calls her the angel. Me . . . I'm too ordinary, I suppose, too many freckles, although there is a market for that too.'

'You said special clients?'

'I cannot say more. No one is allowed to speak of the clients or the place or what happens there.'

'What happened with Agnella?'

'She was pleased to be chosen. It meant more money and she was hoping to save enough to buy herself out of here. After the first time she was a little quieter than usual, but that was all. The next time she went was the last time I saw her.'

'How long ago was this?'

'A few weeks.' Ada was crying. James gave her a handkerchief, which seemed to make her cry even more. 'Help me to find her,' she whispered through her tears. 'Please.'

'Is there anything else you can tell me?'

'Just that one of her clients had a nickname.'

She stopped, her eyes widening. The floorboards creaked overhead. Someone was coming.

'Quickly! Tell me,' James said.

Ada leant forward again and whispered in his ear. 'Agnella called him Il Professore.'

'Ada!' Valeria's harsh voice cut through the room. The effect was instantaneous. The girl leapt away from James and scuttled across the floor as Valeria strode towards her, seized her by her hair and pushed her through a door, slamming it behind her as if she was disposing of unwanted detritus.

'Time for you to leave, signor, I believe,' she said. Her lips had formed a single thin red line.

James hesitated for a moment. Was it worth asking her about what Ada had said? He began to make his way out. Valeria stood behind him as if ensuring that he was leaving. Then he felt her hand on his shoulder.

'One moment, signor. Whatever you heard, if I were you, I'd put it from my mind. It is safer that way.'

James frowned for a second and then allowed her to escort him through the back entrance on to the street. He stopped for a moment in an effort to take in what had just happened. Another missing girl ... when would it end?

Later that afternoon, Lucy sat with Miss Trott in the drawing room, a book on her lap. She was trying to concentrate on its contents, but her attention kept wandering. There was a large grandfather clock in the corner of the room. She listened to its slow, ponderous tick. It was almost four o'clock.

'I'm sure Mr Rambaudi will call as he promised,' Miss Trott said, peering over her glasses. 'What time did he say?'

'He didn't,' Lucy replied. 'He just said that he would come later.'

What did later mean? Her heartbeat quickened at the thought of Francesco Rambaudi. She thought back to his smell – cigars and cologne – and the sensation of his breath

186

on her ear as he whispered into it. She chided herself. The last thing she wanted was to fall in love. Well, not yet anyway. She had other plans. Besides, she had seen what love could do and she wanted no part of it. Her mother had sacrificed everything to be with her father and had been rewarded with a broken heart that had killed her in the end. No, that was not for her. Lucy wanted something different. She wanted a career, like Anna Tarnovsky. She felt a thrill go through her at the notion. Before meeting Anna, it had not even occurred to her that such a thing might be possible, but now it seemed that it might be. Obviously it would not be an easy thing to achieve, but surely James would support her, given his obvious regard for Anna. James and Anna – now that would be a marriage of equals, assuming her husband would release her.

For a moment or two she allowed herself to drift into a fantasy future where she was married to Francesco and he was praising his witty and intelligent writer wife to a crowd of Italian dignitaries. Was it possible to have love and a career? But then even if it was, Fabia was a potential obstacle. She might be sour-faced, but she was also rich and well connected – things that Lucy could not claim to be – and she seemed to have something of an attachment to Francesco already.

The clocked ticked on remorselessly. She tried to read but found herself unable to settle to anything. Perhaps he wouldn't come at all. Maybe he had just been teasing her. He seemed to enjoy doing so, after all. She knew that it should matter, but somehow his disregard for rules and constraints on polite behaviour made him even more attractive.

She heard the sound of the front doorbell ringing and voices in the hall. A wave of excitement surged through her body. He was here! But wasn't that a woman speaking? It didn't sound like Fabia. The voice was light, almost like a small bell chiming. There was a knock at the door and the maid came in bearing a silver tray and a card. Miss Trott took it.

'Signor Rambaudi is here with his sister Bianca. That is a good sign.' She nodded at the maid, who bobbed a desultory curtsey and left, returning a few seconds later to usher in their guests.

Francesco strode over to Miss Trott and bowed deeply. 'Signora, how nice. And, Signorina Lucy, a *particular* pleasure to see you again.' Lucy felt herself blushing reluctantly beneath his gaze.

'Don't tease so, Francesco,' Bianca said. She was still standing by the door, as if uncertain at her welcome. Again Lucy was struck by her plainness in contrast to her brother's striking looks. Dressed in a dowdy dark grey gown devoid of all embellishments, her hair scraped back in a rudimentary coiffure, it was clear that she had no interest in her personal presentation. Her only adornments were the lace trim to her gloves, which she pulled off to reveal stubby fingers and bitten nails, and a red ribbon round her neck, carrying a locket. Lucy wondered idly what it might contain.

'Ah, my dear sister,' Francesco said. 'Where would I be without your advice and guidance? Perhaps you should write it up as a guide to how to behave. Signorina Lucy the writer could help you, I am sure.'

Bianca gave him a thin smile. 'An excellent scheme, if only I had the time, but alas, brother, I am far too busy organising you.'

'Do be seated, signorina, signor,' Miss Trott said, ringing a bell. 'I will organise some tea. I brought some with us, you know. I'm sure you will enjoy it.'

'Tea! So gloriously English!' Francesco said, sitting next to Lucy. 'But you are Scottish, of course. How exotic.'

'I have never heard it called that before,' Lucy said, laughing. 'The weather is not conducive to such excitement. All that rain!'

'I was referring to the evident beauty of its inhabitants, Miss Lucy, not the country itself,' Francesco said. She looked away, unsure how to react to such a level of flattery. He thought she was beautiful!

'Stands Scotland where it did?' Francesco said.

'Alas, poor country,' replied Lucy, relieved that he had chosen a quotation from *Macbeth* she actually remembered. 'Almost afraid to know itself.'

'And are you afraid to know yourself, Miss Lucy?' Francesco asked. Lucy did not know how to reply.

'You are fond of Shakespeare, Signor Rambaudi?' Miss Trott asked.

'Indeed I am – shall I compare thee to a summer's day, Miss Trott?'

Bianca looked over fondly to her brother. 'Francesco has always enjoyed the sonnets. For myself I confess I favour Hamlet rather than Macbeth. He is less treacherous.'

'Quite so,' Miss Trott said. 'Although it is Lady Macbeth who drives her husband towards his crimes.'

'Quite right,' Francesco said. 'Ophelia is a dull stick in comparison to Lady M. I do so admire strength in women.'

'And murder?' Miss Trott asked.

'I believe Professor Lombroso would think Lady Macbeth was not capable of such things, being a mere woman!' Lucy said.

'Now, now, dear. He is not here to defend his views,' Miss Trott said. She turned to Bianca. 'And how is the world of commerce, Signorina Rambaudi? You run your family's rice estate, do you not?'

'That is correct, Miss Trott,' Bianca replied. 'By necessity rather than desire. Our parents are both deceased.'

'Mine too,' Lucy said, noticing that Francesco had paled at the mention of his family. 'It is hard to lose one parent, but two...'

'Oh, I am not sorry about my father,' Francesco said. 'He was a drunken old fool. No one will miss him. But my mother... now there was a real tour de force. Beauty *and* brains.'

'She was certainly clever,' Bianca said. 'Were it not for her, there would be no estate to run. My father was no help in that regard.'

'Bianca has inherited her business sense, if nothing else,' Francisco said. 'But she left me with some other attributes, though I say it myself.'

'And you do say so, dear brother, do you not?' Bianca said. 'Frequently.'

Lucy tried to imagine James speaking so candidly about their parents but simply couldn't. He viewed such things as a private affair. Perhaps it was an Italian characteristic to be so open. There was certainly something refreshing about it. It was clear that Bianca was far more relaxed here than she had been at the marchesa's, which was interesting. Lucy looked at Miss Trott, who was supervising the tea-pouring, a perplexed expression on her face – probably, Lucy thought, at the size of the tiny coffee cups provided rather than the conversation.

'So tell me, Miss Lucy, what did you think of Professor Donati?' Francesco asked.

'I thought he was fascinating, if rather fanciful,' she replied.

'You have had no visitations from Apep, then?'

'None,' Lucy said laughing. She glanced over again to Miss Trott, who appeared to be finding something very interesting in her teacup. 'But then night has not yet fallen and I imagine as a demon he would prefer the darkness.'

'Who would?' asked a voice from the doorway.

'Professor Lombroso! How nice to see you!' Francesco said.

'Well it is my house, so it can hardly come as a surprise, Signor Rambaudi,' Lombroso said, waving away Miss Trott's offer of tea before sitting down in a large armchair. 'Now who is this demon?'

'He's called Apep,' Lucy said.

'Ah yes. As I recall, he resided in eternal darkness. I believe there is some legend about him attempting to eat the Sun Boat of Ra, which would plunge the whole world into darkness.'

'I did not know you were interested in Egyptology, Professor,' Miss Trott said.

'I am interested in many things, madam.' He peered at her. 'I am sure we have met before, which in itself is interesting, don't you think?'

'I am confident that I would have remembered such an encounter, Professor Lombroso,' Miss Trott said.

They stared at each other for a moment as if neither wanted to relinquish their respective positions. Lombroso was the first to look away, leaving Miss Trott with a triumphant expression on her face.

He cleared his throat. 'Tell me, why has Apep entered the conversation?'

'We were visiting the Museo Egizio with Fran ... Signor Rambaudi,' Lucy said. 'Professor Donati mentioned Apep when he was showing us the Book of the Dead.'

'Indeed, it was most interesting,' Miss Trott said. 'The

professor appeared to be something of an expert on Egyptian death rituals.'

'Have you been busy measuring criminals?' Francesco asked. 'I hear you are examining criminal women these days. That sounds entertaining.'

Lombroso nodded. 'It has its moments, although I was engaged in a different kind of enterprise not so long ago.'

'Ah yes. Some spiritism, according to *The People's Voice*,' Bianca said.

'Of a kind, yes,' Lombroso said. 'Though we had not bargained on finding a body, naturally.'

Miss Trott shuddered. 'This was the girl found with the monks, was it not? It said so in the newspaper.'

Lombroso tutted. 'Yes, though quite how that wretched reporter got hold of such detail, I do not know.'

'It said something about the corpse being drained of blood,' Bianca said.

'Indeed . . . quite an enterprise. It must have taken some time to produce that effect,' Lombroso said.

'Well let us not go into that, Professor,' Francesco said. 'There are ladies present.'

'It sounds like something out of Ancient Egypt,' Bianca said, ignoring her brother. 'I believe that the death rituals were quite precise.'

Lombroso looked at her thoughtfully. 'There may be something in that, signorina.'

'Well, quite, but perhaps not a teatime conversation, Professor,' Miss Trott said firmly.

'Are you scolding Professor Lombroso, Miss Trott?' Francesco asked.

Miss Trott raised her eyebrows at him but did not reply.

'You have been most helpful, Signorina Rambaudi,' Lombroso said.

'Perhaps you should pay the Museo Egizio and Professor Donati a visit yourself,' Miss Trott suggested.

Lombroso nodded. 'Perhaps I should do just that . . . Now, Miss Trott, I think I would like to try some of your tea after all.'

21

Because she is unable to destroy her enemies, woman torments them, pricking them with needles of pain and immobilising them with misery. Cruelty, like cunning, is a product of woman's adaptation to the conditions of life. And thus she acquired and developed her ability to torment. In sum, cruelty is a type of defensive as well as offensive reaction in woman.

Lombroso and Ferrero, 1893, p. 68

The following day, James and Sofia started their journey in a horse and cart driven by an acquaintance of Sofia's. She sat up next to the driver, a straw hat on her back, moving effortlessly with the motion of the vehicle, as if she did it every day. He, on the other hand, was sitting at the rear, being thrown from one side to the other as they rattled along the various tracks and poorly maintained lanes that led to their destination. He let out a loud groan as the cart went over yet another of the many potholes.

She laughed. 'Poor signor, you are not used to such humble transport. What a shame.'

He grinned back at her. 'Very funny, I'm sure. We do have such vehicles in Scotland, you know.'

'*Sì*, and how many times have you ridden in one?' she asked.

'A fair point,' he said. 'Is there much further to go?'

Sofia murmured to the driver, who shook his head and mumbled something back.

'We're not far away,' she informed James. 'Look over there and you'll see. The town is close now.'

Sofia's intensity was palpable and it made him worry for her. Perhaps their investigation would bring them closer to finding out what had happened to her cousin. But surely, with the discovery of the bodies, the end result was less and less likely to be a good one. Chiara had almost certainly not run away. It was possible that she was being held somewhere, although for what purpose he did not know. The white slave trade sprang to mind. He hoped it was not that, although the alternative was even worse. Might they find her body at some point, as they had the others?

His dilemma was this: should he allow Sofia to cling on to some hope that Chiara was still alive, or alert her to the reality? Seeing her bright and eager eyes, he knew that the decision had been taken from him. He could not bring himself to take away that hope. It would be too cruel. He would just have to be ready to comfort her if – or more likely when – the horrible and what he regarded to be almost inevitable truth came out. He loved Sofia. He would do anything for her even if that meant lying to her, or at least embroidering the truth. Indeed he had not yet told her of his encounter with Ada, the girl at Madame Giulia's, in case it turned out to be unconnected.

Sofia was right about the proximity of San Callisto, and soon they pulled up in the town square. There was a tavern on the corner and James looked longingly at it.

Sofia shook her head. 'No time for a drink. We must get on. Our friend will wait here for us.'

'Where's the farm?' he asked as he helped her down. She pointed up the road. A few buildings were grouped on a small hill in the distance.

'Come,' she said. 'Follow me.'

Although it was not far, James soon had to take out a handkerchief and mop his brow. The weather was unseasonably hot and the exertion of walking even such a short distance was taking its toll. Sofia, however, seemed almost completely unaffected, probably because she had spent much of her life in physical toil of one sort or another. She strode ahead of him. Desire surged through him. But it was more than that. His sense of loss was mostly of her friendship, and his memories of their brief relationship the previous year were not just of their lovemaking but their conversations, the meals she had prepared for him with such care and all the other things they had shared. How could he have lost her when they were so clearly meant to be together? What a fool he had been. He hoped they would find some answers here, and then perhaps she might begin to forgive him.

After a while they arrived at the small, rather ramshackle farmhouse and knocked at the door. A short, plump lady answered it. '*Buongiorno.* How can I help you?' Everything about her seemed to be cast downwards, from her arms hanging loosely at her sides to her facial features. It was clear that she was grieving.

'*Buongiorno.* We have come about your daughter, Teresa,' Sofia said.

The effect on the woman was startling. Her ruddy complexion paled until she was ashen-faced, and she swayed as if she might fall. 'Teresa? Have you found her?'

Sofia shook her head. '*No, mi dispiace, signora.* But we would like to help you.'

The woman peered suspiciously at them. 'Why? What is my daughter to you?'

'My cousin is missing from the city. She is the same age as Teresa,' Sofia said. 'She used to live not far from here.'

Without another word, the woman took Sofia's hand and led her round to the back of the farmhouse. James followed in silence. He felt like an intruder. They sat in the shade of an olive tree and sipped gratefully on the cool water Signora Mariani brought for them. While she talked, she stared into the distance, as if she could not bear to look into Sofia's eyes, knowing that she would find the same emptiness within.

At the age of fifteen, they were told, Teresa Mariani had left her rural home, like so many other young women, for the excitement and opportunities of Turin. Life in the communities surrounding the city was not easy. There were few local opportunities other than working in the rice fields, which was backbreaking and poorly paid. Teresa had tried that but had found the work too hard. She had hoped that going further afield would allow her not only to make a future for herself but also to send some money back to her family.

'She did not want to go,' her mother told them. 'But she felt there was no other option and we encouraged her . . . God forgive us.' Her voice, which had been flat and emotionless, began to break with the strain of her loss. Sofia put her hand out and touched Signora Mariani's arm. She took it and clutched at it, as though by letting go of it she might lose her precious daughter all over again.

That simple gesture of support moved James unbearably. To see Sofia reach out so selflessly underlined to him how much he stood to lose if she did not take him back. He knew it was selfish given the tangible misery of the two women, but he could not stop himself. In any event, it made him even more determined to help them both.

'Tell us a little more about your daughter, signora,' he said gently. 'What does she look like?'

The woman paused, perhaps wondering if she could trust him.

'It is all right,' Sofia said. 'This man is my friend. He will help us. You can speak freely.'

Signora Mariani nodded. 'She is small and dark, like me. Such a pretty girl! Everyone said so!'

James and Sofia exchanged glances of relief. The description did not fit the girl who had been found in the Abbey San Callisto, and like Chiara, Teresa had disappeared too recently to be the body found in the nearby woods. At least they would not have to break that news to Signora Mariani.

She continued. 'Teresa was a good girl in many ways, but ... she had her flaws.'

'Ah well, we all do at that age,' Sofia said. 'My cousin Chiara is no different.'

'What were Teresa's flaws, if you don't mind me asking?' James said.

'It ... it seems wrong to speak of her this way,' Signora Mariani said.

Sofia patted her hand. 'I know, but it might help.'

'She was ... well I suppose you might call her flighty. She liked the company of young men and did not hide it. It caused her father and me some concern.'

James felt himself lean forward. 'Was there anyone in particular?'

Signora Mariani nodded slowly. 'There was someone, I think, but he was not suitable ...'

'Could she have run away with him?' James asked.

She did not reply for a second or two. 'No, she was running away *from* him, if anything.'

'What do you mean?' Sofia asked.

'She changed.'

James was going to interject, but Sofia gave him an angry look and he realised that she was in control. This was more her world than his. 'In what way?' she asked.

'She used to always be happy – or at least that was the impression she gave. And then . . .'

There was another pause. Her eyes were dull with despair.

'And then?' Sofia said gently.

'It is as I said. She changed almost overnight . . . became subdued. Before, she would always chatter . . . we used to joke about it. And then all of a sudden she stopped talking to me.'

Tears began to fall slowly from Signora Mariani's eyes.

'She abandoned her friends and would not leave the house unless she had to. I asked her many times what was wrong, but she would not tell me. At first I thought she had quarrelled with her man friend and that she would soon recover. But it went on for months.' She paused and tried to wipe away her tears with her hand. James gave her his handkerchief and she held it to her face for a moment, as if she was hiding behind it. 'We were at our wits' end. Then my sister suggested that she leave the town and take up a post in the city as her daughter had done. She said she could arrange it and Teresa leapt at the chance. It was as if she was back to her old self.'

'Then what happened?'

'Teresa would not come back here, so I would visit her from time to time to make sure she was all right. Then one day I went to see her and she was not there. The woman whose house she lodged in said that she had gone to work and had not come home.'

'This is exactly as it was with Chiara,' Sofia said to James. 'Did you make any other enquiries, Signora Mariani?'

'*Sì*, I asked at her workplace, but they did not seem to know anything.'

'What about the police?' James asked.

The woman frowned at him. 'The carabinieri were not interested. They said that she had probably found a better position, or run off with someone.'

'Where did she work?'

Signora Mariani did not answer immediately. 'She was a maid at Madame Giulia's.' She paused. 'I assume you know of the establishment.'

Sofia nodded. James leant forward again. A second girl missing from Madame Giulia's . . .

Signora Mariani continued. 'It was not what we wanted for her, but she was so eager to leave the town.'

'We are not here to judge you or your family,' Sofia said quietly.

'But it would help to know as much as you can tell us. Do you know who the man was . . . the one she was running away from?' James asked.

He looked carefully at the woman, Professor Bell's words in his mind: 'Observe, Mr Murray, observe and learn.' He noticed that her hands were now clasped in her lap, curling tightly into fists so that her knuckles were ivory pale, just like Sofia's when she was waiting for the body to be revealed at the mortuary.

'We cannot help you if you are not willing to help us,' he said.

Her eyes filled with despair. 'I cannot... I cannot... I have said too much.'

James and Sofia exchanged glances, then Sofia took the woman's hands in hers. 'Please, signora, I beg you to tell us what you know. It might help us to find Teresa, and perhaps my cousin too.'

The woman hesitated for what seemed like an eternity. When she eventually spoke, she made her position clear. 'No... there is nothing more I can tell you.' She stood up. 'You must go now. I have chores to do.'

'You know that Teresa and Chiara are not the only girls to have gone missing,' James said. 'Another girl has disappeared from Madame Giulia's place. Not only that, but bodies have been found near here – one in the crypt of the Abbey San Callisto, as well as another female who would have disappeared some time before Teresa.'

Sofia frowned at him. They had agreed not to say anything about Baldovino's findings or the bodies in case they were not connected. Sofia had said that it would be too cruel. But since it was clear that neither of the bodies belonged to Teresa Mariani, James felt it important to at least mention their existence. At first he thought that Signora Mariani was puzzled rather than horrified. Her eyes were blinking rapidly and her posture had changed. Now rather than drooping she seemed upright, tense, as if there was something she was trying to hide.

'Go now, please,' she said. Her tone was harsher, and as before, she would not look either James or Sofia in the eye.

'Before we leave, one more question,' James said, pulling Baldovino's list from his pocket and handing it to Signora Mariani. 'Do you know any of these names?'

'No,' she replied, pushing it back to him. She had barely glanced at it.

She began to chivvy them out. Clearly she could not wait to be rid of them. They heard the door slam as she went back into the house, leaving them to walk back to town in silence, each pondering what they had heard. One thing was clear. Signora Mariani was not just distraught at the disappearance of her daughter. She was afraid.

22

While the woman whom passion leads to crime is very different from the born criminal, who violates the laws of chastity from lust and love of idle pleasure, nonetheless such good, passionate women are fatally inclined to love bad men. Lombroso and Ferrero, 1893, p. 203

James and Sofia sat in silence at a table tucked away in a corner of the local trattoria. The afternoon had not been an easy one, and there were several loose ends that needed to be tied up before they could go back to the city. They had already tried to find the family of Arianna Panico, another girl on the list. But when they had got to the address that Baldovino had given, the occupant, a somewhat dishevelled old man, had denied any knowledge of the girl or her family, telling them that he had lived there for the last ten years and that he thought the previous residents had moved to the city. After that they had decided to stay the night and continue their investigations in the morning.

They both agreed that Signora Mariani was keeping something from them. As well as that, there were now two missing girls who worked at Madame Giulia's, although as Sofia had said when he told her Ada's story, it was possible that her friend had merely managed to escape from her life as a prostitute. Teresa, on the other hand, was a maid, and free to walk out whenever she chose.

And then there was the dead girl at the abbey. Why had she been left there of all places? Something about it was bothering him, and it wasn't just the possibility of a ghostly presence or two, or even the Devil walking about the graveyard. It required further investigation and he decided to make a return visit before they left. He didn't like to bring up a potential link between the dead girl and Chiara, even as a faint possibility, but he knew that if it was in his mind, then it was almost certainly in Sofia's. The strain was clearly telling on her. Her hands were clasped before her and her eyes flitted uncomfortably around the room as if she was unable to settle on anything for more than a few seconds.

There was a bar at the other end of the establishment. Several swarthy-looking men leant up against it, drinking beer. James recognised one of them, a small, wrinkled figure hunched over his tankard. It was Beppe, the burglar who had broken into the abbey for Lombroso. He raised his hand in a mock salute, then smirked and whispered into the ear of his companion, who grinned insolently at James. He considered pointing them out to Sofia but thought better of it. The less attention they got, the better.

The waiter came in with a jug of wine and two bowlfuls of some kind of stew. James had let Sofia order for him, partly because it was simpler given her grasp of the local dialect as opposed to his own ignorance, and partly in an attempt to take her mind off things.

'This looks good,' he said. 'What is it?'

'Try it first.'

He hesitated and examined it more closely. There didn't seem to be anything obviously untoward about it, but Sofia had a mischievous glint in her eye, as if she was playing with him. His diversionary tactic seemed to be working.

She shook her head and laughed. 'It is just a stew . . . a kind of bollito misto. You have had something similar before, I am sure.'

He took a forkful and ate it. It was tender and fragrant; he thought he could detect some rosemary and a hint of garlic. 'It's delicious. Now tell me what it is.'

Sofia grinned at him. 'Not until you have finished.'

James did her bidding and ate heartily. It had been a long day and he was starving, so it was not long before he had cleared his plate. Sofia had left most of hers.

'Not hungry?' he asked.

She pushed her plate away. 'No, my mind is too busy. Did you enjoy it?'

'It was very good. Now tell me what it was.'

'It is oriòn. It means large ears.'

James peered down at his plate. 'Really? Is that what I was eating?'

'Yes and no. You were eating pig's head meat cooked slowly with anchovies, onion, garlic, parsley and rosemary.'

'Including the ears?'

'Of course. We do not like to waste anything here.'

James lifted up his glass. 'Oriòn, I salute you.'

Sofia held her glass up to his. It was the closest they had been since his return to Turin. A warmth spread through him, the kind that he had not experienced for what seemed like an eternity. Might she feel the same? He thought he could see a softening in her eyes.

'James, I . . .' she began.

He reached out to her and took her hand. She left it there for a moment.

'Can I get you anything more?' a waiter asked.

'*No, grazie*,' Sofia said, pulling her hand away quickly. There was a tense silence as their plates were cleared away. 'What should we begin with tomorrow?' she asked.

'We need to find out why Teresa left,' James said. 'It may not be relevant, but...'

Sofia nodded. 'It would be a start. We should talk to her friends here. It is a small place. Someone must know something.' She thought for a moment. 'And then perhaps we should make some enquiries at her place of work. You could do that, couldn't you?'

'Perhaps it would be better if you spoke to the girls,' he said, remembering his encounter with Concetta Panatti.

'Of course,' Sofia said sarcastically. 'One whore to another.'

'That is not what I meant.'

'Did you meet Madame Giulia when you were there?' she asked.

'Yes,' James said, trying not to catch her eye. 'She is an interesting woman.'

'That is one way of putting it. Dangerous is another.'

'Really? She did not seem so to me. In fact I thought her rather charming.'

Sofia's cheeks flushed and she muttered something under her breath.

'What was that?'

'Nothing... Just... she is not what she seems.' Sofia got up from the table abruptly. 'I am tired. I must go to my bed. *Buonanotte*, James.'

He watched her retreating form and for a moment considered following her, but decided against it. He wanted to win her back, but it would take time. He just had to learn to be patient.

*

The next morning James sat in the town square and listened to the small fountain playing softly as he waited for Sofia. She was making some discreet enquiries at the guest house where they had stayed the previous night. Apparently Teresa Mariani had worked there briefly before she went missing. He had asked around but no one had heard of Arianna Panico, so it seemed the old man had been telling the truth.

Sofia was beckoning to him from across the street, her dark hair shining in the sunlight. Next to her stood a tall, thin girl with mousy hair. She was slightly hunched over, as if she was trying to deny her height. He waved in acknowledgement and went over to them.

'*Buongiorno*,' the girl said.

'This is Giovanna,' Sofia said. 'She worked with Teresa. Tell *il signore* what you told me.'

The girl looked around her at the deserted square and lowered her voice till it was barely above a whisper. 'There is not much to tell, but Teresa certainly changed as you suggested.'

'How?' James asked.

'She used to be someone you could laugh with. You need that in a place like this, I can tell you.'

'What do you mean?'

'Secrets . . . the town is full of them. Secrets and lies.'

'What kind of secrets?' James asked.

Giovanna wrapped her arms around herself. He noticed that she kept blinking, as if someone was shining a light in her eyes. 'I'll tell you about Teresa, but that's all.'

Sofia put her hand on the girl's shoulder. 'It is important that you tell us everything you know.'

Giovanna hesitated.

'Go on,' Sofia said.

'Teresa was involved with someone.'

'Who?'

'A boy from the rice estate over to the west of the town, beyond the woods. I don't know his name but I know where they used to meet.'

'Where?'

'At the abbey.'

'Tell the gentleman what happened,' Sofia said. 'As you told me...'

'It was last year, about October. Teresa told me that she had met her friend at the abbey and that something had happened. But she could not tell me what. All I know is that it frightened her, and it was then that she began to change. She became withdrawn. I couldn't get so much as a smile out of her after that. Not long afterwards, she went to work in the city.'

'What about the boy?' James asked.

Giovanna shrugged her shoulders. 'Teresa said that he disappeared.'

'But there is more, is there not, Giovanna?' Sofia said, holding on to the girl's hands.

Giovanna whispered something in Sofia's ear before pulling away from her and walking off.

'What did she say?' James asked.

'Il Diavolo...' Sofia said. 'According to Giovanna, he is the talk of San Callisto. It is said that he has returned to the abbey.'

'And what does he want?'

'Fresh young blood... To be exact, fresh young female blood, because apparently Hell is running dry.'

*

James and Sofia decided to make their way up to the abbey. As they walked through the countryside, they discussed what they had discovered in the hope that together they would reach some kind of conclusion.

'Everything seems to lead here,' James said. 'Teresa and her young man meet here, see something and both disappear. Then we find a body. All the girls are connected to the place. It can't be a coincidence.'

'*Sì*, but what has happened to them?' Sofia asked. 'Do you think it was the rumours about Il Diavolo that made the professor decide to conduct his psychical experiment at the abbey?'

'It would probably tempt him, but the place is well known for satanic rituals, isn't it?'

'Perhaps *too* well known. The professor likes to be different. You know that. For him to go to a place like the abbey for an investigation . . . I think there has to be something more to it.'

James thought back to the dinner where the matter of the experiment had first been raised. 'It was Father Vincenzo who brought up the investigation, though he didn't mention the abbey specifically.'

'But didn't you say that the Church refused permission?'

'Yes, that's right. The abbey still belongs to them. That is why we had to break in.'

'I don't care if Il Diavolo does walk there. I know that Chiara is alive. I can feel it, and if I have to pay Beelzebub a visit to find her, then that is what I shall do,' Sofia said defiantly, crossing herself.

'I still think you should have left this to me. Two girls are already dead. I don't want you to put yourself at risk. '

Sofia stopped. 'No, James. We are in this together.' They stood facing each other in silence. The only sound was the wind whispering in the trees. The colours of the sky and the sunlight filtered through the green canopy and seemed brighter than before. Sofia reached up and tenderly brushed his hair out of his eyes. He took her hand and held it for a moment, looking into her beautiful dark eyes, seeing all the misery and suffering that lay behind them. She leant forward and gently touched his lips with hers. Then suddenly she pulled away from him.

'What is it? What's the matter?' he asked.

'I cannot, James,' she said. 'I am sorry. We can be friends, but that is all.'

'I will wait for you until you are ready.'

'You must not.'

'I will,' he said quietly so she could not hear. 'You know that I will.'

She had already begun to walk through the woods again. He followed her, a new spring in his step. He had thought he had lost her, but that kiss meant that she must still have feelings for him, no matter what she had said. It seemed there was hope after all, and that was all he needed.

The sun went behind a cloud, plunging them into darkness. Sofia held her hand out to him. 'Let's walk together. I feel stronger when you are with me.' He took it and immediately felt reinvigorated, as if their combined will could achieve anything.

Before long the trees began to thin out and the path widened. The outline of the abbey rose in the distance, casting a sinister shadow over them. 'There's something about that place,' James said.

'What? It is just a building like any other.'

'No, I can't accept that. I don't know what happened here,

but whatever it was has left an imprint of some kind, I am sure of it.'

'You have been listening to the professor too much,' Sofia said, laughing. 'He too has an overactive imagination.'

But it seemed to James that her laugh was forced, as if she did not really believe in what she was saying. As they walked out of the woods and further into the shadow of the abbey, he sensed her foreboding. He almost suggested that they turn back, but something made him go on until he could not have stopped even if he had wanted to. Whatever it was drew him in until he could no longer resist its pull. He felt as if he was caught in a dangerous current from which there was no escape.

When they reached the gates, he recalled that they had no means of getting into the place. Last time he had been here, Beppe, the wizened burglar he had seen only the night before, had broken in for them. Perhaps he should have asked him to pay another visit.

'What do we do now?' he asked.

Sofia raised her eyebrows. 'You are forgetting my criminal past,' she said, pulling a pin out of her hair and inserting it deftly into the lock. In a moment the gates opened and they were inside. Together they walked up the wide path towards the entrance. The graveyard was at the side, its stones rising eerily out of a mist that had suddenly descended. The sky was full of clouds now, and the day seemed to have been absorbed into a strange half-light, even though it was still morning.

As they drew closer to the building, it was clear that gaining entry was not to be a problem. The large wooden doors were already open.

23

To kill in a bestial rage requires no more than the mind of the Hottentot; but to plot out a poisoning requires ability and sharpness. The crimes of a woman are almost always deliberate.   Lombroso and Ferrero, 1893, p. 189

The morning was sunny and warm, though there were a few clouds on the horizon. Paola and Gina were taking Lucy to see the museum at the university in the Via Po. As ever, they were accompanied by Miss Trott, who declared herself to be fascinated at the prospect of finding out how the professor's mind worked. Paola had laughed and said there were many who would be interested in that prospect.

When they arrived, Lucy did not know what to make of it. She had been prepared for the experience up to a point. James had already told her tales of his previous trip to Turin. And of course there were quite a few of the professor's artefacts lying around at his house. But the full effect of the exhibits at the museum was another thing again.

'This is Papa's head collection,' Gina announced proudly as they walked into the first room. On one side was a wall of shelves full of skulls of all shapes and sizes.

'Oh my word!' Miss Trott said, fanning herself with a handkerchief she was clutching. 'Who do these belong to?'

Gina cleared her throat as if she was about to give a recitation. 'There are Alexandrian murderers, Sardinian epileptics, barbarians from Abyssinia, and see up there... that is a portrait of a criminal with the flared nostrils, pronounced jaw and cavernous eyes typical of the Mexican and/or Spanish brigand.'

The man in the picture had a large bushy moustache, waxed at the ends. His eyes were dead, as if all the fight had left him. He just looked sad, Lucy thought, not fierce at all.

'Over here are the manacles and chains from various prisons used to restrain the violent criminal, usually habitual. And in this case are daggers and other weapons taken from members of the Camorra.'

'The Camorra?' Lucy asked.

'A group of criminals who work together to do bad things,' Paola replied.

'Let's go to the next room,' Gina said, taking Lucy by the hand and pulling her towards the door. 'There is so much more to see!'

'Wait a moment, Miss Lombroso,' Miss Trott said. 'I just want to take it all in. What made your father begin such a collection?'

Gina looked at her. 'He always tells the story of the skull whenever anyone asks that question.'

'Oh not the skull...' Paola said, groaning. 'I have heard it so many times.'

'Do tell us, Gina,' Lucy said, sensing her disappointment.

'He was examining the skull of a brigand from Sicily, a ruthless killer, a dedicated criminal who had been executed recently. He looked closely at the bones that lay in his hands and realised something that changed his ideas about everything he had studied.'

'Ah yes, how does he put it?' Paola said. 'He holds out the imaginary skull.' She mimed his actions. 'And then he says, "I suddenly saw, like a broad plain on a fiery horizon..."'

Paola joined in with her sister, intoning their father's words as though they were sacred. '"...the solution to the problem of the nature of the criminal, who reproduces in our times the characters of primitive man and even those of carnivorous animals."'

Lucy was amused and a little envious. She used to have a father who made her proud, just like the Lombroso sisters. But now that had been wrenched away from her and all she had left was the faintest of memories of his kindness and affection, overtaken by the vision of his funeral and the mourners staring at them and whispering. She felt a tear make its way slowly down her cheek and brushed at it angrily. Miss Trott came over and offered her handkerchief, but she waved it away.

'So, Miss Gina, take us to the next room, if you would,' Miss Trott said firmly.

Gina nodded and took Lucy by the hand again, this time more gently, leading her away with Paola and Miss Trott bringing up the rear.

The room they entered was similar to the first, except that the skulls were replaced by glass cases filled with alarmingly lifelike heads laid on silk, like the interior of a coffin.

'These are Father's death heads,' Gina said.

'Death masks,' corrected Paola.

'Yes, yes, she is right,' Gina said. 'Once a criminal has been executed, they use their faces to make masks by moulding plaster to them.'

Lucy watched as Miss Trott wandered about the room peering at the men's faces. They even had hair, and eyes that stared up from their cushions like those of decapitated dummies, except, of course, that these were real features. This was what criminals actually looked like. She supposed that her own father had been some kind of criminal. He had been locked away, although she had yet to find out why. But he had not been like this. His eyes were kind and gentle, not staring and full of hatred like these poor excuses for men.

'I think some of them died in prison,' Paola said.

'Prison or the gallows, it doesn't matter,' Gina said. 'They were all born criminals anyhow.'

Paola looked at her sister, her head on one side. 'Well, not *all* born. Even Papa concedes that some have been made bad by their lives.'

'This is all fascinating,' Miss Trott said, waving her handkerchief in front of her face. 'Ooof, it is getting quite warm, is it not? I wonder . . . would you mind if I stepped out for a moment or two? I should like to get a little fresh air.'

'Of course,' Paola said. 'We can look after Lucy.'

'Yes,' Gina said, grinning. 'We haven't shown you the skeleton corridor yet!'

'I will forgo that pleasure, if you don't mind,' Miss Trott said. 'You can describe it to me later, Lucy, in both Italian and English. It will make an excellent exercise.'

She made her way out of the building, leaving the Lombroso sisters and Lucy to complete the tour. The skeleton corridor proved to be exactly as it sounded, with the bones standing to attention like an army unit. Anywhere else this would seem very odd, Lucy thought. But here it was as natural as the dinosaur exhibits in London's Natural History Museum.

A short while later they decided to go outside to join Miss Trott. After all, as Gina said, Lucy had all the time in the world to see the rest of the museum. As they wandered down the steps, Lucy looked around for her companion. At first she couldn't spot her, but then there she was, sitting in a café on the other side of the street, a glass of iced water before her. She was not alone. Seated opposite her, talking animatedly and waving his arms around, was Professor Donati. He was shouting, though she could not tell what he was saying. He threw some papers at Miss Trott, knocking over her drink, then stood and stalked off down the street.

At first Miss Trott sat completely still. Then she picked up the papers and hurriedly stuffed them into her reticule before summoning the waiter and ordering something else. Catching sight of Lucy, she waved hesitantly and then beckoned. The Lombroso sisters were too busy squabbling about something to notice what Lucy had just seen. The question was, should she tell them or keep it to herself? As they crossed the street to join Miss Trott, she remembered a line from a book that James had given her to help with her stories, *Pinkerton's Detection Manual*: 'When observing a subject it is better to keep your own counsel.' So that, she decided, was exactly what she would do. Secrets could be damaging, but information in the wrong hands could be worse.

James and Sofia walked into the entrance hall. The light, such as it was, shone through the stone window frames, making strange shapes on the dusty floor.

'Where do we start?' Sofia said. 'It looks as if no one has been here for a long time.'

'Which is odd in itself. Where are our footprints in the dust? Ottolenghi, Lombroso and I walked through here, but there is no sign of us being present at all.'

'It seems as if someone is trying to hide something,' Sofia said.

This time James knew exactly where he was headed. 'Follow me.' He made his way through the graveyard and down the steps towards the crypt. He examined the stone floor carefully as he went. Footprints were visible, but just one set rather than three. They stopped abruptly by the wall.

'I was certain there would be a door here.'

'Oh, but there is, *caro*... look.' Sofia walked to the left and pulled at a loose stone. A door appeared as if from nowhere and swung open.

'Well that explains the light we saw disappearing when we did our investigation,' James said. 'How did you know it was there?'

'Oh, it was... how do you call it... a hunch,' she said in English.

'You are full of surprises!' James said. Ahead of him was a passage with a room off to the left. Sofia put a restraining hand on his arm.

'Wait, *caro*, we need a lantern, or at least a candle.' She beckoned to him. 'Let's go up to the next floor and see if we can find one. This way, *si*?'

'Yes, but do you mind if we go through the crypt this time. I'd like to take another look.'

'No, I do not mind. We must be brave. There is too much at stake.'

He nodded and allowed her to take him by the hand and lead him into the damp and musty darkness. The dead girl was gone, but her macabre monastic friends remained, still seated upright in an orderly row.

'It's odd,' said James. 'We were so focused on the girl that we hardly paid any attention to these fellows.'

'That is probably because everyone else knew they would be here.'

'Yes, of course. I remember Tullio mentioning it. How come?'

'The story is well known in the city. It is said that an evil presence lives down here.'

'Don't tell the professor, but that doesn't surprise me in the least,' James said, thinking back to his first visit.

'The monks ... well, abbots really ... were left down here to ensure that it could not escape.'

'A monastic guard, then.'

'Something like that, yes. They have been mummified through a natural process.'

'And the weeping angel?'

'She is said to be crying because of the suffering and sinning that she has witnessed.'

James shivered. 'Shall we go and find a lantern?'

Sofia grinned at him. 'It is just a story.'

'I know, I know,' he said as he followed her towards the stairs in the corner. The monks stared back at him from their empty eye sockets. He knew it was just his imagination, but he could have sworn that one of them had moved.

Once they got up to the second flight of stairs, James noticed that there was no dust at all, adding to the mystery.

'Let's try to get into one of these rooms,' he said, indicating the double doors on either side of the corridor.

Sofia pulled out a hairpin and wiggled it about in one of the locks. The doors swung open. The room before them was large and filled with light. The furnishings were plush and the decor ornate. Arranged in clusters throughout were large overstuffed settees and chaise longues. He smelt cigar smoke, perfume and whisky with a hint of incense. It was all familiar, though James couldn't quite place it. Sofia smiled in triumph and replaced her hairpin.

'You have a light touch,' he said. 'Perhaps you should contemplate a new criminal career.'

She stepped towards him. 'And then you could reform me, perhaps? I think I might enjoy that.' She frowned. 'I am sorry. I should not say such things. It is not fair.'

Fair? How could she say that? James thought. He wanted nothing more than to pull her to him and kiss her – but properly this time, a deep and all-encompassing embrace that would show her exactly how he felt about her and how much he regretted all that had gone wrong between them. But before he could touch her, she moved away again. He sighed in frustration. She was right. It was not fair. Why was she torturing him like this?

'Listen,' she said. 'Can you hear it?'

At first James thought she meant his heartbeat, which was thudding so hard in his chest that it was surely audible. But no – she held her finger to her lips. 'Shush . . . footsteps, downstairs.'

'You stay here,' he said. 'I'll go and see if there's anyone there. Shut the door after me.'

She opened her mouth as if to protest, but he put his own finger on her lips, mirroring her movement. 'This time do as I say!' he whispered, inwardly noting the absurdity of telling Sofia what to do. But for once she did not resist. Nodding her agreement, she watched as he began to walk slowly down the stairs, then shut the door as he had asked her.

James stopped halfway down. He heard the creaking of shoes. Was it one pair or two? He couldn't see anything that would serve as a weapon. When he got to the bottom of the staircase, there didn't seem to be anyone there, but as he walked into the gloom, he noticed footprints in the dust. They seemed to be leading to the corridor that circled the entrance hall. He was about to follow them when there was a scream from upstairs.

'Sofia!' he cried, and raced back up the stairs towards her. But when he got to where he had left her, she was gone. On the floor was a handkerchief with the letters CE embroidered in one corner and SE in the other. He picked it up and pressed it to his face. It smelt of cinnamon.

He heard a noise, the creaking of shoe leather. Someone was behind him. Instinctively he put his hands up to protect himself, but he was too late. He felt a sharp blow across the side of his head and his knees buckled beneath him. His last thought before the darkness came was of Sofia.

24

A passion for evil for evil's sake is a characteristic of born criminals, epileptics, and hysterics. It is an automatic hatred, one that springs from no external cause such as an insult or offence, but rather from a morbid irritation of the psychical centres which relieves itself in evil action.
Lombroso and Ferrero, 1893, pp. 186–7

As they made their way through the Turin streets towards home, Lucy thought over what had happened that morning. It all seemed slightly unreal. One thing was sure, though. Miss Trott and Professor Donati made an unlikely couple, whatever their relationship. Lucy tried to imagine them as lovers and dismissed the idea immediately as being too absurd to consider. Once she, Paola and Gina had joined Miss Trott at the café opposite the professor's museum, Lucy had watched her companion carefully to see if she would give anything away. But Miss Trott seemed to act perfectly norm-ally, chatting animatedly to the Lombroso sisters about their father's exhibits and ordering ices for all to cool them down in 'this terrible heat'. Except that it was merely pleasantly warm. Could it have been some kind of a ruse?

She needed to find out more about the address on Miss Trott's piece of paper. What she really wanted to do was to ask

James. But he was away on another research trip, or at least that was what he had told Professor Lombroso, according to Gina, who had overheard the conversation.

As they approached the house, Sofia crossed the road towards them. She looked strange, dazed and bedraggled, her face streaked with tears.

'Miss Esposito, whatever is the matter?' asked Miss Trott.

Sofia's eyes were wide. '*Mi scusi, mi scusi!*'

Lucy gently took her hand. 'What is it, Sofia?'

'It is Signor James! He is gone!' She sank down on to the pavement, as if her legs could hold her up no longer.

'Gone? Gone where?' Lucy asked in alarm.

'They have taken him and it is all my fault. He was helping me to find Chiara, and now he is gone too!'

Miss Trott knelt down and helped Sofia to her feet. Sofia leant on her heavily and continued to sob. Miss Trott beckoned to the sisters. 'Miss Paola, go with Gina and fetch help.' The girls obeyed, glancing back as they left.

Lucy took Sofia by the shoulders. 'Tell me what happened, quickly!'

'We were in the Abbey San Callisto. We were . . .' She paused, as if trying to find the right words. 'We were searching for clues, then we heard a noise. Signor James went to see what it was and I shut the door behind him, as he told me. Then someone came up behind me and put something over my mouth. I must have been drugged, because the next thing I knew I was in the graveyard. I ran back to find your brother, but he had disappeared!'

'How do you know that he wasn't out looking for you?' Lucy asked. 'He might have thought that you'd be here. He could already be back.'

Sofia's face was a picture of misery.

'What is it?'

'I went back to where I had last seen him...'

Lucy looked down at Sofia's hands. They were stained with blood.

The pain wrapped itself around James so completely that he was too weak even to cry out. And even if he had been able to, he was gagged and could not have uttered more than a grunt. His body ached all over and he had a pain in his head that felt as if his brain was being squeezed through a colander. There was some dampness on the back of his neck that might well have been blood, though he could not be sure. But all that mattered was Sofia. Where was she? What were they doing to her? He had to get out of here and find her.

He tried to calm himself by getting his bearings. He was in darkness, but he still had some idea of his surroundings. He was lying on his side. The floor beneath him was stone, and there was dust or dirt of some kind on it. He stretched his foot out as much as he could, which wasn't far given that both his hands and his feet were tied. The walls were also of stone. It was damp and musty-smelling. He might be anywhere.

Slowly and painfully he tried to pull himself upright. It was difficult to get any kind of balance, but eventually he managed to right himself and lean against the wall. He tried to remember what had happened before everything had gone black. There had been footsteps behind him... one set or two? He wasn't certain. He recalled the blow to his head, which presumably was the cause of the pain that he could still feel. But how long had he been here?

There was a rattle at the door, the sound of a key being turned and a light that dazzled him. He tried to get up, but it was impossible on his own. Two men came over to him and hauled him to his feet. His gag was removed.

'Who are you? What do you want?' he asked desperately. 'What have you done with Sofia? Is she all right?'

He was just becoming accustomed to the light when it went again as someone blindfolded him. The cloth smelt of mould and decay, as if it had last been wrapped around something dead or dying.

'This way, *Inglese.*' The voice was gruff but businesslike. He was propelled along at some speed and almost fell at one point.

'*Attenzione!*' This was a second voice, softer, more educated.

After a minute or two they seemed to enter another room. There was no dampness to this one. Instead he could smell wood and polish. It reminded him of Sofia, as it had done the night at the abbey with the professor and Ottolenghi. Was he still there? That might explain the contrast between the two rooms.

He was manhandled into a chair. It was wooden, but the seat was cushioned – a dining chair of some kind, probably.

'Signor Murray, you really must not interfere in matters that are not your affair.' It was the second voice again. It sounded quite gentle, almost conciliatory.

'I was not aware that I was,' James replied.

'Oh, I think you know full well... and you see, therein lies our problem.'

'What problem?'

'Your awareness... your knowledge.' The voice was regretful now. 'It is a shame really.'

'Why?'

'Because it means we must ensure that what you know goes no further.'

'I told you. I don't know anything.'

'Now we both know that you are lying. And that can only lead in one direction.'

James felt someone approach him. He was pulled off the chair and held from behind. Then he was punched, hard, in the stomach, winding him and bringing tears to his eyes. He was punched again and again until he could no longer stand of his own accord. He felt the punches move to his face. Then the blows stopped and he felt himself being lowered back on to the seat with a strange gentleness. The pain was acute and his automatic reaction was to double over with it, but he forced himself to stay upright.

He sensed that someone else had entered the room. The smell of the place altered slightly – a faint hint of a fragrance, nothing more than that. He heard a soft rustling.

'You see, Signor Murray, that is what happens when you are not frank with us,' the voice said sorrowfully.

'I told you . . . I don't know anything.'

'So you say, but how can we be sure?'

James did not reply. He heard the sound of whispering.

'Perhaps there is a solution . . .' the voice said.

'What?'

'Clearly you are unaffected by your own pain, but what of another's?'

James felt himself tense.

'Ah, I see that we have finally got through to you.'

'If you touch her . . .'

'You are hardly in a strong bargaining position, Signor Murray. But I can see that the young lady is your Achilles heel. And then there is your sister, the lovely Signorina Lucy, and your position with the great Professor Lombroso. You are a lucky man in so many ways, Signor Murray. You have so much, but also so much to lose – love, family, reputation.'

'I don't know who you are or what you are doing. I cannot harm you.'

Someone stepped closer to him and he braced himself for another beating. Instead he felt the unmistakable sensation of steel against his cheek, cold and sharp and then stinging as it sliced into his skin. He cried out in pain and shock.

'There – a small keepsake as a reminder. Perhaps you are telling the truth, perhaps you are not. The position is this. If you do anything to indicate that you are interfering in our business again, you will regret it. Do I make myself clear?'

'Yes, very clear,' James replied. A small rivulet of blood was running down his face.

'Good. That is very good. Do not take this amiss, Signor Murray, but I hope we will not meet again, for your sake.'

A command was issued in a dialect that James did not quite understand, and the next thing he knew he was being moved yet again – through corridors and then down some stairs until he felt the sun on his back and could smell fresh air. He was put into what felt like a cart, and a piece of cloth was thrown over him. It smelt of animal dung. He heard the wheels going round and felt the sensation of movement. Before long the cart stopped. He tensed himself again as the cloth was pulled away. He could not be sure that they would not beat him again, just for the hell of it, and this time there was no one to stop them from going too far. He was dragged out of the cart and thrown to the ground.

'*Mi scusi, Inglese,*' said a different voice, and then there was another blow to the back of his head. It only stunned him this time, but he feigned unconsciousness in case they hit him again. He felt his limbs being liberated.

He lay on the ground where they had left him and heard the cart drive away. He stayed there for a few moments, just to be sure, then he opened his eyes and gingerly sat up and touched the cut on his cheek. It did not seem as bad as he had feared, and at least he was free. Now all he had to do was find Sofia. Were they holding her, and if so, where? Had they harmed her? All he could do now was get back to the city and find help. Then and only then could he think about what to do next.

25

Woman's cruelty and her reactions to life's trials stem from her weakness. Because she is unable to destroy her enemies, woman torments them, pricking them with needles of pain and immobilising them with misery. Cruelty, like cunning, is a product of woman's adaptation to the conditions of life. And thus she acquired and developed her ability to torment. In sum, cruelty is a type of defensive as well as offensive reaction in woman.

Lombroso and Ferrero, 1893, p. 68

James lay in bed and looked listlessly out of the window. The sun was shining and he heard the noise of people and carriages as they passed on the street below. It was only two days since his return to the city, but he was already getting tired of being cooped up inside as if he was an invalid. There was a knock on the door and Ottolenghi came in, knocking a pile of books over as he did so.

'Oh dear, I am sorry,' he said, scooping them up and putting them back in an untidy heap on the table.

James grinned at him. 'Don't worry. I'm glad to see you.'

'How are you?' Ottolenghi said.

'I feel like a fraud.'

'Well I don't know why. That was a pretty bad beating you took, James.'

'I know, but I'm recovered now. It's mostly just a few bruises and a bit of a headache.'

'Two cracked ribs, a nasty head wound and lacerations to the face,' Ottolenghi recited. 'I think it will take more than a few days for you to recover. What did Tullio say?'

'Not much. He took my statement, though I couldn't remember a great deal, and said that he would look into it. It was odd, really.'

'In what way?'

'He didn't seem that interested. He was rather brusque, in fact, as if I was wasting his time.'

'That is strange.'

'I know he is busy.'

'Yes, but all the same...'

'Is Sofia all right?' James asked.

Ottolenghi raised his eyebrows. 'She's as well as can be expected, given all that's happened. She has been told to stay at home and rest, which is what you should be doing.' He hesitated for a moment. 'You told the professor that it was over between you, I believe. Is that true?'

'It was when I told him, yes,' James said.

'But you are together now?'

'Difficult to say,' James said, remembering the touch of her lips as she kissed him in the woods.

'Do you still love her?' Ottolenghi asked.

James nodded. There was no point lying. He knew how he felt about her. That had not changed. But her emotions were, as ever, a mystery to him.

'And how does she feel about you?' Ottolenghi said, as if reading his mind.

James shrugged. 'I came back here because she asked for my help. I thought it was because she loved me. I wanted us to start a new life together, but she refused. How could I be so naïve, Salvatore?'

'Love makes us all lose our heads from time to time,' Ottolenghi replied. 'Sofia knows that it might very well destroy you if you were together openly.'

'I don't care! Don't you see?' He cried out in frustration. 'Why can't two people who love each other be together?'

'Sometimes we have to make sacrifices for what we know to be right.'

'It just seems so very unfair.'

'Perhaps, but there are other things to think of now,' Ottolenghi said. 'What happened, James? Why were you taken?'

'I truly do not know,' James said. 'Whoever it was seemed to think that I had found out something.'

'What?'

'That's the problem. I have no idea.'

'And Sofia?'

'They took her in order to get to me, I think.'

'You know what to do, James. You must sever all connection with Sofia. It is the only course of action you can take.'

'I can't,' he said. 'I just can't.'

He knew that Ottolenghi was right. The sensible thing would be to tell Sofia that it – whatever *it* was – could not go on. He should stop looking for Chiara and accept that there was no possibility of a life with Sofia. It would keep her safe, if nothing else. It would be difficult. They had shared so much. James had watched his father descend into insanity and Sofia had suffered as the result of her own father's crimes. Both of them had been damaged, but they had helped one another to survive. Without Sofia, his life would have no meaning. How could he ever hope to understand and accept his past without her at his side? But she had told him already that they could not be together, and now it seemed that there was even more at stake than happiness.

'If you don't end it, you are risking her safety. And, James, it isn't just Sofia.'

'I know. It's Lucy too. They said as much.'

'Well then, what will you do?'

'There is only one thing I can do. I have to get to the bottom of this. If I don't, then we'll never be safe ... any of us.'

Signora Laura Capetti was not, as a rule, a fearful person. Had she been of a nervous disposition, she would not have been walking unaccompanied through the Parco Valentino just as the sun began to rise. Yes, the newspaper had talked of girls going missing in the early morning, but that did not deter her from her journey, even though the solitude and silence made it an eerie experience. Every rustle of foliage, every cry of an animal or bird seemed magnified a thousand times. For Signora Capetti, such sounds held no fear. Indeed, she prided herself on being afraid of nothing and no one, and she could hardly be described as a girl.

Since the death of her husband five years ago, she had been forced to make her own way in the world, which required a certain amount of fortitude. Luckily she had found that fortitude was a characteristic she possessed in abundance. As she had often mused since the beginning of her widowhood, you never really knew what you were capable of until you were forced to find out. Her husband had been a gambler and had left her with so many debts that she had been forced to seek employment in order to make ends meet. She had therefore taken a job at a small souvenir shop in the Borgo Mediaevale, which made her just enough to get by. This was perhaps one of the stranger parts of Turin. It was a perfect replica of a small medieval town built for the Esposizione Universale in 1884. Visitors flocked to it to look at its little shops and its castle, La Rocca – The Stronghold. During the winter months it was open only at weekends, but soon the season would begin again. Today Signora Capetti had been asked to conduct a thorough stock check so that orders could be made in time for the summer, their busiest period.

Many middle-aged women would have been humiliated by such a change of fortune – from middle-class comfort to shop worker in a matter of weeks. Signora Capetti, however, had found that she enjoyed her work. It made her feel useful. She particularly liked stock-taking, as it gave her an opportunity to look more closely than usual at the many wondrous things she sold – history books that told tales of the medieval period, maps of Turin from years ago, lace handkerchiefs and hand-made silk scarves, bottles of cologne and dolls dressed up in medieval clothes. She would place these in order, and by the day's end would have a complete list of stock, and an overwhelming sense of achievement.

All of this meant that as she walked through the park to-wards her place of work on a warm and sunny morning, she did so with a spring in her step. Passing through the main gateway to the castle, she imagined what it might have been like to be a medieval princess wandering her own grounds. And that was when she saw it.

At first she thought it was some kind of mannequin from a dress shop, so perfect did it seem. But on closer scrutiny it became obvious that this figure had once been a living and breathing being. It was the body of a young girl, dressed in a white gown overlaid with gold lace. She was lying prostrate in the small shallow stream that circled the castle and served as a moat. Her long red hair was fanned out behind her and moved gently with the water. Her face was pale, almost as white as her gown. In one of her hands she clasped a few long-stemmed spring flowers of blue and red. More lay at her feet, caught up in the folds of the gown.

For a moment Signora Capetti stood and watched her, entranced. She looked so peaceful, almost as if she was sleeping, just like the painting of Ophelia by Millais. The only sound was the gurgling of the water as it ran gently past her.

Lucy was sitting at James's bedside, reading to him. He was perfectly capable of reading to himself, as he had made abundantly clear. But they had hardly spoken since their arrival in Turin and she was eager to make up for lost time. He had said little about the assault except to tell her in a matter-of-fact tone that this kind of thing was something of an occupational hazard when you were researching criminals. Lucy was sceptical, even though Professor Lombroso had apparently accepted the incident as a random crime. He even seemed disappointed at James's inability to describe his attackers. 'A perfectly good piece of fieldwork entirely lost because of carelessness' was how he had put it, which seemed rather unfair given the circumstances. As she had heard James say afterwards, it was as though he was expected to ask his assailants to pause while they were beating him to allow him to do a quick sketch of the shape of their heads and make some notes. But Lucy had studied the professor's expression as he spoke, and it seemed to her that he was far more disturbed by the incident than he was letting on. There was more to this than met the eye, she was sure of it. According to *Pinkerton's*

Detection Manual, the route to discovery was observation, which sounded like a good strategy.

Lucy had suggested that she should read James a novel – *The Moonstone* by Wilkie Collins was one of their shared favourites – but the book he had chosen was by the professor. She had expected it to be dry and full of scientific terms that she would find hard to understand. She couldn't have been more wrong. Instead it was full of the most blood-curdling anecdotes about this murderer or that, and the language he used was extremely engaging. It was true that he kept wandering off the point here and there, and some of the science was, according to James anyway, rather questionable, but it was a thrilling read and something of a revelation for Lucy.

'Look at these.' She held the book up to show him. '"Before and after pictures of vicious and criminal boys",' she read out. '"William Bender and Tom Wellington – a reformed gang member and a London vagabond who went to Canada."'

James peered at the drawings. 'That's interesting. A criminal can be reformed, even if he was born that way.'

'It is comforting, but there is more,' Lucy continued. 'According to the professor, the crime rate among children is extremely high. He tells the story of a thirteen-year-old who stabbed and killed a companion over some gambling winnings. He had a pointed skull, oblique eyes, protruding cheekbones, voluminous jaws and jug ears!'

'Ugly so-and-so, then,' James said.

'Apparently his brother was convicted six times for theft, his sister was a prostitute and their mother was a criminal who suffered from migraines. His father died of financial anxieties. I didn't know that could kill you, did you?'

'Mmm, interesting,' James said. 'I suppose it might put a strain on the heart.'

'Oh yes, I hadn't thought of that. In addition, his grand-mother died of poisoning and his brother stuttered. The professor says that is evidence of neuroses causing inherited criminal tendencies.'

'The professor isn't right about everything, Lucy.'

'Are you sure? He seems to think he is.'

'Well that is true. He doesn't do much self-doubting.'

'You are so lucky, James,' Lucy said wistfully.

'Why?' he said, shifting uncomfortably in his bed. 'I don't feel very lucky.'

'You study such interesting subjects, whereas all I get to read are dreary self-improving tomes. Aunt Agnes must have sent at least a hundred with Miss Trott.'

He grinned. 'I wondered why her luggage was so heavy. How are you getting on with Miss Trott?'

Lucy hesitated. This could be her only opportunity to tell James about what she had discovered. But together it did not seem to add up to anything much – a note with a mention of an Egyptian demon, the word 'serendipity' and the address of a chemist's shop. Even the altercation between Miss Trott and Professor Donati did not signify anything on its own, although it was something of a mystery. Besides, he had so much else on his mind with the murder of that poor girl that she really didn't want to trouble him with it now. Better to wait until she had found something more concrete and less... now what was the word in *Pinkerton's*... ah yes: circumstantial.

'She seems nice enough, if rather dull,' she replied.

'Dull? Oh, I think dull is good. I could do with some dull,' James said. 'Mind you, it would be nice to get out of this room for a while.'

'You're not well enough yet, according to Dr Ottolenghi anyway.'

The door was flung open and Lombroso bounded in, followed by a sheepish-looking Ottolenghi.

'What are you still doing in bed, Murray? Come along, come along ... there is work to be done!'

'But, Professor, my brother is not yet fully recovered,' Lucy protested.

'I am fine, Lucy. Don't worry,' James said as he started rather gingerly to get up. 'I just need to take it a little slowly.'

Lombroso tutted. 'We cannot take it slowly, Murray. There is too much to do.'

'Why? Whatever has happened?' Lucy asked.

'There's a body, Signorina Murray. The newspapers are full of it. Another young woman, and I would not be at all surprised if she was just like the other one.'

'In what way?' Lucy asked.

'Well, I ...' Lombroso paused.

'Please do not feel that you have to moderate your language on my account, Professor. It is not only my brother who has an interest in such things.'

James frowned at her. 'Lucy!'

Lombroso raised an eyebrow and continued. 'I expect her to be drained of blood for one thing. And for another ...' he paused for dramatic effect, 'I'd put a wager on her being gutted, just like a hare for the pot! We shall find out more at the post-mortem. Tullio has asked me to conduct it, as I found the first body.'

Lucy noticed that he did not seem to care about the poor dead girl. She supposed it was necessary for scientists. Could she really learn to be so detached?

'When will it take place?' James asked.

236

'This afternoon,' Lombroso replied.

'So where are we going now?'

'Ottolenghi and I are going to the university. You are going downstairs.'

'Why?'

'Because you have a visitor.'

'Concetta Panatti is here,' Ottolenghi said. 'She wants to liaise with you about the interviews with her...' He paused for a moment and glanced at Lucy, 'girls.'

'Who is Concetta Panatti?' Lucy asked.

'No one you need worry about, young lady,' Lombroso said. 'Haven't you got something more useful to occupy yourself with than troubling your brother?'

'Lucy was reading to me from your work, Professor, not troubling me at all,' James said quickly, before Lucy could protest.

'Really?' Lombroso seemed to puff out a little, like a cockerel. 'Well I imagine you may wish to read through it again, signorina. It is quite complex, especially for the female intellect. But if you wish to look at some more of my work, there is plenty at the museum. You may borrow it if you like, though I imagine you may need your brother to decipher it for you.'

Lucy was tempted to mention Anna Tarnovsky, who seemed to manage very well, but saw James's expression and thought better of it.

'I shall, Professor,' she said, 'then perhaps we could discuss it. There are already one or two aspects that I find—'

'Wouldn't it be better for you to deal with Signora Panatti, Professor?' James said, interrupting her.

'In an ideal world, perhaps,' Lombroso said. 'But the lady will speak only to you. She seems to have taken something of a shine to you, so you'd better hurry. I don't want her to change her mind about access to the girls. You can meet us at the mortuary later.'

Lucy watched as Ottolenghi helped James out of bed. He was a little unsteady, perhaps unsurprisingly given his ordeal. But there was something else. Professor Lombroso might have been unmoved by the girl's death, but for James it was as if there was something personal in the finding of another body. It was touching him a lot more deeply than he wanted anyone to know. And as his sister, she felt it was her duty to find out why.

26

In the lower animal orders, where the female is more powerful than the male, love is non-existent. The female subordinates sexuality to maternity by getting rid of the male as soon as she has been impregnated. After mating, the female spider devours the male if he has not already fled. Only when the male becomes more powerful, forcing the female to submit to his domination and more ardent sexual demands, does love become linked to reproduction and maternity.   Lombroso and Ferrero, 1893, p. 73

James watched Concetta Panatti through the open door. She was standing by a bookcase, peering at its contents, languidly caressing their spines. For a moment he imagined the feel of her hands on his skin and felt a stirring of desire. Her gown was dark green velvet and hugged her curves provocatively. There was no doubt that she was a beautiful woman. The redness of her hair was striking in its depth. Her features were fine, her skin flawless, pale and delicate, and her eyes . . . well, they were extraordinary: mesmerising, bewitching.

She looked up as he entered. 'Ah, Signor Murray, it is good to see you.' She approached him with a leonine grace. Everything about her was sensual. She embraced him with her presence alone. As during their last meeting, she came so close that he could hear her breathing. Slowly she peeled off her lace gloves, finger by finger, her eyes never leaving his, her lips full, pouting as if waiting to be kissed.

'Your poor face,' she said, running a finger down the cut on his cheek. Her hand lingered there and he felt the heat from it filter through his skin. He suspected that he should stand back and create some distance between them, but he found that he did not want to move. 'I do hope that it will not leave a scar.'

'It is nothing,' he said, struggling to keep his voice steady. This was ridiculous, he thought. Here he was, a grown man, allowing himself to be manipulated by a woman he hardly knew.

'What have you been doing?' she asked.

'I was attacked,' James said. She was clearly not the sort of woman one could lie to. But why would he want to? For a brief moment he wanted to tell her everything about himself, the bad and the good – to lay himself open for her.

She had a sly half-formed smile on her face. 'You must have done something very bad to provoke such a reaction.'

'I have done nothing,' he replied.

'I find that hard to believe,' she said. 'A man like you.'

What did she know about him? What did he know about himself, come to that?

'It was a misunderstanding.'

'I see,' she said, moving away from him towards the window and casually glancing out of it. He willed her to be close to him again. Then he remembered why they were here.

'I gather you wish to make arrangements for our interviews at the university.'

'Yes. I know that you were due to visit me, but I heard that

you were... indisposed.' Her eyes seemed to penetrate him.
'And I could not wait.'

'Another time perhaps,' James said.

'Yes, I would enjoy that.'

'And the arrangements?'

'If you are in charge, I doubt there will be any need for arrangements.' She smiled again. 'I have every confidence that you will treat the ladies with respect. That is all I ask.'

'Of course, signora,' James said, watching her as she approached him again, this time circling slowly round him as if waiting to pounce. From anyone else this would have felt ridiculous, but with her it seemed merely playful.

'I will deliver the girls personally.' She paused for a moment. 'I hear that one of my young ladies accosted you.'

'It was nothing,' James said.

'Ada is a fanciful young woman. I do not know what she told you, but you should put it from your mind, whatever it was.'

Her words sounded familiar. Wasn't that what Valeria had told him? He shook his head. It was hard to think clearly in Concetta Panatti's presence, but he knew he must.

'Have any of your girls disappeared recently? A young woman called Agnella, for instance?'

She hesitated. There was an almost undetectable frisson of disapproval. 'They come and go all the time, Signor Murray. Sometimes they find a man to take them on, or another position elsewhere. It is just one of those things.'

'What about Teresa Mariani?'

'Ah yes, the maid. Domestic staff are no different. She no doubt found work in a different establishment. It happens.'

James nodded. 'Thank you for being so helpful, signora.'

'Delighted to be of assistance. Now is there anything else I can help you with?'

'Signora, I wonder...' James began. He hardly dared to ask, but he could not resist.

'Anything, Signor Murray.' She was next to him again, surrounding him with her musky scent.

'Would you be prepared to talk to us?'

She hesitated. 'I will talk to you, and you alone.'

'I will look forward to it.'

'So will I, Signor Murray. So will I.' She was almost whispering now, her lips close to his ear, her breath caressing him.

The door opened. Miss Trott came in. 'Mr Murray, I wonder if you have seen my... Oh, I do apologise.'

Concetta Panatti stepped away from him. She stared at Miss Trott, her eyes conveying something not far from malevolence.

Miss Trott reddened but did not look away. 'I don't believe we have been introduced.'

'No, I shouldn't think we have. Until tomorrow, Signor Murray.' Concetta Panatti held out her ungloved hand. James took it and held it for a moment. She gave him a knowing smile before sweeping past Miss Trott, passing so close to her that she almost knocked her flying.

For a moment there was silence as both James and Miss Trott adjusted to Concetta Panatti's absence.

'My word, you are a *busy* young man, aren't you, Mr Murray?' Miss Trott said.

'What was it you wanted?' James said, irritated by her comment.

'I have it, thank you,' she replied, holding up a book in triumph. She paused for a moment. 'May I give you some advice?'

'If you must,' James said.

'Take care,' she said. 'A woman like that can cause untold harm.'

'I am quite capable of looking after myself.'

'You will not be able to control her.'

'You forget yourself, Miss Trott. You are engaged as my sister's companion, not mine.'

She shook her head sadly. 'As you wish, Mr Murray, as you wish.'

James watched her as she left. He went over to the window and gazed out of it, breathing in the vestiges of Concetta's scent and thinking about what Miss Trott had said. She had no right to issue such a warning. How could she possibly know anything about a woman like Concetta Panatti? Besides, he was free to act as he chose. Sofia had rejected him, or so it seemed. So much stood in their way that any prospect of a future together now seemed utterly unattainable. Why should he not enjoy the company of another woman? He had no feelings for Concetta, but he was attracted to her and perhaps that was enough. It might even be a relief to stop thinking about a woman he could not have and focus instead upon one who seemed only too willing. But beneath his indignation there was another thought, one that he was doing his utmost to suppress but still it remained there, like a bee with a venomous sting, buzzing around his head. First Sofia and now Miss Trott had issued a warning about Concetta Panatti. Could they really both be wrong?

Lucy stood outside the building and looked up at the window. A small vase stood on the sill in the gap between the ill-drawn curtains. She thought back to last time she had been here, when Sofia had rescued her from the Morals Squad. This time she was on her own errand of mercy, or that was what she hoped it looked like anyway. There was something that had been gnawing away at her ever since her first visit, something she wanted to find out. She had even brought some gifts – a bunch of flowers purchased from a nearby street vendor and a jar of honey from a market stall. As last time, she had not asked for permission for her outing, but she had seen plenty of young women out alone during the day and had therefore decided that it would be perfectly safe to pay Sofia a visit.

She knocked on the door. The wood was of poor quality. She could tell as much from the hollow ring to her rapping. The shabby curtains twitched slightly. A few seconds later the door opened and Sofia stood there smiling hesitantly.

'Signorina, I did not expect a visit from you.'

'May I come in?' Lucy asked.

Sofia stood back and allowed her to enter, following her up the stairs.

Lucy studied the woman in front of her as they stood face to face in the tiny room. She was paler than usual, almost diminished, presumably due to her recent ordeal. Lucy thrust her gifts out before her as if she was carrying a shield.

Sofia took them. 'You are very kind, but it was not necessary,' she said, indicating for her visitor to sit on the small faded settee.

It was not particularly solid and wobbled a little as Lucy lowered herself on to it. 'My mother always taught me never to call on someone empty-handed.'

'Ah, she was Italian, was she not?' Sofia carefully placed the honey on the table and laid the flowers next to it.

'Yes, she was.' Lucy watched as Sofia busied herself opening cupboards and pulling out vessels that might be suitable for the flowers – a jar, a small carafe and so on – until eventually settling for a ceramic jug.

She paused, hugging it to her. 'Why are you here, signorina? I am just a housekeeper.'

'You are more than that, I think.'

Sofia looked down. It was only for a moment, but it was enough.

'What is there between you and my brother?' Lucy asked.

'He is helping me to find my cousin. She is missing.' The reply came quickly, too quickly for Lucy's liking. Sofia was flushed and her hands were still clasping the jug tightly in front of her.

'And that is all?' Lucy asked, her eyes narrowing.

'First Anna Tarnovsky and now me . . . Signorina, you seem very anxious to find someone with an attachment to your brother. I am not sure he is the catch you appear to think he is.' She slammed the jug down on the table and picked up Lucy's flowers, chopping at the stalks with a small knife.

'I would be more than happy if James and Anna were to . . .'

'To what?'

'To marry, I suppose,' Lucy said.

Sofia snorted. '*Madame* Anna Tarnovsky is already married. Her husband is in Prague. They are happy as far as I know.'

Lucy frowned. Prague . . . Not a cruel Russian count then. How disappointing! But then Sofia might be lying – though why would she? 'Really? She has no wedding ring.'

'*Sì*, you are right,' Sofia said, waving the knife around in time to her words, as if to emphasise them. 'She does not wear it. That is because she would not be allowed by the university to work with the professor if her status was widely known.'

'And what about you, Sofia?'

245

'I have told you ... Signor James is helping me. There is nothing more between us.'

'Not from his side, of course, but you?'

'Oh, of course,' Sofia said in what sounded like a sarcastic tone as she laid down the knife. She wiped her hands on her apron and then removed it and hung it on a small hook by the door. 'I am just a servant.'

Lucy nodded, feeling foolish. As if James would be interested in Sofia – it was ridiculous. And Sofia would not allow herself to care for a man like James.

'So your cousin ...'

'As I said, she has disappeared.'

'So that is why he is concerned about the second girl's body?' Lucy said.

Sofia stared at her, horrified.

'You did not know?' Lucy said.

Sofia shook her head. Scooping up her shawl from a chair, she grabbed Lucy by the wrist. 'You should go. I have something I must do.'

Firmly she propelled Lucy to the door and opened it. Standing on the threshold was James.

27

We have discovered that women are less sensitive than men, which explains their greater vitality, but contradicts both popular wisdom and clear evidence that women react more strongly to pain. This apparent contradiction resolves itself when we take into account women's greater excitability and lesser inhibition.

Lombroso and Ferrero, 1893, p. 36

James looked from one to the other. He had not expected this.

'James! What are you doing here?' Lucy asked.

For a moment he considered telling her the truth, but quickly realised that this would be the wrong strategy. 'I could ask the same of you. You know you are not to travel anywhere alone.'

Her face began to redden.

'Wait downstairs, Lucy. I need to speak to Sofia.'

Lucy hesitated for a moment, as if she was considering disobeying him. Then silently she made her way down the stairs.

'Another body . . .' Sofia said, her voice dull. 'I was on the way to the mortuary.'

Instinctively he stepped towards her as if to offer comfort, but she leant away from him. 'There is no need to put yourself through that again,' he said. 'I will tell you if there is any news. I am sure Tullio would have informed you if there was any chance...' His voice tailed off. He did not want to say the words.

'I will escort the signorina back to the house before I go to the museum.'

'Be careful,' James said.

Sofia gave just the ghost of a smile. 'We will be.'

When they got downstairs, Lucy was standing in the doorway waiting for them.

'Sofia will walk back to the house with you,' James said.

'Couldn't we both go to the museum? The professor said that I might borrow some books,' Lucy said.

'I don't think so,' James said. 'We are conducting interviews there this afternoon.'

'Couldn't I assist? Perhaps I could take notes, or be a second observer?' Lucy asked.

'No, I am afraid it is not suitable. You are too young, and you are...' He hesitated.

'Too female?' Lucy said. 'You sound like the professor.'

'Well on this occasion he is absolutely right. This is not for you.'

'What is for me, then?'

'Lucy, this is not the time to argue.'

She did not answer him but instead changed tactics. 'Please, James. I want to do something useful for once. Anna will be there to make sure I am safe. Gina said so.'

'Another time, perhaps, but not today,' he said. 'You must go home with Sofia.'

'But—'

'No buts, Lucy. Three girls are dead. I want you at home where I know you are safe.'

Lucy glowered at him, picked up her basket and stalked off, followed by Sofia. James watched as they walked away together through the busy streets. He already felt alone, but if anything happened to either of them ... He pushed the thought from his mind and began to make his way to the mortuary.

When he arrived he found Lombroso and Ottolenghi waiting outside. 'I thought Tullio had asked you to conduct the post-mortem, Professor,' James said.

Lombroso pursed his lips. 'Machinetti was already there with that drunken fool Gallini, his favourite pathologist. Apparently the scene of the crime, or at least where the body was found, is under his jurisdiction.'

'That doesn't sound right,' James said.

'It isn't,' Tullio said as he approached them. 'I breached his territory so he is breaching mine.'

'Ridiculous,' Lombroso said. 'Well he can't stop me from watching, can he?'

Tullio shrugged. 'I suppose not.' He seemed strangely list-less. Usually he would have been infuriated by Machinetti's presumption, but he didn't seem to have any fight left in him.

'Then let us go in, gentlemen, and see whether I was right about the similarities between the bodies.'

Lombroso strode into the mortuary, followed by Otto-lenghi. James steeled himself for a second before pushing his own way through the large wooden doors. The body lay on a table in the middle of the room, covered demurely by a sheet. Yet again he held his breath, hoping that it was not Chiara.

Machinetti stood in a corner, watching. 'I wondered how long it would be before you poked your nose in, Lombroso.'

'It would be better to have consistency of some kind, would

you not agree, Dottore?' Lombroso said, ignoring Machinetti altogether and addressing his question to Gallini, who merely gave a non-committal grunt in reply. 'Then we can compare the state of the corpses found in the woods and at the abbey with this one. Tell me again, Tullio, how and where was this body found?'

'She was found lying in a stream at the Borgo Mediaevale,' Tullio said.

'That's quite a public place, isn't it?' James said. 'It could not have been there for long. Otherwise it would have been discovered before.'

'I agree,' Lombroso said. 'The killer wanted it to be found, I would think. Do we have any names yet?'

Tullio glanced down at the notebook he was holding. 'The girl at the abbey was a flower seller called Nella Calvi. A friend of hers came in and identified her. We think that this girl is probably another flower seller, Caterina Spirito. She fits the description. They are both on Baldovino's list.'

'Where did he get the names?' Lombroso asked.

'He told me it was from one of his informants,' James said. 'What about the other girls on the list? Have you found anything about them – Arianna Panico, for example?'

'Not much. Panico is proving elusive.' Tullio looked down at his notebook again. 'As is the last one, Susanna Russello. I told you, girls like these go missing all the time.'

Lombroso wandered over towards the body. Machinetti glared at him. 'Get back!'

Gallini hesitated, swaying a little.

'Get on with it, man!' Machinetti barked, looking threateningly at Lombroso. 'And you, keep out of the way or I'll have you removed.' Lombroso took the tiniest of steps back.

Gallini pulled back the sheet. James was relieved. The

corpse was, as Lombroso had said, similar to the one they had found in the abbey, and it was again clear that it was not Chiara. The hair was long and pale red and the skin had a waxy tinge to it, giving it a macabre air like a sinister doll. Gallini began his examination. He was still slightly unsteady on his feet, and occasionally had to stop to support himself by gripping on to the table where his subject was laid out. James watched him with distaste. He knew that the doctor was reputed to have a problem with drink. That much had become clear during the Pilgrim investigation. But he had not realised that the man's alcoholism had got so bad that he would actually be under the influence during a post-mortem. Lombroso stood next to him as he worked, his fingers twitching as if he wanted to intervene.

'What can you tell me?' Tullio asked.

'This is my case. You address your answers to me, Gallini,' Machinetti said..

'The body was found in my jurisdiction,' Tullio said through gritted teeth. 'It is linked to the others, and with regard to the body found in the woods, I have been asked personally to investigate by the mayor.'

Machinetti scowled back at him. 'The link has yet to be established.'

Gallini rolled his eyes and continued examining. Eventually he looked up from his work, a frown on his face. 'Something is not quite right here.'

'What do you mean?' Tullio asked.

Gallini hesitated for a second. Lombroso tutted and interjected.

'After death, certain processes automatically cease and others begin. The heart stops beating and the body starts to digest itself as cells and tissues break down. This is then followed by putrefaction as the bacteria begin their work.'

'Which means?'

Lombroso strode over to the body and began to examine it closely. Gallini moved aside unsteadily.

'Here the processes have been halted. There are only two explanations for this anomaly. The first is that the place where the body was found has an unusual level of some kind of chemical compound, which has resulted in the stalling of putrefaction.'

'Is that likely?' Tullio asked.

Lombroso pursed his lips thoughtfully. 'Possible, yes, but likely . . . no.'

'And the second explanation?'

'Is equally unlikely – that somehow the body has not been allowed to begin decomposition naturally.'

'What could cause that?'

'There is only one possible cause,' Lombroso said, pausing for dramatic effect. It was an old habit, but they had all learnt that it was easier to play along with it.

'Which is?'

'Human intervention, Inspector, human intervention . . . just as in the other two cases.'

Gallini raised his eyebrows. Notwithstanding his drinking habit, he did not look like a man who appreciated drama. He nudged Lombroso out of the way and resumed his own examination.

'As I thought,' Lombroso said, peering over Gallini's shoulder until he turned and glared at him. 'It is similar but not identical to the body at the Abbey San Callisto.'

'Meaning?' Machinetti asked tersely.

'Meaning that both were drained of blood.'

Ottolenghi and James exchanged glances.

Lombroso continued. 'But in this case, rather than all of the organs having been removed, we are missing only one – the heart.'

'Perhaps he was disturbed,' Gallini said.

'Entirely possible, I would say,' Lombroso agreed.

'Anything else in terms of human intervention?' Tullio asked.

'I cannot tell for certain,' Lombroso replied. 'But there does seem to be the residue of a kind of crystalline compound. Can you see?' He took a clean scalpel from a nearby table and scraped it along the surface of the skin. Tiny white crystals were visible on the blade.

'Is that salt?' Tullio asked.

'It might be.' Lombroso rubbed his finger over the body. 'No, actually I think it is something else . . . I believe it is arsenic.'

'As commonly used in the funeral trade,' James said. 'If that is so, then clearly there has been some attempt to preserve the body.'

'Ah yes, I was waiting for someone to say that,' Lombroso said. 'I think that is entirely likely.'

'So the draining of blood and the organ removal means that there is a link between this body, the girl in the abbey and the one found in the woods,' James said.

They stood in silence for a moment, digesting this thought. There was a knock, and an officer came in carrying a bundle wrapped in a cloth. He looked first at Machinetti and then at Tullio, clearly trying to work out which to approach.

'Bring it to me,' Lombroso said.

The officer went to him and gratefully handed over the

bundle. 'This was found at the Borgo, not far from the girl in the stream,' he said, his eyes wandering to her remains.

Lombroso ushered him out, then placed the bundle on a table and unwrapped it carefully as Gallini looked on.

'What is it?' Tullio asked.

Lombroso's brow creased. 'It is a stone pot containing our missing organ, a human heart,' he said. 'And it seems that, unlike the rest of the body, this is cold, as if it has been preserved in ice. It is still absolutely fresh.'

'Of course there is another possibility,' James said.

'And that is?' Tullio asked.

'That the heart does not belong to this body at all. Which would mean—'

Lombroso interrupted him. 'There could be another victim.'

28

In the intense heat of passion, all the moral restraints
that evolution has built up slowly over time dissolve in
a flash, like a fine veil in the flame, with even civilised
men becoming killers and cannibals. Women, in these
extraordinary, transient, atavistic reversions, become the
cruellest of the cruel. They tear out the tongue of the
corpse, disfigure its manhood, prolong their victim's agony,
and demonstrate their thirst for inflicting pain.

Lombroso and Ferrero, 1893, p. 66

Following the post-mortem, James and Ottolenghi had been
sent ahead to the museum at the university to make prepara-
tions for the interviews with the prostitutes from Madame
Giulia's. Lombroso had stayed behind to discuss the case with
Tullio, Gallini and, at his insistence, Machinetti.

As they walked in the warm sunshine across the Piazza
Castello towards the Via Po, James had the chance to observe
his friend more closely. Ottolenghi had been strangely silent
throughout the post-mortem, hanging back where he would
usually be taking much more of an interest. James had always
admired his friend's curiosity and eagerness to learn, and this
reticence was out of character.

'This monster wants to get our attention, as if murder is not enough,' he said.

Ottolenghi merely nodded. It seemed that he just did not want to talk. Undeterred, James tried again. 'You have not told me about Vienna,' he said. 'Do you still think there could be a link to vampirism?'

The vestige of a frown crossed Ottolenghi's brows and he seemed to slow down a little. He paused outside the Caffe Torino. 'Do we have time for a coffee, do you think?' he asked.

'I think so,' James said. 'Let's have some lunch, too. It could be a long afternoon.'

They went in, sat down and ordered. When he had first visited the place, James had thought it splendid, with its marble pillars, elaborate murals and huge gilt mirrors. Now its decor seemed overblown. Lucy would no doubt give it a human personality, saying it was boastful and shallow like an eighteenth-century fop. In his own mind James compared it with the scene in the mortuary – the enticing aroma of coffee replaced by the smells of death and the delicate snacks laid out in glass cases by the corpse of the young girl lying on the table waiting to be dissected. Ottolenghi sat, quiet and pale, staring into a cognac purchased with his coffee, he had said, in order to steady his nerves.

'So, Vienna, then . . . What was it like working with Reiner?' James asked. 'It must have been fascinating.'

'You remember Reiner from last year?' Ottolenghi asked.

'Yes, I do. A queer sort of fellow, as I recall.' James thought back to his encounter with the man during the symposium on criminal anthropology that had been the backdrop to a series of horrible murders. 'He had a rather too fervent interest in sexual murder for my taste.'

'Yes, and that was the nature of his research project. But his particular focus was on the vampire aspect.'

'I don't know a great deal about vampires,' James admitted. 'They drink blood and have an interest in dead bodies, don't they? I have read a short story on the subject, but other than that ...'

'Same here ... or at least that was the case before I got to Vienna.'

'What's the connection between vampires and sexual murder? I mean, they're fictional, aren't they?'

'They don't rise from the dead, if that's what you mean, but they do have certain interests.'

'Such as?'

'Necrophilia,' Ottolenghi said, shivering slightly. 'Arousal by the dead body. Then there is necrophagia – the eating of human flesh – and necro-sadism, which is the abuse of dead bodies.'

James gave a low whistle. 'That is disturbing material for anyone to examine.'

'Reiner claims that a presumption of *Lustmord* – or murder out of lust – is always given when injuries to the genitals are found. The erotic attachment to dead flesh is, according to him, inextricably linked to such crimes.'

'That makes sense, but where does vampirism come in? The story I read had a supernatural element. I can't see Reiner taking much of an interest in that.'

'He claims that the supernatural has in the past been used as an explanation for otherwise inexplicable events, but the reality is more worrying. Apparently there is a long history of sexually motivated crimes where the perpetrator has an interest in the blood of the victim. You may remember the professor mentioning such a case last year.'

'Eusebius Pieydagnelle from Milan?'

'Yes, that's right. The smell of blood in a butcher's shop triggered a condition that led to him murdering six women.'

'But even he did not drain the blood from the corpse. I have not heard of anyone doing that.'

'There have been such cases, and Reiner was keen to collate information on all of them ... very keen, in fact.'

'So are you suggesting that this is the work of such a killer?'

Ottolenghi shrugged. 'I cannot say, but it is at least a possibility that we should consider.'

'And have you told the professor?'

'Yes, after we found the girl in the Abbey San Callisto.'

'What did he say?'

'He was sceptical, as he always is about any ideas that aren't his.'

'I know, I know ... but that doesn't mean he hasn't tucked it away in his brain somewhere, ready to dredge it up as his own theory. And of course, at that point we had no obvious link between the victims, whereas now not only is there another shallow grave but also evidence of preservation, or at least an attempt at it.'

'There was one case that Reiner told me about that does have some marked similarities, in some respects anyway,' Ottolenghi said, drawing closer. The café was crowded, but James thought that most people seemed far too involved in their own conversations to be interested in theirs.

'Go on.'

'It concerns a seventeenth-century Hungarian countess, Elisabeth Bathory. The legend has it that one of her maids accidentally cut herself and blood found its way onto the countess's skin. She thought that she detected a rejuvenation of the area affected.'

'An anti-ageing lotion of some kind?'

'Yes . . . Well you can probably guess what happened next.'

'Girls started to go missing?'

'At first no one thought anything of it. They were all girls from the town and most were thought to have—'

'Run away?' James said.

Ottolenghi nodded. 'Eventually she turned her attention to girls from noble families. This could not be overlooked.'

'But the missing village girls could?' James said. 'Nothing changes really, does it? What happened then?'

'Bathory and a number of accomplices were arrested, and her castle was searched.'

Ottolenghi paused for a moment as their food arrived – two steaming plates of pasta. James began to tuck into his immediately. It had been a long time since breakfast.

'What did they find?'

'Dead girls, dying girls, girls awaiting torture. Some were in cages with spikes on the sides. Others were just found lying on the floor. Bites had been taken out of them.'

'Horrible!' James said. 'What happened to the countess?'

'She was kept prisoner whilst her so-called accomplices were accused of witchcraft and tortured. One had her fingers severed, Reiner said.'

James paused with his fork between his plate and his mouth and stared at his pasta – penne, fat yellow tubes in a deep red tomato sauce. He put the fork down. 'And then?'

'All kinds of rumours were circulating at the time, so it is quite difficult to separate fact from fiction. There were accusations of satanic rituals and various occultists being invited to visit the castle. But none of this was actually proved.'

'And the countess? Was she tried for murder?'

'Due to her position, Bathory herself was never convicted

of a crime, though her servants were. Most of them were executed – decapitated, burnt alive, and so on.'

'Lucky for her,' James said.

'Not really,' Ottolenghi said. 'She did not escape lightly. As far as her family was concerned, she had disgraced them and put their lands and standing at risk. They walled her up in her bedroom with just a few slits left open for ventilation and food. She died a few years later.'

'That's quite a story,' James said. 'It's a very old case. What was Reiner's interest?'

'He thought it was a classic case of *Lustmord*. The mutilations of the victims suggested that Bathory and her accomplices had an interest in necrophagia.'

'So not just a beauty treatment, then?'

'Not entirely, though she *was* beautiful from all accounts. Her skin was particularly fine, apparently – very pale and pure-looking. She was said to bathe in blood drained from the girls in order to keep it that way.'

A vision of the pale body of Concetta Panatti lying naked in a bath of blood came unbidden into James's mind. 'That is interesting,' he said, blinking as if to rid himself of the image. 'We should tell the professor and Tullio. It might well be relevant.'

Ottolenghi nodded and smiled. 'James, you don't know how good it is to talk this over with someone normal.'

James smiled back at him uncertainly. He wasn't sure if 'normal' really described him, but it was good to see his friend looking more relaxed. 'I take it Reiner was ... well, how should I put it?'

'He was very focused on his work ... too focused, I felt. The intensity with which he told me this tale was strange to say the least. He went into every last detail, and really seemed to be enjoying himself.'

'I presume he is safely tucked away in Vienna. He couldn't be a suspect, could he?' James said, half joking.

'No, or at least I don't think so. He was due to give a paper at a conference in Salzburg. He left Vienna at the same time as me.'

'I suppose there could be something in it.'

Ottolenghi hesitated. 'I know it seems rather far-fetched, but as the professor is so fond of saying, we should exclude nothing until we have considered the evidence.'

'And that amounts to the remains of three women, at least two of them with the blood drained from their bodies, and organs removed from all three.'

'It might be someone who is aware of the Bathory case perhaps trying to emulate it in some way,' Ottolenghi suggested.

'Is that what you meant at the abbey?'

Ottolenghi nodded. 'I may have been a little melodramatic, but it seemed so similar, it shook me. I felt as if it had followed me here all the way from Vienna.'

'Perhaps we should be thinking about another question,' James said.

'Which is?'

'What happened to all that blood?'

29

*The born prostitute – lacking maternal and family feel-
ing, unscrupulous in the pursuit of her desires, and mildly
criminalistic – presents the complete type of moral insanity. This fact, too, helps explain her lack of modesty, for
immodesty is characteristic of morally insane women . . .
The fact that the germ of prostitution lies not in lust but
moral insanity also explains prostitutes' sexual precocity,
which is nothing more than an aspect of that general early
propensity for evil which one finds in the morally insane.*

Lombroso and Ferrero, 1893, pp. 216–17

Lucy glanced over at Sofia as they walked back together to the
Lombroso house in silence. Was there really nothing between
her and James apart from her missing cousin? As usual James
had rushed off. But, she thought ruefully, at least he was fully
occupied. The prospect of another empty afternoon with Miss
Trott stretched ahead.

'You seem unhappy,' Sofia said.

'I feel so . . . so . . . trapped.'

'Trapped by what?'

'By everything, everybody! I want to be free.'

'You are free.'

'How? How am I free, Sofia?' She pulled at her drab grey

dress. 'My clothes are chosen for me. My reading is chosen for me. I cannot go anywhere unescorted. I am not permitted to speak to anyone without my brother's permission. I cannot choose my own future. Where is the freedom in that?'

'None of us are really free,' Sofia said. 'You have security. You are loved.'

'What, by James? He is only interested in his own future. He cares nothing for mine!'

'As I have told you before, he cares more than you think.'

'He still treats me like a child. He thinks I am capable of nothing but marriage and children.'

'Would that be so bad?' Sofia asked.

'It isn't that I don't want to be married, but the thought of spending the rest of my days attending to domestic matters...' Lucy groaned. 'I cannot imagine anything worse. There is so much else of interest out there to be studied. Besides, how can I become a great writer if I am forced to spend my time choosing menus and looking after children? I would just be replacing one prison with another.'

'There is nothing wrong with marriage if you have the right man,' Sofia said wistfully.

'Is that what you would like?' Lucy asked, watching her.

'Perhaps... but he would have to be a certain kind of man.'

'What kind?'

'Loving, thoughtful, trusting – able to allow me to do as I wish.'

'And have you met such a man?' Lucy asked.

'I thought I had met him, but we could not be together.'

'If you love him, then you should let nothing get in your way.'

'That is easier said than done,' Sofia said quietly.

'I can make my own way from here,' Lucy said as they approached the Via Legnano. 'Please, Sofia – allow me a few seconds of my own company at least.'

'Make sure you go straight back.'

'I will.' She watched as Sofia walked away towards the museum. As soon as she was out of sight, Lucy took a detour down a side street. She had been given a gift – a tiny morsel of freedom – but she was hungry for more, whatever it might cost her.

When James and Ottolenghi arrived at the museum, they found Sofia standing outside next to a huddle of girls who were laughing and chattering amongst themselves. Their profession was not immediately obvious. They were all dressed in similar hooded cloaks, differing only in colour and the odd detail – a ribbon here and a button there. James noticed that Ada, the girl who had asked him to help find her missing friend, was not among them.

'I do not think the university will like this,' Sofia muttered.

A carriage stood by the entrance. An elegant hand beckoned to Sofia from the window as they approached.

'Signora Panatti,' Sofia said and nodded in acknowledgement.

'Signorina Esposito, how are you?'

Sofia gave a guarded smile. 'I am well, *grazie*. Wouldn't you prefer to wait inside?'

'Yes, I would. Signor Murray is late. I will have to admonish him.' James noticed Sofia raise her eyebrows slightly.

He approached the carriage and bowed. The door opened and he held out his hand to Concetta Panatti, who stepped out elegantly and made her way into the building. As they entered, James noticed the contrast between the cacophony created by the girls outside and the tranquillity inside.

A red-faced Professor Gemelli stood waiting for them.

'What is the meaning of this? Where is Professor Lombroso?'

Concetta Panatti stepped forward and extended her gloved hand towards him. 'I'm sure he will be here soon.'

Gemelli's mouth was hanging open. He took her hand and shook it.

'May I introduce the dean of the faculty, Professor Gemelli,' James said.

'I know the professor. We have met before... many times. Delighted to see you again,' Concetta Panatti said to a now blushing Gemelli. 'I am such an admirer of the university. I find the male intellect so attractive. I am sure my employees will be delighted to see you again.'

Gemelli paused while he recovered himself. 'I take it you are here at the invitation of Professor Lombroso?'

'Yes, the dear man asked me to bring some of my young ladies to the university to be interviewed.'

'Really?'

'Yes, Professor. I do so apologise for the noise. But you see, they are so excited to be here... in a seat of learning, as it were.'

'Well, quite, but they cannot stay there... er, here, rather.'

'Why not? They will be so disappointed.'

'Well, you see... that is to say...'

The door opened and Lombroso backed in. 'Yes, ladies, I will let you in shortly. Please be patient for a little while longer.'

He surveyed the scene: Gemelli standing next to Concetta

Panatti, with James, Ottolenghi and Sofia watching. 'What an interesting tableau,' he remarked.

Concetta Panatti smiled, though not with her eyes, James noticed. 'There! You see, I said that the professor would be here before too long, and here he is, come to rescue us all.'

Lombroso responded with a deep bow.

'That is all very well. But what of the ... er ... young ladies?' Gemelli said.

'That should have been dealt with when they arrived.' Lombroso glared at James and Ottolenghi. 'Where have you two gentlemen been? I distinctly remember telling you to come here directly and organise the interviews. You see, Signora Panatti, what I have to put up with.'

She nodded sympathetically. 'Indeed I do, Professor. You are both very bad!' she said, looking intently at James and smiling slyly again.

'I do apologise,' James said. He noticed that Ottolenghi remained silent.

'I will deal with you both later,' Lombroso said. 'Now can you get on with the work I asked you to do and sort out our subjects outside?'

'About that,' Gemelli said. 'Lombroso ... a word.'

'While you two gentlemen discuss things, perhaps Signor Murray could conduct his interview with me?' Concetta Panatti said.

'Very well,' Lombroso replied. 'Ottolenghi, Sofia – can you deal with the ladies? Murray, why don't you show Signora Panatti around before you talk to her? Now, Gemelli, you wished to discuss something with me. Will it take long? I am extremely busy, as you can see ...'

They strode up the stairs together, Gemelli trying to keep up with Lombroso and talking all the while. James could not hear all of it, but the words 'unacceptable' and 'expressly forbidden' told him all he wanted to know.

Concetta Panatti took his arm and seemed to guide him towards one of the many entrances to the exhibits rooms, as if it was she doing the escorting. Sofia's posture was rigid and her mouth was set in a grim line.

'Would you give me a moment, Signora Panatti?' James said.

'Of course, but do not be too long. There is so much for us to discuss.'

He went over to Sofia. 'It was not Chiara.'

Sofia crossed herself. 'Thank God. Who was it?'

'A flower seller called Caterina Spirito.'

'From San Callisto?'

He nodded. 'Chiara is safe, I am sure of it.'

'I hope you are right,' Sofia said. 'But none of us can know until she is found, and the other girls too. James . . .'

'What?'

'Take care.' She glanced towards the exhibits rooms for a few seconds before leaving to help Ottolenghi in his efforts to organise the girls.

Concetta Panatti swept back in. 'Signor Murray, you are neglecting me.'

'I do apologise. There was something I needed to deal with.'

'It is of no matter. I found your colleague,' she said, indicating Anna Tarnovsky, who was waiting for them by one of the exhibits. 'She has been most helpful, although I imagine she is too busy to join us.'

'Not at all, Signora,' Anna said, smiling. 'After you, James.'

He led the way through the door. 'This is the corridor of skeletons, Signora,' he said as they wandered along the passage lined with the bones of executed criminals. She ran her fingers over them lightly, caressing them as she wandered past, and again he imagined pulling her to him, pressing his lips against hers and feeling her respond to his touch. Suddenly he thought of Sofia, with whom he had had a highly charged encounter in this very place when they had first met. He felt disloyal for a moment but pushed it out of his mind. Sofia had rejected him, and although he still had hopes for them as friends, he no longer believed that anything more was possible.

'How fascinating,' Concetta Panatti said. 'What do you think, Signora Tarnovsky?'

'I agree, they are very interesting.'

'But, of course, one might ask why the professor has collected them. Should they not have been buried? What about their families?'

'They were all criminals, Signora Panatti,' Anna said. 'As I am sure you know, they would not be buried in consecrated ground.'

'Still, their loved ones might wish to remember them, for all their badness in life,' Concetta Panatti said.

'I would not have thought you would be so sentimental,' Anna said. 'A criminal is a criminal for all eternity . . . unless of course he has seen fit to confess his sins before God prior to death.'

'Now it is you who sound sentimental.'

'Not a God-fearing woman then, signora?'

'I fear no one, deity or otherwise.'

'Perhaps we should try another room?' James said, hoping to dilute the tension, though he suspected it was his alone.

'I think not,' Concetta Panatti said. 'I think it is time we started our interview.' She glanced at Anna. 'You need not trouble yourself. I am sure the Professor will have some tasks for you to perform.'

Anna narrowed her eyes. 'I will leave you to it, then.'

'Thank you, Anna,' James said. He indicated a small office. 'Shall we, signora?'

'How kind,' Concetta Panatti said, smiling insincerely at Anna.

'*Too* kind,' Anna murmured before mouthing a good luck to James.

He was relieved to be away from the crossfire. Now he just had to deal with one force of nature rather than two.

'So, Signor Murray... May I call you James?' Concetta Panatti asked.

James attempted a reply. 'Well, Signora Panatti...'

'Concetta, please.'

'I do not think the professor would approve.'

'But he is not here, James, so when it is just you and I...'

James nodded, making a mental note to try not to use her name at all. He could not say why, but it just seemed wrong... too intimate, too personal.

'Your questions, then, James,' Concetta said. She unfurled herself effortlessly on to a chaise longue until she was reclining elegantly as if posing for a portrait.

'Am I right in thinking that you have declined to use the professor's lie-detecting equipment?'

'That is so, James. I have no secrets – not from you – so I did not see the point. You can be certain that I will tell you the truth. And I am sure our relationship is such that you will do likewise.'

James cleared his throat. She always seemed able to unnerve him. 'May I ask you about your upbringing?'

'It was uneventful. My parents were unexciting people who

269

lacked imagination in almost every aspect of their lives, with the obvious exception of producing me.'

'Is there anything in your past that is significant?'

'In what respect?'

'In relation to your current profession.'

'I am a businesswoman, James.'

'Yes, but at least one of your business interests is considered by some to be immoral.'

'Running whores, you mean?'

He flinched at her terminology. 'You are trying to shock me.'

'I am sorry that you find my frankness disconcerting. For some reason I thought that you of all people would be more . . .' she paused, 'open. You must understand that I see what I do as more of a service to mankind. Men need physical love, James. You will know that. And that is the commodity I supply. It is no different to any of my other business concerns.'

'You say that, but you do not advertise your association with Madame Giulia's, do you?' James said.

She nodded. 'True, but that is because I prefer to maintain a certain position in society. As I have said before, people can be so judgemental.'

James hesitated. Ada's absence troubled him to the extent that he felt he could not ignore it.

'Tell me, do you have another place similar to Madame Giulia's?'

The smile froze on Concetta's face for an instant. 'What makes you ask that?'

'Oh, just something I heard.'

'Really? Well, as it is untrue, I think it better that you put it from your mind.' Her voice was harsher now, though still low and sensual.

'I notice one of the girls is missing... Ada, is it, the red-head?'

'You are very observant, James. I suppose it is because you are a scientist.'

'Perhaps,' he said. 'Where is she?'

'You would have to ask Valeria. She takes care of the girls. I did hear that one of them was... how shall I put it... indisposed? She had to leave us after she became diseased. I suppose that might have been Ada. As I have told you before, these girls come and go. Now, are you going to ask me some proper questions?'

James studied her. Her expression wasn't exactly hostile, but it was clear that the subject was closed.

'As you wish. Could we return to your past? Was there something in it that may have led to your work?'

She paused, her head tilted slightly, as if summing him up. 'I will tell you if you will tell me. What in your past provoked your interest in studying criminals? It will go no further. Just think of it as the affirming of trust between us.'

He paused for a moment. Could he trust her? He doubted it. 'I hope you do not think me rude, but I am here to interview you, not vice versa.'

There was a silence as she scrutinised him, her eyes narrowed as if she was trying her best to claw her way into his mind.

'It will be something to do with your father. It always is.'

He caught his breath. How could she possibly know? Who could have told her?

'I am right, am I not? From your reaction it must have been something extreme.'

'There is nothing to react to,' he said carefully.

'You are lying, James. I thought we had an understanding.'

'Why did you say "It always is"?' James asked. 'What did your father do to you?'

She laughed, but without humour. 'Everything and nothing.'

'Go on,' he said.

'Not until you tell me something personal about yourself.'

'What sort of thing?'

'A memory.'

'I have no memories that I wish to share.'

'Really? Then perhaps I will have to think of one for you. What about your work? I think there is a little frisson of excitement that goes through you when you see a question that needs to be answered. Am I right?'

He was unable to maintain eye contact with her.

'Now I wonder . . . your father, he is the one who taught you about desire . . . the desire to know, no matter what the price.'

'I don't know what you are talking about.'

'More lies, James. You should be ashamed.' She studied him. He could see that she was enjoying the effect she was having on him. 'I see that you *are* ashamed. What did he do, your father? Why has it had such an influence on you?'

'We must talk about you, not me.'

She shook her head in triumph. 'I think you are afraid of something or someone. Yes! You are afraid of yourself. Of what you are.'

Those words again. How should he react? He decided on caution. 'I will not say any more, signora. You agreed to talk to me. If you are not proposing to do so, then perhaps we should end this interview.' He prepared himself to leave.

'Wait!' she commanded. 'I have not finished.' She cast her eyes over him in appraisal, then smiled, but there was no pleasure in it. He thought he could detect something else. What was it? Scorn, perhaps? An underlying derision? She began to speak.

'It happened when I was thirteen. I had an encounter with one of my father's employees. He thought that I was his for the taking. I was not, as he learnt to his cost.'

'You hurt him?'

'I killed him.'

James had not been expecting that. She had spoken defiantly. It was clear that she felt no remorse. 'And were there consequences?' he asked.

'I told the truth – that it was self-defence – and no charges were brought. The man's family were paid off at my mother's insistence, but my father . . .'

'What did he do?'

'He did nothing, but he made it clear that he did not believe me. He told me that I was born bad.' She hesitated, leaning back and closing her eyes.

'And?'

'He was certainly right. In fact I have spent the rest of my life proving him so.'

'You run a brothel. There are worse things.'

She got up from the chaise longue and stepped towards him. He found himself flinching as she laid her hand upon his face, caressing it slowly before tracing the shape of his lips with her finger. Instinctively he gripped her wrist and moved her hand away. Again she mocked him with her smile. 'Oh, I have done worse things,' she whispered into his ear. 'As have you.'

She went to the door and turned the key, then walked back to him until they were so close that he felt her breath on his face – an earthy aroma like a forest after the rain. She brushed her lips lightly over his, sending a frisson of longing through him. Her response was another kiss – long, deep, sensuous. It was as if the world around them had ceased to exist. She did not want it to end there, that much was clear.

He did not love her. She was not that kind of woman. But in that instant, part of him wanted to be possessed by her. She had him now, and if he did not stop her, he knew that she would never let him go. His path to self-destruction was only too clear. He had betrayed Sofia with that kiss, but then he did not deserve her love. This... this was what he deserved. Because unlike Sofia, Concetta Panatti knew what he really was.

At that moment, he understood that if he allowed this to continue, then his life, all that James Murray was and could ever be, would begin slowly and inexorably to unravel. That was too high a price to pay. He had others to think of.

He pushed Concetta Panatti away.

She stood back, contempt in her eyes. 'Too late, James, too late.'

30

In England under the Restoration, masses of women assisted in the hideous tortures of the Puritans. These were acts of impotent cruelty, a type that gives pleasure without any expenditure of energy. Like all human activities in which a power outside the individual produces pleasure, so too, ferocious or cruel activities can cause delight, the delight of blood intoxication.

Lombroso and Ferrero, 1893, p. 67

Lucy stood in the main hall of the Museo Egizio and viewed her mummified companions lying snugly in their sarcophagi. It reminded her of when she and James had been taken by their father to the British Museum to see the collection of Egyptian artefacts. She had found the experience profoundly moving, and James had teased her a little for being tearful over an account of the death and burial of a young boy. Her father had been far more understanding, or so she had thought at the time. But that was before everything had changed. Lucy's memories of that period were odd, disjointed things: the sound of muffled voices raised but indistinct; her mother sobbing inconsolably and James kneeling at her feet trying to comfort her; and an overwhelming feeling that something dreadful had happened. But the worst memory of all was that of her increasing and terrible realisation that her father's absence was permanent because of something bad that he had done. Somehow she had decided that it must be her fault too, and she had tried to make amends by bargaining with God in her prayers. But it had not worked, and now her father was dead and her mother too.

The mummies, or rather their cases, were elaborately decorated with pictures and hieroglyphics. They had tried to cheat death by planning an existence in the afterworld, and they too had been let down by their gods. Perhaps that was why she felt their pain so acutely. She certainly seemed to be sensitive to such things, as Professor Donati had pointed out last time she had been here. But that was not the reason for her coming here today. Miss Trott had met with the Egyptologist and argued with him. Lucy wanted to know why.

'Signorina Murray, I am delighted that you are visiting us again.' Professor Donati was behind her, smiling enigmatically. He did not look suspicious or guilty, or even remotely shifty, Lucy thought. But perhaps that was an act in itself.

'Professor Donati, thank you for agreeing to see me.'

'Not at all. I had hoped you would come.' He glanced behind her. 'No Francesco today, or anyone else?'

'No, Professor. Today I came alone.'

She scrutinised him. When she had first met him, she had thought him dapper, but now she could see that his face was fleshy and slightly dissipated. He might have been considered handsome in his youth, but that was no longer the case, and in his heart he knew it. He stared back at her. His eyes were a deep brown and had a tendency to wander, as if he was searching for something worthwhile to focus on. Disconcertingly, once they had alighted upon her, it felt for a moment as if he was inside her mind.

'Ah, you are a modern young lady then. That is refreshing, I suppose. Have you told anyone that you are here?'

'I have not, Professor. But then I do not see why my brother can travel anywhere he chooses on his own whereas I am expected to seek company whether I want it or not.' He looked a little anxious, presumably in response to the suggestion of female emancipation. 'Perhaps modern is not strictly accurate. I see myself more as an explorer in a foreign city.'

'You are certainly that, signorina. What is it you wish to explore?'

'I wanted to discuss the artefacts you showed us last time I was here. Would that be possible?'

'I am working with some new exhibits down in the basement. Would you care to accompany me? Strictly speaking, of course, you should be chaperoned, but as you are so progressive in your outlook, perhaps you would not mind?'

Lucy hesitated for a moment, but then nodded her acceptance. 'I would think that the search for knowledge should always take precedence over niceties, Professor. Thank you.'

'Excellent. Please follow me. We will be undisturbed down here.' He started to walk down some broad stone steps into the bowels of the building, humming the same tune as when they had first met. Lucy followed him. He was not wearing his long coat or skullcap today, but was dressed in a sombre suit. She noticed that it was worn in places and the sleeves were fraying at the cuffs.

There were no windows in the room where the professor was working, so it was darker and more oppressive than the others she had seen. They were quite alone. A number of metal tools were lying on a nearby table next to some pieces of stone. Could one of them be a scalpel? Lucy started as she saw some figures staring back at her from the corner. She relaxed when she realised that it was just a facsimile of a tomb with wax representations of the participants.

'A scene from the Book of the Dead, signorina. I thought it might interest you.'

Lucy peered at the figures. 'It is unusual to find such a thing in a museum, is it not?'

The professor nodded in a not entirely convincing show of humility. 'We are the first to include waxworks, I believe. They will go on display in the next week or so. I felt it was important to give the visitor a sense of what it was like to be at such a ritual.'

'To bring it to life?'

'Indeed, though I accept that given the subject matter, the motive might be seen as somewhat ironic.'

Lucy shivered.

'I hope I have not frightened you, signorina,' the professor said. He was standing close to her now and leaning towards her. He smelt of cheap cologne. She stepped away from him and his beady eyes followed her.

'No, no. It is a little cold, that's all,' she said.

'Ah yes. We deliberately keep it cool down here in order to preserve some of our rarer exhibits.'

Lucy studied the decorations on the robe worn by the priest overseeing the ritual. There it was again, she noticed – the green and gold serpent . . .

'I see you are looking at Apep, the evil demon,' the professor observed. 'He is an interesting character. Or deity, perhaps I should say. One would not want to upset him. He is an extremely powerful entity.'

'In what respect?' Lucy asked.

'In every respect. If crossed, he has the power of complete

destruction. He is the encircler of the world, the dark demon, the spirit of evil.'

'You speak of him as if he was real.'

The professor hesitated. 'Well now, who are we to say that he is not?'

'Are there people who believe in Apep?'

'He has a following in some quarters, and his wife as well, of course – Tawaret, the demon goddess.'

'I didn't know that gods and demons got married.'

'I imagine it was a rather different institution from the one that we enjoy today.'

Lucy thought his use of language interesting. She wasn't at all sure that marriage was something to be enjoyed, particularly if you were a wife. 'So people actually worship Apep?'

'There are all manner of gods.'

'Something for everyone, then.'

'It is not a joking matter, signorina. It is entirely possible that those who follow these gods or demons, whichever you prefer, are a danger to themselves and perhaps even others.' He frowned at her. 'I do hope that you are not—'

'Oh no, I am asking merely for information, Professor. But I am interested in any rituals that might be connected.'

'And the nature of your interest?'

'Purely academic, Professor.'

'You are a very self-assured young lady.'

Lucy considered this. She hadn't felt anything of the kind when she arrived in Turin. Might that have changed? She decided to maintain her apparent boldness. 'How well do you know Miss Trott?'

'What an extraordinary question! I don't, except of course for our meeting when you were present. Why do you ask?'

There was no point in shilly-shallying. No self-respecting

detective would do that. 'I saw you together at a café in the Via Po.' Was it her imagination, or did the professor's brows furrow ever so slightly at this?

'Yes, of course. My apologies. I had quite forgotten. We met by chance. She is a charming lady.'

'You didn't seem to find her so,' Lucy said. 'In fact you seemed to be shouting at her, if anything.'

'You . . . you must have been mistaken, signorina.' He took a few steps towards her. Again she backed away, but this time he continued until she was trapped against a wall.

'Forgive me, Professor Donati, but I must go. I have to meet someone.'

'I thought you had told no one of your visit here.'

'I was mistaken.'

He hesitated for a second before standing aside. 'Then I wonder if I might escort you out. I am afraid that I too have remembered an appointment.' He moved towards the door and waited for her.

'Of course, and thank you for showing me the exhibit. Perhaps we shall meet again soon.'

'Perhaps,' he replied in a tone that made it clear that he would rather they didn't. 'But I would have thought that a young lady like yourself, with such a pure kind of beauty, should be concentrating on more appropriate matters – marriage and children, for instance.'

'There will be time enough for that,' Lucy said. 'For the present, I prefer the pursuit of knowledge to that of a husband.'

'Be careful, Signorina Murray. Too much knowledge can be a dangerous thing.'

'I am not sure that you have that quite right, Professor,' Lucy said.

Donati merely raised his eyebrows and gave a supercilious smile as he gesticulated towards the steps.

Lucy obediently followed him upstairs. At the entrance, she said goodbye and began the short walk home. She forced herself to look back and saw him watching her intently. After a moment, he swivelled on his heel and went back into the museum. Looking down, she noticed that her hands were trembling. She shook them gently and focused on the facts. What exactly did he mean by 'a pure kind of beauty'?

All in all, she felt that had discovered very little. Still, what she had found out seemed significant. Anna Tarnovsky was married, so if James was involved with her it was an illicit liaison. Sofia was hiding something, and that something was to do with James. Miss Trott was in Turin for a purpose other than being her companion, but its nature was as yet unknown, although it seemed there was some connection with Professor Donati. Whether or not it was related to Apep, the evil demon, was still a mystery, but of one thing she was sure: Donati had lied to her about his relationship with Miss Trott. In fact he had been quite menacing towards her. What Lucy didn't know was why.

As James walked into Lombroso's laboratory, he was immediately taken back to the last time he had been in Turin. Even the equipment that Ottolenghi was setting up seemed no different.

After what had just passed between him and Concetta Panatti, it was a relief to get back the comparatively mundane nature of the experiments with her girls. He could still smell her musky scent on him. It made him feel unclean. She had consumed him so completely that it was hard to shake the memory away. Something else was there too – an overwhelming sense of guilt that gnawed at him even now and could surely only become more marked as time went on. Dealing with the professor's experiments would provide a welcome distraction.

'The plethysmograph – is that your lie-detecting machine, Professor?' he asked.

Lombroso was standing next to it. The expression on his face was that of a father watching as his beloved child took its first steps. 'Yes, I suppose so, although there is a sphygmograph needed too. I have made some changes so that it is more responsive. And I would not call it a lie-detecting machine. Really, Murray . . . you should know by now that to name it so would be overstating the capability of what we have here.'

James nodded, realising that it would be utterly pointless to remind the professor that it was he who had named the equipment in the first place.

'Anyway, the most it can tell us about these girls is how their vascular system responds to various questions,' Lombroso added. 'That is what we are about today.'

'I suppose what we are really examining is the extent to which the body betrays itself,' Ottolenghi said as he tugged on some wiring.

James walked over to his friend, who seemed to be struggling rather. His face was a study in concentration as he twiddled with various knobs. It was an odd-looking piece of equipment. At its heart was a kind of airtight glove attached to a rubber membrane. This in turn was connected to a pen that rolled over the surface of a rotating drum.

'Remind me, Professor, how does it work?'

'Really, can't you remember from last time, Murray?'

James shrugged. A lot had happened to him since then.

Surely it was not reasonable to expect him to recall every last detail. But then reasonableness was not one of Lombroso's strengths at the best of times.

'Well do me the courtesy of listening now, and try not to forget again,' Lombroso said slowly, as if addressing a small child, another of his less than endearing habits. 'The speed of the pen varies with the subject's blood flow. We believe that when someone tells a lie, the stress of deception affects his or her heart rate and blood pressure. If the researcher watches and observes the deviations traced by the pen, then he might be able to tell if and when the subject is lying.'

'I see. So how do you wish us to conduct the experiment? Do you have a list of questions?'

'I do. Ottolenghi kindly worked on them before he left to study fairy tales with Reiner.'

'They're not fairy tales, Professor,' Ottolenghi protested. 'Some of what he told me—'

'Yes, yes, we don't have time to go into it now,' Lombroso said, shaking his head impatiently. 'Let's get the first subject in. Are you ready?'

Each subject had to be connected up to the machine, which was not an easy task in itself. The girls tended to wriggle about and pull off the wires if they found them uncomfortable. The machine was accurate in some cases but not in all. The results were interesting, according to Lombroso, apparently indicating that the subjects were, for the most part, lying about their pasts. They were far franker about the present, it seemed, which Lombroso said was only to be expected, given their weak moral sensitivity and lack of feeling. James was not certain that he agreed completely with the professor's summary of their findings. It seemed to him that most of the women they had spoken to were quite frank about their motivations for embarking on a career in prostitution. The only lies they told were to themselves, and related to the future rather than the past. Many seemed convinced that they would escape their situation and retire either through being rescued by a respectable man or becoming the exclusive property of a rich one.

'Women keep tears in their pockets,' Lombroso declared. 'Not only that, but they also have two sorts of tears: one for sadness and the other for deceit.'

'And are these results from previous experiments?' James asked, half joking.

'No, they are well-known Italian proverbs,' Lombroso replied, as if that amounted to scientific discovery and fact. He was very fond of proverbs, James had noticed, as well as anecdotes. But was it really science?

One of the last girls to be seen was Nora, who had been measured at Madame Giulia's. She was slightly older than the others they had encountered, and had reminded James a little of Sofia – or more accurately of what Sofia might have become had Lombroso not rescued her.

Ottolenghi showed her in and guided her to the couch. She sat down and stared at the equipment. 'What in heaven's name is that?'

'It is a device for measuring the blood pressure and so on. Murray, will you strap the lady in?'

Nora laughed. 'Lady? It is a long time since anyone has referred to me as such. And to have such learned gentlemen dance attendance on me – what a treat!'

Carefully James pushed Nora's sleeve up and put her arm into the airtight glove. 'You have a very gentle touch, Dottore,' she said.

'Now, Signor Murray here will ask you some questions. Here, Murray, take these.' Lombroso handed him a list.

'What is your name?' he asked.

'Ah – an easy one to start with. I am called Nora Santorini, these days anyway. I did have another name, the one I was christened with, but that was so long ago now I have forgotten it.'

'I find that hard to believe, signorina.'

'Yes, yes. Get on with it!' Lombroso said impatiently.

'How did you come to your current profession?'

'How very polite you are! But then that is an English trait, is it not?'

'I am from Scotland, actually. Can you tell us how you became a...' He paused, not knowing how to put it.

'A whore... You can say it, Signor Scozzese. I do not mind speaking plainly.' Her smile had left her. 'I left my home in the countryside to come to the city to find work. The Morals Squad found me on the streets and... let's just say they found a use for me.'

'You were forced into prostitution?' James asked. He had heard of the dreaded Morals Squad from Sofia, but had not quite believed her account. Perhaps he had been wrong to doubt her.

'*Sì*, it is a common enough story.'

'Do you enjoy your work?' Lombroso asked.

James frowned at the list. The question was not there.

'I am good at what I do. Would you like an appointment, Professor? Perhaps I could demonstrate it to you.'

'With all due respect, signorina, that is not the same as enjoyment,' Lombroso said. 'Does it fulfil you, make you happy?'

'Make me happy? You would like to believe that, I think.

All my clients would, too. But you want the truth, don't you? Now let me see . . . do I enjoy lying on my back for any man who wants to buy the privilege, however old or dirty, allowing him to grope and grunt, to hold me down until I bruise, to salivate over me before he mounts me or to make me kneel before him for his pleasure . . .' She stopped and shrugged. 'And that is a good customer on a good day. Enjoy? What do you think?'

James focused on the machine. It was a good deal easier than looking Nora Santorini in the face. If she was lying, he would expect to see the pen moving up and down furiously as she spoke to reflect the change in her blood pressure. Instead it maintained a flat and steady line. There were no lies here. Perhaps the professor's machine was more efficient at the detection of lies than he had thought. Encouraged, he decided to try something.

'Have you been chosen for the other place?'

Finally the machine responded, and yet she had not spoken.

'What other place, Murray? What are you talking about?' Lombroso asked. 'That is not a question from the list!'

'No. I have not,' Nora said.

'Do you know about it? What goes on there?'

'I do not.' The machine continued to respond.

'What happened to Agnella?'

There was fear in Nora's eyes.

'Where is Ada?'

She ripped off the wires that attached her to the equipment, got off the couch and left the room.

The few remaining interviews had taken longer than James had anticipated. He had been forbidden by Lombroso to ask any further questions; they could not, he said, afford to lose any more girls. Given Nora's response, it seemed more and more likely that Agnella had not merely run off as Concetta had suggested, and that something had also happened to Ada. For the moment, however, he was forced to concentrate on the matter at hand.

Eventually Lombroso looked at his watch. 'I have to go, Murray. I have work to do. Can you complete the final experiment?' And then, before James could answer one way or another: 'The girl is waiting outside. I'll send her in.'

James was tired and hungry. Everyone else had been permitted to leave. Ottolenghi had departed to work on one of the professor's papers. Even Sofia had gone. Now he had another girl to interview before he too could make his way home.

'*Buonasera.*' The girl slid in through the door as if she did not want to be seen. 'Are you ready for me, Dottore?'

James did not recognise her. She had not been at Madame Giulia's when he had conducted the measuring experiments with the professor. She was blonde and well built in an obvious kind of way. No doubt she would be sought after for such charms, though they left James cold. There was something about her face... Her teeth protruded slightly from her full lips and her eyes were narrowed and sly. He doubted that he would be hearing much in the way of truth from her.

'Sit down on the couch, if you would,' he said. 'Now, could you roll up your sleeve?'

The girl obeyed. He attached the equipment with some care. She seemed to have positioned herself so that he had to lean over her to get everything into the right place, and he was acutely aware of the rise and fall of her breasts as he tightened the various wires.

'You seem nervous, Dottore,' she said. 'Perhaps a little

287

tumble might relax you. I wouldn't charge . . . well, not the first time anyway.'

James gave a thin smile. 'No thank you. I am perfectly relaxed already. Now, shall we get on?'

She grinned. 'Yes, let's.'

'Name?'

'Gabriella.'

'And how did you get into this line of business, Gabriella?'

'Through my family.'

'Could you explain a little?'

'My mother was a whore, my father was a thief.'

'So you were born into it?'

'You could say that, I suppose.'

'And how long have you been in your current position?'

'About five minutes,' Gabriella replied with a raucous cackle. 'I wouldn't mind staying in it a bit longer if only you'd take up my invitation.'

She was all smiles on the surface, but there was something else there too.

'The thing is, Gabriella, I don't think you want to be what you are.'

She stopped smiling immediately. 'Yes I do.'

The pencil swung up and down.

'Why?' James asked. 'Tell me. I genuinely want to know.'

'Do you? It's all very well for someone like you. You've never had to worry about where your next meal is coming from or whether you'll have a roof over your head. You stand there all fancy and la-di-da, doing experiments on us like we're nothing.'

'So I am right, then?'

'What comes next? Don't tell me. I suppose you want to

rescue me... Well I've been rescued before, *caro*. It's just more of the same.'

'I have no intention of rescuing you, as you put it. I am just curious, that's all.'

'Oh, I've had enough of this.' Like Nora before her, she ripped off the various wires and stood up. 'People like you make me sick. You want to examine us, hiding behind your science, when really you're just as bad as any of our clients. '

James shrugged and showed her out of the room. She stood by the door, her hands on her hips. 'Come on then. Escort me out.'

They went into the hall together and he was about to send her in the direction of the kitchen and the rear entrance when she turned to him.

'Oh no, Dottore. If I'm good enough to be researched, then I'm good enough for the front door.'

He tried to usher her through it quickly, but she stopped and gave him a disdainful stare. '*Arrivederci, Dottore*. I am sure we will be meeting again before too long.'

She made her way down the steps and walked over to a carriage that seemed to be waiting for her. The door opened and she got in. James watched as it drove away. He thought he caught a glimpse of red hair through the window, but he could not be certain. He rubbed his eyes. It had been a very long day.

31

Prostitutes are both sexually frigid and sexually precocious. They present us with a real tangle of contradictions: an eminently sexual profession, practised by women in who sexuality has almost been extinguished; and women who, despite their weak sexual drive, devote themselves to vice at an age when they are barely ready for sexual intercourse. What, then, is the origin of prostitution? Psychologically, as I will show, it originates not in lust but moral insanity.

Lombroso and Ferrero, 1893, p. 213

At dinner that evening, Lucy was decidedly on edge. First and foremost in her mind was whether Miss Trott could be involved in some kind of criminal enterprise. She decided to observe her carefully with a view to making some notes in her journal later. That was exactly what *Pinkerton's Detection Manual* would advise, she had no doubt.

She took a sideways glance at her companion and watched as she examined her food thoroughly before taking a mouthful. Each foray to the plate began as a mere speculative enquiry as to the fitness of the chosen morsel; once satisfied that it was indeed worthy, she would put it delicately into her mouth and chew it carefully.

No one could say that Miss Trott was an obvious candidate

for criminality. Of course, Lucy could consult the work of her esteemed host to assist her. She made a mental note to re-examine the volume *Criminal Man*, which, despite its name, did have some minor references to criminal women. No doubt Paola and Gina could also help in that regard. According to them, the professor had some pictures of female criminals, which might well be useful for identification purposes if nothing else. Perhaps she should consult him. Lucy tried to imagine the conversation but somehow couldn't.

Gina and Paola were talking animatedly to one other. They were evidently having some dispute, and their mother and Anna were acting as arbiters. Gina stabbed at her food with a fork, waving it around occasionally to emphasise her argument. Her mother gently took hold of her wrist and guided it back to her plate. Paola was more thoughtful, but Lucy could see that her points, though made with less passion, were more compelling, judging from the expression on Anna's face. Gina was losing the argument and she knew it.

Ottolenghi and Lombroso were deep in their own discussion, and as she studied them, the source of Gina's passion for argument became clear. The professor also waved his cutlery around as he spoke, though his movements were more expansive and his views delivered with a confidence that Gina did not yet possess. Naturally no one dared to guide his hand back to his plate.

Ottolenghi had his own version of passion, but it was more understated than the professor's. He had seemed initially to be a quiet sort of man, but here in the middle of some kind of debate he was bright-eyed and alert. He had a habit of pushing his round wire-framed glasses up the bridge of his long nose as he listened and nodded. He occasionally paused to eat, and when he did, he attacked his food, spearing it like a hunter, and then added his view on whatever was under discussion, as if spearing ideas too.

James was seated between the professor and Ottolenghi. Their conversation seemed to ebb and flow around him while he sat like a small island in the midst of it, staring into space and pushing his food around his plate. He was hunched over it in that way he had when he was worried about something, as if the burden had become so great that he could no longer sit upright. Lucy wished that he would confide in her. She knew he still saw her as a child, but she was mature enough to understand that something was wrong. He had been so confident and relaxed when they were travelling here, delighted and excited at the prospect of a new life. But now that man seemed to have disappeared completely, to be replaced by the old James: diminishing in stature almost daily after their father's illness had begun, as if he wanted nothing more than to shrink into the shadows of anonymity for ever more.

'I think our findings will reveal some interesting traits, both physical and emotional,' Lombroso said with a self-satisfied smile spreading across his face. 'Don't you think, Murray?'

James blinked and shook his head slightly.

'What? You do not agree?' Lombroso boomed. 'Then you must say why.'

'I'm sure you're right, Professor,' James said. 'Although as there is quite a lot of variation between the subjects, I am not sure that any patterns of behaviour will be established.'

Lombroso stroked his beard thoughtfully. 'That is true. They are by their nature contradictory. Some, for example, are both sexually frigid and sexually precocious. It is a real tangle.'

'Cesare, really!' Signora Lombroso shook her head at him. 'This is not suitable conversation for the dinner table. I do not know how many times I must say it.'

'I apologise, my dear,' Lombroso said airily. 'Murray here has opened up an interesting area for discussion.'

'Well discuss it later, please.' Signora Lombroso turned to Lucy. 'Are you looking forward to the marchesa's ball?'

'Yes, I am, signora, very much,' Lucy said, not entirely truthfully. She had not given it much thought recently. Still, it would be an interesting experience. She had not been to a ball before. Aunt Agnes did not approve of such things.

'We are going too,' Gina said. 'I cannot wait.'

'We shall be leaving early,' her mother said firmly. 'And I do not want any arguments or fuss when the time comes.'

'Very well, Mama,' Gina said, though from her expression it seemed that both fuss and arguments were more than likely.

'It sounds as if it will be quite an occasion,' Anna said. 'The marchesa tells me that she has done her best to invite everyone of interest in Turin.'

'Of course, those are very subjective criteria,' Lombroso said. 'What I find of interest and what the marchesa does might well be different.'

His wife smiled. 'I imagine your guest list would include members of the criminal fraternity, and I don't think the marchesa has that in mind.'

An image flashed into Lucy's mind of various convicts in prison uniforms shuffling in shackles around the marchesa's palazzo. Now that really would be interesting.

When dinner came to an end, as it was not a formal occasion, they all gathered in the drawing room for coffee, rather than separating according to gender. This was with the exception of Miss Trott, who had retired early again, pleading another headache. Freed from her surveillance, Lucy watched Anna take out a small, slim cigar, which Ottolenghi lit for her, and sit back in her armchair as she joined her male colleagues in their conversation, every inch their equal.

'Isn't she marvellous?' whispered Gina. Lucy nodded, but she knew it was not as simple as it appeared to be. It seemed to her that equality was dealt out when it suited but could be snatched away in a moment when it did not. She moved a little closer to the group under cover of studying one of the professor's criminal artefacts, which were arranged on a small shelf in a corner.

'I think the next step is to meet tomorrow morning, pull together all we have, including the data from Prague, and think about how it could be disseminated,' Lombroso was saying.

'Could we do this in the afternoon?' James asked. 'I have some business to attend to outside the city in the morning.'

His tone was anxious. What on earth was so pressing that he would take time off from his beloved research to attend to it?

'Very well, Murray,' Lombroso said. 'I am sure we can accommodate you, but make sure you are on time. I am anxious to present our findings to the wider world.'

'It will be particularly interesting to see if the findings reflect mine in Prague,' Anna said.

'Ah yes, the question of moral insanity – I suspect that will turn out to be significant, but we shall see.'

Her attention wandering, Lucy went over to the floor-length window and looked idly out at the deserted street below as she sipped her coffee. The contrast between the darkness outside and the large bright room full of people chattering and laughing was distinctly unsettling. A figure emerged from the house on to the street and paused briefly beneath a gas lamp. It was Miss Trott. She began to walk slowly along the Via Legnano. After a moment, she stopped and glanced up at the window. Instinctively Lucy drew back, and when she looked out again, Miss Trott had disappeared.

The following morning, James was up bright and early to go to San Callisto. He had told nobody of his intentions, not even Sofia. After what had happened during their last visit, he was only too aware that this might be a dangerous course of action, and he didn't want her involved. He was convinced that the supposedly disused abbey held the key to a number of things, not least his own abduction. But before he went there, he had another call to make.

He pounded on the shabby front door, making it shake so precariously that he softened his knock in case he broke it down. The occupant would probably deserve it, but James wanted something from him, and this was almost certainly not the way to achieve it. Eventually he heard a shuffling and some swearing as the door opened.

'*Merda!* It's practically dawn, and on a Sunday too. What do you want?'

'*Buongiorno,* Baldovino. I see you're as well dressed as ever.' James pushed past the reporter and made his way into the house.

'Hey! What are you doing?'

'I'm here to get some answers.'

The door slammed behind him and Baldovino came in tucking his stained shirt into his equally stained trousers. 'I've told you everything I'm going to. I gave you the list. That was the arrangement.'

James grasped him by his shirt and pulled the man towards him until they were face to face. 'I don't care about any arrangement. I want to know how you got the names in the first place. Who tipped you off?'

'We've been through this already. I can't tell you that. It's more than my life's worth.'

'Who was it?'

Baldovino struggled until James released him, pushing him onto a grubby chair – the same one he himself had slept on when he had tried to drink his way to oblivion after Sofia's rejection.

'What's got into you, *Inglese*?'

'Let's just say I'm tired of being so damned polite. Now give me the name.'

Baldovino got to his feet and tried to square up to him. 'It'll cost you.'

'Give me the name!'

'That won't get you what you want.'

James took a step towards him.

Baldovino lifted his hands in submission. 'All right, all right! If it's that important to you . . .' He went over to a small desk in the corner and pulled out a piece of paper from the back of a drawer. 'Here, take it. I doubt it'll help you. It certainly didn't bring me anything but grief.'

'What do you mean?'

'I made a few enquiries, but then . . .'

'What?'

'I was warned off.'

'So that's why you gave me the list. You wanted me to do your work for you. How were you warned off?'

'Some bastard shoved me down some steps and told me to mind my own business.'

'Did you see who it was?'

'No, and I don't care either, though I'm guessing they were

intimately acquainted with the name on that piece of paper. Still, it's always the quiet ones, as they say.'

'Did you find out anything before you were warned off?'

'Not much, but I did uncover something about that girl in the abbey.'

'What?'

'It'll cost you . . .'

James said nothing.

Baldovino shrugged. 'Suit yourself . . . Nella Calvi was a flower seller.'

'I know that already,' James said, exasperated.

'There's more. Apparently she did some whoring on the side.'

'Really? That *is* interesting.'

'Do you know her professional name?'

'No, I don't, and I'm not sure it really matters.'

'Fair enough. Mind you, it's a shame to end our little arrangement. I thought you could give me some information in return. Some little titbit about the old professor, perhaps.'

'First tell me the girl's other name.'

'All right. You can have this one on account, as it were. As a mark of my goodwill. Nella Calvi's professional name was Agnella. Nice touch, don't you think?'

'Why?'

'Agnella means pure . . . Interesting name considering her occupation. Now, about our arrangement . . .'

'No thanks,' James said.

'Are you sure? There would be a fee. You could spend it on your woman . . . not that she'd appreciate it. Her type never does. Once a whore, eh, *Inglese*?'

James had heard enough. His frustration overwhelmed him, and he charged towards Baldovino, picked the man up and pushed him against the wall. 'If I ever hear you so much as whisper her name, I'll...' He let the journalist fall. Finishing the sentence just didn't seem worth it. He had got what he'd come for after all.

He made for the door, leaving Baldovino lying on the floor muttering to himself under his breath: 'You'll be sorry for that, *Inglese*... very sorry indeed.' He almost pitied the man. What could someone like Baldovino do to him? Threats were all he had.

He slammed the door as he left, and grinned with satisfaction as it fell halfway off its hinges and swung pathetically back and forth. He stopped for a moment and leant on a nearby wall, hunching over in an effort to gather himself. A year or so ago he would not have dreamt of threatening violence to get what he wanted, but now everything was different. *He* was different. He thought about his father and what the man had become in his later years. Was he the same now?

The chill of the early morning was seeping into his bones. He pulled the piece of paper from his pocket and read the name that was written on it. It made no sense to him. After a moment or two he straightened up and began to walk up the narrow cobbled street towards the main road to hail a cab to San Callisto, the name of Baldovino's source tucked safely back in his pocket and Agnella's real identity in his head. He was annoyed with himself. He should have worked out who she was for himself. Still, it was clear that his visit to the abbey was vital and timely. It seemed that he might be a few steps closer to solving the mystery, and perhaps even finding Chiara.

32

The scarcity of the criminal type and lack of ugliness may cause many to doubt our theory that prostitutes are not only equivalents of criminals but, in fact, have the same characteristics in exaggerated form. However, in addition to the fact that true female criminals are much less ugly than their male counterparts, in prostitutes we have women of great youth in whom the 'beauty of the Devil', with its abundance of soft, fresh flesh and absence of wrinkles, masks anomalies. Another thing to keep in mind is that prostitution calls for a relative lack of peculiarities such as a large jaw and a hardened stare which, if present, might cause disgust and repulsion . . .

Lombroso and Ferrero, 1893, pp. 142–3

Lucy sat in the drawing room pretending to read a book and watching Miss Trott write a letter. She allowed her imagination to run riot. Could it be to some criminal mastermind, perhaps, or was it a coded letter for the head of a smuggling ring?

'I am just writing to your aunt, dear. Do you have any messages?' Miss Trott asked.

Lucy was about to reply when Sofia came in. 'This arrived for you,' she said, handing her an envelope.

Lucy read the note. It was from the Rambaudis, though she suspected it had been written by Bianca rather than Francesco. It was an invitation for her and Miss Trott to take lunch with them that day at their villa on the outskirts of the city.

'I think we should accept,' Miss Trott said. 'It would do you good to venture outside the city and see the countryside. I believe there are some pretty views in that area, and the weather is perfect for such an outing.'

'It is a pity that James can't join us,' Lucy said.

'He is busy at his work, as befits a young man of his intellect.'

'He had some business to conduct outside the city. I heard him say so last night.'

'You *over*heard him, you mean,' Miss Trott said. 'Wherever he is going, that is his business. Eavesdropping is not at all ladylike, and neither is poking one's nose into the affairs of another.'

Was she trying to make a point? Her expression was still rather vague, as if she was somewhere else entirely, or perhaps wished that she was. It did not seem as if she was being pointed.

'It wasn't intentional. I just happened to hear, that's all. He's my brother. I worry about him.'

'Do you? Whyever would you do that?' Miss Trott asked. 'He is old enough to look after himself.'

'I know, but after all that business with Sofia, and being hurt by those men, whoever they were, I can't help it.'

'I suppose that is natural. But you really mustn't worry. I am sure he was simply the victim of some kind of misunderstanding.'

'That is pretty much what he said.'

'Then that is what it was.'

'Still . . .'

'Still nothing. He is a young man, and sometimes they get into scrapes. It is just one of those things. My advice is to leave him be. He won't thank you for interfering. Now, have you thought about what you will wear for our outing?'

Lucy forced herself to stop worrying about James. Miss Trott was right. There was no point. He would not listen to anything she said anyway. Instead she allowed herself to think about Francesco, and a shiver of anticipation went through her. Did this invitation have any underlying meaning, or was it something more casual? She tried to tell herself that it didn't matter. After all, it would be pleasant to get out of the city for a few hours on a beautiful day like this.

James narrowed his eyes in the sun. He was sitting in the square in San Callisto, considering what to do next. He thought about what he knew, trying to make sense of it. Two of the girls on Baldovino's original list had now been identified. Nella Calvi, the girl found at the abbey, had worked at Madame Giulia's as a prostitute known as Agnella. Teresa Mariani had also worked there as a maid. According to her mother she had been upset about something, possibly a boyfriend she used to meet up with at the abbey. Both were now missing. The body found at the Borgo belonged to a girl called Caterina Spirito, a flower seller friend of Nella/Agnella. That left Arianna Panico, Susanna Russello and Chiara.

He had made further enquiries and had been given a similar story each time. All the missing girls had originated in or near San Callisto but had gone to work in the city. Arianna Panico's family seemed to have left the area long ago. The other families had all been told by the local carabinieri that the girls were most likely to have gone elsewhere, either for another job or because they had met someone. They were left to hope that one day they would be contacted by their missing daughters.

The note with the name of Baldovino's informant on it was still burning a hole in his pocket, and now his mind too. Someone he had trusted had lied to him . . . but why? He pushed his thick dark hair out of his eyes.

An image of Sofia came into his mind. He had betrayed her. Even though he had not instigated the kiss with Concetta Panatti, he had responded. If Sofia found out, that would almost certainly be the end of their friendship. She had always made it clear that trust was more important to her than anything. He leant back and closed his eyes. Why did he always make such a mess of things, allowing his heart to rule his head?

Still, perhaps it was a sign. As Concetta had said, he had done worse things . . . things that would no doubt horrify Sofia if she knew. Once she discovered what he had done, she would walk away from him for ever, and she would be right to do so. All he could do now was to try his best to find Chiara for her. Perhaps it would be enough to retain her friendship. He knew now that he could not expect her love.

Later he would pay another visit to the abbey to see if he could work out why he had been threatened. But first he had to try to find Teresa Mariani's missing lover. According to her friend Giovanna, the young man had worked at the rice estate to the west of the town. James was not sure if he would discover anything there, but it was the only lead he had, so he had decided to pay a visit and ask some questions.

He chose to walk, as it was not too far. Even though it was

cooler up here away from the city, and the path led through woodland, it was still very warm for early spring, and he had taken off his jacket and slung it over his shoulder as he went. He stopped for a moment to rest, sinking down on the mossy ground beneath a tree and leaning against it whilst he took out his handkerchief and wiped his forehead. The breeze rustled the tops of the trees, making them sound like waves breaking on to a beach. Their pale green leaves were outlined against the clear blue sky. He breathed in the aroma of pine needles mingling with the scent of earth. The familiarity was comforting. Closing his eyes for a moment, he thought of Scotland, and expeditions into the countryside with his friends from medical school during hunting and fishing holidays.

He heard the crack of a broken twig. He sat completely still, listening carefully for any sound that might indicate the presence of someone else, but there was nothing. He shook his head and laughed at his folly. Perhaps it wasn't surprising that he should be sensitive to such things given what had happened during his last visit. He picked up his jacket and got to his feet. He was about to set off again when he thought he heard a rustling sound. He told himself that it was probably just an animal – a squirrel perhaps, or a fox. He returned to the path and continued his journey towards the abbey. Every now and again he thought he heard something, but dismissed it as a sign of an overactive imagination.

Before too long the woodland began to give way to sparser shrubland. As the land became flatter, he could see fields full of what he assumed were lush green rice plants divided into grids by shining lines of water. Dotted among them were women, most of whom were bent double, moving rhythmically as they planted and weeded. Mesmerised, he paused for a moment to watch them. In the near distance there was a large villa in honey-coloured stone with a number of outbuildings set slightly away from it. It seemed that he had found the estate where the missing boy worked. Now all he had to do was find out who the boy was and why he had disappeared. Had anyone emerged from the forest behind him? No, he was alone. Heartened by this, he began to make his way down the valley towards the fields and the estate.

As he walked past the fields, some of the women straightened up to watch him, calling out greetings and occasionally ribald comments. It seemed like a good opportunity to ask some questions, so he stopped by one of them and smiled at her.

'That looks like hard work, signora.'

'*Sì*, signor. I would not recommend it,' the woman said cheerfully. She was ruddy-faced from the sun despite the fact that she was wearing a large straw hat. Her skirts were tucked up, revealing sturdy legs covered in bites.

'You should get some ointment for those,' James said, the doctor in him taking over for a moment.

The woman nodded. 'I would if I could afford it. Mosquitoes and frogs . . . they won't leave us alone, whatever we say to them. Thank God it isn't for long!'

'How long are you here for?'

'A few months. Mind you, even that's too much for some. We've had a few give up on it before the season is over.'

'Hey, Perla! Who's your new man?' cried one of the women.

'Has he got a friend for me?' shouted another.

'Don't mind them, signor,' Perla said. 'Any diversion is welcome here, especially the male variety. Did you want to know anything in particular?'

'Do you know of a young man who works on the estate? He may have gone missing recently.'

Perla paused for a moment. 'Do you mean Bruno Ferranti? He worked here last season. I thought he'd moved on, but I think I caught a glimpse of him up at the house a few weeks back.'

'Did he have a friend ... a young girl called Teresa?'

'I don't know if that was her name, but he did hang around with a girl for a while. Haven't seen her recently, though. We mondine usually keep ourselves to ourselves.'

'Mondine?'

'That's what we're called – the rice weeders. Most of us come down from the mountain villages to work at places like this in the summer. There are a few from nearby, but not many.'

'Just one more thing,' James said. 'What do Bruno and the girl look like?'

'He's handsome enough, I suppose, in an obvious sort of way, except for a scar on his cheek from a knife fight a year or so back. A bit like yours, if you don't mind me saying, only his is bigger and deeper ... much more noticeable.'

James held his hand up to his face and felt the thin line of the mark left by whoever it was who had cut him. Perhaps Bruno had had the same experience.

Perla continued. 'He's quite sturdy ... looks like he can handle himself. Funny, though, he used to be quite mouthy, something of a troublemaker, but then he seemed to calm down till he wouldn't say boo to a goose. Mind you, there were rumours ...'

'What kind of rumours?'

'Some say that he got too close to the estate owner's wife

when he was still just a boy. She died a few years back. I suppose that might explain why he's not such a loudmouth these days.'

'And the girl?'

'Short, dark, pretty . . . that's all I can remember.'

James thanked Perla for her time and began to make his way towards the buildings. At last he felt he was getting somewhere with this puzzle, or a strand of it at least. He was certain that Teresa Mariani and her friend Bruno lay at the heart of it. All he had to do now was find them.

Lucy looked idly out of the window at the scenery as she and Miss Trott rattled through the countryside in their cab. The road was uneven in places, so there was a certain amount of rolling to and fro, as if they were voyagers on a stormy sea. Miss Trott bore the discomfort with fortitude, commenting only on the heat and the lack of any breeze as she fanned herself with a large straw hat.

The vista was attractive – mostly rolling green hills punctuated by woodland. As they drove, Lucy noticed a series of fields in the distance with their crops planted in straight lines. It reminded her of the old corded doormat that used to be in their summer house – a grand name for a not very grand building; more of a large shed at the bottom of the garden really. When she was younger, Lucy liked to sit and write there, pretending to be a great lady novelist. Her father would come and sit with her, puffing on his pipe and asking questions about her stories.

'I think we must be almost there,' Miss Trott said, indicating a large villa not too far away.

Lucy pictured Francesco's face with its delicate features and rakish smile, and felt a slight rolling in her stomach that she supposed must be butterflies. As they approached the gates to the villa, she peered out of the window to admire their intricate design.

'Oh look. I see we are not the only guests,' Miss Trott remarked, pointing out a grand carriage that blocked their path so that they could not drive through the gate.

The cab driver, a fat, balding man with a small bowler hat pushed to the back of his very large head, muttered something about stopping here.

'Oh really, that is too bad!' Miss Trott complained. '*Non accettabile!*' she shouted loudly, as if the man was hard of hearing.

The driver ignored her completely, looking into the distance as if hoping that she would disappear.

'Well now, come along, signor. We cannot sit here all day!' she said, poking him with her parasol.

Eventually the man alighted and helped them down on to the driveway. Miss Trott paid him, slowly and deliberately counting out the coins and refusing to leave a tip. It was lucky that Francesco had suggested in his note that he would take them back to the city. Lucy doubted their cab would have materialised for the journey home, if the muttering coming from the driver was any indication.

As they walked past the grand carriage, Lucy noticed the insignia on the door: a large flower – a lily perhaps. It matched the design on the gate. As they approached the front door to the villa, it opened and Francesco came out, followed by several dogs. One of them barked and leapt up at Miss Trott, who was slightly ahead of Lucy.

'Get down, wretched animal!' she cried, beating it off with her parasol, which was clearly a versatile piece of equipment. This merely had the effect of whipping the dogs into a frenzy of excitement, as they seemed to think that it was some kind of game, and Francesco had to restore order, clapping his hands and shouting until the dogs retreated into the house.

There didn't seem to be any real alarm in Miss Trott's face, and yet again Lucy was struck by the feeling that at least some of this was for show, although what the purpose might be she couldn't say.

Francesco gave a deep bow. 'Come this way, ladies, come this way. We are eating outside today, as we have been lucky with the weather.'

'Al fresco . . . how very Italian,' Miss Trott murmured appreciatively as they followed their host round the house into beautiful though somewhat overgrown gardens.

'Here we are,' Francesco said, indicating a large terrace with a dining table and chairs on one side and wicker chairs to the other. It was exactly as Lucy had feared. Seated on the latter, next to Bianca Rambaudi, were their fellow guests, the marchesa, Professor Donati and – in the centre, in the position of guest of honour – Fabia Carignano. She was semi-reclined on her seat and yet still managed to look elegant, Lucy noted with irritation. She was not sure what she felt about Professor Donati. He had seemed threatening last time they met, but now he was polite, giving a little bow of his head and taking off his hat in greeting. She supposed she was safe here as long as she was in company. It would be interesting to watch the interaction between him and Miss Trott.

'Signorina Murray, how nice,' Fabia said icily.

'Likewise,' Lucy replied.

Francesco beamed at both of them. 'A cool drink is what we all need, I think. Do take a seat, ladies.'

Lucy sat next to Miss Trott, who had made a beeline for the seat next to Professor Donati. He sat bolt upright and wore the hunted expression of a man who was about to be caught out at something. His eyes darted around and his brow shone with perspiration. An awkward silence descended upon them like a damp blanket.

'How are arrangements going for the ball, Marchesa?' Bianca asked.

'The invitations are about to be sent, I believe.'

'Of course, we have already asked our most intimate friends,' Fabia said. 'Francesco and Bianca received their invitations some time ago.'

'What Fabia means is that she brought them with her today because she was coming to lunch,' Bianca said. 'Isn't that right?'

Fabia blushed but did not answer.

'But we were delighted to receive them, weren't we, Bianca?' Francesco said, as a maid arrived with a tray bearing glasses of lemonade, which she passed round with great ceremony, as if distributing the nectar of the gods.

'Indeed we were,' Bianca agreed. 'It is so nice to have a real occasion to look forward to.'

'And we look forward to seeing you there,' the marchesa said. 'All of you.'

'I know that everyone in our household is excited about it,' Miss Trott said.

'Even Professor Lombroso?' Francesco asked. 'He doesn't look to me like a man who would appreciate that kind of thing.'

'You'd be surprised,' the marchesa said, smiling. 'The professor loves an audience, so any crowd is appealing to him.'

'Ah, but is he appealing to any crowd?' Francesco said, making Lucy smile.

'I have heard that he has quite a popular following,' Professor Donati said.

'Do you know him, Professor?' Francesco asked.

'We are acquainted, yes. I find his ideas very stimulating.'

'Tell me, Professor, how did the Ancient Egyptians view crime?' Miss Trott asked.

Professor Donati hesitated for a moment. 'Their criminal justice system was not dissimilar to our own, although the punishments were rather more savage.'

'As I recall, they executed murderers by impaling them on a stake,' Francesco said.

Professor Donati nodded. 'That is correct. Burning was also used, as a kind of purification, though of course it denied the wrongdoer an afterlife as there would be no body to preserve, which is somewhat ironic.'

'I have always wondered how they made their mummies,' Miss Trott said.

'It is a very intricate process, I believe,' Francesco said.

'Yes, it is, and a fascinating one. You see, the body has to be completely free of fluid,' Professor Donati explained, clearly enthused by his subject. 'That is how the purification process begins.'

'Let's change the subject to something less morbid,' the marchesa suggested hastily. 'What does your brother think of Professor Lombroso's theories, Signorina Murray?'

'He is employed by the university?' Fabia asked.

'He is assisting the professor in his research, yes,' Lucy replied. 'I believe he admires him greatly.'

'The professor must be gratified to have such a slavish follower.' Fabia's lips formed a small, tight smile.

'You make it sound as if Signor Murray is indiscriminating, Fabia,' Bianca said.

'I am sure he is nothing of the kind,' declared the marchesa.

'Professor Lombroso has many admirers, and I am among them.'

'He is lucky to have your patronage, Marchesa,' Professor Donati said, 'particularly after that business with the murders last year.'

'Ah yes, and I believe your brother was involved too, was he not, Signorina Murray?'

'That is not a topic of conversation to be raised over lunch, Fabia,' the marchesa said before Lucy could answer.

'Speaking of which, shall we eat?' Bianca waved at a manservant who was waiting patiently in the doorway. Lucy immediately wished that she had brought her notebook. He was extremely tall and broad – the word 'immense' came into her mind. His face was most peculiar in that he had a vast, domelike forehead, large ears that stuck out at right angles and slightly drooping features. He reminded Lucy of one of the pictures of criminals that she had seen in Professor Lombroso's book. She gazed past him to the interior of the house. She couldn't see a great deal, such was the man's bulk, but she was left with the impression that no expense had been spared. Everything looked new. The paintwork was gleaming and the wallpaper was vivid, one might even say garish, particularly when compared to the faded grandeur of the marchesa's decor.

'Cosimo, can you tell the kitchen that we are ready?' Bianca said.

The man grunted an incoherent reply and loped into the house. A few minutes later, the first of a parade of tempting dishes were brought out and lunch began in earnest. Lucy could not remember when she had eaten a finer meal. There was risotto, of course – made from 'our own Carnaroli rice', as Bianca announced proudly – a local speciality called risotto alla piemontese, a creamy concoction made with fragrant rosemary and veal marrow. There were delicate courgette flowers stuffed with ground beef and gelatina – or aspic, as Miss Trott insisted on calling it. There was a broth made from veal shanks and various spices and aromatic vinegar, sieved, according to Francesco, and left to set in a cool cellar. Fresh sheep and goat's cheeses were also on offer. These were milky, fresh and buttery and served with local honey to drizzle on them. To finish, apparently in Lucy's honour, which made Fabia scowl, was *zuppa Inglese*, or English trifle. Despite bearing no relation to the true English version, as Miss Trott reminded everyone, it was a delicious dessert made with layers of sponge generously soaked with a spiced Italian liqueur called Alkermes, apricot jam, and vanilla and chocolate custard.

Lucy tucked into it all with great enthusiasm. She had never been one to peck at her food, unlike Fabia, who, Lucy noticed, had the art of self-denial perfected. She ate very little and cut everything into tiny morsels before chewing each one thoroughly, whilst wearing an expression that made her lack of enjoyment clear.

After lunch, Francesco stood and extended a hand towards Lucy. 'Would you like to see some of the estate? Our gardens are renowned for their beauty.'

Fabia got to her feet. 'I should like to come too, Francesco, if I may.'

'Oh no, Fabia, it would only bore you,' Francesco said.

'It wouldn't at all!' Fabia replied. She was pouting, Lucy noticed, which made her look a little like a goldfish.

'You know it would. Last time you yawned throughout!'

'Why don't you two go ahead and then Miss Carignano and I can follow on?' Miss Trott suggested.

'What an excellent idea,' the marchesa said, which decided the matter, much to Fabia's annoyance.

Francesco held out his arm to Lucy, who took it, and together they began to walk around the grounds of the Villa Purezza.

33

Thieves, like prostitutes, covet bright-coloured clothes, necklaces, chains, and even earrings. They are the most ignorant and gullible of the criminal species. Almost always nervous about being caught, they talk nonsensically and constantly change the subject. Assuming that those who speak their jargon are worthy colleagues, they make friends hastily. They sometimes feign romantic love, but prefer prostitutes, their natural allies.

Lombroso, 1876, p. 73

James stood by the back gate of the rice estate. What should he do next? The whole expedition had taken him longer than he had anticipated, and it seemed highly unlikely that he would get back to the city in time for his afternoon meeting with Lombroso. He squinted up at the sun. It was noon already. How would the professor react? He thought he could probably guess. Lombroso hated lateness of any kind, except of course his own. Both James and Ottolenghi had been kept waiting on many occasions whilst the professor lost track of the time in the middle of some experiment or other. Then when he finally arrived, they would be told that they should be more flexible and he did not know what the fuss was about. But if they were late, he would tut and sigh and go on about it for ages. Not showing up at all might be considered a step too far, but it couldn't be helped. He would just have to deal with the consequences when they arrived.

In the meantime, he needed to work out what he should do next. The place seemed deserted, which was inconvenient, as he needed to ask some questions about Bruno Ferranti's whereabouts.

'Hello? Is anyone about?' he called.

There was no reply. He listened out for voices, but all he could hear was the birds singing. He rattled the gate for a moment, and to his surprise it swung open. He walked through into the courtyard. There were a few pieces of farm machinery strewn about the place, as if someone had been working on their maintenance but had been called away. He started to examine an old plough. He had always been fond of taking things apart and putting them back together again. Any form of mechanism or machinery fascinated him.

'Hey, what are you doing? Thief!' A man ran towards him, grabbed him by the shoulders and pushed him to the ground.

'I haven't done anything,' James protested.

The man kicked at him. 'You were trying to steal something. Well, we'll see what the boss has to say.'

'I was looking for someone, that's all.'

'I don't believe you.' The man shouted over his shoulder. 'Bruno! Cosimo! *Vieni qui!*'

Two more men appeared from another of the buildings. One of them was one of the largest men James had ever seen. The other was much younger, little more than a boy really. There was a long, deep scar on his cheek.

'Search him, Bruno,' the first man ordered.

'*Sì*, Marco.'

The bigger man, presumably Cosimo, pulled James to his

feet and held him while Bruno went through his pockets. Before long, James's notebook was found and duly handed over to Marco, who looked at the first page and nodded. 'Put him in the stables. I'll tell the boss.'

James was dragged away to a small room, where he was unceremoniously dumped on the floor in the middle of a large pile of manure. He lay there for a moment. Had coming back to Italy been worth it? Suddenly the prospect of a practice as a family doctor in a small Scottish town with a nice, quiet, undemanding wife seemed very attractive indeed. Still, he thought, as he pulled himself up and out of the manure, he had found Bruno, the missing boy. And as far as his own well-being was concerned, at least things couldn't get any worse.

Lucy was enjoying herself. The gardens were beautiful and quite extensive, even including an ice house, which Francesco pointed out to her with some pride. Indeed, the further they went, the clearer it became that the Villa Purezza's grounds were very close to Francesco's heart. Lucy studied him as he led her through the tree-lined paths to the various sections, explaining how his mother had designed them to represent different deities, each one symbolising purity. His eyes were full of passion as he related the story of the research and care that had gone into the creation of the place. The more he told her, the closer to him she felt. She had only ever seen passion like that in her father's eyes although James sometimes got near to it when he was talking about Turin. It made her want to reach out to Francesco and touch him. In fact, it was only the close proximity of Fabia and Miss Trott that prevented her from doing so. She could hear the distant rise and fall of their conversation. Although she was not close enough to make out the exact words, Fabia's irritation and Miss Trott's failed attempts at conciliation were clear. But none of that mattered. She was alone, or almost, with Francesco, and with every moment that passed, she was becoming increasingly convinced that she was falling for him.

'So you see, Lucia, how very clever my mother was,' he said. 'And the tragedy is that she had just completed it all when she was taken from us.'

'She sounds like a remarkable woman. You must both miss her terribly.'

'I do, very much, although I am not so sure about Bianca.'

'Really? What makes you say that?'

'Oh, nothing... just a feeling I have, that's all.' He stopped outside a tall wooden gate. 'This is the last part of the garden. I have never shown anyone before.' He took her hand and kissed the palm gently. It felt to her as if a feather had been passed over it. She could hardly breathe. He took a large key from his pocket and began to unlock the gate.

'Are you certain of this?' Lucy asked.

'I have never been more certain of anything.'

They heard the voices of Fabia and Miss Trott approaching. 'Quickly!' Francesco said. 'Before they see us.'

He pulled her through the gate and shut it firmly behind them. They stood away from it to one side, and Lucy heard Fabia's voice: 'Oh really, this is too much! Where have they got to?' Then a determined Miss Trott: 'Do not despair, Miss Carignano. We shall find them. Follow me.'

She was so close to Francesco that she felt his breath on her cheek. It made her feel faint with what she thought must be desire, though she had nothing to compare it to. It was a curious sensation – as if she was slowly melting from the inside out. Was that how love felt, or was it the heat?

Once the two women had passed, Francesco took Lucy by

the hand and led her into the garden. She caught her breath at the sheer beauty of what she was seeing. In front of her was a summer house built in the style of an Egyptian temple.

'Do you like the house?' Francesco asked.

'Very much,' Lucy said.

'My mother used to come here all the time. I think she saw it as somewhere to escape to. It has several rooms. There's even a wine cellar.'

In front of the summer house was a landscaped pond in the shape of a cross. It was strewn with water lilies in all shades of red, from crimson to the palest of pinks. At its heart was a small fountain with a stone statue of a young Egyptian woman holding a sceptre.

They walked towards it. 'May I introduce you to Maat, the Egyptian goddess of purity, amongst other things,' Francesco said. 'She wrote one of the spells in the Book of the Dead – the forty-two declarations of purity.'

The statue's features were perfect. Her gaze was cast down, as if she was afraid to catch their eyes.

'She is beautiful,' said Lucy. 'Did your mother commission it?'

'She did. It was her last gift to me.'

He took hold of Lucy's hands. She closed her eyes as he drew her closer, waiting for him to kiss her. It seemed like the right thing to do under the circumstances.

'Francesco? Are you in here?' There was a knocking at the gate. Francesco released her hands. 'Later,' he whispered in her ear. 'Yes, we are here. What do you want, Bianca?'

'There is some trouble at the house. Can you come back and sort it out?'

He rolled his eyes at Lucy, who smiled back. Whatever had

just happened between them could happen again, she was sure of it. The question was whether she wanted it to.

'Very well. I will be there shortly,' Francesco called.

'Don't be long!' Bianca said. 'See you in a moment, Signorina Murray.'

'Our secret is out,' Francesco said, grinning. 'Come on. We had better go.'

As they made their way back to the house, a new closeness between them, Lucy thought about all the great literature in the world, talking of love and how it could be gained and lost and found again. And yet it seemed as if she might have fallen in love without any difficulty at all. Not only that, but it looked as if her feelings were reciprocated. Was that what love felt like? Somehow it was far too easy. Surely there had to be more to it than that.

They arrived back at the house to see everyone seated as they had been before lunch. Fabia glowered at her, and Lucy couldn't help but smile triumphantly back. If this had been a competition for Francesco's affections, it appeared that she had won it. Bianca was standing to one side and whispered to her brother. He nodded and looked over to Lucy. 'Apparently we have had an intruder,' he announced.

'Really? How very alarming!' exclaimed Miss Trott.

'There is nothing to worry about, signora,' Francesco said. 'The rogue has been caught and is being brought here as we speak.'

Why was Francesco insisting on dealing with the matter in front of them all? Was he showing off a little? Lucy wondered.

'We often have problems with tramps and the like,' Bianca said. 'They think they can come here and help themselves to anything they want.'

'Indeed. Crime is a problem in this city as in any other,' the marchesa agreed. 'We must all be vigilant.'

'I am not sure that I wish to see this ruffian.' Miss Trott fanned herself with her hand. 'Is he violent?'

'He resisted, Bianca tells me, but he was no match for my employees,' Francesco said. 'I thought it might be of interest if he was asked to explain himself. It might teach him a lesson.'

'A good idea, Francesco,' Professor Donati said. 'His kind should be made to account for their actions.'

'How will you deal with him in the end?' Fabia asked.

'I am not sure,' Francesco replied. 'He will either get a whipping or, if the matter is serious, I may call in the carabinieri and have him arrested.'

'I think you should do both!' Fabia said. 'The wretch is a criminal when all is said and done.'

'What do you think, Lucy?' Francesco asked.

Lucy thought for a moment. 'It depends on what he says. But there is no excuse for breaking in, in my opinion, and if you let him go, I expect he will just do it again. Professor Lombroso calls them habitual criminals, I believe. They cannot help themselves, as they are born to it.'

'Huh! That sounds like an excuse to me!' Fabia said.

'I think Professor Lombroso knows more about criminals than any of us here,' Miss Trott pointed out.

'I do not believe the professor is suggesting that anyone can shirk responsibility for crime,' Lucy said. 'Just that they are primitive and so have a propensity for such behaviour.'

Francesco nodded. 'Sound thinking. Ah, here they come. We shall see how primitive this chap looks.'

Lucy heard a scuffling sound in the distance, together with cries of protest. 'Let me go! There's no need for this. I wasn't doing anything wrong!'

No, she thought, it couldn't be . . . It must be a coincidence.

The servant Cosimo and another man brought the trespasser towards them, holding him tightly as he struggled between them. He made a sorry figure in his stained clothes, his face covered in cuts and bruises, not to mention a layer of what looked like mud. The men finally reached the assembled party and the prisoner was thrown to the floor in front of them.

'So what do you have to say for yourself, you scoundrel?' Francesco said.

The young man got to his feet and began to straighten his clothing, before noticing Lucy.

'James, what on earth are you doing here?' she said in horror.

'You know this man?' Francesco asked.

She nodded miserably. 'He is my brother.'

'Your brother is a thief, Signorina Murray?' Fabia said, hardly managing to contain her glee.

'Dr Murray is no thief!' Miss Trott said firmly. 'There must have been some misunderstanding.'

'Well I am sure we are all waiting to hear what it is,' Francesco said, his voice heavy with sarcasm. 'This is really your brother?'

'Yes, I am afraid so.'

'Lucy,' James said. 'I can explain.'

Lucy looked at him with distaste. 'I do not want to hear it.'

'Perhaps we should go,' the marchesa suggested.

'Oh must we, Aunt?' Fabia said, looking smugly at Lucy.

'Yes, I think we must. We are taking Professor Donati home. May we do the same for you, Signorina Murray, Miss Trott?'

Lucy nodded. 'Thank you, that would be most kind.'

The marchesa glanced at James. 'We shall wait for a few moments, Signor Murray.'

'Thank you.'

Lucy turned to say goodbye to Francesco, but he was resolutely ignoring her so she said it instead to Bianca, who gave a small embarrassed nod in return. Lucy began to follow the marchesa and Fabia to the carriage, closely followed by Miss Trott. Bianca walked after them after glaring balefully at James.

'Lucy, wait, please,' James called out. 'Let me speak to you.' He tried to follow, but was stopped by Cosimo, who stood in his path as Lucy marched past.

The way she was feeling, James would be lucky if she ever spoke to him again.

34

At least half of hysterical women are normal in intelligence, but they are easily distracted. Due to their profound egotism and total self-absorption, they adore scandal and public attention. They are extremely impressionable and as a result subject to sudden anger and unreasonable likes and dislikes. Their will is always unstable; they delight in speaking evil; and if they cannot attract attention through baseless trials and outrageous forms of revenge, they embitter the lives of their associates with continuous quarrels and disputes.

Lombroso and Ferrero, 1893, p. 234

James stood before his accuser and waited to hear his fate. It was bad enough being accused of being a common criminal, but being labelled as such in front of his own sister, and Miss Trott and the marchesa too, made it a thousand times worse.

'What do you want to do with him, boss?' Cosimo asked.

There was a pause as Francesco Rambaudi viewed his prisoner with contempt.

'I didn't do anything. You must know that!' James said.

'Your sister didn't seem so sure.'

'I can see why you might want to question me, Signor Rambaudi, given the circumstances, but what I can't understand is why you felt the need to humiliate Lucy.'

Francesco gave a mocking smile and nodded towards Cosimo. 'Let him go.' The servant did as he was told and lumbered off down the hill, back to the estate.

James stood for a moment waiting for an explanation. When none came, he began to walk towards the marchesa's carriage. Francesco stood in front of him and laid a restraining hand on his wrist. 'A private word before you go, Signor Murray. What were you doing trespassing on my estate?'

'I was looking for someone.'

'Who?'

James hesitated. 'A young man who works here, Bruno Ferranti.'

'Why are you looking for him?'

'I ... I can't really say.'

'Perhaps I should call the carabinieri after all. Then you can tell them when they get here.'

'No, no, please ... I am just trying to help a friend. A girl has gone missing. The boy might know something, that's all.'

'I will make enquiries. If he knows anything, I will inform you.'

'Thank you.'

'Just one thing, Signor Murray. I trust that we shall not see you here again.'

James nodded his agreement, gave a short bow and left to join the marchesa. When he got to the carriage, he found that there was further humiliation to come. Unfortunately the whiff of manure he carried on his clothes was too much for the ladies. He was forced to sit with the driver, and even he leant away from him at every opportunity.

He held onto the side of the carriage as it passed through the ornate gates on to the road home. It was typical of Rambaudi to have such vulgar taste, but then the man was clearly no gentleman. He had known that James was the intruder but had still insisted on parading him in front of Lucy and his other guests. That was unforgivable in itself.

But it was more than that. Francesco Rambaudi was not to be trusted, and as a consequence, Lucy was not safe in his company.

The following day, James was summoned by the professor to his study. He had assumed that Rambaudi had complained, and was thus surprised to see Anna and Ottolenghi sitting in two of Lombroso's more uncomfortable chairs, both looking embarrassed. Ottolenghi had a newspaper in his hand, which he handed silently to James. It was a copy of *The People's Voice*. James scanned the front page and felt his stomach churn.

SCANDAL!

It has come to the attention of this newspaper that a certain foreigner currently residing at the home of one of our city's leading citizens, Professor Cesare Lombroso, has been consorting with prostitutes under the guise of university business. It is also said that the same man has been conducting a scandalous liaison with one of the professor's servants, herself an ex-prostitute.

This newspaper is not able to say at present whether Professor Lombroso knew of his guest's activities or the background of his servant. But if he did, it must surely call into question his own standing. We call upon the university to institute an immediate investigation in order to establish the facts and root out such base immorality wherever it is found. More on pages 4, 5 and 6.

He forced himself to turn the pages. There was an editorial entitled 'Clean up our city!', which discussed at length Turin's moral decline, largely brought about by foreign visitors 'coming into our midst, infecting our minds with unsavoury ideas and lax morals'. If there had been any doubt about whom this was aimed at, then it was removed by the features section and letters page. The former contained an interview with someone described as 'an employee of Madame Giulia', who described an incident at the university where a foreigner made lewd suggestions to her under the guise of conducting an 'anthropological experiment'. To cap it all, this young woman's account was endorsed by Madame Giulia herself, who described an incident in which the same man attempted to force his attentions on her. That was not how James would have described it, but none of that mattered now. The damage was done. Presumably this was what Concetta had meant when she had told him it was too late.

The letters page apparently endorsed this view, with the great and good of Turin condemning his actions and demanding everything from his deportation to a public whipping.

'I have asked your colleagues to be present because your conduct affects us all,' Lombroso said, glowering at him.

'My conduct?' James asked. 'But you can't believe any of this nonsense, surely?'

'Explain yourself,' Lombroso said.

James told them what had happened, including Concetta Panatti's kiss.

'Now that's interesting,' Ottolenghi said. 'It sounds as if you were tricked, James.'

'Ottolenghi is right,' Lombroso said. 'It seems to me that both the Panatti woman and the girl had been given instructions.'

'What kind of instructions?' Anna asked.

'Both were told to inveigle Murray into a compromising position,' he replied. 'I'd also be willing to bet that the girl was told to leave by the front door, and that somewhere down the line a witness will come out of the woodwork saying that they saw her leaving in a dishevelled state or some such nonsense.'

'So it was a trap?' James asked.

'It would seem likely,' Lombroso said. 'Perhaps Panatti is motivated by revenge. You did reject her, after all.'

'Surely she wouldn't ruin him just for that,' Anna said. 'There has to be more to it.'

'My dear Anna, you know as well as I do that women are far more vengeful than men,' Lombroso said. 'It is in their nature. They simply can't help themselves.' Anna glared at him, but he went on. 'If you offend such a woman, you may well find yourself in the hands of an almost inexorable executioner. She is quite capable of pouring torments on her victim, drop by drop and at great length.'

'That's comforting,' James said.

'We need to find out for certain if there is another motive,' Lombroso said. 'But before we deal with that, I should tell you, Murray, that I have received a further complaint about your behaviour.'

'From Francesco Rambaudi?' James asked.

Lombroso nodded. 'I see you were expecting something from the gentleman.'

'Gentleman!' James said. 'He is no such thing.'

'What is James supposed to have done, Cesare?' Anna asked.

'Signor Rambaudi tells me that he broke into his estate and was found tampering with some farm machinery. '

'What on earth were you doing, James?' Ottolenghi said.

'Rambaudi is not entirely accurate. The gate was open.'

'He insists that it was locked and that you broke in,' Lombroso said.

'He has been misinformed. I tried the gate and it opened.'

'Well, that aside, what were you doing there in the first place? If you wanted to see your sister, it would have been more sensible to go to the house, surely.'

'Lucy was there?' Anna said.

'She was lunching with them apparently, although I didn't know it. Well, not until he exhibited me in front of her and his other guests as if I was a common thief.'

Lombroso stared at him. 'So why go there at all? It is a mystery to me.'

'I was making enquiries for a friend.'

'What friend?'

James paused. 'I was helping Sofia to look for her cousin.'

'What would she be doing at the Rambaudi estate?'

'It wasn't her I was trying to find exactly.'

'Have you decided to become an enquiry agent on the side? Do I not give you enough to do?'

'As you know, Chiara is not the only girl to have gone missing. One of the others, Teresa Mariani, had a male friend who also seems to have disappeared.'

'We have discussed this before, Murray. The girls are most likely to be runaways and I daresay the boy is no different.'

'Actually I've found him, or at least I think I have, and I'm not sure he's a runaway exactly. Also, the girl at the abbey, Nella Calvi, worked as a prostitute at Madame Giulia's. She went missing from another establishment ... a secret one.'

'So Panatti is running a second brothel. That is interesting.'

'And another of the missing girls worked there as a maid.'

'Also interesting,' Lombroso said. 'Anything else?'

'And then there are the bodies of the girls, all with organs removed, signs of exsanguination and attempts at preservation through mummification or embalming.'

'I have been thinking about that myself. It is a peculiar thing to do to someone, going well beyond the actions of any habitual criminal that I have come across. And of course we don't know if this was the cause of death, although nothing would surprise me in this case.'

'You think they may have been bled to death . . . that they were tortured . . . That is terrifying!' Anna said.

Lombroso frowned. 'Why drain the blood? That is what I do not understand. Why kill them in this ghastly way?'

'I might be able to help with that,' Ottolenghi said. He repeated what he had told James about Reiner's research.

Lombroso leant back in his chair, his hands together in front of him as if he was praying for a solution. 'Perhaps it is some kind of sect. We are plagued with them in this city.'

'But this woman, Bathory, died hundreds of years ago,' Anna said.

'The Devil is older than that, but satanists still worship him,' James said. 'What if someone has decided to repeat Bathory's work? Reiner seems to think there is a particular criminal type who is aroused by the drinking of blood.'

'I have read his case files. There are many examples of deranged killers who drink the blood of their victims,' Otto-lenghi said.

James shuddered. 'Which would explain what happened to the blood.'

'It doesn't, however, explain the attempt to preserve the corpse,' Lombroso said.

James nodded. 'True, but that could just be an extension of the criminal's perversion.'

'It would certainly fit with the profile of moral insanity,' Lombroso agreed. 'But such a manifestation would be rare indeed.'

'You have said yourself that such men exist, Professor. Look at all we went through last year. How was it that you put it in your book?

'"They are born to savour evil and to commit it",' Lombroso said slowly.

'Well someone here in Turin is doing exactly that,' Anna said. 'Girls go missing, then bodies are found – and it surely can't be a coincidence that as soon as James investigates, he gets into trouble.'

'Panatti must be involved somehow,' Lombroso declared. 'We need to find out more about her.'

'And how do we do that?' Anna asked. 'The woman is devious and manipulative. I was there the day she kissed you, James. She could not wait to get rid of me. Now I know why.'

'Sofia warned me about her . . . something to do with visiting the good and keeping well with the bad,' James said.

'An old Italian proverb, and definitely a warning. Panatti is clearly known as a bad lot in certain circles,' Lombroso said.

'Perhaps I'd better speak to her,' James suggested.

'No. Keep away from her for now,' Lombroso said. 'She's obviously dangerous, particularly as far as you are concerned. We need to be careful how we deal with her. I am told she is likely to be at the marchesa's ball, so we must plan our strategy.'

'Well, I hope you all enjoy it.'

'None of that, Murray,' Lombroso said. 'You will be there too. The article does not name you. That, I am certain, will be good enough for the marchesa.'

'But after all this, surely my presence will be controversial.'

'Perhaps, and I will of course speak to the marchesa to canvass her view. But I suspect she will not withdraw her invitation. Your attendance might just give us some idea about why this is being done to you. It is an excellent opportunity to gather information. I want all of us to be alert, particularly if there is anyone of the criminal type present.'

'Any particular type, Professor?' Ottolenghi asked.

'We may well be looking for an example of moral insanity, so asymmetry in facial features, unequal ears, thick lips, large jaw and mouth, malformed teeth, perhaps with some missing, scanty beard...'

'Sounds like half of the carabinieri,' James murmured to Anna.

'Are these likely to be characteristics in the marchesa's guests?' she asked.

'If they are morally insane, then yes,' Lombroso replied crisply.

'Reiner says that such people are often very precocious and have a ferocious bloodlust,' Ottolenghi commented.

'Indeed, then we must be on our guard,' Lombroso said.

'And what if Concetta Panatti is the sole instigator here?' Anna asked.

'I find that an incredible proposition,' Lombroso said. 'She is a criminal woman and therefore inherently inferior in intellect. Besides, a morally insane woman would have a virile physiognomy, and we cannot say that of her at least.'

Ottolenghi grinned. 'Certainly not, or James would never have kissed her!'

Lombroso glared at him. 'That is not helpful, Salvatore, though no doubt it is true. Of course Panatti is shameless and lascivious, traits found in both the prostitute and the morally insane. Though she is not imbecilic, which is interesting.'

'Why would the marchesa invite her to the ball?' James asked.

'She is a leading businesswoman and her association with Madame Giulia's is not generally known. And I know she interests the marchesa.'

'I will watch her closely if she is there,' Anna said. 'I look forward to it.'

'Right . . . well, we all know what we are about,' Lombroso said. 'I am confident that by the end of the evening we will understand more about this whole business.'

James hoped he was right. The prospect of attending the ball had never been particularly inviting. He had always found formal occasions a little daunting, and had been hoping to blend into the background and observe rather than partici-pate. But now he faced the prospect of being talked about and perhaps judged by people he had never even met.

What worried him more, however, was the thought of Lucy having to endure the same fate when she, unlike him, was blameless. It was ironic, really. He was accustomed to being the subject of tittle-tattle as the result of his father's actions, and now the cycle seemed to be repeating itself. It seemed that Lombroso might have been wrong to reassure him about his provenance at the end of his first visit to Turin. Perhaps he was a born criminal after all.

35

Hysterics, like epileptics, often suffer from delirium, either melancholic or mono-maniacal. The maniacal form of the disorder is accompanied by hallucinations, impulsiveness, constant agitation or a need for movement, and desires to smash whatever lies in their way. These symptoms will appear in a flash in someone in good health, last just a short time, and leave without a trace. Suddenly a person will run from a ballroom and throw herself in the river. A girl will break all the dishes and pour boiling water over her brother's head and then fly from the house to the woods, where she may be found building a stone altar for the celebration of her imaginary marriage. These crises, like those of epilepsy, come and go.

Lombroso and Ferrero, 1983, p. 236

The evening of the marchesa's ball was warm and humid. The sunshine and showers of late spring had subsided, to be replaced by a heavy dampness, and the city seemed to shine as if it was sheathed in a thin film of perspiration brought about by the anticipation of the festivities to come.

Lucy felt the same. Her gown, pale blue silk, had been lent to her by Anna Tarnovsky. Already it was clinging to her and she had not even danced a single step. Whilst she waited for the rest of her party to alight, she watched carefully as other carriages began to arrive and the marchesa's guests, also dressed in their best finery, emerged. This might be a scene in her novel, with Lydia Loveday posing as a guest in order to detect a notorious jewel thief, watching her suspects as they mingled and wove their way through the throng, waiting for one of them to make their move. Lucy was just as alert, although her targets were less obvious. Miss Trott and Professor Donati were her suspects, though their crime, if there was one, was as yet unknown. But there were, of course, other things to consider.

Overall, the last few days had been odd to say the least. James was avoiding her, which was to be expected after the incident at the Villa Purezza. But she had known that something else was going on. There were meetings behind closed doors, raised voices on occasion, and even Gina and Paola had been unusually distant, apparently concentrating on their studies according to Signora Lombroso. Miss Trott would not be drawn on the matter, preferring to try to distract her with gallery and museum visits.

Finally Anna had taken her aside and explained things to her. James had been subjected to a campaign that was clearly calculated to destroy his reputation. He had unwittingly helped it along, but all the same, most of it – particularly the most recent 'revelations' – was untrue. Fortunately the marchesa had made it clear that she had no interest in the subject, and both Lucy and James had her full support.

Everyone of note in the city of Turin would be there, and Lucy was glad of the opportunity to observe them. Somebody was doing their utmost to hurt James, and she was determined to find out who and why. Now that they were here, it was clear that the professor was of the same view. When it was time to go in, he issued instructions to everyone as if it were a military operation. Lucy heard James whisper to Ottolenghi that Garibaldi himself would not have done better.

The professor led the way with his wife and daughters and Miss Trott, followed by James and Lucy with Ottolenghi and Anna Tarnovksy in what James called a rearguard action. This had the effect of demonstrating support for James and also protecting him from the glares and whispers that surrounded them as they entered.

Lucy was familiar with this kind of thing up to a point. When their father had been taken away from them to the asylum, the entire family had become the subject of local fascination. James and Aunt Agnes had done their best to shield her from this unwanted attention, but she was still aware of it, although the details of exactly what her father had done to deserve his detention still eluded her.

Once they entered the main ballroom, she had thought they would find a discreet corner somewhere to settle, but that was not Lombroso's way. Instead he insisted that they choose a central table, and once they were seated, he took great pleasure in rising to greet people as they passed and then performing elaborate introductions to Lucy and James.

'May I present my assistant, Signor Murray, and his sister Lucy, from Scotland. He is heading up my new research project, you know ... a very intelligent young man! We are lucky to have him in our city.'

Of course this did not stop people from staring at them, and no doubt there was plenty of gossip circulating about the newspaper article, but the professor's obvious support did seem to be working up to a point. However, it was when the marchesa actually took the trouble to come over and greet them personally that Lucy could tell the tide of public opinion was turning.

'I am so glad you could come this evening, Signor Murray,' she said, shaking him warmly by the hand.

'I am honoured by your invitation,' James replied.

'I would be interested to hear of your work with the professor. Perhaps you would visit me soon and we can discuss it.'

'I would be delighted.'

'It is wonderful that our city is at the heart of such wide-reaching endeavour, Professor,' the marchesa said to Lombroso before turning her attention to Lucy and smiling at her. 'And, Signorina Murray, how nice to see you also, my dear. I hope that you will enjoy the dancing later.'

'I look forward to it, Marchesa.'

With that, she left them to greet some of her other guests. All of this gave those attending the ball something of a dilemma. It was clear from the attention that James was attracting that most people were aware of the newspaper article. Yet he had been acknowledged by the marchesa herself, which in itself gave him a certain respectability. In the end it seemed that most preferred to ignore him, which was certainly better than being openly snubbed.

Lucy was content for the time being to sit with her party and observe her fellow guests, which was fascinating. There were many enthusiastic greetings, both true and false, the bonhomie pouring from honeyed tongues. The ladies whispered to each other about who was wearing which gown and the extent to which it suited them. Gossip was exchanged, music began to play and drinks were served. The ball was under way.

Lucy noticed that the priest who had been at Lombroso's dinner the first night they were in Turin seemed to have

336

assumed the role of social commentator to the marchesa. Earlier she had made her grand and glittering entrance to the usual sycophantic applause, but having performed her function as hostess, it seemed that she, like Lucy, was content to observe. Occasionally those who had been chosen for the honour were presented to her, but for the most part she sat, resplendent in her diamonds, watching as a piece of theatre she herself had created played out before her.

Fabia, of course, was in her element. The ball was in her honour and she was making the most of the fact. She was dressed in a beautiful silk gown of pink and silver that sparkled as she moved. Lucy felt quite drab in comparison. Standing next to Fabia was Francesco. Lucy expected her heart to lurch when she noticed him, but there was nothing more than slight regret. He had not tried to contact her and she had assumed from this that James had offended him so much that he would not have anything to do with her. He was paying court to Fabia, watched intently by Bianca, who was standing at his side. She murmured something into his ear, and he looked over to Lucy's table. Fabia followed his line of sight and simpered. Francesco waved as if nothing had happened and began to make his way over to her.

'Signorina Lucy Murray, how nice to see you!' he said, bowing deeply.

'Signor Rambaudi,' she said with a brief nod of acknowledgement.

'Would you do me the honour of dancing with me?'

Lucy hesitated for a moment. This would be an opportunity to make amends, but it would also be her first dance at her first ball. She had attended dancing lessons, but this was different. Hundreds of people were watching. Would she remember all the steps? Fabia was frowning at her. That decided it. 'Yes, thank you, signor,' she said, and taking Francesco's arm, she followed him into the ballroom.

'A waltz, how enchanting,' Francesco declared.

In a moment she was in his arms, being expertly steered around the dance floor. It was an intoxicating experience. She had never been in such close proximity to a man. The feel of his hand in the small of her back and the lightest of touches as his fingers intertwined with hers was almost overwhelming. Perhaps she loved him after all.

'You waltz well, Signorina Murray.'

'Thank you. But Miss Trott has told me that one is not supposed to converse whilst engaged in a dance.'

'Ah, the magnificent Miss Trott. We must bow to her infinitely superior wisdom.'

'Oh, I don't mind talking. She doesn't know everything.'

'And have you informed her of this startling revelation?'

'You are teasing me, Signor Rambaudi!'

'Francesco, please. We have no need to be formal, you and I.'

'I am sorry for what my brother did, Francesco.'

'It doesn't matter. I imagine he had his reasons.'

'He was helping a friend.'

'From what I have read, he seems to be a very friendly sort of fellow altogether.'

Lucy did not reply. Perhaps Miss Trott was right. Silence was better after all. Besides, it was difficult to know exactly what to say, since James was so evidently in the wrong. Should she really have to defend her brother? They continued round and round to the music and it seemed to her that they were increasing their speed with each turn.

Out of the corner of her eye she noticed a tall, gaunt-looking man with a piercing gaze. He looked familiar – where had she seen him before? Somehow he did not seem to fit in with his surroundings. Then round and round they went again, faster and faster. Who was the man talking to? She couldn't see. He was standing behind a pillar . . . oh, move, why don't you . . . round and round again . . . they seemed to be having a very animated conversation . . . not altogether friendly . . . spinning and spinning . . . ah, he had moved . . . it was Professor Donati . . . funny how he always seemed to be upsetting people . . . round and round . . . must keep up with Francesco. He was grinning at her and she felt herself smiling back. Then it was as if they were the only people in the room. Everyone else had melted away.

Abruptly the music stopped and they came to a standstill. Francesco bowed to her, led her from the floor, and then he was gone. She stood there, confused, not knowing what to do. She had expected to be escorted back to her party, but now she had been abandoned and, having lost her bearings, did not know where they were. In an instant, James was standing next to her.

'My dance next, I think,' he said quickly, leading her on to the floor for some kind of quadrille, with the dancers lining up in rows.

''I don't know the steps for this,' she said.

'Neither do I. Let's make it up.'

'James, we can't!' Lucy said, half in alarm and half laughing at her brother's sudden carefree attitude. 'What will people say?'

'They will say whatever they want. I'm already in disgrace. I'm sure a few misplaced dance steps will not make it any worse.'

'But *I* am not in disgrace,' she protested.

'Look. We're in luck. It's a cotillion. We will be directed

in our steps.' He indicated an elderly autocratic man who had positioned himself at the head of the lines, like a general about to direct his forces into battle. 'It will be just like dancing the reel at home.'

'I'm not sure it will,' Lucy said.

'Shush now. We need to concentrate.'

'James, I really don't think—'

She was interrupted by an elegant red-haired woman in an emerald green and gold gown who, with her partner, took her place next to James, readying herself for the dance.

'Well, well, Signor Murray. I did not expect you to be here this evening.'

'Nor I you, Signora Panatti. I did not have you down as a dancer.'

'I am here as the guest of Judge Carraldi.' She indicated an elderly man with a pronounced stoop. 'I wonder, Judge, shall we wait a little until dancing again? I do not find the company to my liking.'

'Very well, my dear,' he replied.

Lucy glared at her. According to Anna, this was the woman who had claimed that James had misbehaved so disgracefully.

'Perhaps you should go,' Signora Panatti said as she was leaving the floor. 'Nobody wants you here.'

'I do not think so, Signora,' James said. 'I have done nothing wrong, as I am sure you are well aware.'

She laughed mirthlessly. 'That is not what I have been told.'

'What do you mean?'

'I have many friends, Signor Murray. They come from all over the world and they tell me all kinds of useful things.'

'I am very happy for you, Signora Panatti.'

'At least one of them knows you of old, apparently. In particular he has been very talkative about your family. In fact, I am told that he knows better than all of us exactly what you are.'

'What is this woman talking about, James?' Lucy asked.

'I have no idea.'

Signora Panatti smiled. 'I think you have some explaining to do, Signor Murray. You see, my dear,' she continued, addressing her comments to Lucy, 'even without his penchant for ladies of a certain kind, your brother is hardly a paragon of virtue.'

She leant over to him and spoke in a low voice. 'I have only just begun.'

The other dancers were staring at them and murmuring to each other behind hands and fans.

'You are despicable,' muttered James, and taking Lucy forcibly by the arm, he began to propel her from the dance floor back towards the professor, who was watching with concern.

'You can't say I didn't warn you,' Signora Panatti called after them.

Having delivered Lucy into the safe custody of Miss Trott and Professor Donati, who had joined their table, James accompanied Lombroso, Anna and Ottolenghi outside on to a nearby terrace to discuss matters.

He leant over the balustrade and peered out into the fast-approaching darkness. It had rained recently, and the raindrops were shining like moonstones in the fading light.

'What was all that about, Murray?' Lombroso asked.

James faced them. The two men were standing and Anna was seated, all of them as if frozen in time, creating an elaborate tableau depicting some kind of inquisition.

'I don't know what she wants from me,' he said, speaking slowly, stretching the words out as if they were elastic. His breath came in short bursts and he felt a small bead of sweat trickle down his cheek, following the path of his new scar.

'If it was unclear before, it is certainly clear now. Panatti definitely has some kind of agenda,' Anna said. 'She seems absolutely set on destroying your reputation.'

'We still need to establish her motive,' Lombroso said.

'Perhaps you have found something out, or she thinks you have,' Ottolenghi suggested. 'After all, as you have said yourself, James, she has an influence in all kinds of areas, many of them illicit.'

'The only thing I have been doing is searching for Sofia's cousin.'

'Then, as we have said, it must be something to do with that,' Lombroso said. 'Is there anything you might have stumbled upon during your investigation?'

James frowned. 'The trouble is, I can't remember much from after I was assaulted.'

'Try your best, Murray. This second establishment of Panatti's is the most likely.'

'It doesn't sound as if it is state-registered,' Ottolenghi said, 'so it's probably secluded. That would make it a good place to commit murder, particularly if one wanted to drain blood from a body.'

'I thought I saw Panatti speaking to the Rambaudis a few moments ago,' Anna said. 'They are acquainted, then?'

'I'm not sure,' Lombroso said. 'I know the family, but I am not aware of any link between them and that woman. I imagine they were just being polite.'

'What about their background?' James asked. He had seen that Lucy had formed some kind of attachment to Francesco Rambaudi but had assumed that it had ended after his appearance at the rice estate. After seeing his sister dancing with the man that evening, he was no longer certain that this was the case, which was a potentially disturbing development. And if Rambaudi knew Concetta Panatti...

Lombroso stroked his beard, deep in thought. 'The parents are both dead. The father succumbed to the effects of drink a few years ago now, and the mother more recently from some illness or other. It was quite sudden, I believe.'

'I think Panatti could be responsible for the murders,' Anna said. 'Both Nella Calvi and Teresa Mariani worked for her, which surely cannot be a coincidence. I have encountered her criminal type before, utterly ruthless and quite without conscience. I am certain she would be quite prepared to kill, if it became necessary.'

Lombroso shook his head. 'You are wrong, Madame Tarnovsky. These killings are almost certainly the handiwork of our morally insane criminal, who is obviously a man. As I have said before, Panatti, if she is involved, is just an accomplice.'

'How can you be so certain, Cesare?' Anna asked.

Before he could reply, there was the sound of a commotion from the main ballroom.

'What the devil?' Lombroso said.

Professor Donati came running on to the terrace. 'Signor, Professore... your presence has been urgently requested by the marchesa...'

'Whatever has happened?' asked Lombroso.

'It is Fabia Carignano,' Professor Donati said. 'She seems to have gone missing.'

36

To society's shame, many occasional prostitutes are recruited through violence and traded as black slaves were. They are enlisted by some scoundrel who, pretending to find them work as waitresses or something similar, takes them to foreign countries where they have neither friends nor supports. He shuts them up in brothels where everything encourages them to give in: cajolery, threats, liquor... *Most are raped and maliciously prevented from leaving their brothel-prison. They end up by adapting to the prostitute's life, and they continue with it because escape is so difficult.* Lombroso and Ferrero, 1893, p. 225

She wakes slowly. Her head is pounding. She opens her eyes, but what she sees is not what she expects. She sees that she is in some kind of cell. The walls are made of stone and she can smell dampness, though it is underpinned with something sweet... no, not sweet... overripe, decaying. Beneath her is straw. She tries to move but discovers that she is chained to a wall by her ankle, tethered like some kind of animal. She cries out in anger and frustration and pulls at her shackles as if doing so will tear them from the solid stone they are so securely fastened to. She realises that it is more of a pit than a cell, for there is no door. Above her is an iron grid through which there is some natural light. It was night when she was taken, so how long has she been here? All she remembers is getting a note inviting her out on to the terrace. Once out there, she heard someone whispering her name in the gardens and walked towards the voice. In a moment someone had placed a cloth over her face and everything went dark.

She shivers and hugs herself. She is still dressed in her thin ballgown, a magnificent creation in varying shades of pink and silver with beaded embellishments that shone so prettily in the flickering candlelight. It is short-sleeved and low-cut, and seemed so daring when first chosen. She loved it when she put it on. It made her feel like a queen. But now she is wishing that she had chosen something warmer, or at least had a shawl to keep out the cold.

She shifts around a little. She needs to relieve herself, but how? She sees a bucket in the corner. No. She is an aristocrat. She will not sink to such depths. Suddenly she is overwhelmed by fury and pride. How dare they, whoever they are, bring her to such a place? A girl – no, a woman – of her standing?

'Let me out of here!' she cries. 'If you do not, you will be sorry.'

She hears a noise from above. There is someone leaning over the edge of her prison, watching her.

'You can shout as much as you like, but no one will hear you.' The voice is strange ... musical, like a small bell. She cannot tell if it is male or female.

'Listen to me,' she says. 'If you release me now, I will say it was all a joke. Nothing will happen to you.'

'I cannot. You must atone.'

'Atone?' she says. 'Atone for what? I have done nothing wrong! If anyone should atone it is you. You have abducted me and brought me here. The longer you keep me here, the worse it will be for you.'

'Atone . . . you must atone.'

The figure moves away. The light from above dims slowly and there is a scraping sound. A cover of stone or wood is being hauled over the opening above.

'No! Don't leave me here! Come back!'

But it is no use. The lid of her stone box is in place and she is left in darkness, like an exhibit in a museum. She starts to weep. Her defiance has left her. This was not how this day was meant to be. It should have been full of wonderful things – admiration, adulation and gifts. For today is a special day. It is her birthday. But if what she suspects is right, it might well be her last.

James perused the newspapers cautiously over breakfast. The events of the previous evening were covered on all the front pages and, unsurprisingly, had taken precedence over further discussion about his own activities. Clearly it was one thing for servants and flower sellers to go missing, but quite another for a member of the aristocracy to be snatched at a society event. He and many others had searched the surrounding area, but there was no trace of Fabia except for a solitary shoe found in the gardens. It seemed as if she had been smuggled through the back gates. No one had seen anything; it had been carefully planned.

Apprehensively, he opened *The People's Voice*, and there he found his worst suspicions confirmed: an attempt to link him to the abduction. Firstly it was mentioned that the ball had been attended by some foreign gentlemen who 'may be under suspicion', although that could refer to any number of people present. Secondly, in the centre of the newspaper there was a feature about him written by Baldovino. James wasn't named, but he might as well have been. There was even a cartoon depicting a scientist with a large head and a tiny body ensnaring a young woman in a butterfly net. 'Leave me alone!' she was saying. 'I don't want to go to Scotland. It's far too cold!' The headline was THE SCIENTIST AND THE MAIDENS? and the article was, James thought, absolutely ludicrous. It suggested that foreign scientists were 'infiltrating our university'. 'Who knows what their intent might be?' it asked, and then suggested that there might be some link between their 'malign presence' and the 'disappearance of a number of girls from our city'. The implication was clear. This was plumbing new depths, even for Baldovino.

As he was reading, Lombroso came in, closely followed by Ottolenghi, who had stayed with them due to the lateness of the hour.

'More nonsense in *The People's Voice*?' Lombroso asked. James handed over his copy. 'Try to rise above it, Murray,' he advised. 'In a few days it will all be forgotten. The search for Fabia Carignano is bound to take precedence, as indeed it should.'

'It is a terrifying business,' Ottolenghi said, 'but at least the carabinieri should act now.'

Lombroso nodded. 'Apparently there are to be extra patrols on the streets, and all leave has been cancelled. The marchesa has insisted on meeting the mayor to discuss the investigation.'

'It is a pity that all this wasn't put in place when the other girls went missing,' James said bitterly, looking down at the newspapers on the table in front of him. 'They're hardly mentioned except for Baldovino trying to imply that I am involved.'

'No one will take that seriously,' Ottolenghi said. 'Reporters always like to make connections where none exist. Look at how he suggested a link to the Abbey San Callisto and the monks.'

'No doubt that will turn out to be my fault as well.'

'Even Baldovino would find it hard to connect you to something that happened a century ago,' Lombroso said.

'We did find a body there,' James pointed out.

'Indeed – one of a series of unexplained events: missing girls, dead girls, missing blood, mummified monks, reports of haunting, you being beaten and threatened, and of course last night's abduction.' Lombroso looked thoughtful. 'We need to put our anthropological thinking caps on and see what we can find.' He sat down at the table. 'But first we must take a good breakfast. After all, hunger provokes crime, as the Tuscans say.'

Having no appetite, James retired to Lombroso's small library and tried his best to work, though he was finding it difficult to concentrate. All he wanted was to get out there and investigate Fabia's disappearance in the hope that it would lead him to Chiara. But thanks to that stupid article, he had been advised to stay here. Sofia had been sent home and he did not know what she had been told, although he was certain she would have read the articles. She must be beside herself.

Before long, Ottolenghi came in and sat opposite him. Lombroso had asked them to continue with the tasks he had set; he himself had a meeting with Gemelli, presumably about the articles and other matters. Ironically, they were going through the data collated from the interviews with Madame Giulia's girls, with whom James was accused of consorting.

They had been asked to pick out quotations from what the girls had said to them, in order to illustrate the truth or otherwise of their comments.

'It will be all right,' Ottolenghi said. 'The professor will sort it out.'

'I have been such a fool!'

'You are being very hard on yourself.'

'I should have listened to you when you warned me about Sofia. It would have been better for us both if I had kept away from her.'

'You fell in love. That is not a crime,' Ottolenghi said. 'And no one could have foreseen that Baldovino would have been quite so vengeful.'

'I did rough him up a little.'

'I know, but that sort of thing would normally be like water off a duck's back to a man like him.'

'It does seem extreme. And it is not just my life that is affected.'

'So you think Baldovino is acting under Panatti's influence?'

'He did mention that he had been threatened.'

'Who by?'

James looked at Ottolenghi. In all that had happened, he had almost forgotten Baldovino's treacherous informer. 'He claimed that he didn't know. Whoever it was told him to mind his own business. That was why he gave me the names of the girls.'

'You do his dirty work and he reports it. Is that how it worked?'

'Something like that.'

There was a knock at the door and a maid came in with a note for James. She handed it to him, then ran off without waiting for a reply, as if she was afraid he might attack her.

When he had read it, he crumpled it up in disgust and threw it on the fire, watching as the flames flared up and consumed it

'Who was it from?' Ottolenghi asked.

'Baldovino. Apparently he has some information for me.'

'Will you go?'

James hesitated. 'I suppose I'd better.'

'Are you sure that's a good idea? The professor told you to stay here. It might make things worse.'

'How could they get any worse, Salvatore? My reputation is in ruins, not to mention that of my sister. I might lose my job and I've almost certainly lost Sofia. Do you really think I should just sit here and wait for it all to blow over? Baldovino might know something. At the very least, he could tell me who's behind these stories.'

'Do you want me to come with you?' Ottolenghi asked.

'No,' James replied. 'This is between me and Baldovino. Just cover for me if you can.'

'I will. But be careful. Whoever threatened Baldovino is dangerous.'

James acknowledged his friend's warning as he left, but he knew it would make no difference. He had to solve these riddles before anything else happened. He remembered the words of his captors when he had been abducted. They'd told him he had a lot to lose and they were right.

Then there was that Panatti woman. 'I have only just begun,' she had said at the ball. At least some of this was her doing, but why, and how much? Perhaps Baldovino held the key. He was certainly involved. James knew it was risky, but too much was at stake. He had to find out.

*

Baldovino's broken door was still hanging off its hinges, as it had been the last time James was here. He pushed it open.

'Baldovino, are you there?'

There was no reply. He stepped inside, then stopped to take in the scene. The place had never been particularly tidy, but now it was completely wrecked. Pieces of china were strewn around. The windows were smashed. Every stick of furniture had been pulled apart. Even the shabby sofa had been slashed with a knife. He heard a groan from behind it and went to investigate. It was Baldovino. He had been stabbed as well as severely beaten. His blood seemed to be everywhere. James knelt down beside him and opened his collar. He was still breathing, but only just. Something was tucked underneath him. James lifted his coat and pulled it out. It was a large knife.

'What do we have here, then?' said a voice from the doorway. James stood up quickly, the knife still in his hand. Two carabinieri officers walked into the room.

'Put it down, son. You've done enough.'

'You can't think that I did this.'

'Drop the knife,' the second man said, stepping towards him.

James obeyed and held up his hands in surrender. The first man knelt down by Baldovino and felt for a pulse. He nodded at his colleague.

'You're under arrest for attempted murder,' said the man, handcuffing him.

'I did not do this,' James protested.

'Funny, that's what they all say . . . to start with, anyway.' He escorted James out of Baldovino's room and into the street.

'I need to get home,' James said.

'The only home you're going to is jail,' said his captor. 'You won't be seeing anywhere else for a while.'

James had been told that if he interfered he would regret it. He had chosen to ignore the warning and he had been wrong. The threat had been carried out, and regret it he certainly did.

37

Every mental abnormality makes its own contribution to criminality. The idiot is given to explosions of rage, assaults, murder, rape and arson for the mere pleasure of seeing the flames. The imbecile and feebleminded, succumbing easily to their first impulses or the suggestions of others, become accomplices to crime at the slightest prospect of gain. Lombroso, 1889, p. 275

Lucy sat at the breakfast table, still thinking about poor Fabia. Where was she now? Was she even still alive? Gina and Paola were poring over the newspaper, much to Miss Trott's disapproval.

'It says here that the carabinieri are questioning everyone who attended the ball,' Paola said.

Gina sighed. 'I wish we had not left early. We might have seen something.'

'If you'll excuse me,' Miss Trott said, 'I have to go out shortly. I have some things to do. I doubt I'll be back before lunchtime. I am sure you can occupy yourself until then, Lucy.'

'Do you think you should, Miss Trott?' Paola said. 'The editorial warns against going out unaccompanied. It says here that no one is safe.'

Miss Trott glared at her. 'I think that young ladies should not be reading at the breakfast table!' She got up, snatched the newspaper away and stalked out.

Gina watched her leave. 'I wonder where she's going.'

'Probably shopping or visiting a gallery or something,' Paola said as she nibbled delicately at a pastry.

'She might be going to the Via San Pellico,' Lucy said. 'Let's follow her.'

Gina waved her butter knife enthusiastically. 'That's a very good idea.'

'But what about the warning?' Paola said. 'Won't Mama object?'

'She won't mind if we don't tell her. Besides, we'll be together.'

Lucy nodded and got up from the table. 'We should hurry. We don't want to miss her.'

The girls waited in Lucy's room until they heard the door to Miss Trott's bedroom open and close. The game was afoot.

Miss Trott was a fast walker. The day was warm and humid and the sun was unrelenting, so keeping up with her was no easy task. *Pinkerton's Detection Manual* was, as ever, invaluable in its advice, giving ten tips for successful pursuit of suspects:

1. Keep your distance.
2. Ensure that you are never directly behind your subject.
3. Be discreet.
4. Wear a disguise where necessary.
5. Do not make loud noises.
6. Do not lose sight of the subject.
7. Carry a newspaper so that you have something to hide behind if your subject suddenly stops or you are spotted.
8. Do not under any circumstances run.

9. Carry a likeness of your subject so that you can ask passers-by if they have seen him in the event you lose sight of him.
10. Always carry a notebook, pencil, a map and pocket watch.

They had all agreed that most points were rather obvious and that number 4, although inviting, was likely to be a recipe for disaster. Gina was tempted to dress up as one of her father's criminal types, but this was rejected because, frankly, it was far too warm. They were going to take a newspaper, but Professor Lombroso was reading it. However, they did manage to equip themselves with a notebook, and Lucy said that she would use her silver propelling pencil, a gift from her mother. The only map they could find was not of Turin, and the pocket watch and likeness of Miss Trott were equally elusive. In fact they spent so long trying to get ready that they almost missed their quarry altogether. Had it not been for the fact that Miss Trott had evidently forgotten something and was forced to return to collect whatever it was, they would have failed before their mission had even begun.

Despite the teething problems, they managed finally to follow Miss Trott, and a merry dance she led them. It was odd, Lucy thought, that she did not seem to be going to one particular place to conduct her business. Instead she meandered through the streets, turning down alleyways and even at one point doubling back on herself, forcing her pursuers to take evasive action that involved ducking into a millinery shop, where they examined the merchandise with some care. In fact, such was Paola's attention to detail that she had to be almost dragged away from a pretty straw summer bonnet and reminded of their aim.

Eventually, after an exhausting hour, Miss Trott seemed to be walking with more purpose, and it was not long before she began to slow down and examine the buildings she was passing with more care. Then, quite suddenly, she stopped. Fortunately the girls were able to slip into an alleyway and observe her from a distance. She stood and peered at the building for a moment as if undecided. Then she drew herself up, put her shoulders back and her chin in the air and marched inside.

'Let's see where she went,' Lucy suggested. 'Then we can decide what to do next.'

'No need. I know where she has gone,' Paola said. 'Papa has pointed it out on more than one occasion. It is the headquarters of the carabinieri.'

Baldovino lived only a few streets away from the carabinieri's headquarters, so James had to suffer the ignominy of being escorted on foot. A crowd made up mostly of small boys began to follow them, jeering as they went. There were also a couple of enterprising street pedlars who supplied snacks where requested. It was, after all, not every day that a gentleman was arrested, and the officer seemed to take great pleasure in slowing their progress at every available opportunity. After what seemed like an age, they arrived at their destination, and their followers melted into the background as if they had never actually been there. When James made as if to go through the front door, he was directed round a corner.

'Tradesmen's entrance for you today,' the officer said firmly.

He was taken to a shabby reception area, and then to a holding cell, where he was shoved onto a bench and told to wait until someone came for him. There were a number of other prisoners also waiting, and a motley crew they were.

Two of them had obviously been in a fight and were nursing various wounds and glaring at each other. Another was clearly drunk and sat in a corner moaning to himself, a pool of vomit at his feet. A woman with heavily rouged cheeks and a large feathered hat winked at James and blew him a kiss. James began to think that perhaps Lombroso had a point in his description of the criminal type. They certainly resembled some of the photographs he had seen in the professor's study.

'Wait here. You will be taken through to be interviewed when someone is available,' the officer said.

'Who?' James asked.

'Whoever is here.'

'I want to see Inspector Tullio.'

'Oh do you?' said the officer. 'And will he want to see you?'

'Yes,' James said decisively. 'He will. I am innocent.'

'Oh, I see. Well that makes all the difference,' the officer said sarcastically.

'Please... the inspector will understand.'

'He's a busy man. The marchesa's niece has been abducted. The whole city is up in arms.'

'I want to see him now. I did not do this.'

'So you've said, but that's for the courts to decide. Maybe he'll come and see you in jail.'

'Please. Just tell the inspector that I am here.'

The officer shrugged and walked away, leaving James trying to avoid the glances of his companions and contemplating what Lombroso would say when he heard about this. As for Aunt Agnes... He sighed in frustration. He should be out there looking for Chiara and Fabia and the other girls, not stuck in a cell.

A few minutes later he heard the sound of a key in the

outer gate. The bars rattled ominously. Was he about to be taken to prison? A familiar face came into view.

'Tullio, thank God!' James said.

Tullio, unsmiling, nodded at the man who had opened the gate and pointed at James. 'You, get up and follow me.'

James did as he was told, and soon he was sitting in a small room with Tullio. It was almost normal except for the fact that he was shackled to the table and the inspector, rather than sitting, was standing uncomfortably in a corner looking anywhere but at him.

'We need to get the professor on to this first of all,' James said, 'and Ottolenghi. If you can bring them to the scene and then to Baldovino's bedside, that would be best. Once he comes round, it should be a simple matter, but I don't know when that will be. How is he?'

'He is in a bad way. He may not recover at all.' Tullio's voice was cold.

'I feared that might be the case. He was badly injured when I found him. Well, we will just have to examine the scene carefully. It will exculpate me soon enough.'

'The evidence is damning,' his friend replied.

'You must know that I did not do this, Tullio!'

Tullio shrugged. 'I cannot help you, James.' He looked pale, and new lines seemed to have formed around his mouth and on his forehead.

'Is it because it was you who tipped off Baldovino?'

Tullio's eyes darted towards him. 'I don't know what you mean!'

'I think you do. You gave him the names of those missing girls. What I can't work out is why.'

'Whether I did or didn't makes no difference to this. I

cannot change the evidence. There is a clear motive, and you were found holding the weapon.'

'What? You think I half killed a man just because of a few stupid newspaper stories?'

'Men have been murdered for less.'

'Perhaps, but not by me! You know me better than that.'

'I will make sure that the professor is informed. But that is all I can do.'

'Is that it? Tullio, what is wrong with you?'

'I'm a policeman, James. I have to do my job. It isn't personal.'

The inspector got up to leave, but then hesitated briefly. Just for a moment James thought that he would go back to being the old Tullio, but he was wrong. He opened the door and called the jailer back before walking quickly away. James stared at the grey walls and wondered how on earth he was going to persuade a jury that he was innocent if could not convince his friend of the same thing.

Lucy, Gina and Paola stood in a huddle wondering what to do next.

'What could she be doing there?' Lucy said.

'Giving herself up?' Gina suggested. 'I still think she might know something about the abduction.'

'That doesn't seem very likely,' Paola said.

'It is possible,' Lucy said. 'She must either be reporting something, or she's witnessed a crime.'

Gina groaned. 'So we are no further forward.'

'We will be if we go inside,' Lucy said.

'How can we do that without being detected?' Paola asked.

'We can't, but it may not matter. Follow me.'

'Are you sure this is a good idea?' Paola said, her voice quavering.

Gina gave her a withering look.

Paola tutted. 'All right . . . if you really think it will help.'

They walked into the building. Miss Trott was standing at a counter having a heated argument with a carabinieri officer.

'I do not wish to speak of these matters here. I want to see someone in authority!'

The officer gave her a puzzled look. His mouth was open. 'Signora, you need to tell me first. Then I will decide.'

Miss Trott tutted loudly. 'Really, that will not do. It is a confidential and important matter.'

The man shrugged and began to speak slowly and carefully, as if addressing an idiot. 'You tell me what it is, then I will decide.'

'No, no, no! Is Marshal Machinetti available? It is vital that I see him. Or perhaps Inspector Tullio.'

'He might be,' the officer said hesitantly. He was clearly impressed that she knew both of them.

'Then I suggest you find him immediately!'

'There are other people waiting,' the officer said, gesturing towards Lucy, Gina and Paola.

Miss Trott frowned at them. 'What in the world are you doing here?' she said sharply.

'We happened to see you come in, Miss Trott,' Lucy said. 'We were concerned and thought we might be able to help.'

For a brief few seconds Miss Trott narrowed her eyes, then suddenly, as if she had remembered who she was, her manner changed completely. 'Oh . . . good gracious me . . . how kind of you. It is nothing really.'

The officer looked confused. 'Not vital, then?'

'Just my parasol ... I left it somewhere and wondered if it had been handed in.'

'You wanted the marshal for a missing parasol?' the officer said.

Before she could answer, there was the sound of a door being unlocked in the corner.

'Stand back, ladies, please. A prisoner is coming through.'

Lucy was interested at first. She had little experience of criminals. But then she saw James being led through a barred door, handcuffed, surrounded by carabinieri officers, his face a picture of misery. At first she was paralysed with shock. She could not believe what she was seeing. Wasn't he meant to be working in the professor's study? How could he be here, and chained up like that? Had Francesco got him arrested? She took a step towards him. 'James ...'

She felt Miss Trott's restraining hand upon her arm.

'Don't you worry, Dr Murray. Clearly there has been a terrible error. I will ensure that this is sorted out straight away.'

'Tell the professor, please,' James said as he was propelled firmly through another door. 'Lucy ...' he began. But in a second he was gone, and Lucy sank onto a nearby bench feeling lonelier than she had ever done in her entire life.

38

Maintaining the death sentence does not mean using it often. It is sufficient that it should be suspended like a sword of Damocles over the most terrible criminals, those who have attempted to kill innocent people. This removes the last justifiable objection to capital punishment, that it is irreparable. Lombroso, 1896–7, p. 348

There was an expectant hush as James appeared in the dock. The courtroom was large and suitably imposing, with a preponderance of wood panels and red leather seating. He blinked as his eyes became accustomed to the comparatively bright light.

It was hard to believe that he was here. He had been held at the police station over the weekend, and during that time he had tried again and again to explain his presence in Baldovino's rooms, but nobody believed him. His attempts to contact Tullio had been fruitless, which was perhaps not surprising. He had been seen with a knife in his hand leaning over a stabbed man. Not only that, but he had ample motive given the articles that had appeared in *The People's Voice*. And if Baldovino died, well then, that was the end of that. They still had the death penalty here, although it seemed likely to be abolished soon, if Lombroso was right. But how would that help him?

Lombroso was sitting at the front of the public gallery with Ottolenghi beside him. The professor lifted a hand in acknowledgement. It seemed that James had not been completely abandoned. But he was going to prison, at least until trial. There appeared to be little doubt about that. At the back was a flash of red hair. Concetta Panatti sat and smiled at him – not in greeting, but in satisfaction. She was almost certainly behind his downfall, but why? What had he ever done to her to warrant this? And who else was involved?

There was absolutely no sign of Sofia. She had probably given up on him altogether. He thought of her half-smile and felt an ache of longing. If only he could see her, even if it was for the briefest of moments, just to tell her how much she meant to him. But there was little chance of that. He would be spending a good few months in prison before his trial, he imagined. By then, even if he was acquitted, which in itself seemed unlikely, she would have moved on. He had tried his best to find Chiara for her, but he had failed comprehensively. He deserved to lose her and she was better off without him.

James stood as the judge came in – a small man with a pinched face and a mouth that looked as if it was permanently pursed. The proceedings were brief, as he had expected. The prosecution's lawyer read out the facts of the accusation against him. The charge was attempted murder. His lawyer, an elderly man appointed by the court, seemed to be dozing throughout and had to be poked by his clerk into responding.

'The matter of bail, your honour?'

'Under the circumstances, I do not think that is appropriate. Given the facts of this case, the prisoner might as well accustom himself to custody.' So much for an unbiased hearing. The judge's voice was thin and reedy and his expression dour. James imagined him sitting with Aunt Agnes, comparing sins or something similar. They would get on like a house on fire.

There was some rumpus going on in the public gallery. A note was passed down from Lombroso and eventually found its way to the judge, who tapped his long, thin fingers impatiently as he waited for it to be delivered. He opened it and his eyebrows shot up in surprise. After a long pause he spoke. 'The prisoner should stand.'

James got to his feet and braced himself.

'It appears that you have influential friends. A bond has been lodged with the court, which, given its provenance and size, is enough to persuade me that you should be released until your trial. It is conditional on your residence at the home of Professor Cesare Lombroso in the Via Legnano. If there is the slightest hint of any misbehaviour, then to prison you will go. Have I made myself clear?'

James could not quite believe what he had just heard. He had thought that prison was inevitable. He hesitated as he took it in.

'Well?' the judge said impatiently.

'Yes, your honour.'

'You may go.'

As James was released from the dock, he noticed that Concetta Panatti's seat had been vacated. Whoever his influential friend was, it certainly wasn't her.

Lombroso approached him and shook his hand warmly. 'Come this way, Murray. We are taking you home.'

As James walked through the courtroom to freedom, a feeling of dread overcame him. He would be seeing this place again, he had no doubt. And the next time perhaps he would be leaving through another entrance altogether.

Lucy was whiling away the morning by trying but failing to read one of the books that Aunt Agnes had sent with Miss Trott. The last few days had been almost unbearable, but despite all she had been told about the accusations that James faced, she was absolutely certain of his innocence. He just didn't have that level of violence in him.

There were sounds from downstairs. It seemed that the professor and Ottolenghi had returned from court. She hoped they would not come in here. She knew the outcome of the proceedings. It was inevitable. But she did not want to hear those words – *James is in prison*. She could imagine it only too well: his pale and handsome face peering out at her through bars. He would try to smile, not wanting to upset her, but she would know. How could she not? His eyes would betray him, as they always did, and she would see in them his abject misery and fear of what the future held. The question was, did she have the inner strength to support him, or would it be too much for her?

Then she heard the sound of someone bounding up the stairs. The door flew open and, by some miracle, there he was, standing in front of her and grinning like an idiot. James was home.

39

Another, and very serious indication of moral insanity is the lack of maternal feelings that makes the born prostitute the twin sister of the female born criminal. Lesbians, especially, are completely indifferent to maternity and indeed terrified of pregnancy.

Lombroso and Ferrero, 1893, p. 214

'The only way we can prove that you are innocent, Murray,' Lombroso said, 'is to find the real culprit.'

'I know,' James said. 'But how can we do that unless Baldovino recovers and identifies him?'

He was sitting with Lombroso, Ottolenghi and Anna in the professor's study after lunch, enjoying a glass of grappa. Given what he had been through, and the prospect of what might be in store for him, it seemed to James that everything tasted a little sweeter.

'Surely this is all part of the same mystery,' Anna said. 'James has been framed for this assault by the people who threatened him before. Their identity is the key to everything.'

'Anna is right,' James agreed. 'That is what I need to focus on. Anyway, at least I'm free to investigate. Thank you for the bond, Professor.'

'It wasn't me that bailed you out,' Lombroso said. 'You have Sofia to thank for that.'

'But she has no influence.'

'No, but the marchesa does,' Ottolenghi said. 'Sofia went to her and asked for help.'

James could barely contain his joy. Sofia cared! She still cared after everything.

'That is very good of the marchesa, considering that her niece has been taken,' Anna said. 'She must be beside herself.'

'Well, it was not entirely altruistic,' Lombroso said. 'Both Sofia and I have spoken to her about your enquiries, Murray, and she believes that you may be able to help in finding her niece. Any ideas?'

'If Teresa Mariani's friend Bruno Ferranti is working on the Rambaudis' rice estate, then we should talk to him,' James said.

'*Eccellente!* We can talk through criminal types on the way.'

Lucy stood on the grand Renaissance steps of the Duomo and watched Sofia walking across the piazza towards her. She wanted to help James, but since he was clearly keeping things from her, she had concluded that it was time to get some answers from the only person she thought would not lie to her. It had not been easy. James had made it clear that she should not leave the house unaccompanied, given Fabia's abduction. But he had gone straight into the professor's study after lunch and Lucy had taken the opportunity to slip out, hoping that he would not notice.

Sofia smiled hesitantly as their eyes met. All Lucy knew for certain was that there was something between James and Sofia. The part Sofia had played in freeing James proved that. And if they were as close as Lucy was beginning to suspect, then he would have told Sofia about his past – that was the sort of man he was.

'Signorina, I am here as you asked,' Sofia said when she reached her.

'Thank you for coming. I know it must be difficult for you at the moment, with Fabia being taken.'

'Your brother is free now and he will help, I am certain of it.'

'I am sure you are right. It is my brother I have come to talk to you about. Shall we walk?'

Sofia agreed, and together they went into the cathedral. It was quiet. There were just a few people there, dotted about, looking at the interior or praying. Lucy had selected it as a venue because she wanted somewhere calming, and it seemed that she had chosen well. They began to walk along the main aisle until they reached a small chapel. Lucy followed Sofia in and watched as she gazed at a statue of a woman at prayer.

'I need you to be truthful with me.'

Sofia's expression was difficult to read, but there was something. It was no more than a flicker in her eyes, but it was enough for Lucy.

'Tell me, Sofia, do you love my brother?' she asked in a low voice.

Sofia hesitated for a moment and then nodded slowly. '*Sì, sì*. You must believe me when I say that I have always loved him. But...'

'But what?'

She had tears in her eyes. 'As I have already told him, we cannot be together.'

'I know about your background, and it will be difficult, but if you love him...'

'It is not enough.'

'Why not? Is it James that you do not love enough?'

'No, it isn't that. But I have others to think of. I cannot say more.'

'When you were with him, I imagine you shared a lot. You must have done, to love each other so much. You know he still loves you, don't you?'

Sofia nodded. 'It would be better for us both if he did not.'

'Did he speak about our father?'

'Yes, he did often, and it troubled him. We found that we were very similar... Our fathers both sinned in the worst way possible and left us with the consequences.'

'How did James describe our father's sins?'

Sofia paused. 'I do not know that I should tell you. It should come from him.'

'He will never tell me. He thinks I cannot cope with the truth, that it will hurt me to know what our father did. But not knowing is far worse.'

'Your father became obsessed with his work.'

'I have seen that in James too,' Lucy said.

'He fears that in himself, I think.'

'So what happened?'

'Your father operated on someone using experimental techniques and it went horribly wrong. James found out; they argued violently. After that, your father took to drink. He got involved in a brawl, stabbed someone and ended up in his own asylum.'

Lucy felt faint and held onto the wall for a moment. She had not expected Sofia to be so direct. 'Father killed someone? Why didn't James tell me?'

'He didn't want to hurt you... and also...' Sofia hesitated.

'What? What is it?'

'For some reason he blames himself for your father's

downfall. But it is not just that. He is afraid that part of your father lives on in him. That is why he came here to the professor . . . to see if it was true.'

'To consult him, you mean?'

'Yes, though I am not sure that he got the answers he was looking for.'

'What did the professor tell him?'

'I think he reassured him, or tried to, but James was still not sure. His fear is lodged too deeply inside him. I can tell that it is still on his mind. He is very troubled.'

'And someone is using that uncertainty to destroy him,' Lucy said.

'I think so too. I am sure that Panatti woman is involved, but there is more to it than that.'

Lucy grasped Sofia's hand. A memory had come to the forefront of her mind – a gaunt-faced man and what had seemed like a strange comment to make at a funeral. 'I have to go, Sofia. There is someone I must speak to.'

'Will it help James?'

'I hope so.'

'Then you must try.'

'I must succeed,' Lucy said firmly.

In its introduction, written by Pinkerton himself, the manual stated that any good detective must be resolute and persevere until the investigation was complete. She would follow the instructions to the letter. Nothing less would do.

James looked wearily out of the window as the carriage jolted its way towards the Rambaudi estate. Lombroso was holding forth about his profile of the killer.

'He is a morally insane epileptic, of this I have no doubt.

We are looking at someone with a number of telltale physical characteristics.'

'Ah, yes,' Ottolenghi said, still very much the student at the feet of his master. 'I have taken the liberty of noting these down, Professor, as you have mentioned them throughout the investigation.' He took his now battered notebook out of his jacket pocket and consulted it. 'Our killer has asymmetrical facial features, a big jaw, jutting cheekbones, large mouth, thick lips with malformed teeth. If he has facial hair, it will be scanty. He enjoys sexual perversion of all kinds and the drinking of blood. He is intelligent but unable to tell the difference between good and evil.'

'Could the killer be a woman?' Anna asked, holding onto the carriage door as they went round a corner at speed.

'No,' Lombroso replied. 'Not enough physical strength and, besides, a woman would not be intelligent enough to do this.'

'There are plenty of female killers,' Anna said, clearly unwilling to let the possibility go. 'You have seen my own photographs and read my research.'

'No, I do not think this killer is a woman,' Lombroso said firmly.

'But my data reflects yours, Cesare!' she protested. 'I too found asymmetry of the face. Remember the two women who killed their husbands? And the others . . . the demi types who did not fit the profile completely but still had big jaws, deep-set eyes and dark hair.'

Lombroso gave her a patronising smile, and she pursed her lips as if with the effort of not interrupting. 'These are domestic murders, though, my dear Madame Tarnovsky, quite different from our man – and it is a man, I am sure of it.'

'Your description is very precise, Professor,' Ottolenghi said carefully.

'Quite!' Lombroso said, beaming at them. 'A man like that shouldn't be too hard to find.'

'Aren't we concentrating too much on these characteristics? Because frankly...' James hesitated. He did not know exactly how far he should go with this, but he was becoming increasingly frustrated by Lombroso's fixation on appearance.

'Out with it, Murray! If you have an idea, we should hear it, you being such an expert.'

'I just think we would be better served by examining what this person has done and trying to work out why,' he said.

'Studying the description of the location where the bodies were found and the state they were in might well be helpful also,' Ottolenghi said.

'I don't doubt that both of these approaches might be of use, and I commend you for your attempts at adding something to the investigation.' Lombroso's face was reddening with each word. 'But may I remind you both that my theories have been tried and tested over many years, so I think we will stick with them if you don't mind.'

James did not trust himself to reply. Instead he merely nodded and allowed Lombroso to continue outlining his increasingly outlandish ideas as the carriage took them, he hoped, nearer to finding a solution. They passed through the imposing wrought-iron gates resplendent with their fleur-de-lis design. Why could his colleagues not see what was staring them in the face? The answer to this mystery was not in criminal types but criminals. Lombroso's talk was merely a distraction. James was convinced that Bruno Ferranti held the key, and he hoped that he would shortly have the chance to question him in person.

40

Female criminality increases with the march of civil-isation. The female criminal is an occasional criminal, with few degenerative characteristics, little dullness, and so on; her numbers grow as opportunities for evil doing increase. The prostitute, on the other hand, has a greater atavistic resemblance to the primitive woman – the vagabond Venus – and thus she had a greater dullness of touch and taste, greater fondness of tattooing, and so on.

Lombroso and Ferrero, 1893, p. 148

Lucy studied the wooden sarcophagus in front of her carefully and scribbled some notes down in a notebook she had purchased on her way to the Museo Egizio. The artefact was the same one she had seen on during her first visit with Miss Trott. It was magnificent, highly varnished and covered with elaborate depictions of rituals, animals and gods. She started to sketch it, wondering if it might be a good place to hide a body for Lydia Loveday to discover. She noticed that there were several other scholars paying similar attention to various exhibits. Clearly if one wanted to study the history of Egypt, this was very much the place to come. They were mostly much older than her, and male. The only exceptions to this were a couple who had arrived at about the same time as she had.

He was a handsome young man with a shock of dark hair that he kept pushing impatiently out of his eyes, just as James did. She noticed a deep scar running down his face and wondered idly if it bothered him. The girl was short and dark. She was studying a statue of Sakhmet, a fire-breathing goddess with the head of a lion. Lucy had wanted to examine it herself, but the other girl had got there first. The pair certainly seemed to be together, and Lucy soon concocted a fledgling romance for them: love amongst the dead, or some such. There might be a short story in there somewhere, although she doubted she would ever write it. Detective rather than romantic fiction was her forte.

She rubbed the bridge of her nose to relieve an itch. It was important to blend in when conducting surveillance of any kind, which was why she was wearing a pair of wire-framed spectacles borrowed from Paola, who with Gina had helped her prepare for her visit. The sisters had wanted to accompany her but she had managed to dissuade them, quoting from *Pinkerton's*, which claimed that 'the best surveillance is carried out alone'. The spectacles were perched uncomfortably on the end of her nose. She hoped they would make her look learned and perhaps a little older than her years, but now she wished that she had left them at home. Still, no one seemed to be taking the slightest notice of her, which was the main thing.

Lucy could see the steps down which Professor Donati had led her during her previous visit. Her intention was to confront him in his lair. She had to know what he had been discussing with that man at the ball, the same man who had made such a fuss at her father's funeral. Who was he, and what was he doing in Turin? With luck, Donati would at least be able to name him.

She stretched and feigned a yawn. It would be only natural

to take a break and look at the other exhibits, wouldn't it? She wandered over to an impressive Sphinx by the stairs and pretended to examine it closely. Her scholastic companions did not seem to have noticed her. Satisfied, she made her way down the stairs towards Professor Donati's workshop.

Striding along the basement corridor of the Museo Egizio, she was pretending to be a good deal braver than she actually felt. The place was deserted, and every now and then she would catch a glimpse of a statue of a god or a frieze with Egyptians solemnly standing in a line, arms raised, worshipping something or somebody. Eyes seemed to be everywhere, but none of them were human, or alive at any rate. Finally she reached the room where Professor Donati had been working. The door was open, so she went in. There were the waxworks, looking even more eerie and lifelike than on the last occasion, but of the professor there was no sign. Lucy decided to wait for a few moments in case he had stepped out for a moment.

She examined a piece of papyrus that was lying on a table. Clearly Donati had been looking at it recently. Next to it was the sheaf from which it seemed to have come, neatly rolled and lying in a box decorated with gold and turquoise. On a piece of paper were some scribbled notes. The heading was 'APEP: Book of Spells'.

She leant forward and squinted at it in the half-light, trying to make sense of what was written beneath. So intent was she on deciphering Professor Donati's script that she did not hear someone approaching her from behind. Suddenly a strong arm grabbed her and a hand clamped a cloth over her mouth and nose. The smell was chemical, but with a strange sweetness to it. She understood immediately what was happening and attempted to prise the hand away from her mouth, but the grip was too strong. She tried to hold her breath, all the while struggling as hard as she could, grabbing at the face behind her, hoping to get her fingers into his eyes, and pulling at his hair. All she could think was, no! This must not happen to me! I must survive! But it was hopeless. Her assailant was too strong for her. The last thoughts that went through Lucy's head before the blackness descended were firstly regret that she might never know the solution to the mysteries she had encountered, and secondly that her life might be over before it had scarcely begun.

'How strange to see you here again, Signor Murray,' Francesco Rambaudi said as he lounged elegantly on a wicker chair in the courtyard of the Villa Purezza. He had not even bothered to stand up in order to greet them, which, given Anna's presence, was unforgivable.

James tried to put his personal dislike to one side, the better to assess Francesco's character.

From his expression, it was clear that Rambaudi was amused. 'I thought we had a gentlemen's agreement on the matter. But then of course you are not really much of a gentleman, are you? Or so I have heard. What is it you are accused of? Oh yes – a serious assault, perhaps even attempted murder. Well, my personal knowledge of you would certainly seem to confirm your propensity for both dishonesty and violence. I will, of course, testify to that effect at your trial. It should be a most interesting experience. And let's face it, prison is where you belong.'

James tried to keep his temper. He knew that Rambaudi was goading him, and that if he responded, he would play into his hands. Ottolenghi's comforting presence was there behind him, but nonetheless it was going to take a supreme effort of will to maintain his equilibrium.

'Signor Rambaudi, thank you so much for seeing us. Please be assured that we will not detain you for long,' Lombroso said. 'We merely wish to question one of your staff.'

'Well, Professor Lombroso, do you know, I am not minded to allow it.'

Lombroso raised his eyebrows. He was not accustomed to people saying no to him in such a forthright manner. 'May I ask why?'

'I rather think that is my question.'

'This particular young man has been reported as missing but has been seen here.'

'I assume that your assistant is your witness. Hardly a reliable source.'

Lombroso continued. 'The young man's name is Bruno Ferranti. Can you confirm that he is employed by you? Then we could at least reassure his family. His mother, in particular, is worried about him.'

Rambaudi hesitated, as if he was summing up the pros and cons of being difficult. 'Very well, Professor. I agree that family is important, especially mothers. Yes, he does work for me. Strange, though. I was told that he did not have any family. Still, I must take your word for that.'

'May we speak with him?'

'No, you may not. He is busy working for me. He does what he is told, as all servants should. But then . . .' Francesco smirked at James, 'it is so difficult to find obedient, law-abiding staff, don't you agree, Professor?'

James stepped forward but Ottolenghi placed a restraining hand on his shoulder.

'Yes, that's right. Always best to keep servants and animals restrained in company,' Francesco said. 'How's that sister of yours, Murray? A pretty girl . . . such a pity she's not from better stock.'

A light voice came from behind them. 'I do hope you are being hospitable to our guests, Francesco.' Bianca walked over to her brother as if in solidarity.

'I have done my best under the circumstances, sister dear.'

'Signorina Rambaudi,' Lombroso said, bowing. 'We have no complaints.'

'To what do we owe this pleasure?' Bianca asked.

'We just had a business matter to discuss,' Lombroso replied.

'I usually deal with such things,' Bianca said. 'Francesco has no head for business. He is far too sensitive.'

'They were enquiring after Bruno,' Francesco told her.

'I think he is working away from the estate today. I will send him to you, though, if you wish to speak with him.'

'That is most kind, Signora,' Lombroso said. 'Well, I think that concludes our business here. We shall leave you both in peace.'

With that they began to walk up the drive to where their carriage was waiting. James paused and took a last look at the house. He doubted he would be able to visit again. There was something forbidding about it despite its golden stone – a kind of coldness, perhaps. Unhappiness almost seemed to seep from its walls.

'That was interesting,' Lombroso said as they reached the end of the drive, 'although not particularly helpful.'

'I agree,' Anna said. 'There was very little of consequence that was actually said. Signor Rambaudi seemed to be interested in insulting James rather than anything else.'

James was silent. He had found the conversation far more illuminating. As he knew only too well from Professor Bell's own techniques in the analysis of conversation, it was not always what was said that was important. Sometimes what was left out was far more significant. Francesco knew of his interest in the servant from their last encounter, but neither he nor his sister seemed remotely curious about why Ferranti had been reported missing or what reason they had for wanting to speak with him. As Professor Bell often said, the only reason for a lack of curiosity was surely that the facts were already known.

41

Even born criminals for whom sex is not all absorbing are livelier before puberty than normal women, but their vivacity gradually disappears. Almost all of them begin their careers by fleeing with a lover; and prostitution is always one of their many sins, although not the most serious. They feel a strong attraction towards men and are more curious than other women about the mysteries of sex.

Lombroso and Ferrero, 1893, p. 172

When they arrived back at the museum, they found Machinetti waiting for them in one of the exhibits rooms. With him was a tall, pale girl with long fair hair tightly plaited and wound so closely around her head it looked like a bid to prevent it from escaping. She stood next to the marshal, glancing uneasily at both him and the walls, which were lined with various artefacts including some of Lombroso's death masks and jars of pickled human remains.

'Ah, Lombroso, at last,' Machinetti said. 'I have someone here who may be of interest to you.' He pushed the girl forward. 'Tell them your name.'

'I am Susanna Russello.'

'Well go on, girl! Tell them what you told me,' Machinetti said.

'I have been working in Vercelli recently, but I came back to see a friend. She told me that a policeman had been asking about me. Until then I did not know that anyone was looking for me.'

'And there we have it,' Lombroso said. 'This, Murray, is why we should take care not to leap to conclusions about these girls, Sofia's cousin included.'

'But we have three dead bodies, and I don't suppose Fabia Carignano has run off to work in Vercelli,' James pointed out.

'We are looking carefully for the marchesa's niece, of course,' Machinetti said.

'Fortunately, so are we,' Lombroso said, glancing at the marshal. 'The bodies are a matter of concern. All I am saying, Murray, is that we should be focusing on those and the abduction of Signorina Carignano and not worrying too much about the Esposito girl.'

'Which is what I have been saying all along,' Machinetti said smugly. 'Now I must go. I have an appointment with the mayor.' He swept out, leaving Susanna Russello standing awkwardly in the middle of the room.

'I will see you out, signorina.' Anna began to usher her towards the door.

'No, wait,' the girl said.

'What is it?' demanded Lombroso.

'Before I left for Vercelli, something happened to me. I was frightened and that's why I left Torino.'

'Go on, signorina,' James said.

Anna led her over to a chair and she sat down on its very edge, her hands clasping and unclasping in front of her.

'It was on the first of November. I was walking to work at the market at the Porto Palazzo so it was early... about five o'clock, still dark.'

'Was there anyone around at that time?' James asked.

'No, it was deserted as usual... well, mostly. But I could hear a carriage behind me. It was driving slowly, as if it was following me.'

'What did you do then?' enquired Anna.

'I began to walk more quickly, but it seemed to gather speed. Eventually it drew up beside me.'

'Did you see anyone in the carriage?' James asked.

'I could not see clearly. It was still quite dark, though the street lights were gone. But it looked as if a woman was sitting inside.'

'Did you see her hair?'

'Not really. It was covered, I think. There was a flash of something red, but...'

'What happened then?' Lombroso asked.

'I heard someone walking behind me. Then I felt someone try to grab me... but an old man came out of an alleyway and started shouting and waving his hat around. Bits of straw were coming off it and flying everywhere. The carriage drove off. I think someone jumped onto it, but I could not be certain.'

'Did you notice anything else?' James asked.

'No, I'm sorry. It all happened so quickly. The old man might be able to help, if you can find him.'

'That is unlikely, I'm afraid. It is a great pity that you did not come forward earlier,' Lombroso said, peering at the girl over the top of his glasses.

'I... I did not know... I was frightened.'

'Never mind,' Anna said firmly. 'You have been most help-ful, signorina.' She took the girl by the hand and led her out, giving Lombroso a look of disapproval as she did so.

'Well it seems pretty clear to me, whatever Machinetti

thinks,' James said. 'Somebody is abducting girls and killing them.'

'A morally insane epileptic, I'll be bound,' Lombroso said.

'Perhaps... but it would help to look at the victims. I'll try to be as organised as I can... by date is probably best.'

'That sounds like an excellent plan to me,' Anna said as she came back into the room.

'May I?' James picked up a piece of chalk and walked over to a blackboard in the corner. Lombroso pursed his lips as his assistant rubbed off his drawings and began a list of the missing girls, reciting it as he wrote.

1. Body in the woods – unidentified. Signs of attempted preservation. Organs removed. <u>Missing for at least six months.</u>
2. Teresa Mariani – San Callisto. Maid at Mme G's. <u>Missing from city – 1 October.</u>
3. Agnella/Nella Calvi – body found at Abbey of San Callisto. Prostitute at Mme G's. No sign of attempt at preservation except for organs removed. <u>Missing 1 January.</u>
4. Chiara Esposito – maid at marchesa's. <u>Missing 1 March.</u>
5. Caterina Spirito – flower seller, friend of Nella Calvi. Body found in the Borgo. Signs of attempted preservation with arsenic, and organs removed. <u>Missing 1 February.</u>
6. Arianna Panico – <u>missing 1 December.</u>
7. Susanna Russello – maid. <u>Attempted abduction 1 November.</u>
8. Fabia Carignano – marchesa's niece. <u>Missing mid-April.</u>

'We can see from this that the disappearances took place on a monthly basis,' James said. 'In fact all the girls, except for Signora Carignano and possibly the body in the woods, went missing on the first of the month.'

Anna tapped a pencil on the table in front of her, deep in thought. 'There must be some significance in relation to both the date and the frequency.'

'Why does he choose those particular girls?' Ottolenghi asked.

'There is some variation in appearance, so that doesn't seem to be influencing him,' Lombroso said.

James looked at the blackboard. There was something bothering him about the list. He breathed in sharply.

'What is it, Murray?'

'We have only found three bodies so far.'

'So where has he left the others?' Anna asked.

'Nowhere, yet.'

Lombroso looked at him in surprise. 'What do you mean?'

'They are not dead.'

Lombroso shook his head. 'Nonsense! Just because we haven't found them yet doesn't mean that they are still alive.'

'He is keeping them,' James said. 'Whoever is abducting these girls is holding them somewhere. That is why there is a gap between the abductions.'

'But what about the bodies?' Anna asked.

'He kills them eventually, but not until he's ready.'

'And the state of the bodies?' Lombroso asked.

'He tries to preserve them using various techniques, then he leaves them to be found – posed. Which means...' James hesitated for a second.

'He is a morally insane epileptic!' Lombroso said. 'There, you see! I knew I was right.'

'Which means that he is a curator,' James said, ignoring Lombroso. 'The killer is abducting girls and putting them in his collection.'

'And the killing only happens when he is ready to share,' Anna said.

'Yes, that's right. He is not just leaving the bodies for us to find ... he is putting on a display.'

'But didn't you say that the first body was laid to rest?' Lombroso said. 'Really, Murray, as I am always telling you, a scientific approach means that consistency must be maintained.'

James exchanged glances with Ottolenghi and Anna. Lombroso had his own unique way of dealing with such matters. If something wasn't consistent, he would simply go back and alter data until it was. 'I have considered that. Given the state of the body, it is likely that it belongs to a much earlier victim. I think at this stage he was still practising his art. Preservation of a body is not a simple task, particularly for an amateur. He would need to learn by experience.'

'That would explain how the bodies were found – the embalming, the draining of the blood, the removal of the organs and so on,' Lombroso said.

Ottolenghi nodded enthusiastically. 'That would fit in with the mummification ... Weren't organs removed during Ancient Egyptian death rituals?'

Lombroso beamed. 'Well done, everyone! I knew you would get there eventually. It is so very gratifying to see one's protégées shine.'

'So you knew already, Cesare?' Anna said, giving James a sideways glance.

'Of course, although I have to concede that Murray here filled in some of the detail.'

'Very generous of you, Professor, I'm sure,' James said.

'Not at all! Now, of course, we have to fix these theories to something a little more solid.'

'Meaning?' James asked.

'Meaning – where might we find a morally insane epileptic with an in-depth knowledge of Ancient Egyptian death rituals?' Lombroso smiled. Clearly he knew the answer to his own question. 'There is only one person in Turin with those credentials. Although come to think of it, I don't know if he is an epileptic, or morally insane... though he could be both.'

There was a sharp rap on the door and it opened to reveal an agitated Miss Trott accompanied by a tearful Paola.

'Mr Murray, a terrible thing! Oh, I have been so lax!' Lucy's companion could hardly get her words out, she was so breathless. 'We came as soon as I realised.'

'Realised what, Miss Trott?' James said. 'You're not making any sense.'

'Paola, what is it?' Lombroso asked.

'I am sorry, Papa, Signor Murray. But it is Lucy.'

'What about her?' James said.

'Apparently she went off on her own on some silly mission after speaking to Sofia.' Miss Trott glared at Paola.

'She said she knew who had been trying to hurt you, Signor Murray,' Paola said.

'She must have meant Concetta Panatti,' James said. 'The woman made it clear that she had more planned for me. Did Lucy go to Madame Giulia's?'

'No. She went to the Museo Egizio,' Paola said. 'She said that she had to see Professor Donati.'

42

The graffiti I have collected from women's prisons and hospitals for syphilitics indicate an excessive libidinousness in four out of seventy-eight examples. For example, one graffito read 'Dear dickybird'; another said 'Always thus' under a sketch of an immense penis; and a third said, 'Bring me a bird to my taste and I'll bring one to you, and when I am free you will find that I am just as hot and tight as you want...' But these graffiti were created by prostitutes who were also born criminals. In the graffiti of others, insofar as it exists, eroticism is latent, as in 'I kiss my little brother', or else the writings express only sentimental love or desire for revenge.

Lombroso and Ferrero, 1893, p. 173

The movement of the carriage was bumping Lucy up and down, this way and that. They had travelled some distance, she thought, given the length of the journey. Whatever had been used to drug her had quickly worn off, perhaps because she had held her breath. Despite this, escape was impossible, as her hands and feet were now both tightly bound. She had to content herself with feigning unconsciousness and trying to work out where she was being taken. The terrain was smooth to begin with but then had become rough, which meant, she assumed, that she was being transported from the city to the countryside. But just as she was becoming accustomed to travelling, they came to a halt and she was lifted and thrown over someone's shoulder as if she was a sack of potatoes. She risked opening her eyes for a few seconds and managed to catch a glimpse of what she thought were farm buildings. She tried to look further but she could hear another person approaching so she had to shut her eyes again.

'Put her in number three. That's free now.'

The voice belonged to a woman – youngish, Lucy thought. Number three? That meant that there were at least two more.

She heard something being slid back; it might be a stone or a piece of thick wood. It was hard to tell. Then she was put in some kind of a basket and lowered down into a hole or a pit. She started to panic. What if she was being buried alive? No, someone was coming down after her. She could hear them. There must be a rope ladder, she thought, as she couldn't hear any scraping sounds. Rough hands pulled her out of the basket, laid her down and untied her. It was a man, she was certain. He set about shackling her to the wall by her ankle. He slid his hand surreptitiously up her leg. She tried not to flinch.

'Stop that!' The voice came from above – a different sound, softer. The man straightened up and cursed softly, then pushed Lucy roughly aside with his foot as if she was a piece of meat before starting back towards the ladder. Lucy opened one eye and almost gasped when she recognised him. It was the young man from the museum. He must have been watching her – the girl too, perhaps. But surely they couldn't be in charge. They were too young.

'I see you are awake already,' said the second voice. It was light-sounding, as though it was chanting a mantra. Not real, Lucy thought. Someone was disguising their voice. But why?

'It will do you no good, Signorina Murray ... no good at all. Deceit is not what is needed here. Only humility will help you. You must atone.'

'And if I don't?' Lucy asked.

'Then I will kill you sooner rather than later ... and that would be a shame.'

'Who for?' Lucy asked. 'You or me?'

The voice laughed. It was like little bells, the sort you might find on a sleigh at Christmas time in the snow.

'For that, my dear, you can go hungry. A little suffering will speed up your repentance. You will be pure enough before you know it.'

The lid or grid or whatever it was began to move, and soon she was plunged into darkness. Frustrated at her helplessness, she pulled on her shackles. But they were of thick metal and could not be shifted. She sat back against the cold stone wall. A solitary tear slid down her cheek.

'No!' she said. Then more loudly: 'I am Lucy Murray and I will not be afraid!'

'Lucy? Is that you?' The voice was muffled. It sounded as if it was coming through the wall.

'Fabia?'

'Yes, it's me. How long have I been here?'

'Two days,' Lucy replied, thinking how typical of Fabia it was to put herself first.

'Really? It seems like more.'

'Are you hurt?'

'No, not hurt, but, Lucy ...' There was a pause. 'I'm so frightened. I keep hearing noises.'

'What kind of noises?'

'Crying mostly, some talking . . . but screams, too.'

'From one girl?'

'I don't know. I just don't know.' Fabia's voice trembled. 'Who are these people? Why are they doing this?'

Lucy closed her eyes and leant back against the wall. She felt like crying too, but she knew that she had to be strong. 'Fabia, listen now. This is important. You said you heard talking. What was said? Tell me exactly.'

Fabia sniffed and Lucy pictured her wiping away her tears. 'When the girl was crying, he told her to stop and that she had to atone.'

'That's what was said to me.'

'Me too,' Fabia said. 'But what are we atoning for, and how are we supposed to do it?'

'I don't know,' Lucy said.

'Perhaps if we ask them and do what they want, they'll let us go.'

'Maybe.' Lucy was doubtful. No one else had been released, and she had a terrible feeling that unless they were rescued, whatever they said or did the end result would be the same.

'Someone will come for us,' Fabia said. 'My aunt will make sure of it.'

'Perhaps,' Lucy replied. 'But we don't know how much time we have.'

Fabia cried out. 'Don't say that!'

'I just mean that we need to find our own way out of here. Let me think.' She began to go through escape routes in her mind, each less possible than the last. As she did so, she heard someone crying.

'Fabia, is that you?'

'No . . . it's that other girl.'

'Hello! Can you hear me? What's your name?' Lucy called.

The crying stopped. 'Arianna . . .'

A noise came from above. Someone was coming. There was talking. It was quiet, but Lucy could just about make out what was being said.

'I told you, Bruno. We cannot wait. Those that have failed the test must be purified.'

The voice was familiar, but she could not place it. It was too quiet.

'We can't do them all together. Start with December. The latest one is a replacement for November. She has yet to be tested. We'll wait for that and then you can do April.'

'I want to do April first. If I have to listen to her complaining just one more day . . .'

'Sssh, Bruno, just follow the path. That is all we ask.'

'What about March? Isn't she ready yet?'

'No. Her atonement is incomplete. It is December's turn.'

'Do we use the drugs?'

'No. Do it without this time. There aren't enough left.'

'She's going to be awake for everything? Won't someone hear?'

'Foxes scream all the time, don't they?'

At James's insistence, Sofia was sent for and told to meet them outside the Museo Egizio. He knew that meant they might be seen together, but frankly he had ceased to care. As soon as she saw him, she came to him and took his hand in hers. 'We will find her.'

'I haven't found Chiara. What makes you think Lucy will be any different?'

'Have faith.'

'In God? That hasn't worked out well so far.'

'In yourself, James, *caro*.'

He allowed her to lead him into the museum. Lombroso and Ottolenghi followed behind at a discreet distance. Anna and Miss Trott, both of whom had insisted on accompanying them, waited outside.

'Lucy told me that she had been to see Donati before. He took her down to a workshop in the basement,' Sofia said.

'That sounds like the right place to go,' Ottolenghi said.

'Yes,' Lombroso said. 'He would need somewhere secluded where he could easily subdue his victims and do whatever he liked without detection.'

Sofia squeezed James's hand. 'Do not listen to him,' she whispered. 'You know how he likes to dramatise.'

James nodded. He couldn't really blame Lombroso. It wasn't as if similar thoughts had not entered his own head on the way there.

The museum was almost empty. A few scholars remained, but they were far too caught up in their own studies to notice the party as they made their way down the broad stone steps to the basement. Once down there, they began to walk slowly and silently along the main corridor, Lombroso inevitably taking the lead. There was no evidence of anyone else being down there, as far as James could tell. The passageway was lit by gas lamps, but they were few and far between. There were rooms on both sides. Were they cells? Was Lucy tied up in one of them? Ottolenghi peered in each as they went, shaking his head as he found them to be uninhabited.

Lombroso held out his hand and stopped them. The sound of whistling was coming from one of the rooms further along. The tune was familiar. James was certain he had heard it before. Where was it from? An opera, he thought. Ah yes, 'La donna è mobile', the aria from ... *Rigoletto*, was it?

The whistling grew a little louder, and in a moment Donati

was standing in the corridor staring at them, his eyes darting about in alarm. The whistling stopped.

'Ah, Professor,' Lombroso began. 'We thought that we'd pay you a visit.'

Donati ran. James went after him. Ottolenghi was behind him, huffing and puffing as he tried to catch up.

All at once Donati seemed to disappear. Had he gone into one of the rooms? James slowed down to a walk and made his way into a large chamber. Sarcophaguses lined the walls. Some of them had depictions of people on the front. Their eyes seemed to follow James as he walked slowly round. He stopped and listened carefully. Was that breathing from one of the coffins? He put his hand up to remove the lid.

'Murray, did you have to go so quickly?'

James was briefly distracted by Ottolenghi, who was almost bent double near the doorway. The lid pushed into him, making him stumble, and Donati ran past him, shoving Ottolenghi aside as he went.

'Are you all right?' James asked his friend.

'Yes,' Ottolenghi said, picking himself up. 'Go after him! I'll search the rest of the rooms.'

James ran back out into the corridor. Donati was just visible in the distance. He went up some more stairs and James followed him through what appeared to be a back door. On they went, right round the museum towards the front entrance, Donati gaining the advantage by taking short cuts. Miss Trott and Anna were standing outside at the bottom of the steps. Miss Trott went towards Donati as he ran past and gamely did her best to tackle him, but he swerved and she missed him, though only just. James went after him but was so far behind that he couldn't catch him.

Ottolenghi came down the steps. 'There is nowhere for a

girl to be kept in those rooms. But I did find these.' He held up a pair of spectacles. 'They were on the floor underneath a table in Professor Donati's workshop.'

'Those are Paola's!' Miss Trott said. 'Lucy must have borrowed them as a disguise. Such a resourceful young woman!'

'So it seems there is little doubt that she was taken from here against her will,' Lombroso said.

'But where to?' James stood there hunched over as Sofia tried to comfort him, but even that could not help assuage his guilt. He had been so concerned with his own affairs that yet again he had let Lucy down, and now he felt utterly powerless. A chill spread through his body. What if he could not save her? What if he had lost her for ever?

Lombroso strode over to him, making Sofia step back in surprise. He took James by his shoulders, forcing him to straighten up. 'Now listen to me, Murray. We are experts in crime and criminals and we will not be beaten by the monster that has done this. We will go back to the museum, sit down and do some hard thinking. We shall not stop until we have solved this and found both your sister and Sofia's cousin.'

Before James could reply, Tullio arrived. He was slightly out of breath.

'You have heard about Lucy?' James asked. 'We think Donati has taken her.'

Tullio shook his head. 'That is not why I'm here.'

'What is it?' Lombroso said sharply.

'Machinetti is on his way.'

'Good. We need the carabinieri to start searching,' James said.

'No,' Tullio said. 'That's not it. He is coming for you, James.'

James looked at him in confusion.

'The girl in Baldovino's article. Gabriella.'

'What about her?' Lombroso asked.

'She has gone missing and James is a suspect. Machinetti is coming to arrest you. Your bail has been revoked.'

43

One essential trait of the most serious cases of moral insanity and epilepsy in women is premeditation. The crimes of insane women are sometimes even more remarkable than those of ordinary female offenders in terms of skill, premeditation, steps taken to establish an alibi, and efforts at covering up.   Lombroso and Ferrero, 1893, p. 228

Lucy looked around her. Escaping from her cell pit, as she had begun to think of it, was clearly going to be no easy task. The walls were steep and at least twice her height. But as *Pinkerton's Detection Manual* was fond of saying, 'There is always a method – it is just a question of finding it.' She thought back to her arrival. She had been lowered down in a basket, and there was also a rope ladder allowing access. That meant that all she had to do was get up high enough to pull either the ladder or the basket down. Then she might be able to climb out. Hopefully she would be able to push the lid aside far enough to escape.

The first thing to do was to get out of her shackles. That shouldn't be too much of a problem, if her memory was accurate. She had researched this problem for an early Lydia Loveday story called 'The Captured Orphan', a complex tale in which an evil aunt engineered the abduction of her niece in order to get her hands on a substantial inheritance.

She put her hands up to her hair, which was held back by a large decorative clip given to her by Miss Trott. She pulled it free and examined it carefully. If she bent part of it back, it would leave a sharp point. She began to wiggle it in the lock on the chains, just as the orphan had done in her story. To her amazement, the lock sprang open. She was free. At least the first stage in her plan had been accomplished. Now for the rest of it, which, she had to admit, might be rather more difficult to put into action.

She began to scrape at the wall with her fingernail. A small cloud of sand came out, making her cough. This confirmed her suspicion that some of the bricks were loose. Might it be possible to work enough of them loose to enable her to climb up using the gaps as footholds? She did some more scraping, but it was hard work and before long her fingers were red raw. She pulled at the brick. It was definitely looser, but not by much. It would take forever to get just one of them free. She slumped back against the wall and stared miserably into the darkness. It was hopeless.

She pulled herself to her feet and walked around a little. As she did so, her foot hit something small and hard. She bent down and picked it up. A smile spread slowly across her face. It was a spoon. It wasn't exactly a pickaxe, which was what she really needed, but it might speed her bid for freedom up a little. She moved back to the brick that she had been working on and began to scrape again. This time her new tool meant that she made more progress. As she worked at the brick, a chilling thought came to her. How had the spoon got there? Had another captured girl had the same idea as her – Sofia's cousin Chiara, perhaps? Could she have left it there in a bid to help her successor? If so – and this was the worst part of it – where was she now?

James stood in the shadows and tried to catch his breath. Tullio had turned a blind eye, allowing him to leave before Machinetti arrived to take him in for questioning. Everyone had pledged their support and promised to do their best to help him, but he could not go to the museum, the Via Legnano or Sofia's place for fear of being found. It was imperative that he remain free to search for Lucy. Whoever had framed him for Baldovino's assault would clearly not be satisfied until he was behind bars. He was a wanted man with no safe haven. All he could do was carry on looking for his sister and hope that he would not be detected.

With that goal in mind, having recovered a little, he continued to make his way along the back streets, walking with his head down and hoping not to bump into any carabinieri officers. Soon he found himself in the small courtyard outside the back entrance to Madame Giulia's. A figure came out, her identity almost obscured by a large basket of washing. Seeing the red curls bobbing above it, however, James knew immediately who it was.

'*Buongiorno*, Ada,' he said gently, taking the basket away from her.

She stepped back and peered at him fearfully, her eyes darting this way and that. 'I cannot talk to you. Gabriella—'

'Do you know where she is?'

She did not answer. Her arms and face were covered in scratches and bruises. 'Did Valeria do this?' James asked.

'*Sì*, and if you do not go, she will do it again. I have already been turned into a scullery maid. I don't want any more trouble.'

'What about your friend Agnella?'

Ada shook her head. 'She has not returned. I don't think I will see her again.' There was a noise from inside the house. 'Please go. Leave me alone. I don't know anything.'

'I will, but first, is there anything else you can tell me about your friend's client . . . Il Professore, wasn't it?'

She hesitated for a moment as if weighing up the risk of saying more. Then she picked up her basket again. James thought that was that, but he was wrong. 'Agnella gave him that name because he was so clever. He used to talk of faraway places and their history – Egypt and suchlike.'

'Why did he choose Agnella?'

'He said that he liked pale girls because they were untroubled by sin.'

James thanked her and carefully laid some money on top of the washing.

'Wait . . . one more thing,' Ada said in a whisper. 'The other place . . . it smelt strange. It reminded Agnella of going to church.'

There was the sound of footsteps coming towards the door, so James quickly walked around the corner so that he was out of sight. As he moved away, he heard the unmistakable harsh tones of Valeria scolding poor Ada. He resolved to ask Anna to help the girl. It was the least he could do.

As he turned into the main street, Sofia ran towards him. *'Aspettami!'*

'What is it? What's happened?' James asked as she reached him and grasped his arm, catching her breath.

'We need to find the old man.'

'What old man? You're not making any sense!'

'The woman who came to see you . . . the one who was nearly taken.'

'Susanna Russello?'

'*Sì*, that's the one.'

'What about her?'

'According to Madame Tarnovsky, Susanna said there was an old man who saw it happen.'

'I know that, but we don't know who he is. It could be anyone.'

'No. That is what I am trying to tell you. I know him!'

He hesitated.

'What is it, *caro*?'

'Sofia, if you are found with me, you will be locked up too.'

She checked that no one was near and he thought she was about to leave, but then she pulled her to him and kissed him. It was all he needed.

Sofia set off across the street with James behind her. They could not be seen together. It was too risky. Fortunately she had brought an old hat and a large overcoat for him to wear, which helped to disguise him. As they rushed through the city, one question preyed on his mind. What was it about all these girls, Lucy and Fabia included, that had made them targets for this monster?

Lucy was working harder than she had ever done in her life. But then this was the first time that her life and those of others had depended on her industry. She scraped away with her spoon at the grouting holding the bricks together, desperately trying to forge sufficient hand- and footholds to allow her to climb up and escape. She knew it would be difficult. The walls were high and there was no guarantee that she would be able to get enough purchase to get to the top. But she knew that at least she had to try. From what she had heard, it was obvious that they were running out of time.

She had to work harder. She scraped with renewed ardour. She had already removed two bricks, although they had been loosened already by the passing of many years, no doubt. Now she was working on a third.

'What are you doing?' Fabia asked.

'My best . . .' Lucy replied, wiping the sweat from her forehead.

'They've taken the other girl away. Did you hear?'

Lucy could hardly have missed it. Arianna had wailed and screamed and it sounded as if she was putting up quite a struggle. In the end, her increasingly desperate protests had suddenly stopped. Someone had evidently hit her with such force that they had either knocked her out or subdued her. Then she had been dragged away to her fate, whatever that was.

As if to underline the desperation of their predicament, there was a scream – or the vestiges of one. It came from outside but was still loud enough to make the suffering that had caused it only too clear. Lucy stopped for a moment to inspect her handiwork. She wiggled the brick – it was definitely loose. If she could just . . . She moved it up and down and then . . . there! She finally pulled it free. Time for the next one. She put the spoon in her mouth and began to climb. This time of course she had to go higher, and so had to rely on the holes she had already created. She clung to the sides of the wall and pulled herself up until she was in position. As she took one hand away to get the spoon out of her mouth, she lost her balance and fell back on to the hard floor.

She lay there for a moment, winded by the impact. Every muscle and bone in her body felt as if it was bruised. She looked up miserably at the stone that was her makeshift ceiling. It wasn't going to work. Soon – it could be minutes, hours, days or even weeks – her captors would come, and she and Fabia would be dragged away to suffer the same horrible fate as Arianna was enduring. Part of her wanted to weep and wail at the injustice of it all. What had she done – what had any of them done – to deserve this torture? But another part of her was furious at whoever was depriving them of the life they had yet to live. She sat up. Giving up was not an option. She had to fight on, even if it proved to be fruitless.

She was about to pull herself to her feet when she realised that the darkness was becoming lighter. She looked up. The stone was being pulled free. She was too late. It was her turn to die.

44

Nymphomania transforms the most timid girl into a wild and shameless reveller. She looks at every man with longing and flirts outrageously, even to the point of violence. Often she is extremely thirsty, with a dry mouth and bad breath, and she swings her hips almost as if in intercourse. She tends to bite everyone she meets, as if rabid, so much so that she is sometimes repelled by liquids and feels that she is being strangled.

Lombroso and Ferrero, 1893, p. 229

James and Sofia were still searching for the old man, who was proving elusive. According to Sofia, it was almost certainly Pietro, whom they had seen sleeping off a night at La Capra when they were trying to trace Chiara's last footsteps. The day was coming to a close and the shops were shutting. Sofia had said that as far as she knew, the man lived on his wits, or what was left of them, and did not have a home as such. Occasionally he was arrested for loitering, but usually the carabinieri just ignored him, preferring to avoid the bother of taking him to a cell and filling in forms.

'I think it was around here that Susanna Russello says they tried to snatch her,' James said as they reached an alleyway off a winding cobbled lane near the market.

'Yes, this is certainly one of the old man's haunts,' Sofia said.

They moved up the narrow passage. The height of the buildings on either side had made it dark despite the fact that the sun had not yet set, and even though it was in the middle of a busy city, it was quiet and secluded.

'This would be a good place to snatch someone,' James commented.

'Look, I think that might be him.' Sofia indicated a pile of newspapers in a doorway with a battered straw hat balanced precariously on top of it. They approached quietly. The papers rustled gently in the breeze and the telltale sound of snoring emanated from beneath the hat, which now had a jaunty striped ribbon tied around it. A wrinkled, liver-spotted hand held a half-full bottle of cheap brandy.

'Hey, *svegliati*! Wake up!'

The snoring continued. James poked the body gingerly with his foot. The snoring stopped for a moment and then went on.

Sofia shrugged, knelt down beside the apparently sleeping form and snatched the bottle from its hand. The body seemed to erupt like a small but contained earthquake, newspapers falling left, right and centre until a small, shabby figure emerged.

'Eh, give it back!'

'*Un attimo!*' Sofia said, and held the bottle aloft, forcing the old man to struggle to his feet and stretch up in an attempt to get it away from her. He began to leap up and down, desperately trying to get hold of it.

'Wait, signor, wait!' James said. 'Answer my questions and you'll get it back with interest.'

The old man grunted and stopped jumping. He gave James a bleary-eyed stare. 'What do you want to know?'

'It's Pietro, isn't it?'

The old man nodded suspiciously.

'A friend of ours told us that you saw someone try to snatch her off the street near here.'

Pietro's eyes widened in fear and he shook his head vigorously. 'She is mistaken.'

'Are you sure? She was very certain.' James got some notes out of his wallet and waved them under Pietro's nose. The old man paused and peered at them, his nose twitching as if testing their scent. He tried to snatch them from James's hand, but he was not quick enough and could only watch as they were held aloft, out of his reach.

'La Capra,' he said, and pausing only to pick up a tatty woollen blanket that he wrapped around him like a cloak, he stomped off in the direction of the bar.

Sofia looked heavenwards and began to follow him, James running to catch up. 'Why do I always end up at La Capra?' he said.

'It is Hell's back door,' Sofia said, as if it was obvious.

'No wonder I never leave there sober.'

In a few moments Pietro was slumped at his usual table nursing a large glass of grappa. James had been forced to lurk in a corner while the drink was bought so as not to be recognised. Gambro, the barman, gave him a curious stare when he came across to collect some dirty glasses, but then simply shrugged as if to accept him into the criminal fold that made up his usual clientele.

'You have your drink, Pietro, and you will have your bottle back. So tell me what you saw,' James said.

There was a pause. 'A carriage. I saw someone try to pull the girl into a carriage.'

'Who was there?' Sofia asked.

'A man ... a young man ... he tried to grab her. I shouted ... I wanted him to stop ... Leave her alone!'

'What did the young man look like?'

'Dark, he might have had a scar. He was driving the carriage.'

'Who was in the carriage?' James asked.

'A woman ... that's all I know. I just saw her gloves ... lace ... very fancy.'

'What about the carriage itself?'

'That was fancy too ... had a picture on it ... Some kind of flower ... white, I think.'

'Did you see the woman's face?'

Pietro hesitated and looked down into his drink. He was wheezing, as if the effort of remembering was impeding his breathing.

'No ... not her face.'

'Her hair, then?' James asked urgently.

Pietro shrugged.

'Did you see red hair?'

'Can I have another drink?'

'In a moment ... Did you see red hair?' James repeated.

Pietro nodded. '*Sì*, I think so ... something red anyway.'

'So the man tried to snatch the girl,' Sofia said.

'Yes. She struggled, wriggling around, kicking and screaming. He was trying to get his hand over her mouth, but she bit him. Don't take her! I said ... then he dropped her and jumped into the carriage, which went off.' Pietro's eyes widened again and he peered into the distance, as if he could

406

see the scene right in front of his eyes. 'It was the same the second time.'

'Second time?' James said, leaning forward.

Pietro nodded. '*Sì*, a couple of months ago . . . but that one did not get away.'

Lucy stood up tall and straight as she waited for the inevitable. Whatever her fate, she was not going to make it easy for her tormentors. The lid was slid back with relative ease and light flooded into her cell.

'Do exactly as you are told and you won't get hurt.'

She winced as the light hit her unaccustomed eyes. She shaded them with her hand and squinted towards the voice. It was high, but definitely male. She could not place it. 'Who are you?' she asked in confusion. 'Why have you brought me here?'

'Silence. Do not move until I tell you.'

The rope ladder was thrown down.

'Climb up slowly.'

She hesitated for a moment and then obeyed. After all, what other choice did she have? At least she would get out of this pit.

'Lucy, what's happening?' It was Fabia.

'Be quiet. Your turn will come soon enough,' the man said.

When she got to the top, he pulled her out. A second figure stood in the shadows. Lucy was pushed roughly to the ground, her wrists were bound and a blindfold was put on. She struggled.

He pulled her hair with one hand. 'Keep still or your friend will get a visit she won't forget. Understand?' Lucy nodded. He pulled her to her feet. 'Come on, *puttana*. Time to go for a little walk.' She felt herself being dragged along by a rope like an animal being taken to market. She had no idea where he was taking her, but wherever it was, it seemed as if she would not be returning.

45

*Among the morally insane, Krafft-Ebing has observed
early signs of sexual perversion and sexual overindulgence
followed by impotence, a phenomenon I have seen in
criminals. 'The sexual impulses of the morally insane,'
Krafft-Ebing continues, 'are often precocious or unnatural
and preceded or accompanied by a ferocious bloodlust.'*

Lombroso, 1884, p. 215

James and Sofia left a happy Pietro in his usual corner in La
Capra. He had been well paid for his information and had
already begun the process of drinking his earnings.

'That must have been Chiara's abduction he saw the second
time,' James said. Sofia was crying. He took her in his arms
and she leant against him, convulsing as she wept. Now it
was beyond question. Chiara had been taken just like the
other girls . . . just like Lucy. But she had been missing for two
months, which meant that she might well be dead already.
He could not admit that to Sofia, though, and take away her
last vestiges of hope.

'She is gone! She is gone!' Sofia said through her tears.

'Sssh now, *cara*. We don't know that for certain. Think
about it. If she is dead, where is her body? We must not give
up on her . . . or Lucy.'

Sofia wiped her eyes and nodded. 'You are right. There is no time to be lost. We must tell Tullio and the others what we know.'

'I can't . . . not yet. Machinetti might be waiting there for me. You find Tullio. I am going where no one will look for me.'

'Where?' Sofia clung to him. 'Will you be all right, *caro*?'

'I need to rest and think. It is better that you do not know where I am.' He took her hand. 'As I said before, you're just going to have to trust me. Can you do that?'

She nodded. '*Sì*, but then what choice do I have?'

She kissed him on the cheek and left him. He watched her as she hurried through the dying light of the terrible day. When she was out of sight, he took the risk and hailed a cab. Walking would take far too long. He had lied to Sofia. It was not rest that he needed. James had to act now and hope that he would be in time.

Lucy was tearful with pain and humiliation. The man was dragging her along some kind of track, but he was going so fast she was finding it almost impossible to keep up.

'Please stop,' she begged. To her surprise, they came to a halt. This was it, her only chance.

'Can you loosen the blindfold a little? It is hurting.'

She heard a sigh. Her captor came up behind her and began to fumble with the knot at the back of her head. Sensing that he had released the tether, Lucy gave him an almighty shove. She heard him stagger back. She managed to pull off the blindfold and began to run for her very life, desperately trying to loosen the rope around her wrists as she did so.

She was on a rough farm track leading towards fields. Some labourers were finishing work and making their way towards a group of buildings, presumably to eat and then sleep in readiness for another day. Should she try to make it there, or might the workers be party to whatever dreadful plan was being enacted?

Beyond and to the left was a wood. If she could get there, she would find cover at least. She knew where she was. She recognised Francesco's rice estate. Should she make her way to the Villa Purezza? No, it was too far. She hoped the town was nearer. Yes, that was the best plan.

She looked behind her. No one appeared to be in pursuit. She allowed herself to slow down and catch her breath a little. It seemed strange that she had not been followed. She made her way through the damp fields to the wood. Someone was standing there, hands on hips. He moved towards her. Lucy hesitated for a second and then began to run sideways in a bid to avoid him. Her skirts were sodden with water and mud and weighed her down so she could barely move. In a moment he was upon her. She tried to move away but stumbled. He took hold of her and punched her to the ground, where she lay in a damp mass, frogs leaping around her and mosquitoes buzzing round her tear-stained and throbbing face.

He stood over her and laughed. He was close enough for her to see his scarred cheek as he stared at her. 'That was your last journey, Bella. I hope you enjoyed it.' Then he pulled her up and began to drag her again by the rope back towards the stony track, where a cart was waiting. She tried to resist, pulling away from him, but he grabbed her and held her to him, his lips close to hers. His breath smelt of garlic and stale tobacco. 'Try that again, *puttana*, and I'll have you right here. You never know, you might enjoy it.'

She turned away from him.

He grabbed her face and twisted it towards him. 'What's

the matter? Too fancy for the likes of me? Well you wait and see what's in store for you. Then you'll be begging me to end it.'

Lucy summoned up her courage. 'How dare you! Wait till I tell Signor Rambaudi. He'll have you flogged.'

The man laughed again.

'What is so funny?'

'Wait and see, *puttana*, wait and see. Let's go.'

When they reached the cart, he put her in the back, tying her to its barred sides.

'We're going on a mystery trip. I don't want to spoil the surprise,' he said, before blindfolding her again and throwing an old piece of sacking over her. As they drove, she tried her best to push it off so that she would be visible, but to no avail. He had tucked it in around her and she just could not shift it.

After a short journey, the cart stopped. Lucy strained to hear something, anything that might provide a clue to where she had been taken. There was the sound of running water. After she had been untied, her captor led her into what felt like a hallway and down some stairs. He took off her blindfold, tethered her to a door and went over to light a series of lanterns.

As her eyes adjusted to the candlelight, she could see shapes emerging from the shadows. To one side was a beam with some manacles. The floor surrounding it was covered in bloodstains. There were a number of large glass jars with liquid in them. On a shelf were more jars, but these were smaller and made of stone, with carvings on them. They looked familiar. When Lucy remembered where she had seen them, her blood ran cold. They were like the canopic vessels of Wahibra that Professor Donati had shown her, designed to hold organs removed from a body in Egyptian death rituals. But that was not all.

In the centre of the room was a table. When she saw what was on it, she had to use every ounce of will left in her to fight her instinct to cry out. It was a girl, naked and pinned out as if she was a butterfly in a natural history museum, her skin peeled back in two neat flaps like one of the illustrations in her father's anatomy books. The girl's face was pale – translucent almost. Her mouth hung open as if in a silent scream and her lifeless eyes stared into the distance. Underneath the table was a bucket of blood, and a tray containing a pair of kidneys and a human heart.

As the cab made its way out of the city towards his destination, James considered what he knew. Professor Donati had a workshop in the basement of the Museo Egizio and Lucy had clearly been there. He had met her there before, and had also been at the marchesa's ball from which Fabia had gone missing. He had expertise in Egyptology, and when they had found him, he had run away. All these things suggested that he had to be involved, although James suspected that someone else was in control – and he had a good idea who that was. The question was, where had Donati and his employer based themselves? To keep several girls at one time you would need space. It would need to be somewhere secluded. If they were being tortured, they would be making a noise. He pictured Lucy covered in blood, screaming in pain, crying out for him. It felt as if somebody was ripping his heart out of his chest. He leant forward, urging the cab to speed up.

46

Paradoxically, in some cases maternity and sexuality, instead of working against one another as usual, join together in incest, and the mother becomes the lover of the son, adoring him partly as a son and partly as a lover.
Lombroso and Ferrero, 1893, p. 186

'Soon that will be you,' said the man as he pushed Lucy into a small room with a bucket of water in the corner. He threw in a parcel and locked the door behind her. 'Wash yourself and put this on. Your hair should be loose.'

'No, I won't!' Lucy said.

'Want me to come in and undress you myself? It would be a pleasure.'

'Turn your back.'

He gave a sly smile and obeyed her. Quickly she slipped off her clothes. In the parcel was a long white robe, Grecian in style. She put it on and took her hair out of its pins, shaking it out until it tumbled down her back. Was there any chance of escape? Might it be worth keeping hold of one of her hairpins? After all, it had worked before.

'I'll take those,' the man said holding his hand out through the bars. She gave them to him and he pocketed them, still smiling soullessly at her.

'What happens now?' she asked.

He was silent for a moment, then he said simply, 'You won't have to wait long.'

'Why are you doing this?'

The man did not respond.

'Tell me.'

This time he spoke. 'I am doing it for her. She was there for me when I needed someone. This is my way of repaying her.'

'Who?'

'You'll find out.'

There was a noise from above. Footsteps. Someone was coming.

'It's time.'

Lucy readied herself. Her only chance was to make her escape once she was released from her cell. The man turned the key and pulled her out.

There was a sharp rapping sound above. Someone was knocking at a door. Was it James? Had he managed to find her? The footsteps stopped. The rapping began again. Whoever was upstairs went to answer it. The man held her tightly against him, his large sweaty hand over her mouth and his other arm round her neck so she could hardly breathe. She knew that she had to get away from him and run upstairs, but the more she struggled, the tighter his grip became. She heard the door opening.

James stood outside the door. He had knocked but there was no reply. He considered trying to break in, but the place seemed to be almost impregnable. He knocked again. Were those footsteps he could hear? His hands tightened around his cane. The door started to open.

*

Lucy relaxed in the man's arms in the hope that he would loosen his hold, but instead he whispered into her ear: 'One word from you and I'll break your pretty neck.'

She heard a muffled voice as the door was opened. It sounded as if whoever it was had been asked to come in. The invitation had clearly been accepted, because the door was shut firmly behind the visitor. Had James come to rescue her? She hoped so. Be careful. Please be careful, she pleaded silently.

'Yes, that's right . . . down the stairs. Watch yourself. They're quite steep.' She thought she recognised the voice, but surely she must be wrong.

There was creaking as the visitor negotiated their way down. Then they seemed to change their mind and went back up. Lucy brought her heel down hard on her captor's foot, and as his grip was momentarily loosened, she wriggled free and made a break for the stairs. He came after her and caught hold of her skirts. She tried to cry out, but he had his hand over her mouth again before she could.

'Oh my word. What is that noise? Do you have an intruder?'

'It is nothing,' Francesco said. 'Now tell me, how can we help you, Miss Trott?'

James stood and stared in consternation at Beppe, framed in the large wooden doors of the Abbey San Callisto. 'What are you doing here?'

Beppe raised his eyebrows. 'I could ask you the same thing, *Inglese*. Aren't you on the run? What's up? Looking for somewhere to hide? It'll cost you.'

James lifted his cane in what he hoped was a threatening gesture. 'Stand aside.'

Beppe shrugged and did as he was asked. 'No need for that. I'm just the caretaker. You can pay me later.'

James walked in quickly and stood in the hallway, listening, but there was only silence.

Beppe followed him and shut the door behind them with a crash. 'There's no one here. The whorehouse is closed until later. The girls haven't even arrived yet.'

James ignored him and ran up the stairs to the room that he and Sofia had broken into just before they had both been taken away. This time the door was wide open. There it was again – the faint aroma of incense and beeswax polish. Beppe was right. It was deserted.

He walked in and wandered around the room. Its purpose was clear. Couches and chaises longues were arranged artfully about the place. There were paintings on the walls – classical depictions of gods and goddesses, but engaged in distinctly ungodlike pursuits. Various doors lined the room, and he opened one. There was a bed, a dressing table and an armchair. It would have seemed perfectly normal were it not for the rack of fearsome-looking leather riding whips, manacles and chains on the walls. Beppe had joined him and was leaning on the doorpost leering at him.

'Like what you see, *Inglese*? Want to bed down here? I could arrange some company for you.'

James frowned. 'I take it that when you broke in for Professor Lombroso, that was just a performance?'

Beppe laughed. 'The boss knew he was coming, so they cleared out for the night. I just hung around in the right place and there he was, asking me for a bit of help. Did you enjoy my lantern show, by the way?' He grinned and waved his arms in the air, moaning softly.

'What about the girl's body?'

'Don't know anything about a body.'

'And who is your boss? Donati or Concetta Panatti?'

'None of your business, and if I were you, I'd keep it that way. Now, signor, it's time to go. I don't think it's worth the risk letting you stay, you being a fugitive from justice and all. Besides, sooner or later the boss will be back, and then you'll just get another beating, like the last one, and maybe a scar to match the one you've already got.'

Ignoring Beppe, James ran down the stairs until he was near the crypt. There was the door that Sofia had found. He knew it led to underground rooms. That must be where Lucy and the others were being kept.

'Lucy! Fabia!' he called.

'What are you doing, *Inglese?*' Beppe had joined him.

'Let me in,' James demanded. 'I know the girls are there.'

'What are you talking about? I've told you. No one is here.'

'Open up.'

Beppe did so grudgingly, then stepped back and bowed. 'Be my guest, but you won't find anyone.'

James barged past him and walked along the stone corridor. It was musty and damp. He stopped. Silence. 'Lucy?' he called again.

He walked on. There were several rooms branching off the corridor. Most seemed to be used for storage. One had a desk and a couple of chairs. He noticed dark red marks on the floor and bent to examine them. They were drops of dried blood – hardly the pool that one might expect if someone had been exsanguinated. But the room felt familiar. He winced as he remembered the feel of the knife slicing through his cheek. Was this where it had happened? He wondered if the girls had ever been here. Certainly there was no evidence to suggest that anyone was here now.

He heard a noise. Beppe was standing behind him. 'Time to go, signor.'

James followed him out. When they reached the front door, Beppe held it open for him. 'If I were you, signor, I'd keep quiet about this place,' he said as James walked past him. 'They don't take kindly to interference, as you know.'

James waved a dismissive hand at him and left. He had no time to lose. He knew now that Concetta Panatti's unregistered brothel was at the abbey. Presumably Agnella had never left after her second visit, ending up in the crypt with the mummified monks. Had Panatti been responsible for her murder? It seemed likely. But why drain the blood from the girl's body? Was she trying to cover up something by making the death look like the work of a lunatic? He still could not be certain that she was responsible for the missing girls, or Lucy and Fabia's abductions. But if it wasn't her, then who had taken them, and where?

He thought back to the old man Pietro and his description of the woman in the carriage. Had he actually said that she had red hair? He couldn't recall. He did say something about the carriage, though. What was it? Something about a picture – a flower of some kind? Where had he seen something similar before? When he remembered, a cold shiver went down his spine. He had been so convinced that Panatti and the abbey were at the heart of all this that he had ignored everything else the old man had said.

As he ran down the hill, a carriage seemed to come from nowhere and overtook him. Then it stopped. The door opened. Someone stepped out and began to walk towards him.

47

If one goes back over reports of female cruelty, one can detect a common element, whether they be about epidemics or individuals, the demoniacal atrocities of certain queens and criminals, or the smaller vulgarities of spitefulness and daily persecutions. That common element is woman's tendency to inflict the largest amount of pain – not to obliterate her enemy but to martyr him slowly and paralyse him with suffering.

Lombroso and Ferrero, 1893, p. 68

It was dark now, and the moon was obscured by cloud. A tall, shadowy figure was getting ever closer. 'James!' it hissed.

'Ottolenghi? Is that you?'

'Yes, hurry! Before you're seen.'

'Ah, there you are, Murray,' the professor said as James climbed in, having given instructions to the driver. 'We were beginning to think that you'd gone back to Scotland.'

'Where is Sofia?' James asked as the carriage bumped along the rough road.

'She guessed that you had gone to the abbey, so we came to find you. She and Anna will follow on once Miss Trott has reappeared. Apparently she had yet another errand to run. Odd timing, but there we are, that's women for you. Now tell me what on earth made you go back to the abbey, and where we are going now.'

'It's a long story . . . but never mind that. I know where the girls are.'

'Indeed. Well, better late than never.'

'The insignia that the old man saw was almost certainly a lily, which symbolises purity . . . hence the Villa Purezza.'

'Really? You think young Rambaudi is responsible? I was beginning to think that he might be a mattoid.'

'What does that mean?' James asked.

'A mattoid is another variant of the insane criminal. They are prophets of a kind . . . self-appointed, naturally; revolutionaries who rise up from the lower classes to spout utopian ideas.'

'How does that fit with Rambaudi?' Ottolenghi asked. 'I thought you said the killer was a man with large ears, a scanty beard and a propensity to write erotic poetry?'

Lombroso shook his head vehemently. 'No, no, no, Ottolenghi! I do wish you would listen! Rambaudi sees himself as someone who has a profound moral insight. His actions reflect that. It is his way of spreading ideas.'

'He is certainly courting public attention,' James said, 'but I would hardly term him a revolutionary.'

'Perhaps you are right,' Lombroso conceded. 'I did think he fitted the hysterical criminal type – egotism, self-preoccupation, leading to a desire for scandal and public attention – but that can't be correct.'

'Why not?'

'Because they are almost always women, Murray. And I knew all along that this was the work of a man.'

'See. There it is,' James said, pointing out the lily on the gates as they approached the entrance to the Villa Purezza.

The place was in almost complete darkness except for some gas lamps by the house.

They alighted from their carriage and walked up to the front door. 'Should we ring, do you think?' Ottolenghi asked.

'We don't want to alert him at this stage,' Lombroso said, pulling the bell rope. 'We are merely paying a call, finding ourselves in the area.'

James could not quite believe what he was hearing. 'Why aren't we tearing down the door? We're here to find Lucy, Fabia and Chiara, not make a social visit!'

'I think it best if I do the talking,' Lombroso said, frowning at him. 'We must be careful. Lives are at stake.'

The door opened to reveal Cosimo, the enormous servant who had dealt with James during his last visit. He gave James a hostile glare.

'Would Signor or Signorina Rambaudi be at home?' Lombroso enquired politely.

'I'll see,' he said and slammed the door in their faces.

'A certain lack of finesse there,' Lombroso said. 'Probably a born criminal of the most basic type. All the primitive atavistic features are present.'

The door opened again. 'This way,' Cosimo said, ushering them into the hall. 'Signor Rambaudi is out, but the signora will see you in the library.' He pointed to a room in the corner and left them.

Lombroso shrugged and walked over to the door. He knocked and entered, James and Ottolenghi following behind. Bianca Rambaudi was sitting in an armchair reading. She stood up to greet them. 'Ah, Professor, an unexpected pleasure.'

'I do apologise ... Your manservant ...'

'Not at all, Professor. Cosimo is a little rough and ready, I know. But he is obedient and loyal. What more can one ask in this day and age? Were you and your colleagues here for anything in particular?'

'It is a rather delicate matter.'

Something of an understatement, James thought, but it had to be said.

Bianca raised her eyebrows. 'I see. Then you had better all be seated.'

'It is about your brother. I am so sorry to have to say this, but it appears that he may be responsible for the abduction of a number of young girls.'

There was a long pause as she assimilated this information. She seemed oddly composed, although James thought that her eyes told a different story.

'Exactly what evidence do you have for that outrageous suggestion?' she asked eventually.

'A witness saw a carriage with your family's insignia at the scene of two abductions,' Lombroso said.

'That does not mean Francesco is responsible.' She spoke precisely, positioning her words like a medieval typesetter.

'Nonetheless, we would like to speak to him. If he is not responsible, he might be able to help us find the real culprit. Whoever it is has almost certainly murdered at least two young women, and others are at risk.'

Her hands were folded primly in her lap. The left forefinger had been rhythmically tapping her wrist. When murder was mentioned, it stopped.

'It is true that my brother has been behaving erratically since the death of our mother. They were very close.' She stared into the distance, as if she was seeing something that was hidden from everyone else. Her whole body had stiffened. 'I suppose that grief might have clouded his judgement. But he would not abduct anyone, let alone harm them. He doesn't have it in him to do such a thing.'

'Perhaps, but we are searching for the girls. Do you know where he might have taken them?'

'I do not.'

James had had enough. It was all too damn polite and it wasn't getting them anywhere. He raised his voice. 'He *has* taken Lucy, and you know where, don't you?'

She blinked at him, her face still devoid of expression.

'Is there a place that is special to him?' Lombroso said with a sideways glance of warning at James.

She thought for a moment and nodded. 'Follow me. There is only one place I can think of.'

'Lucia, you look even more beautiful each time I see you,' Francesco said. 'That dress suits you. It fits exactly. Bruno, release her immediately!'

'What if she runs off again?'

'She only did that because she didn't understand. Isn't that right, Lucia?'

Lucy nodded. Miss Trott stood and watched in silence.

Bruno shrugged and obeyed. Francesco held out an arm. 'You will join me for dinner, won't you, Lucia? I have some guests who are dying to meet you.' He paused for a moment. 'Just think of it as a test. If you pass, you will live here with me, happily ever after.'

He turned to Miss Trott. 'I do hope you will join us. Our guests will be delighted to meet you.'

'I came only to retrieve my parasol, Signor Rambaudi,' Miss Trott said, her eyes flicking to the body lying on the table. 'I came here because I could get no answer at the house. It is of sentimental value, you know. My dear late father gave it to me as a gift. However, I can see it is not here, so I will not trouble you further.'

'Not at all, Miss Trott. I would not hear of it,' Francesco said, standing in her path, preventing her from getting to the stairs. 'You will join us. Then you can see if Lucia passes her little test.'

'And if I don't?' Lucy asked. She forced herself to walk over to Francesco and take his arm, knowing that she had no choice. Her skin crawled as he patted her hand.

He glanced at the body, the beam with the manacles, the bloodstains, and smiled sheepishly at her. 'Then I fear you will follow the same path as Arianna, and you don't want Miss Trott to witness that, I am sure.'

He led Lucy carefully up the stairs, followed by Miss Trott escorted by Bruno. Lucy didn't know what the test might be, but one thing was for sure: she had to pass it to survive.

As they emerged from the cellar area, she finally realised where they were – Francesco's summer house, or rather his late mother's. The statue of Maat was gleaming even in the darkness.

'Now let me look at you. I want to make sure you are presentable.' Francesco arranged her hair and straightened her dress a little before standing back to admire his handiwork. 'Yes, I do believe you are ready. Follow me.'

They stepped out into the garden in front of the summer house. There a table was laid with crystal glasses and fine white linen. Candles were lit, and baskets laden with bread and fruit waited for them. A heavily veiled woman dressed in white was seated at the head of the table. Lucy presumed that she was the guest of honour. Miss Trott nodded at her charge almost imperceptibly, as if telling her to play along with their host, not that she had much choice.

'Of course if you are to be my consort, then you will need servants.' Francesco indicated a young woman in a maid's uniform. 'Curtsey, girl!' he said sharply. 'Show some respect to your new mistress or you know what will happen.'

Lucy gasped. It was Fabia. She looked both terrified and crestfallen. She bobbed to Lucy. 'Good evening, madam,' she said shakily.

Another girl dressed as a maid was at the far end of the table, pouring wine. She was small with dark hair and looked uncannily like Sofia.

'Chiara?' Lucy said. She nodded and curtseyed too. At least they were alive, Lucy thought. Now all she had to do was work out what this test was and ensure that she passed it. It would buy them some time at any rate.

Francesco led her with great ceremony to the head of the table, where the guest of honour was sitting. As he gently drew aside the woman's veil and bent to kiss her cheek, Lucy recoiled in horror. The figure before them was not a living woman but the mummified remains of one. Her leathery brown skin was stretched over the bones of her face and her mouth was set in a ghastly parody of a smile.

Francesco pulled her closer to the figure. 'Now, Lucia, I don't believe you have met my mother.'

48

While the woman whose passion leads to crime is very different from the born criminal who violates the laws of chastity from lust and love of idle pleasure, nonetheless such good, passionate women are fatally inclined to love bad men. They fall into the hands of frivolous, fickle and sometimes depraved lovers who later abandon them, often adding to betrayal the even greater cruelties of scorn and slander. Lombroso and Ferrero, 1893, p. 202

James stood at the entrance to the storage barn. 'Why here?'

'It is where Francesco spends most of his time,' Bianca said. 'He is usually with Bruno.'

He walked over to one of the grain pits, pushed aside the lid and looked down into it. There was a bucket and some scraps of food on the floor. 'This is where he keeps them?'

Bianca came over and looked down. 'So it seems. I had no idea. Still, it does not mean that he has hurt anyone.'

She was standing next to him, completely still, her hands clasped loosely in front of her. As before, she was hardly reacting at all. Her voice was neutral. Her face was devoid of expression. There was not even a raised eyebrow. Did she not understand, or was it that she didn't care? Perhaps she was in shock. She unclasped her hands. There were small red crescent-shaped marks where her nails had been digging into her flesh. She both understood and cared, it seemed, but did not want to show it.

James and Ottolenghi went to each pit in turn to see if anyone was still there, but they were all empty.

'There must have been some indication,' Lombroso said.

'There have been one or two incidents with girls from the area. He and Bruno would befriend them, and sometimes we had to make payments to smooth things over when they got out of hand.'

'Teresa Mariani, for example?' James asked. 'You paid her mother, didn't you?'

'Yes,' Bianca said. 'The girl works for me now, so she did well out of it.'

'What happened to her?'

'Bruno violated her. But we sorted it out,' she said casually, as if it was a trifling matter. 'We have to beat her now and then, sometimes put her in a pit for an hour or two. But she usually does what she's told.'

James looked at her in disgust. 'Where else might he have gone?'

'I don't know of anywhere else . . .'

'Yes you do. I can see it in your face. You're lying. It would be better for him if you told us. We need to find the girls before . . .' James could not bring himself to say it. 'If you tell us where they are, I will do all I can to help Francesco.'

She hesitated for a few seconds. 'Follow me. It is not far.'

A few minutes later they were standing at a small wooden door encircled by roses. James could smell the sweet scent of them in the still warm air. Bianca took a key from her pocket and opened it to reveal a garden with a large pond in the shape of a cross. A statue of a young woman stood in the centre in front of a small fountain. Beyond it was a summer house, built in the classical style, complete with fluted pillars and frescoes. The murmur of conversation wafted over the water with the chink of glasses. Someone was laughing. Bianca stopped for a few seconds, as if halted by the sound, then beckoned to them. They followed her in silence towards a terrace at the front of the house.

At its heart was a large table, laid for dinner. Two maids stood by. One of them appeared to be Fabia Carignano and the other also looked familiar. Might it be Chiara? The young man James assumed was Bruno Ferranti watched as two of the diners appeared to lean in and whisper to each other like lovers. James felt his heart lurch. One of them was Lucy, ashen-faced, her eyes full of fear. Francesco had his hand clamped over her wrist. Miss Trott was sitting uncomfortably next to the fourth figure in the flickering candlelight. She gave him a small, tight smile.

He looked more closely at her companion. Repulsed, part of him wanted to turn away, but the sight was so strange and so terrible that it was oddly compelling. Seated at the table between Francesco and Miss Trott was the mummified corpse of a long-dead woman, her silver hair still strangely intact and held up with pearl combs like a macabre Miss Havisham. Could this be Francesco and Bianca's dead mother? His thoughts scrambled around in his mind in an effort to make sense of what he was seeing.

'Bianca?' Francesco said. 'I wish I'd known you were bringing guests. I'd have had the servants lay more places.'

Bianca moved towards him, as did James. In one quick movement Francesco pulled Lucy to her feet and held her, his arm across her chest. In his other hand was a knife.

'I didn't want her bled like the others, Bianca. I really think that she's the one.' He spoke in a strange sing-song voice, as if mimicking his sister.

Again James made as if to go to Lucy, but Ottolenghi pulled him back. Miss Trott edged away as Bianca continued to move slowly towards her brother.

'What's that?' Francesco said, looking towards his mother. 'Are you sure?' He flinched slightly. 'Yes, Mother, if that is what you want.' He spoke quietly to Lucy. 'Mother doesn't think you are suitable after all, Lucia.'

'Then let her go, Rambaudi,' James said. 'She has not harmed you.'

'I must kill her, Bianca,' Francesco said. 'Mother wants me to.'

He lifted the knife and brought it down on to Lucy's throat. A few drops of blood trickled down towards her collarbone. She looked back at James, her eyes wide. He couldn't lose her!

Francesco laughed. It was a light sound, almost musical. 'Oh, she is wicked. Mother says so. She is mocking me, and what is worse, she is mocking my dear sweet mother. She is just like all the others.'

'Francesco, hush. You do not know what you are saying.' Bianca took another step towards him.

'Lucy is different,' James said carefully. 'She would never mock your mother. She has lost her own.'

'Don't come any nearer, Bianca,' Francesco warned, 'or I will tell them everything.'

'There is nothing to tell,' Bianca said.

'Go on, Signor Rambaudi,' James said. 'We are listening.'

'Mother wants me to find a wife. Isn't that right?' He looked at Bianca, who did not respond. 'But I haven't found the right girl. There were plenty of candidates, but none of them were pure enough.'

'Tell me why not.'

'How could any woman measure up to Mother? Lucia here is no different.'

'Please, Francesco!' Lucy said.

'Hush, Lucia, hush. You see, that has always been your problem. A woman should be strong, and from that inner strength comes purity. That is the mistake they all made, with their childish pleading and crying. How can a woman be considered pure if she does that?'

'How did you find the girls?' James asked, hoping to divert Francesco's attention from Lucy.

'Usually Bianca found them. Some were from the estate, some from San Callisto itself. Then when that got too risky, we took local girls that Bruno knew who had moved to the city, to make sure they would not be missed.'

James was curious. 'Why did they have to be local?'

'Purer stock. One always needs to check pedigree if one wishes to breed.' Francesco glanced down at Lucy, who shifted slightly. He responded by moving the knife a little so it was resting against her neck. He went on. 'Eventually Bianca decided that the experiment was failing because of class, so she selected some more upmarket fillies, as it were – Fabia, and then Lucia – although Bruno and I found the girl from the abbey. I really thought she was special. She was so pale already, and so submissive. She used to call me Il Professore . . . I liked that.' He sighed. 'But then she ruined it all by asking me for money. We gave her the chance to atone, but it did not work. How could it? She was just a whore, when all was said and done. They all are at heart, even my dear sister.'

'What form did this atonement take?' James asked.

'We kept them until they were cleansed outside and in.

Then they were introduced to Mother. If they were polite and she accepted them, they would live here as my bride.'

James imagined that the likely reaction of any girl in that situation would be one of horror. No wonder they didn't pass the test. 'What happened if they did not atone?'

'After Bruno and I had amused ourselves, Bianca took them away.' Francesco tightened his grip on Lucy. 'Now, I think we have had enough of talking. The time has come for Lucia here to bid you all goodbye.'

Lucy's eyes were full of terror. He had to do something. He could not let her die. But if he made a move, Rambaudi would kill her. The knife touched her throat.

'Stop there, Mr Rambaudi!' A voice rang out from behind them. 'If you move an inch, I will shoot you!'

Miss Trott was standing next to Ottolenghi, her legs apart, her arms raised, a determined look on her face. She had a derringer pistol in her hands.

'I am a very good shot, Mr Rambaudi. I will not miss. Move away from Lucy and drop your knife.'

'Euphemia Trott,' Francesco said, still smiling dreamily. 'I just knew you and Mother would get on.'

He lifted his hand again. Miss Trott braced herself.

'What is it, Mother?' Francesco said, bending towards the corpse. He loosened his grip on Lucy for a split second, but it was enough for her almost to wriggle free. He still had hold of her dress and for a moment it seemed as if he would drag her back, but then a shot rang out. He glanced up in shock, and Lucy pulled away and ran to Miss Trott. Francesco fell to his knees and looked down at his stomach. Blood seeped from it.

There was a scream. Fabia had been seized by Bruno Ferranti. He dragged her away through the garden, holding her in front of him as a shield. James blocked his path and grabbed

432

the struggling girl, pulling her free. Then he launched himself at the man, knocking him to the ground. They wrestled for a moment, but Ferranti escaped, leaving a dazed Fabia sitting nearby. Ottolenghi chased after him.

Francesco was lying in Bianca's arms. The knife was in her hand. As James walked towards her, she held it up in warning. 'Stop, Signor Murray.'

James did so. Lombroso slowly walked over and stood next to him. 'You must leave him to us, signorina,' James said gently. 'You have done all you can for him.'

'You don't understand. He must die.'

'If you allow me to stop the bleeding, then he can be saved.'

'No.'

'Why?'

'Because I love him.'

'Despite all he did to those girls?' Miss Trott said quietly.

'He just played with them a little. The rest was down to me.'

Miss Trott looked at her, aghast. '*You* murdered them?'

'Many years ago, Francesco and I were close. We barely spent a minute out of each other's company. But when he was about seven years old, our mother, Sylvana, began to take an interest in him.'

'What kind of interest?' Lombroso asked.

'The kind that my father denied her. Francesco knew no better. She told him it was a special kind of love that only a mother and son could share. He believed her. Why would he not? He worshipped her.'

'And how did that make you feel?' Miss Trott asked. Taking advantage of this attempt to distract Bianca, James tried to move slowly away. He wanted to see if he could approach her from behind and get to Francesco that way.

'Lonely, neglected... second best. She would flaunt their relationship, leaving doors open so that I could see everything they did together. Then, when I turned away, she made me watch.'

This time Lombroso asked a question. 'When did she die?'

Bianca's face slid into an insincere smile. 'A few years ago. A wasting illness... a terrible thing...'

'Poison will do that,' Lombroso said.

Bianca laughed. 'How clever of you, Professor. Yes, but she had to die. You do see that, don't you?'

'How did Francesco react?' Miss Trott asked.

The smile left Bianca's face in an instant and she looked down at her brother. 'He was devastated, inconsolable. I offered myself to him but he was not interested. I told him that she would have left him soon anyway. I could see the signs. She wanted the boy, not the man. But he would not accept it.' She looked up. 'If you could have seen him... He was distraught, dying of grief. I could not lose him like that, so I tried to preserve Sylvana for him. I even kept her heart in our ice house.'

'The heart that was found at the Borgo?'

'Yes, that's right. A nice touch, don't you think? A heart was the one thing my mother never really needed.'

'And after Sylvana?' Miss Trott said.

'Francesco was grateful at first, but then he wanted more, so I found him a girl – one of the mondine.'

'Teresa Mariani?' Lombroso asked.

'No. She's just Bruno's little plaything. We kept her alive to amuse him. The mondine come and go all the time, so I knew that no one would miss them. When I got him the first one, he toyed with her a little but then he discarded her. He said she did not measure up to Sylvana because she was not

434

pure enough.' Bianca ran her bony fingers across Francesco's cheek. 'I wanted to please him, so I locked her up in the grain store and told her to atone. I waited until she had her monthly visitor so she would be clean, and then I drugged her and purified her for him.'

'Purified?' Lombroso asked.

'The Egyptians bled their dead and removed their organs to cleanse them for the afterlife. We learnt this from Francesco's tutor, Professor Donati. So I did the same, though of course I did not wait for death. To achieve real purity, one needs to conduct the process while the subject still lives. I hung her up, with the help of dear Bruno, then I bled her, removed her organs and embalmed her. I wanted to see if I could preserve her beauty better than I had managed with my mother, so I tried a different technique, but it didn't quite work.'

'So you got Bruno to bury her in the woods,' Lombroso said.

'Yes. I gave him the exact specifications for where to dig the grave. I wanted to be precise. It is very important, don't you think?' she said, her head coyly to one side. 'Francesco thought so. He could see what I was trying to do. He and Bruno, my mother's other little pastime. So I kept doing it, and I gave the bodies to Francesco to play with. Chiara's monthly visitor never arrived – I think she was too young – so we kept her as a sort of pet.'

James thought of the anguish that Sofia had gone through. Bianca was a monster, whatever the cause, and her brother was no better. Still, he should not be allowed the solace of death. He inched closer as the questioning continued.

'What about the girls in the abbey and the Borgo?' Lombroso asked.

'Francesco was bored. He was becoming more interested in

living girls, like Lucy here. But I had grown attached to my work. I was getting quite good at it, you know. I decided to put it on display. I selected my subjects carefully. Bruno gave me their names. Then once I had created my pieces, I wanted to share my first collection. Did you like it?'

'And Lucy and Fabia Carignano?' Miss Trott said. 'Why did you take them?'

'As I said, my brother needed a wife. It was going to be Fabia due to her stock. We thought that made her pure enough, but she was so objectionable we decided on Lucy. Francesco made Fabia wait on her. Don't you think that was amusing? He knew it was the thing that would hurt her most. He was always inventive in his cruelty. He learnt that from my mother. I would have killed Fabia for him when he tired of her . . . Lucy too if he'd wanted me to.'

'I do not think it was love for your brother that made you kill,' Miss Trott said. 'Now was it, dear?'

Bianca smiled her dead smile.

Miss Trott went on. 'First he took your mother's love from you, and then when she was gone he rejected you. You never forgave him. Poor Bianca . . . always the odd one out. They loved each other but never had time for you, even when one of them was dead.'

James had almost reached them when Francesco stirred. Bianca kissed her brother's forehead. Then, without warning, she lifted her arm and brought the knife down on his throat, slicing through it from side to side. Before anyone could act, she did the same to her own. The blood poured from their wounds and mingled on the ground beneath them, uniting them in death.

James heard shouting in the distance. Anna, Sofia, Tullio,

Ottolenghi, Machinetti and a crowd of carabinieri ran through the gate towards them. Bruno Ferranti was in handcuffs.

Sofia broke away from Anna and embraced Chiara as if her life depended on it. James waited for Machinetti to approach him. He knew he would be arrested, but now that Lucy was safe and Chiara found, it didn't seem to matter. He would be taken to prison, which after all was where he had always belonged.

49

The chief motive for female crime is vengeance. The inclination towards revenge that we noted even in normal women becomes extreme in criminals. Because their psychic centres are irritated, the smallest stimulus can provoke an enormous reaction. But usually the female born criminal revenges herself more slowly than men. She has to develop her plan little by little because her physical weakness and fearful nature restrain her even when her reason does not.
Lombroso and Ferrero, 1893, p. 186

At the marchesa's private dinner, held to mark the return to her care of her niece, the mood was subdued rather than celebratory.

As they took their seats, she remarked pointedly, 'It is hard to believe that so many girls could be taken and so little was done.'

Lucy noticed that the fat little policeman, Machinetti, had the good grace to blush at this at least. He had taken great pleasure in arresting James at the Villa Purezza because of a girl who had apparently gone missing. It had looked for a while as if James would have to await trial in custody. Fortunately his friend Tullio had received a tip-off and the girl was found at Madame Giulia's, claiming that she had never been missing in the first place.

All involved with the Rambaudi case, as it was now known, had been invited to the dinner, including Chiara and Sofia. Lucy noticed how her brother made sure that they did not feel uncomfortable, including them in the conversation whenever he could and discreetly demonstrating how each course should be tackled. It was clear how he and Sofia felt about each other. He would touch her affectionately on the arm or hand at every opportunity. Sofia was less openly demonstrative, but her emotions were clear. Chiara was watching them carefully, just as Lucy was, and now and again they would catch each other's eye and exchange knowing smiles.

James was still tense, of course, though he was doing his best to hide it. His freedom was in question. The trial would be upon them soon enough, and Lucy could only guess how apprehensive he was about its possible outcome. Baldovino was still unconscious, and much of the evidence was damning. The professor seemed confident that they would win, but Lucy could see that James did not share his certainty.

Fabia was quieter than Lucy had ever known her, which was not surprising, considering her ordeal. Thanks to James's intervention, she had largely escaped physical pain. But she had been humiliated, and that, for Fabia, was a form of torture in itself, as Francesco had known so well.

Perhaps they were all dreaming in the same way, reliving their experiences. Sometimes it happened even when Lucy was still awake. Just closing her eyes could conjure up Francesco's face and the expression on it as Bianca had sliced through his throat, or the sight of his mummified mother seated at the head of the table. She had already decided to write it all into one of her stories. She would never show it to anyone, but she was finding that pouring her feelings onto the page in the form of fiction was comforting, and comfort was exactly what she craved.

She observed the remaining guests with care. Tullio, the other policeman, looked pale and tense as he listlessly pushed his food around his plate. His eye would twitch occasionally and his smiles were strained. Every now and then he would glance at James and close his eyes as if he did not dare to look at him directly. Why was he so worried? The case was over and it was not he who was about to stand trial.

Miss Trott was the opposite. She was relaxed and chatting animatedly to the marchesa and Anna. Her eyes were shining as if a burden had been lifted. Nothing further had been said about her part in the rescue. Lucy had thought her companion to be so dull. Who would have thought that she would save the day, and with the help of a derringer too!

After dinner, they all gathered in the marchesa's drawing room. Professor Lombroso was going to address them about the murders, and 'other crimes', as he had put it. He said that it would help them all to understand what had happened, and Lucy was inclined to agree.

'Francesco Rambaudi was not a born criminal, but his immorality became instilled in him at an early age due to the attentions of his mother, Sylvana.'

'Should the young ladies be hearing this?' Miss Trott asked.

'Thank you for your concern,' the marchesa said. 'But given their ordeal, I think it appropriate for them to hear the background from experts in the field, assuming they wish to stay. As the professor says, it may help them to understand it, insofar as it can be understood.'

Lucy nodded vigorously, as did Fabia and Chiara. Lombroso continued.

'As his sister told us, Rambaudi developed an obsession with Sylvana, both physical and sexual. When she died at Bianca's hands, he needed to find a substitute. This was the motivation for his actions. Assisted by Bruno Ferranti, a young man with overdeveloped sexual impulses, he began his search amongst some of his employees.'

'The mondine?' James asked.

'Correct, Murray. As your research led me to that conclusion, perhaps you would care to continue.'

James got to his feet, his face serious and intense. His tone was measured and authoritative. Lucy didn't think she had ever felt as proud of him as she did at that moment.

'The mondine are the itinerant seasonal workers who come to labour in the rice fields of the region, planting, weeding and harvesting the crop. They live and work together, but that work is hard, back-breaking in fact. I questioned one of them, a woman called Perla, and she confirmed that girls from surrounding villages came to work there but that the turnover was high. For many of them the work was too unpleasant and they left. This means that no one noticed when some of them disappeared. Everyone just thought they had gone to work elsewhere.'

'What happened to them?' Ottolenghi said.

'The first was a young woman called Teresa Mariani,' James said. 'Sofia, you remember how her mother reacted strangely when we talked to her?'

'*Sì*, she did not seem surprised about the finding of the bodies.'

'That's because she knew Teresa was not dead. Bruno Ferranti chose and befriended the girl. But after a while she became frightened of him and wanted to leave him. He threatened her, so she ran off to the city. But he found her and took her back, forcing her to work for the Rambaudis. Her mother knew this but was too frightened of what they might do to her to intervene.'

'Was she the girl with Bruno at the museum?' Lucy asked.

James nodded. 'Yes, but it was not her choice. She was as much a victim as you.'

'What will happen to her?' the marchesa asked.

'She is helping us with our enquiries,' Tullio said. 'I doubt she will be charged, unlike Bruno Ferranti.'

'What about the body in the woods?' Anna asked.

'May I?' Lombroso asked. James nodded graciously and sat down. The professor was treating him as an equal, Lucy thought. Good for him!

'This was the first victim. She was abducted, murdered and then some form of experiment was performed on her by Bianca, assisted no doubt by both Francesco and Ferranti. Francesco was always interested in Egyptology, so he no doubt influenced Bianca as she tried to re-create their death rituals in order to preserve her handiwork.'

'So Professor Donati had nothing to do with it?' Lucy said.

'He gave some advice but we cannot be sure that he knew its purpose.'

'I'm sure he did,' Anna said. 'Why else would he run away from us at the museum?'

'Yes, he must be guilty of something!' Lucy declared.

'We will hear more of him in due course, dear. Be patient,' Miss Trott said.

'This led to the forming of a pattern of behaviour. A girl would be abducted, an experiment conducted, and then she would be kept at the summer house as an exhibit before being disposed of. Moral insanity at its most extreme.'

'Where are their bodies?' Anna asked.

'I am guessing that a search of the woods and perhaps even the grounds of the estate would be fruitful,' Lombroso replied.

'I have sent men to do just that,' Machinetti announced.

'It is a wonder you did not do so when the first body was found,' the marchesa said, looking on disapprovingly as Machinetti flushed and shifted in his seat.

Lombroso continued. 'The bodies at the abbey and the Borgo were left there for us to find. As you may remember, Baldovino helpfully publicised my investigation. Bianca had tired of keeping her experiments to herself and was also aware that rumours were beginning to circulate amongst the mondine. She needed to target a different set of victims and so took the opportunity to develop a new approach, which she wanted to show off.'

'How did she select her victims?' Anna asked.

'By name,' James said. 'All the girls had names that signified purity in one way or another. Chiara means clear bright light, Lucia means graceful light, Susanna is graceful lily, Ariana is chaste and holy, Caterina means pure and so does Agnella.'

'Why did Bianca arrange for Agnella to be left at the abbey?' Ottolenghi asked.

'She worked at the abbey as a prostitute and Francesco was her client. He told Bianca that he wanted her, so she complied, then exhibited the body where she knew we would find it.'

'What does Fabia mean?' Chiara asked.

'Bean farmer, I believe,' the marchesa said with an affectionate glance at her niece, who was scowling.

No wonder she didn't pass Bianca's test, Lucy thought. And it might even have been her own name that saved her.

'How did Baldovino find out about the missing girls?' Anna asked.

'I told him,' Tullio said.

'What?' exclaimed Machinetti. 'You passed on information to a reporter? You will answer to the mayor for this!'

'Why, Tullio?' James said.

'I was getting nowhere and he has certain contacts. I thought it might assist. Sometimes you have to use unconventional means to achieve a result.'

'As you did in relation to Concetta Panatti,' Lombroso said.

'Please tell me you have not been using her as an informant!' Machinetti said.

'We have been investigating the abbey for some time. The suspicion was that Concetta Panatti was running an illegal brothel there. The mayor and Father Vincenzo asked me to be discreet, as a number of establishment figures are implicated, including members of the Catholic clergy. I asked the professor to go up there and look around under the guise of one of his psychical investigations.'

'Is that why we had no relevant equipment?' James asked.

Lombroso looked sheepish. 'Yes ... well, actually, other than a camera and a thermometer, there is no equipment for such an enquiry.'

'For the avoidance of doubt, the rooms on the first floor are where the brothel is,' James said. 'Ada, one of Concetta Panatti's girls, told me about its existence, and about her missing friend Agnella, or Nella Calvi, who worked there.'

'Can you bring Concetta Panatti to justice?' Lombroso asked.

'Not yet ... perhaps not ever,' Tullio said. 'It has been difficult to prove anything because of all the vested interests involved. She has kept her association at arm's length.'

'I went there looking for Chiara,' James said. 'My visits and

Ada's information were enough to ensure that I was threatened and beaten. Why didn't you warn me, Tullio?'

'I couldn't,' Tullio said. 'It would have ruined the investigation. And . . .'

'You were being threatened too?' James asked quietly.

Tullio nodded. 'I was told that my family would be harmed if I did not stop investigating.'

James was looking at his friend's face, pale and strained, and Lucy could see that he understood the stress that Tullio must have been under. 'Is Panatti behind the assault on Baldovino and the supposedly missing Gabriella?' he asked.

'It is possible, but again we cannot prove it,' Tullio said. 'No one will speak up, such is her hold.'

'She is a blackmailer,' Lombroso said. 'An unusually intelligent example of female criminality.'

'I thought you said that women were incapable of such things, Professor,' Lucy pointed out. 'What makes Concetta Panatti so exceptional?'

'An excellent question, Lucy!' Anna said. 'What is your answer, Cesare?'

'She is of course physically incapable of satisfying her perverse instincts. However, superior intelligence in a criminal woman can be explained by two things – the fact that she is a born criminal and the originality of her crimes. She has combined prostitution, pandering and blackmail with legitimate business interests – a lethal mix that makes her almost invincible.'

'And she is ruthless,' Ottolenghi said. 'Look at what she has done to James. First she flirts with him, and when that doesn't work, she has him physically assaulted. Then she tries to seduce him, attempts to discredit him with that nonsense in *The People's Voice* and frames him for an attack on Baldovino.

When he gets bail, thanks to the marchesa, she cannot allow him to be free, so she arranges to hide Gabriella so he will be arrested.'

'Do you agree, Tullio?' Anna asked.

Tullio nodded forlornly. 'I do. It was one of her girls who told us about Gabriella's whereabouts.'

'Ada?' James asked.

'I cannot confirm that for security reasons,' Tullio replied. 'Panatti's influence cannot be underestimated. She has collated information on so many members of the establishment, particularly in high places. I am sorry, James. I wish we could do more.'

'I understand,' James replied.

Lucy was confused. He was being framed for a crime that he had not committed. Why wasn't he shouting out his innocence for all to hear?

'We can only hope that more is revealed at the trial,' Lombroso said.

'Indeed,' Miss Trott said. 'I am making my own enquiries. I am confident that they will be fruitful.'

'Ah, the redoubtable Euphemia Trott,' Lombroso said. 'But we have met before, have we not? You were a nurse at St Euphemia's Hospital in Pavia when I was working there all those years ago.'

'Indeed, Professor, you are correct. I took my pseudonym from the hospital. You stared at me so when we first met, I thought my cover was blown right at the beginning of my mission.'

'What is Serendipity?' Lucy asked.

'It is the code name I am known by at the agency.'

'Agency?' James asked. 'Is that where Aunt Agnes found you?'

'Hardly,' Miss Trott said. 'It is a detective agency. My name was given to your aunt by Professor Bell, who happens to be my cousin. Both of them wanted some protection for you and your sister, so I was asked to watch over you.'

Lucy gazed at Miss Trott in admiration. It was ironic. She had been writing about a lady detective when all the time there was a real one in their midst. No wonder she kept disappearing. 'That wasn't your only brief, though, was it, Miss Trott?'

'No, dear, it wasn't. As I was coming here anyway, my agency asked me to look into another matter.'

'Professor Donati?' Lucy asked.

'A thief,' Miss Trott said. 'That is all there is to say really. He stole from the British Museum what is reputed to be the demon god Apep's book of spells. It was not his only acquisition. Scotland Yard have been after him for some time. He operates from an address in the Via San Pellico, a chemist's shop.'

Lombroso beamed at her. 'I knew it! An expressive face, manual dexterity and small wandering eyes . . . all classic signs of the criminal type.'

'Perhaps, Professor,' Miss Trott said. 'But generally speaking I prefer to use more old-fashioned methods – intelligence from fellow criminals, surveillance and, naturally, deduction. It is, after all, what led me to both Donati and Francesco Rambaudi.'

'Your methods certainly seem to be effective,' James said.

'They played their part, Dr Murray,' Miss Trott said. 'But let us not forget that your detective work also took you to the Villa Purezza.'

'Eventually, though I allowed my suspicion about Concetta Panatti to divert me from the truth. I was so intent on catching her that I heard only Pietro's mention of seeing something red through the window of the carriage when he witnessed the abductions.'

'You thought he was talking about Panatti's hair,' Ottolenghi said.

'But what was it?' Anna asked.

'It was the red ribbon round Bianca Rambaudi's neck!' Lucy said. 'I noticed it when she came for tea because it was so unusual. It holds a locket.'

'Bravo!' Miss Trott said. 'You have excellent observation skills.'

'You put me to shame, Lucy,' James added, looking downcast. 'If only I had been as astute.'

'You saved Fabia from that man Ferranti, Signor Murray,' the marchesa said. 'I will be forever in your debt for that.'

'Yes, well done, Murray,' Lombroso said, shaking his hand. 'And I have to admit that I was wrong about Donati.'

'You were wrong, Cesare?' Anna said. 'Can we have that in writing?'

'Very droll, Madame Tarnovsky, very droll,' Lombroso said. 'But I still think that Francesco Rambaudi suffered from epilepsy . . . the hidden variety, of course. It is difficult even for me to distinguish such criminals from the merely morally insane, so I can understand Murray's mistake. '

'So in fact you were right?' James said.

Lombroso nodded. 'Quite so, Murray, quite so. I knew you'd get there in the end. We'll make a criminal anthropologist of you yet.'

James grinned. 'Oh I do hope so, Professor, I do hope so.'

50

Contradictions within the legal system lead to trials marked by wasted money, scandalous publicity and uncertain outcomes... Numerous cases demonstrate the complete ignorance of most jurors.

Lombroso, 1896–7, p. 335

James sat in the dock and tried discreetly to observe the jury. They did not seem to like him, and based on what they had heard so far, who could blame them? Not only had he been discovered standing over the victim, Baldovino, with a knife in his hand, but he had also been the subject of critical pieces by the man in *The People's Voice*, giving him motive, means and opportunity. In addition, the clothes taken from him at the police station had been produced, now covered in blood, even though James was sure that there had been no more than a few drops when he had been arrested.

Despite the fact that the marchesa had paid for an expensive lawyer and that Lombroso himself was about to give evidence on his behalf, it was not looking hopeful. Having seen the expression on the judge's face, he had resigned himself to a good few years in Le Nuove at best, and at worst...

James's lawyer, a serious grey-haired man with a monocle,

asked the professor his first question: 'How long have you known the accused?'

'Almost a year. He has worked as my assistant.'

'And during that year, what impression have you formed of this man?'

'I have found him to be extremely sound. He is honest, intelligent, hard-working and an excellent employee.'

'He is accused of a violent crime. Is he capable of such an act, in your expert opinion?'

The prosecution lawyer, a sharp-featured younger man, sprang to his feet. 'Is this witness here to speak to character or expertise?'

'Both,' replied James's lawyer.

The judge peered down his glasses and indeed his nose at Lombroso. 'I will allow an answer, but keep it brief.'

'So is he capable of this crime?'

'No.'

The defence lawyer sat down and the prosecution stood up. James wanted to shout: *Is that it?*

'Professor Lombroso, as you have given evidence relating to your expertise in crime and criminals, I wonder if you could tell us about heredity in crime?'

'That is a most interesting question. The main thing to note is that criminality can be hereditary.'

'I see, and how does this relate to alcoholism?'

'Oh, that is a fascinating phenomenon, for I have found that parental alcoholism is an important factor in inherited propensity to violence.'

James put his hands over his eyes in despair as Lombroso warmed to his theme, bringing his conviction closer with every sentence that he uttered.

'I studied a boy with thick dark hair and pale skin whose

father was an alcoholic and a killer. He himself was only twelve years old when he committed his murder. And of course the ferocious Galetto of Marseille was the grandson of Orsolano, the cannibal rapist, Dumolard was the son of an assassin, and the Cornu family was filled with murderers from father to son, and those are just a few examples.'

'Thank you, Professor, that is most helpful. Can you also confirm that the father of the accused was confined to an asylum for the criminally insane after he stabbed someone to death in a bar brawl?'

There was a long silence. Lombroso fiddled with his glasses, and his beard twitched as if a small animal was living in it.

'Professor, can you answer the question,' the judge said impatiently. 'Was the father of the accused a killer?'

'Yes, I suppose he was.'

'Thank you, no further questions.' The prosecution lawyer sat down with a satisfied grin on his face. The jury murmured to each other and the packed public gallery did likewise.

James sat there helplessly, watching as Lombroso left the witness box. It was all over. He was going to prison. His career, Sofia, Lucy ... everything was to be taken from him, and all for something he had not done. But it didn't matter. It was better for everyone if he just accepted his fate. He might not be guilty of this crime, but he had committed another, just as heinous.

He saw a flash of red hair in the public gallery. Concetta Panatti gave him a smug smile. Next to her was a gaunt man wearing a scarlet cravat.

'I know what you are,' he had said when they had first met. And now he was about to get what he had wanted all along: revenge.

*

451

The speeches had been made and the jury were out. James was waiting in a tiny room with a barred window for his fate to be announced. He had asked to see Lombroso, Ottolenghi and Anna, and before long they were ushered into the room. He felt calm. He knew what was coming and it was almost a relief. Finally he would get the punishment that he truly deserved.

'I have something to tell you,' he said. 'Something that I think may explain what has happened and why I deserve my sentence even though I did not commit this crime.'

'You do not know that you will be convicted, Murray.'

James gave a wan smile. 'I am certain that I will be, but it is all right.'

'It is nothing of the kind! I am so very sorry, Murray. I had no idea they would bring your father's case up. I do not know how they found out,' Lombroso said.

'I think I do,' James said. 'Do you remember last year when I first told you about my father?'

'Indeed I do. He performed illegal brain surgery on a young man in the asylum where you both worked, did he not?'

'Yes. I told you that I was assisting at the asylum on an ad hoc basis in order to gain some experience in the field.'

'Yes, I remember.'

'Sir Henry Gadd, the father of the young man who was operated on by my father, is here today.'

'And what business does he have with you?'

'As you know, the operation was not a success. Richard Gadd was transformed from a patient troubled by hallucinations and blackouts into little more than an idiot.'

'What does that have to do with the trial?' Ottolenghi asked.

'Richard committed suicide earlier this year.'

'I can see why Sir Henry would be angered, of course, but this was due to your father's actions, surely,' Lombroso said.

There was a silence as James closed his eyes and wished that he was anywhere but there. His shoulders dropped and he began to stoop as if a burden had been placed on his back.

'I was there.'

'You were present at the operation?' Ottolenghi said incredulously.

'Yes.'

'You lied to us, then?' Lombroso said.

'I lied to you and I lied to myself. I did not condone the operation but I did assist. I tried to prevent my father from conducting it, but . . .'

'But what, James?' Anna said gently.

'He was adamant. I thought that at least if I was taking part, I might be able to ensure Richard's safety.'

'But you were not able to do so?' Lombroso said.

James shook his head. 'I was not sufficiently experienced to know how. I was arrogant. I thought that I knew more than I did. It seemed to me that it went well, or as well as it could do.'

'And when you discovered the consequences?' Anna said.

'I argued with my father. There was a terrible row and the rest is as I have already told you.'

'And now?' asked Lombroso.

'Sir Henry holds me responsible for the death of his son . . . and he is right.'

'So he has engaged the services of that Panatti woman to assist in this?'

'It is more likely that she has her own reasons. First I visit the abbey and find the brothel, so she has me abducted, beaten and threatened. I persist in my enquiries, so she tries to seduce me in order to control me, and when that doesn't work, she manipulates Baldovino into writing those pieces in *The People's Voice*. Finally, perhaps encouraged by Sir Henry, she frames me for murder by forging a note from Baldovino getting me to visit him. She wanted to discredit me and found the ideal way to achieve it. It is clear that she did her research. No doubt Sir Henry was happy to assist.'

'Then the trial must be stopped. We must tell the authorities immediately,' Lombroso said.

'No. I deserve this. What you said in court was right. I have inherited my father's morals and his propensity for violence. Look how I threatened Baldovino.'

'This is nonsense, James,' Anna said. 'You tried to stop your father. And threatening a reporter is hardly demonstrative of a propensity to violence.'

'It's done. I'm going to be locked up where I belong. I could have saved Richard but I did not. I am a born criminal like my father before me. I need to be put away before I do more damage. I deserve this.'

'Don't be ridiculous, Murray,' Lombroso said. 'You are no more of a born criminal than I am. You must believe me. I know what you are!'

James flinched at the irony of the words.

'But James—' Anna began. She was interrupted by a knock and the door opened. 'Time's up,' the jailer said. 'The jury is back.'

'Take care of Lucy, Anna,' James said. He watched calmly as his friends were shown out. Anna gave him a tearful wave before she disappeared.

Back in the dock, he watched as the jury filed into their seats. Sir Henry sat in the gallery, still smiling.

The judge strode in and shuffled his papers about before

454

nodding at the court clerk. He in turn nodded to the fore-man, who stood to deliver his verdict. The jury refused to look James in the eye. His fate was sealed.

Outside there was a kerfuffle and some shouting. Then the door was flung open and a small rat-like man in a bowler hat limped in with the aid of crutches, closely followed by Miss Trott.

'What is the meaning of this interruption?' the judge said, glaring at the man.

'I am the victim, your honour, Baldovino of *The People's Voice*, and I demand to be heard.'

There was a pause as the judge pursed his lips. 'Very well, swear him in.'

Baldovino took the oath. Would he tell the truth? It was impossible to tell from the look on his face. The prosecution lawyer got to his feet. 'Can you identify the man who attacked you?'

Baldovino paused and looked round until he found James, then he smiled and gave a mock salute. 'No.'

The prosecutor frowned and tried again. 'Is the man who attacked you sitting in this court?'

'No.'

'Who was it who attacked you?'

'I don't know who they were, but it was not James Murray.'

'Are you sure?'

'Yes. I *was* there, you know.'

The prosecutor scratched his head for a moment and then had a whispered discussion with the man sitting behind him. It seemed to go on forever.

'Well, what do you want me to do?' asked the judge.

The prosecutor shrugged.

The jury began to talk amongst themselves, then the foreman stood.

'Yes, what is it?' enquired the judge.

The foreman looked over at James. 'We find the prisoner not guilty, your honour.'

The court erupted. There were cheers from the public gallery and James was patted on the shoulder as he was released from the dock. In all the chaos, he noticed one face focused unerringly on his own.

'I know what you are,' Henry Gadd mouthed at him. 'I know what you are.'

51

Woman's sensitivity is notably different from man's, as the anatomy of her organs itself suggests. Her eye is smaller and more on the surface of the head; her nose and ears are shorter. Lombroso and Ferrero, 1893, p. 58

'You know why I am here,' James said as he walked into the kitchen at Lombroso's house. Although it had been a few weeks since the trial, he was still coming to terms with his freedom. Lombroso had given him some more work to do to keep his mind occupied, and that had certainly helped, but he knew that there were matters to resolve. The marchesa had visited that day and made it clear that she would do anything she could to assist him. She held him responsible for the return of her niece, chastened a little by her experience, but unharmed.

'How can I help you?' she had said, and he had told her.

Sofia was baking bread, as she had been when they shared their first kiss. He realised now that they were destined to be together no matter what. He was here to claim her and make her understand that he would fight for her until the day he died.

'We can't keep pretending,' he said. 'It is meant to be. I think you know that.'

She sighed. 'I have to be honest now. I know this, *caro*. There have been too many lies already. I do love you. I have never stopped loving you.'

He pulled her to him and held her. 'Then I will ask you again. Will you marry me?'

She did not move away from him, but she did not respond either.

'I cannot.'

'You can, Sofia. We can be together. The marchesa has arranged everything.'

Sofia shook her head. 'No, I cannot.'

'I have a teaching position in America. Lucy can come too. I want you to be my wife.'

She shook her head again and pulled away from him. 'I cannot do that. I want to with all my heart, but I cannot.'

'Why not?' James asked. 'There is no reason for us to be apart.'

Sofia's tears were dropping onto the loaf she had been kneading. He took her in his arms again. 'We can't keep saying goodbye,' he said. 'What is stopping you? I know our lives, our backgrounds are different, but we can get over all of that. We love each other and that is all that matters. We have a future.'

She put a hand up to his cheek and caressed it before leaning forward and kissing him. As he held her to him, for a moment it felt as if nothing could touch them as long as they were together. But then the dampness of the tears on her face told another story. 'What is it, Sofia? Tell me!' he begged.

'Chiara,' she said.

'I got her back for you. She will be all right now.'

'I know, and I will never forget what you did for us.'

James held his hands out. 'So, what then? We will ensure

that Chiara is in good hands. Your cousin has a position with the marchesa.'

Sofia paused. 'Chiara is not my cousin, *caro*. She is my daughter, and I must put her first.'

'Are you sure you have to go, Miss Trott?' Lucy said as she watched her companion pack her things into her carpet bag.

'Yes, dear, I must. I have been called back to my agency. Apparently they have another assignment for me.'

'What's it like?'

'What do you mean, dear?'

'Being a detective. Is it exciting?'

'It can be. But it can also be monotonous, tiring and dangerous. I would not recommend it unless one had no choice.'

'And did you? Have a choice, I mean?'

'Yes, I suppose I did. I was to marry, but my fiancé died. Once he had gone . . .' She looked wistfully into the distance as if he was waiting there for her. 'No one could replace him, so I did not even try. Besides, I wanted to make my own way in life. And it turned out that I had particular talents.'

Lucy looked at her in admiration. In a way, she envied Miss Trott. She knew where she was going and what her place was in the world. Lucy herself had no such certainty. After her experience with Francesco, she had no interest in love . . . not for the time being. She too wanted to make her own way. The only question was how.

She had been working closely with Anna in the months since her abduction, and had found it both stimulating and fulfilling. Indeed, Anna had asked her if she would consider continuing their work back in Prague. But before any decisions about her future could be made, she had to sort out

James, who had been miserable ever since his trial despite his exoneration by Baldovino.

Chiara knocked on Miss Trott's door. 'Signorina Lucy, I am here as you asked.'

Miss Trott looked up from her packing. 'Is there something I can assist you with?'

'Yes,' Lucy said. 'There is. We are both worried about James and Sofia.'

'Ah yes. I understand that your mother has told Mr Murray she cannot go with him to America.'

'It is so wrong!' Chiara said. 'She is giving up everything for me when I do not want her to!'

'Then you must tell her,' Miss Trott said.

'I have tried, but she will not listen.'

'I see,' Miss Trott said. 'Then perhaps you need to tell her again but in a different way. Let me explain.'

James was sitting in the drawing room looking disconsolately out of the window. He had thought that everything was about to change, but it was not to be. Sofia's confession had seen to that. In some ways it was a relief. It explained why she had rejected him. She had other responsibilities and had been left with little choice. She had given birth to Chiara when she herself was scarcely a child, and the baby had been looked after by a family member who lived in San Callisto. When the woman had died, Chiara had returned to Sofia, who had explained to her who she really was.

'I want to be with you, *caro*,' she had told James. 'But I cannot abandon my daughter again.'

Now he had nothing, or at least that was how it felt. He would still go to America, and hopefully Lucy would go with him. But he was done with love. No one could ever take Sofia's place.

There was a knock at the door and Lucy came in. Behind her were Chiara and Sofia.

'Sofia, would you sit down?' Lucy asked.

Chiara nodded at her mother and sat next to her.

'Chiara and I have been talking,' Lucy said to James. 'There are a few things we need to explain.'

James frowned. 'You do not need to worry. Sofia is to stay here with Chiara. You and I . . . well, I have some plans for us.'

'No, James. I am afraid that will not do. Chiara and I have plans of our own.'

'*Sì*, we have,' Chiara said. James could see the likeness between her and Sofia now. She had a way of half smiling that was almost identical to her mother's.

'Plans . . . what sort of plans?' Sofia said, looking mystified.

Chiara turned towards her. 'Mamma, you must go to America with Signor James and be happy.'

'I cannot leave you,' Sofia protested. 'We have only just found each other again.'

Chiara took her mother's hands and held them tightly. 'Don't you see? I want you to be happy, and I know that this is the only way.'

Sofia hesitated and looked carefully into her daughter's eyes. 'Really? Are you sure, *cara*?'

'I have never been more sure of anything,' Chiara said. 'The marchesa has offered me a new position and I have decided to accept it. It will be quite challenging and will involve some travelling, but I think it will be very fulfilling.'

'It won't be dull, that's for sure,' Lucy said.

'No, indeed,' Chiara said, smiling. 'I am to be Fabia Carignano's companion.'

'*Santo cielo!* Are you certain? She is a handful, that one,' Sofia said. 'You'll have your work cut out.'

Chiara laughed. 'Remember, I have seen her in a maid's uniform, curtseying to Lucy. If she gets too much, I will remind her of that.'

'But what about Lucy?' Sofia said. 'Perhaps she is not so sure?'

'I don't want to go to America,' Lucy said, 'if that is what you were hoping for, James. Because I too have been offered a position, of a kind.'

'What position? You're not thinking of going back to Scotland, surely!' James said.

'Certainly not. I have changed, James. You must see that. I'm not sure Aunt Agnes would approve of the new me. The thing is . . .' She paused, as if she was trying to find the right words. 'Anna is going back to Prague. She has decided to conduct her own study on women and crime, inspired by what happened here. She has asked me to go with her to assist. She wants me to use my experiences to further her knowledge on the subject. I will stay with her and her husband, so I will be well looked after.'

'So there you are,' Chiara said. 'We have made our arrangements; now you can make yours. We will visit, though. You can be certain of that.'

James held out his hand to Sofia. She walked over to him and took it. 'Signora Murray,' he said. 'I like the sound of that.'

'If we are going to America, then it will be Mrs James Murray,' Sofia laughed. 'I like the sound of that even more!'

Mr and Mrs James Murray stood on the deck watching the famous Statue of Liberty come into view as they approached New York. He kissed his wife and breathed in her scent of cinnamon and lemons – still there even though they had left Italy weeks ago.

Saying goodbye to their friends and family had been hard for both of them. They had married in a quiet but beautiful ceremony, surrounded by those who were dearest to them. Lombroso, who had given Sofia away, had seemed quite tearful, though he claimed to have something in his eye.

James noticed that the professor had wasted no time in replacing him at the museum. A serious and studious young man called Guglielmo Ferrero was to take his place on the research project. Now there was a new case to write up, that of Francesco and Bianca Rambaudi and their mother Sylvana. It seemed that Lombroso had been right after all. Women could be crueller than men, and none more so than the two who had manipulated Francesco until he was nothing more than a shell of a man completely at their disposal.

That was all in the past. Now James Murray was the happiest of men. He had everything he wanted: the woman he loved at his side, an interesting new position in a thriving and exciting place. It was all going to be perfect. He squeezed Sofia's hand and she laid her head on his shoulder as they looked out across the harbour to their new life.

But on that harbour stood a familiar figure, smiling with satisfaction at the prospect of the Murrays' arrival. It was a year or more since their encounter in Turin, but he had not forgotten them. The epitome of a well-to-do American, he carried a silver-topped cane and wore a distinctive coat, smart and elegant, with an astrakhan collar. He watched as the ship came closer, but before it reached the harbour, he turned and walked away. It would wait, he thought. *They* would wait.

Because murder should never be rushed.

Author's Note

Cesare Lombroso (1835–1909) is known as the father of modern criminology. His theory of the born criminal dominated thinking about criminal behaviour in the late nineteenth and early twentieth centuries. Essentially he believed that criminality was inherited, and that criminals could be identified by physical defects that confirmed them as being savage throwbacks to early man.

Lombroso and women

In 1893, together with his assistant Guglielmo Ferrero, Lombroso wrote *Criminal Woman, the Prostitute and the Normal Woman*. Here he applies his ideas about the born criminal to female offenders, and in doing so tries to explain the nature of female crime by applying his born criminal theory.

However, this was not a straightforward perspective. Lombroso had already made his view of women, whether criminal or not, quite clear in *Criminal Man*, claiming that they were inferior, less evolved and in some cases no more than 'big children'. Surely it would follow that they would have more of a propensity to commit crimes?

The problem was that female criminals were then, as they are now, a relatively rare phenomenon. Once his critics had pointed this out, Lombroso and other criminal anthropologists were therefore forced to argue that women were less criminal than men *because* they were inferior to them, being essentially too weak and stupid to be bad. Women were so passive that they were incapable of reaching either the intellectual and moral heights of men, who were normal, or the primitive, atavistic depths of the male born criminal (Gibson, 2002, p. 68). Such female born criminals that did exist were much more savage, morally deficient, vengeful, jealous, inclined to refined cruelty and possessed more evil tendencies, as well as being physically scarred with imperfections and abnormalities.

Criminal woman, Lombroso insisted, was a true monster. This viewpoint was not easy to maintain. Lombroso turned to science, and was one of the first criminal anthropologists to use a control group of 'normal' women, and to try to define deviance in a scientific manner and to identify the boundary between normality and abnormality (Gibson and Rafter, 2004, pp. 7–9).

One might assume in the light of his theories that, like many men of his era, Lombroso was something of a misogynist. The views expressed in *Criminal Woman* certainly seem to suggest that this was the case. In his private life he was surrounded by strong women. Both of his daughters, Paola and Gina, were academically gifted, and it is likely that they were influenced by Anna Kuliscioff, a socialist feminist and physician and a regular visitor to the Lombroso home. Russian physician Pauline Tarnowsky was a fellow criminal anthropologist, on whose work with Moscow prostitutes Lombroso drew heavily. (The character of Anna Tarnovsky is fictional but loosely based on an amalgam of both of these women.)

Interestingly, Lombroso's translators, Nicole Rafter and Mary Gibson, speculate that Lombroso was apprehensive about his daughters' growing independence, and that this might explain in part his irritation and frustration when writing about woman's nature. They point out that he also apologises for his harsh words about women, perhaps because he was mindful of arguments at the family dinner table about the roles and status of women and wished to keep the peace. It is worth noting that although both daughters were well educated, arguably neither reached their full potential, being held back by the ideals of their time (2004, pp. 13–14). Paola organised a series of children's books, thus buttressing the family and Gina became her father's secretary (Gibson 2002, p. 89).

The 1880s and 1890s saw the beginnings of the formal Italian women's movements, which Lombroso found troubling, notwithstanding his relatively liberal political stance. Perhaps that is why, as his translators Rafter and Gibson suggest, he was so dismissive of clever women and insisted that maternity was their proper aspiration. I know that while I was researching this book by reading his works, there were many times when I would have cheerfully slapped him. However, I also had to remind myself that despite his attitudes, which did after all reflect the times in which he lived, and his somewhat slapdash research methods, Lombroso was creative, passionate and influential.

Lombroso's influence

Given his sometimes eccentric views, it is easy to dismiss Lombroso as being ridiculous and therefore unimportant. This is, to my mind, a simplistic viewpoint. His theories were certainly flawed but, as Rafter points out, he was responsible for transforming criminology into a fully-fledged science (2008, p. 84). The impact of *Criminal Woman* was far-reaching, particularly as a version was published in English in 1895. It was the first book to focus on the causes of female crime and remained so for many years. As a result, the idea that women who commit violent crimes do so for biological reasons is still with us.

Lombroso and the paranormal

Another of Lombroso's interests was paranormal investigation, particularly ghost-hunting or, as P. J. Ystehede puts it, 'going around the town on the lookout for ghosts' (2012). Essentially, like many others of this period, Lombroso wanted to prove that crime had its roots in the possession of such things as malign and evil spirits. He even studied ancient and modern witchcraft in the hope that his work would help to gain acceptance for the idea that the supernatural did exist.

Lombroso the man

Lombroso was an ebullient, enthusiastic, energetic and provocative man with an interest in many things. I particularly liked the description of a typical day in his life written by his daughter Paola (cited by Nicole Rafter 2008, p. 79):

> ... composing on the typewriter, correcting proofs, running from Bocca (his publisher) to the typesetter, from the typesetter to the library and from the library to the laboratory in a frenzy of movement ... and in the evening, not tired and wanting to go to the theatre, to a peregrination of two or three of the city's theatres, taking in the first act at one, paying a flying visit to another and finishing the evening at a third.

Rafter also cites the historian Delfino Dolza, who writes of Lombroso's almost total inexperience with the practical aspects of existence, his childlike innocence and a gullibility so extreme that his children felt a need to protect him.

Lombroso's museum

A born collector, as his daughter Gina would later describe him, Lombroso began to assemble artefacts when he was still a student himself in the 1850s. These included skulls and brains and other pickled body parts, death masks, skeletons and examples of prisoners' art (Montaldo, 2012) all of which he brought with him to Turin and kept in his house. One can only imagine his wife Nina's reaction to that! Eventually, and no doubt much to her relief, he moved these items to his laboratory at the University of Turin. In 1892 it opened to the public for the first time, and although it closed again in 1914, the museum reopened in 2009.

Sources

I have drawn on a number of academic sources in my research, most of which are listed below. If there are factual errors then they are, of course, mine.

Bibliography

Gibson, Mary (2002), *Born to Crime: Cesare Lombroso and the Origins of Biological Criminology*. USA: Greenwood Press

Gibson, Mary (2006), 'Cesare Lombroso and Italian criminology: theory and politics'. In P. Becker and R. F. Wetzell (eds), *Criminals and their Scientists* (pp. 137–58), New York: Cambridge University Press

Horn, David (2003), *The Criminal Body: Lombroso and the Anatomy of Deviance.* London: Routledge

Lombroso, Cesare (2006), *Criminal Man* (M. Gibson and N. H. Rafter, trans.) Durham and London: Duke University Press. (Original work published 1876–97)

Lombroso, Cesare and Ferrero, Guglielmo (2004), *Criminal Woman, the Prostitute and the Normal Woman* (M. Gibson and N. H. Rafter, trans.) Durham and London: Duke University Press. (Original work published 1893)

Montaldo, Silvano (2012), 'The Lombroso museum from its origins to the present day'. In Paul Knepper and P. J. Ystehede, (eds), *The Cesare Lombroso Handbook.* (pp. 98–112). London: Routledge

Rafter, Nicole (1997), *Creating Born Criminals.* Chicago: University of Illinois Press

Rafter, Nicole (2008), *The Criminal Brain: Understanding Biological Theories of Crime.* New York: New York University Press

Ystehede, Per Jorgen (2012), 'Demonising Being: Lombroso and the ghosts of criminology'. In Paul Knepper and P. J. Ystehede (eds), *The Cesare Lombroso Handbook* (pp. 72–97). London: Routledge.

Acknowledgements

The Devil's Daughters started taking shape at an Arvon course in Moniack Mhor, Scotland. My thanks go to the staff, all of the 'Arvonites' and our tutors Val McDermid and Andrew Taylor for an inspiring and joyous week.

The writing of this book would have been a much more difficult task had it not been for the advice of my PhD supervisors from the University of Southampton, Rebecca Smith and Professors Peter Middleton and David Glover.

Thanks as ever both to my editor Jemima Forrester, who has again guided me through the writing process with her customary intelligence and charm, and my lovely agent Luigi Bonomi for his invaluable guidance and support.

Fellow writers are always a great source of comfort in those darker days when you just can't finish a chapter or sometimes even a sentence. Thanks for being there when I needed you Will Sutton, Tessa Ditner, Tom Harris, Matt Wingett, Christine Lawrence, Zella Compton, Sarah Baxter, Carolyn Hughes and Claire Holland.

Thanks to Nicole Hahn Rafter and Mary Gibson for allowing me to quote from their translations of Lombroso's work.

My colleagues at the Institute of Criminal Justice Studies at the University of Portsmouth have again been a great source of expertise and support. Thanks in particular go to Dr

Paul Smith and Jenny Weaver for some informative if rather hair-raising conversations about forensics, blood draining and female sex offending, among other things.

Thanks to my husband David for reading drafts, offering advice, solace, tea, cake and white wine, always with patience and love.

And lastly, to my wonderful mum, without whose influence and encouragement I would never have become a writer in the first place. I miss you.